Dordrecht Dimension

A Novel

Jim Otte

DEDICATION

Dordrecht Dimension is dedicated with love and gratitude to
Nancy Otte, my wife and companion for 53 years.

AUTHORS NOTE

The physical and cultural setting of *Dordrecht Dimension* is a fictionalized version of the western Michigan area where I was born and raised and where Dutch immigrants replaced the original people of the Odawa tribe. With a deep respect for both cultures, I describe the changes that have occurred over the last decades of the twentieth century from the perspective of someone who has left and lived elsewhere for decades. The characters are also fictional. Real people inspired some aspects of each character, but no character is or is meant to be a representation of any specific person. I hope readers enjoy this story from the points of view of Joe, Harry, Amy, and Pete.

I could not have written Dordrecht Dimension without the encouragement of my wife, Nancy. Her patience in adding ideas to the story and correcting errors in each of many drafts was invaluable. Any errors that remain are my own. Nancy has written her memoir, *A Matter of Life and DeaF*, which is available on Amazon in paperback and on Kindle eBook.

Contents

Dordrecht Dimension

Chapter 1–Pete, Fall, 1972

There was a man under a tree, propped up as if taking a nap, with his head falling to the right. Singapore County Deputy Sheriff, Pete McAdams, moved back from the tree, trying to get a feel for the larger scene. The sky had darkened since he arrived. Rain was in the forecast after a weeklong dry spell. The edge of the pond was about fifty yards to the north. He noticed a duck blind along the right side of the pond thirty yards away. The road, little more than a wagon trail, was visible as it wound through a clearing and passed the pond about 150 yards to the right as it headed north to County Road 18. Behind him, it continued south-southwest to CR22.

The acreage belonged to the Dordrecht Fish and Game Club, known as the DFG. It had been owned since the 1920s by club members from Dordrecht, fifteen miles north in Nederland County. It was a small city of almost four thousand residents that was settled in 1849 by immigrants from a town of the same name in the South Holland province of the Netherlands to which more than ninety percent of the current residents still traced their ancestry.

The one square mile of the DFG Club, a 640-acre section that was prime land for waterfowl hunting with several ponds created by muskrats and expanded by the members, was bisected by a large creek that led to the Singapore River on the western edge of the property. Much of it was reclaimed marshland. There was a large section of higher ground, alternately woody and grassy, to the northeast, where hunters could find pheasant and even deer in season.

Pete was familiar with the area. His mother's extended family, the Toussaints, a mixed French and Native family since the early 1800s with Odawa, Potawatomie, and French ancestors, still owned eighty acres farther south on the Singapore River. In the 1920s, other family members had sold half of the section forming the DFG to the Dordrecht residents who wanted a place close to their town to hunt, fish, and socialize. Pete's grandfather did not sell his acreage.

The man's shotgun was angled across one leg haphazardly. He no longer had a face, ear, or neck on his left side. The blast from the gun had destroyed them. It was not a direct hit, but it was effective enough at close range for the bird shot to cause instant death. Pete thought he recognized him, but he knew he was correct when he found his ID in his wallet and a badge to go with it. He was George Bosch, the Chief of Police of Dordrecht. Pete had met him several times when they dealt with inter-county investigations and enforcement issues.

Pete tried to be calm and careful, but his mind was still in disbelief. He was surprised he did not feel the nausea veteran deputies had warned him about. It could be his Native DNA or his time in the US Army Military Police in Saigon. Not only was this the first time as a deputy sheriff at the scene of death that was neither natural nor a traffic accident, but knowing the deceased was clouding his mind as he tried to analyze the scene the way a professional should. His suspicion was enhanced as he recalled a presentation by a storyteller at a powwow he attended months earlier: During border skirmishes on hunting grounds in eastern Minnesota with the Ojibwe and Odawa people, Sioux warriors would prop up their kills against a tree facing west to intimidate their enemy.

Buck Johnson, the caretaker of the DFG Club land, had found the body in the early weekday morning while looking for unauthorized hunters who would often try their luck on weekday mornings before the club members came in the afternoon. Deputy McAdams had given up waiting for a medical examiner to arrive from Wakazoo, the county seat four miles to the south, but he was sure that the body had been dead twelve to twenty-four hours. The ground and the roads were drier than usual for the second week of October. There were no visible tracks, vehicle or human, that he could see. A crime scene team could check further. But Pete realized that rain forecasted to arrive later in the day would wash out some of the evidence. He had already radioed to headquarters and caught the sheriff, Jimmy Dickerson, in his office. Jimmy, as usual, had come to a quick conclusion.

--It's obviously suicide, Pete.

Pete had tried to agree. He had only been a deputy for less than a year. Jimmy was a former state police officer who had just been elected to his third term as Singapore County Sheriff.

--It does look like it could be, Sheriff. But it feels like something else.

3

--Just let it go. We don't have the budget for wild goose chases.

--I know we don't have anyone qualified for this, but we could ask for a state team from Lansing to supervise the investigation and forensics.

--It would be a timewaster for everyone. Get the body to the morgue. Bernie will take care of it.

Pete followed Sheriff Dickerson's order as he had learned to do as an MP in Vietnam, but only after he canvased the area more extensively, taking measurements and notes while snapping some photos with his Polaroid camera. He put on a pair of knee-high boots that he retrieved from the trunk of his patrol car before wading into several areas of cattails to check for more evidence. He found nothing that would change the sheriff's mind. He did wonder why there were no more shells left in the three-shot chamber since he only found one spent cartridge.

Later that night, after discussing it with his wife, Flo, Pete decided to apply to the Michigan State Police for an entry-level position. He felt his degree in criminology, combined with his military police experience, could be put to better use in a more ethical and professional organization. The higher pay would help, too. He hoped he could land a slot allowing him to continue living in Wakazoo, which had been his family's hometown for generations.

Chapter 2—Harry, First Sunday, 1998

Harry Berendts was surprised at his apprehension on a rainy fall Sunday afternoon as he drove his rental Accord into the DeVos Funeral Home parking lot two blocks from downtown Dordrecht. He had been here when his mother, Rosemary, died six years earlier, but his father's death brought up different emotions. Joe Berendts was a complicated man. He had finally died from congestive heart failure after living with its increasing complications for almost a decade. When a stroke two years previously had reduced him to a semi-invalid, Harry's sister, Amy, had arranged for in-home help, allowing Joe to stay in the Dordrecht house he had lived in for over forty years. As she had told Harry, she hoped to avoid his fear of wasting away in an assisted living residence. Harry thought preserving Joe's financial resources was her real motivation, but he had no right to complain. Until six weeks earlier, Harry had been back to Dordrecht only once to see Joe after his mother's funeral. He made that trip because he knew he would feel a burden of guilt if he missed Joe's seventy-fifth birthday celebration.

Harry was coming directly from the New Leiden airport without stopping at the Amsterdam Inn, which had recently been built near the Interstate 296 exit between Middleburg and

Dordrecht. He was already late but did not need to change since he was traveling in a business casual sport coat that was his uniform when he took trips for his company. Coming back to Dordrecht always gave him a constricted feeling in the pit of his stomach and caused him to withdraw into himself. It was not only a typical midwestern small town, but he always felt that Dordrecht's strict Calvinist roots gave the town an extra restrictive patina due to their effect on the residents' psychological makeup and social interactions.

He and Joe had not been close for decades. Harry never felt safe due to Joe's frequent mood changes. Joe was a religious man who attended church regularly and was known to attest to his beliefs publicly. He would be mourned and celebrated at the funeral service in the Second Reformed Church. He was also a businessman who was connected to the most influential and powerful men of Dordrecht. He was socially gregarious and well-liked by those in the seven Reformed and Christian Reformed churches in Dordrecht. On the other hand, his reputation for less-than-honorable business practices and the rumors that he followed a second, not-so-Christian lifestyle apart from his family and his church caused many of the Godfearing folk of Dordrecht to withhold their admiration and approval.

Harry was aware of the dichotomy. He had personally experienced Joe's unrighteous wrath and selfish motivations. He did not doubt the rumors, believing as he did that the religious devotion of most of the Calvinists in Dordrecht was colored with diverse hues of hypocrisy. He was thankful that Joe had pulled strings to get him in the National Guard, but he always wondered if Joe had ulterior motives, perhaps trying to assuage his feelings of guilt about the relationship with his son.

Harry's six months of active-duty training and two years at Western Michigan University had felt like a release from custody. He vowed not to live in Nederland County for the rest of his life. After one of Joe's friends arranged a job for him as an installation technician at DeJong Office Furniture for their new open-office system, Harry volunteered for every out-of-town installation opportunity and did not hesitate to accept when a permanent job in Denver with one of DeJong's dealers was offered to him. He soon married Monica Ellsworth, a teacher he met on a ski weekend with mutual friends. Her being a lapsed Catholic made Harry determined to sever the last of his ties to Dordrecht and its churches.

As he walked through the entry hallway, he was relieved there would not be an open casket with Joe's lifeless body on display, as was the custom in Dordrecht. When his mother died of breast cancer, she was severely emaciated and insisted that she be cremated, feeling even before her death that she and her body were no longer connected. Joe also opted for cremation. His ashes would be buried with Rosemary's in their plot in the Dordrecht Cemetery.

He did not miss Monica on this trip. She had only visited twice in the twenty years of marriage before they had divorced two years prior. But he did wish his kids were with him. David was a junior at the University of Colorado in Boulder, where Jennifer was now in her first year of medical school. They had not been back to Michigan since their grandmother had died when they were still in junior high. They had never felt close to Joe, perhaps because of their empathy for Harry.

As he entered the visitation room, Harry saw his older sister, Amy, with her current live-in partner, Doug Mason. It seemed to him that she had aged more than the three years since he had last visited Joe. She was still a classic Dutch beauty with part of her white-blonde hair pulled up--the same Frisian hair that Harry had also inherited from their mother. Perhaps she had just lost weight, causing a few more lines on her face. Dressed in a burgundy pantsuit with just the right jewelry and the perfect medium black pumps, she looked as if she owned a designer clothing boutique, which she did.

It took a moment for him to recognize the couple she and Doug were talking with. Marilyn and Butch Bosch were old high school friends. It was no surprise that the body language of the group was tense. Butch and Amy had dated seriously, as had Harry and Marilyn. After Amy had moved on from Butch, Marilyn dropped Harry for Butch during their senior year. Harry had not seen them since their twenty-fifth class reunion, the only reunion he had ever attended. That visit coincided with Joe's birthday party, Harry's divorce from Monica, and a convenient trip to attend NeoCon in Chicago. None of his close friends had shown up, so he left the reunion early, reminding himself that he had good reasons to have left Dordrecht behind.

Just as he realized that he had been watching them for too long, Marilyn spotted him, and their eyes locked for more than a moment. He turned away and looked for anyone else that he knew. Luckily, he almost bumped into Larry Vandevoss, his best high school and college friend. Larry was hard to miss—six feet six and at least 280 pounds, his curly red hair still thick but duller than in their student days. He was already open-armed and gave Harry his patented bear hug.

--I was wondering if you had changed your mind about coming.

Larry's gravelly voice often made him seem as if he were growling, even as he whispered into Harry's ear. Harry gently hugged him back and answered quietly.

--I did have thoughts. But I wouldn't want to miss a chance to hang out with you.

--I'm sure. I would express my sympathies, but you know that I know how things were between you and your dad.

--Ja, I know you're right, but I can't say I don't have any guilt feelings to go along with relief.

--I know you should circulate, and I have things to do. Can we get a bite later?

--I still need to check in at the Amsterdam Inn after I'm done here. How about eight at Der Kroeg? Is that too late for you?

--No, that'll work. See you.

Harry watched him walk out with a wave of nostalgia. They had been inseparable from seventh grade through their sophomore year at Western, where Harry was a backup placekicker, and Larry was a second-string tight end. All that time, 'Harry and Larry' was almost a single person's name. When Harry left for Denver, Larry was already into the second year of his enlistment as a US Army MP in Germany. After his military service, he joined the Michigan State Police, finished his criminology degree, and retired early the previous year. They had always remained close friends, staying in touch on the phone when they couldn't find the time to see each other in person.

As Harry's attention returned to Amy, Marilyn and Butch appeared beside him. Butch unenthusiastically said, 'Hello Harry' as he offered a weak handshake. Marilyn touched his arm and offered standard condolences. After a short conversation about each other's children and details of Harry's stay, they nervously excused themselves and moved toward the exit.

Harry was dangling until he saw Amy talking to two sets of uncles and aunts, his mother's sister and brother, and their respective spouses. Sensing a safe opening, he walked over to join them. Harry's mother's younger sister, Judy, had married Ben Veenstra, a real Dutchman who had emigrated from the Netherlands to teach European history at Covenant Christian College in New Leiden, a large city twenty miles east of Dordrecht that was now less than ten percent Dutch. Being from Groningen, a city and province in the northern part of the country where a part of the traditional Calvinist remnant still existed, he fit in with the West Michigan religious environment much better than in any Dutch university. Judy now gave him a loose hug and asked about his kids. Harry was more comfortable talking about anything other than Joe. They, too, probably found it difficult to talk about Joe, even though their issues with him differed from Harry's. Rose, Judy, and their brother Al, who now gave Harry a firm handshake, were the children of Reverend Hendrick DeHaan, a fixture in the Christian Reformed Church, which was the second largest and one of the more conservative branches of the several American Dutch Reformed denominations.

Reverend DeHaan had not been pleased when Rose dated and then married Joe. As time went on, he was even more displeased, not only about Joe's failing to understand or have any interest in the nuances of Calvinist and Reformed doctrine but also because his lifestyle was libertine compared to that of the DeHaan family. Judy, Ben, Al, and Al's wife Winnie were very much on the Reverend's side. Even Rose had returned to her hyper-Calvinist upbringing as time went on, especially after she began to lose her fight with breast cancer. However, Harry's problems with Joe had little to do with religion.

Amy slipped away as the five of them continued to catch up with the latest news of Harry's cousins and their families. Harry saw her talking to two men and a woman, all three of whom were a generation younger. One of the men and the woman were shorter and darker than the others in the room, but the second man was lighter and taller. He fit right in with the Dutch folk. Harry did not recognize them. He had been away from Dordrecht for a long time, so he was no longer fazed by interacting with darker-skinned people, but being in Dordrecht made it seem strange. He thought their conversation was not about offering condolences or recalling memories of Joe.

He felt a touch on his shoulder and, as he turned, was greeted with an enthusiastic voice.

--Harry Berendts! How long has it been?

He drew a blank for a moment before he recognized Randy Veltmaan, another old high school friend, or at least they had hung around with the same jock crowd. He was now at least forty pounds heavier and had less hair, fashioned into a moderate combover. Everyone was shocked when Randy decided to enter the ministry.

--Hello, Randy, it's been a long time. Your wedding, I think. Before I went to Denver, and you left for LA.

--That's right. Amy tells me you are still in Denver. You're divorced with two kids, as I remember.

--Ja, she got that correct. And I have heard, though not from Amy, that you are back in the area. I hear that you have a church in Middleburg.

--Yes, I do. It's been five years now.

--How's business?

--Um.... Although I don't think of it as a business, we are being blessed. We've had over five hundred people at both services lately. Many people who have left the traditional Reformed Churches are winding up with us at Joyful Spirit. Like I have said since I became a pastor, folks want more joy, hope, and faith and less guilt and doctrine, including your sister.

--Really? Is she a regular?

--Absolutely, in the winter when her store is not busy. She is back singing and playing the guitar for our bluegrass praise band. She's starting a Christian yoga group. She's even had Joe coming with her at times.

--Amazing! If you've pulled her back in the fold, you must be one heck of a preacher or an even better salesman. I thought she had sworn off churches forever. She's always been partly hedonist and, simultaneously, a new-age mystic.

--You should come next Sunday. You know I was with the Crystal Cathedral for fifteen years. I've patterned our mission after theirs. You might find out you like it or—need it.

--I'm not staying that long, although I may return next week. I don't want to waste your time or mine even if I do. I don't think you could succeed if my mom and her family couldn't bring me back to the fold.

--I would like to try. Even Joe would have switched from Second Reformed if it were not for Lydia.

--Lydia? His sometime girlfriend?

--Yes. She was here earlier talking to Amy. Oh. Here's Amy now.

--What about Lydia? I'm sure you are sorry you missed her, Harry.

--Hello to you too, Amy. Missing Lydia is one of the benefits of being late. We were discussing how she kept Dad from going to church.

Randy became uncomfortable.

--I think I will work on my remarks for tomorrow. I'll see you both before the service tomorrow.

Amy watched him go and then looked back at Harry.

--I didn't think you cared about churches, Harry.

--I don't. But Randy does. He's roped you in.

--There was no roping involved. I like being part of something. And, at Joyful Spirit, there is no judgment. I can believe and think what I want.

--I'm for that. But if he is giving the sermon, what will Reverend Scholten do? He was Dad's minister, and it's his church.

--Randy is not doing the main sermon. He's just giving remarks. He'll make me feel more comfortable.

--Oh my gosh! I'll need to listen to two sermons! It's too bad Grandpa DeHaan is no longer with us. We could explore three kinds of heaven, or hell, that Joe may be experiencing. But anyway, what did Lydia have to say?

--Nothing new. She cried a little and said how much she cared about Dad and couldn't understand why I disliked her and why I tried to keep them apart. She looked a lot older. She must be seventy by now.

--And you told her it wasn't personal but that you just wanted to make sure she didn't spend his money or be able to get her hands on any more of it?

--F. you! You know there is nothing left.

--I know there is not much left. I don't know where it all went.

--F. you again. I'll show you if you want to meet with the accountant. We also need to decide when to inter Dad's ashes. I assume you'd like to do that with us.

--Can we do it tomorrow morning? I'm flying out to see a site in Madison right after the service.

--No way. I have too many things to take care of. I'm going to a personal retreat later this week. Can't you stay another day or two so we can take care of everything?

--I'm afraid not. I'm trying to broker what, for me, is a big deal. The earliest I could be back is Saturday. By then, the deal will either be done or dead.

--I have other plans for the weekend. But we could meet Bill–the accountant–next Monday morning and do the ashes in the afternoon.

--That'll work. I can stay through Monday. I wanted to hang out with Larry a bit on the weekend anyway. What are we doing with the ashes?

--We'll have a little ceremony and put them in the plot with Mom's. I'll save some that Dad wanted to have spread at the DFG Club.

Amy looked around as if looking for an escape from the conversation.

--Oh, there is Reverend Scholten. I need to talk to him about tomorrow. We need to meet with him at the church with just the family at one thirty. Okay? And we still plan to meet next week on Monday.

--Ja, I'll be there. Both days.

Harry watched her go and looked around to see if he could sneak out. He met some other high schoolmates to reminisce with, along with several old Second Reformed Church friends of Rosemary and Joe. He was stopped by a group of employees with whom he had worked at DeJong Systems. All the conversations were the same: condolences, updates about families, and some gossip—lots of talk with the Systems folks. By then, the crowd had thinned. He felt he had done his duty and left for the Amsterdam Inn.

When Harry checked in, a message was waiting for him at the desk from Allen Zuverink, an elementary school friend, asking him to call. He brought his suitcase and garment bag to his room, only unpacking his shaving kit, knowing he would check out before noon. He checked his pager and his new Nokia cell phone. He was proud of his new pocket phone but only used it in Denver or for emergencies. He hated paying the roaming charges, and the service was inconsistent in many places. Finally, he called his message service from the room phone to check for work-related calls. Feeling more settled in, he returned Allen's call.

The conversation with Allen was short. He had missed Harry at the funeral home and would not be able to stay for the reception at the church after the funeral. Not only did he want to offer condolences, but he also wanted to give Harry some information he had come across about Joe. They agreed to have breakfast together in the morning.

Allen had been a friend of Harry's longer than Larry. They had been neighbors as children, becoming best friends even before they attended the local Christian elementary school together through sixth grade. The school was associated with the Christian Reformed Church. Rose and her father had insisted that Amy and Harry attend. No longer willing to pay the tuition, Joe had forced them to transfer to the public school beginning in junior high. Allen continued along the Christian school path through the Christian high school in Middleburg.

Since Larry always played on the junior high football, basketball, and baseball teams after school, Allen and Harry were still after-school friends in junior high, often hanging out at Joe's Diner. The Joe of Joe's Diner was a different Joe, a lone Italian Joe who somehow had landed in Dordrecht. They played the two pinball machines in the back room when not shooting hoops or tossing the football at the schoolyard. Even in high school, Allen and Harry always kept in contact, including spending even more time together during their high school years when Allen began to date a friend of Harry's girlfriend, Marilyn, setting up many double dates.

Harry's friendship with Larry started in junior high when Harry was the new kid at the public school. He knew some others from Second Reformed Sunday School but not those who, like Larry, had attended First Reformed or other churches. Still pre-puberty, short and skinny, even blonder than the other Dutch kids, Harry looked more like a fifth grader, a prime candidate to be tormented by the bullies who would try to outdo each other in their meanness. Larry was the biggest of the bullies but far from the meanest. Harry felt that his heart was not in it. On the third day in seventh grade, he noticed Larry trying to complete the math homework in the five minutes before class and only getting a '50' with the assignment half done. The next day, he slipped Larry a prepared answer sheet, which Larry frantically copied, earning him a '90' and a surprised look from the uncool, studious girl who cross-graded with him. Harry had given him one wrong answer so no one would be suspicious. When the lunch break came, Larry punched Harry in the shoulder and said to follow him. In the lunchroom, Larry told the others that Harry was his buddy. The bullying stopped. From that time on, the two of them were inseparable.

Harry grabbed his coat and headed out to meet Larry. Der Kroeg was a new pub just outside the newly expanded northern city limits of Dordrecht. It had to be outside of town because Dordrecht had always been alcohol-free. In its earlier incarnation, Der Kroeg had been little more than a roadhouse dive bar called the Beeline with a disreputable image. With changing times, it had recently been completely gutted and rebuilt and was now a fashionable spot for the more liberal Reformed folk to have a drink and feel less separated from the broader American culture. Larry was at the bar, waiting, with two IPAs. They grabbed a table in a far corner. He seemed uncomfortable as he raised one of them.

--Here's to Joe; he was neither the worst nor the best person I've known.

--Is that the best you could come up with?

--I'm sorry. I'm not very eloquent. He was hard to figure out.

--Yes, he was. Laughing and fun-loving one minute, bitter and angry the next, and then vulgar and cynical. That made him hard to live with—and hard to trust. As a son, I loved him, but I was always waiting for the mood to change.

--Do you think you were abused?

--Not physically. He hit me a few times but always stopped before he did any real damage. Like many Dutchmen of his generation, he was raised that way. Psychologically, he could be cruel at times. But so could my mother, in her way. She took her Calvinism seriously.

--So, you're grading on a curve?

--Ja, I am. I think I need to. I could only minimize the damage and get on with my life after I learned to see them as imperfect human beings. On the other hand, I did need to get away from them and the whole culture. I don't care to point fingers or assign blame. I just needed to be away. My perspective is different now.

--What were the best parts of Joe?

--His humor was great. We had fun times when he was feeling good about himself. And don't forget that we wouldn't be friends if he hadn't gotten me out of Christian School.

--Really? That was him?

--Oh yeah, my mom and grandpa put up a real fight about it. The Christian School was part of their faith. He also taught me how to fish and hunt; don't forget that.

--How could I? He taught me, too. My old man didn't have the time. He ran his gas station sixty to seventy hours a week. Sundays were church time.

--Joe also supported me when I wanted to be a field goal kicker.

———————

During their seventh-grade year, Allen and Harry had felt left out by not being athletic enough to make the junior high teams. Larry was a three-sport guy, leaving Harry with free afternoons. When Allen's Christian School friends made their basketball team, he and Harry became after-school partners. In the spring, they decided on a plan of action so they would not be left out the following year. Both hoped to improve their chances when puberty brought along a growth spurt. They decided to work together every day to improve their skills. They had played little league baseball together but did not often get to play except for the mandatory one-inning and one at-bat. Allen thought he had some hope as a pitcher, so he pitched, and Harry caught. The same in football. They would practice routes with Allen throwing to Harry. Their one-on-one basketball games usually resulted in Allen winning, although Harry usually won the H-O-R-S-E contests. They soon decided that Harry would never have the speed to be a receiving end, so they devised the idea to make him a kicker. It was a failure at first, but then Allen suggested he try soccer-style kicking. A light was turned on. He could only kick a little further than extra point distance, but he could make nine out of ten. Harry was confident enough to show off his new skill by the start of tryouts in August. The coach kept him on the eighth-grade team.

When Harry brought the good news home, Joe treated him with surprising respect. The following week, Joe announced he had found a kicking coach in Lansing. The rest of the season and again in the spring, Joe drove Harry the ninety miles to the Saturday clinic and followed that up with a two-week camp in the summer. Joe's pride and that of his buddy Larry, the team's best player on both sides of the ball, swelled when Harry kicked ten of twelve extra points and three goals in the six-game ninth-grade season. By the start of his sophomore year, Harry was the kicker for varsity. His work, training, and puberty had added fifteen yards to his kicking range. The older, bigger guys, for whom kicking was a sideline, had more length, but they did not have Harry's consistent accuracy.

Meanwhile, Allen had made the eighth-grade team basketball team at the Christian Junior High School and, after adding a foot in height during puberty, made the JV team at Middleburg Christian High in his sophomore year. In his first year in high school, Larry was already practicing with the varsity football team before becoming a starter as a sophomore.

_____

--Oh yeah, I remember that too. One day, I'm the star, and the next, you lead the team in scoring.

--That's what a kicker does; he scores. Too bad it didn't work with the girls. Speaking of girls, Marilyn was at the funeral home with Butch. Did you see them?

--Yeah, she looked great! She's still got it.

--She did look amazing, but not happy.

--I don't think he's a dutiful husband. He always had a roaming eye.

--I don't want to be the typical dumped boyfriend, but she deserves him. I was miserable for a few months.

--Don't I know it! It took the girls at Western to heal your wounds.

--True. But I still have scars. Anyway, back to Joe. Those were the best years for us. But by the time I was a junior, my parents were having severe problems. Later, they finally split up. Of course, I sided with Mom. His chasing women and partying with his gang finally caught up with him. She let him return after he went to rehab when I went to Western, but I never forgave him. And he never forgave me for not supporting him. That's when I started to call him Joe instead of Dad.

--That 'gang,' as you called it, was something else. From what my dad told me, they started just like some guys who started playing cards after they hunted together at the Dordrecht Fish and Game Club, what they call the DFG now.

They created an in-town Monday poker night back in the fifties. It gradually grew into something bigger. That banker, Herm Den Arden, was one of the guys. The Visser brothers—they own the Honda dealership in Middleburg now. Ole Hank Plagmeyer, and Dennis Whatshisname, the farm co-op guy. They were all there. Even old Herbert DeJong. He must have been eighty. Guys started coming from Middleburg, New Leiden, and even Chicago.

Larry took a big gulp of his IPA and then continued.

--One of my uncles was a hanger-on. For my twenty-first birthday, he took me to their weekly party just before I was heading to basic training. It was in a room upstairs above the front section of the bowling alley that Dennis also owned. By then, they had a fully supplied cash bar, two poker games, a blackjack dealer, an actual roulette table, and a guy taking bets on the Lions game the following Sunday. The bartender, the two servers, and the dealers were real babes who looked like they just missed the cut at the Playboy Club in Chicago. Butch Bosch was even there with his dad, the Chief of Police.

--I guess that's why they were protected. Can you believe my wonderful sister worked behind the bar on Monday nights? She also worked here when it was still the Beeline Bar and Grill. Its specialty was an excellent burger, fried chicken, and Saturday night fights.

--Uh, I remember a couple of those fights. If my information is correct, the protection went beyond a small-town police chief.

--Did you get involved when you joined the state police?

--Nope, it was shut down by then. Plus, I always worked on the east side of the state. When George Bosch shot himself, the core guys, which included Joe, packed it all up and acted as if it never existed.

--I either didn't know or had forgotten all that. I was in Denver by then. I mostly tried to put Joe and Dordrecht behind me. Did Butch's dad really shoot himself?

--Well, maybe not, from what I heard. Let's say that the Singapore County Sheriff made the call. No one tried to prove otherwise. Tell me more about Amy. You've told me before that she had a wild spell. How did she get in and out of it?

--I'm not sure she ever got out of it. You know more than I do. She had a reputation for being wild. She was always dating older guys as soon as she got to high school; they took her to drinking parties before she was ready. Before Joe and Mom separated, she studied art and fashion design at the Art Academy in Chicago. The following year, she dropped out either because she flunked out or left because Joe was experiencing a weak business period and couldn't come up with the tuition. I've heard several reasons. But she stayed in Chicago for a while. Joe got a friend from DeJong to get her a job at their showroom at the Merchandise Mart. She screwed that up, too. After an outpatient rehab stint at the Christian Reformed Psychiatric Center in New Leiden, Mom convinced her to live at home with her and Joe. That did seem to help some. As far as I know, she never completely gave up the booze, pot, or even coke, but she controlled it.

--How did she meet that guy she married? Wasn't his name Bolinyk? I heard he was convicted of drug dealing and spent some time in prison.

--Ja. She met Theo at the Beeline. Joe introduced them. I guess he and Theo were out slumming. Theo got Amy to move to New Leiden, where his sister, Stephanie Goodman, gave her a job in her clothing boutique. She fit in, worked well with Stephanie, and found a career. When they married, Theo and Joe became even closer buddies. They also maintained a business relationship. Theo was known to frequent the Monday night card game, which, you're telling me, was much more than a card game. Somehow, Joe was never caught up in Theo's drug deals. Amy also became closer to Joe. Mom gave up on her at that point.

--She lives in Singapore now?

--Yeah. Theo developed a real coke problem and had a wandering eye. At that point, he still had some money, so she got a divorce settlement and opened a boutique in Singapore, partnering with Stephanie. It seems to have done well. Enough about my family. What about you? How is semiretirement and the private eye business?

--Hey, don't call me a private eye, although I just got my license. I don't chase errant husbands. I am a security consultant. See! Here's my card. During my last six years with the state police, I was assigned to the white-collar crime unit for the Attorney General's office. With my experience, I'm now offering my professional services to investigate internal crime at private corporations. I even have a part-time employee. She said she's your second cousin.

--Who's that?

--Bonnie van Draght. She's a couple of years younger than us. She's retired from the state police, too.

--I think I remember her. She was a tall girl. Wasn't she all-state in basketball?

--Ja. And softball. I am planning to double my income with half the work. I'll have time to be a grandfather. The rest of my life will be spent golfing and fishing here and in Florida.

--No new female companion picked out?

--Absolutely not. I've been a free agent for five years. I like it that way. What about you?

--No. I've not been interested. These days, I've been traveling way too much—no time for dating. But I am also ready to cut back on work if I can. You're making semiretirement sound surprisingly good.

--So, how would you pull that off?

--My partner and his son want to buy me out. We brought his son into the business five years ago. I initially spent half my time buying and selling and the rest in operations and inventory. My partner was the money guy. As I've told you, we purchase and sell used office systems like DeJong manufactures. When a company needs to start over with a new system, we buy the old one or sometimes tear it down and pick it up at no cost. That allows us to save someone else a lot of money by setting them up with a custom-designed layout with used system pieces. My partner did the accounting and general management. Later, his son, who was somewhat of a computer genius, joined us. He customized an off-the-shelf program to control all our inventory, which could be stored in several locations nationwide. In real-time, we now know what we have, where it's going, and who's installing it. We are handling triple the inventory and double the installations with half the office staff. I am rightfully out of half my job. The other half has grown, and it's been successful. But I am getting burned out by too many hours, working on weekends, and too much traveling.

--So, how do you get off the treadmill?

--They want to buy out a firm in San Jose so we can be more competitive in California. I am not up for that for many reasons. I'm ready to get out. The California company has people who can do my job. They won't need me. We're close on price. This deal I'm working on is the largest we've ever done. My override and annual bonus will be over half my base salary this fiscal year. I can take my time organizing my future. I'll need to have some income, of course. I plan to downsize, so I won't need as much as I'm used to. The buyout money will be my retirement fund. I'll need to stay in the same field because it's all I know. I'll need a non-compete agreement that allows me to keep working. That's part of what we are negotiating. I may wind up being a freelancer and consultant just like you.

--Wow, good luck with all that. Will you have time for golf or hunting before you leave?

--No and yes. I'm flying to Madison right after the funeral and then to Atlanta to close this deal. I'm coming back on Saturday to meet Amy and her accountant on Monday, so I'm free on Saturday afternoon and Sunday.

--Great! It could be too wet for golf. But there are a few days left in duck season. We could try our luck at the DFG.

--I'd like that. I haven't been hunting in more than a decade. My son, David, didn't want to shoot animals, so I gave it up. But I don't have my old Remington or any hunting clothes. Do you have a membership?

--Not a problem. My son is living in Middleburg, and he does belong. He has an extra bedroom in the basement where I stay when I'm in town, which is most of the time now. We can be his guests at the club. He's about your size. I'll borrow some clothes from him and his Remington. It's a lot newer than yours.

--So, do we have a date early Sunday morning?

--Absolutely! I'll pick you up at the Inn at six. Call me when you get in. You have my business card. The phone number is my direct line in my son's basement. That's also my temporary office now.

While they drank two more IPAs, they talked more about Larry's divorce and his kids as well as old times, sports, women, and all the other things men talk about while they are re-bonding.

Chapter 3—Joe, Fall, 1969

J oe Berendts woke up in the Howard Johnson Motor Lodge on the state bypass between Dordrecht and Middleburg, his head throbbing as usual. He called down to the restaurant and asked Peggy, the receptionist, to send a pot of coffee, scrambled eggs, and toast to his room. HoJo's didn't have room service, but Joe was a friend of one of the franchise-owning partners and a good tipper. The server, Jennifer, could quickly bring a tray down a hallway on the first floor. By the time he showered, his breakfast had arrived. He gave Jennifer a twenty, telling her to share the change with Peggy. He knew them both from the Beeline, where they were regulars at the Friday night happy hour. They were still young and good-looking enough to get free drinks and bar food from older men in a party mood. He sat up on the bed, picked at the eggs, and sipped the coffee with a sigh and regret, more regret than he was used to. He was in deep trouble this time, triple deep, too deep to work out of it. He always thought he could get out of anything. This time, all the ways out were blocked.

It was three days since Rose had kicked him out of the house. For the first time, it lasted more than one night. He was sure he would be divorced by now if she and her father were not dead set against it, even if adultery was a legitimate reason. His drinking only got worse when he was away from Rose. His friend Hank Plagmeyer was trying to get him to an AA meeting. Although Joe realized his drinking was uncontrollable, he did not want to quit. He did not dare stop. He could forget his problems only during the first couple of drinks of his nightly self-medicating, even if he stayed home and hid from his other life outside of work and home. As he drank more, the effectiveness of the alcohol depreciated, and his thoughts returned to his troubles. That damned Lydia had called Rose and told her she should divorce Joe because he was in love with her, not Rose.

Two years previously, Joe had tearfully promised Rose that he would never see Lydia again. Joe knew he was captivated and could not resist her, especially after drinking, but he never considered being with her permanently. Two weeks later, she surprisingly showed up at the Beeline. It did not take more than a look and a smile for them to hook up again, resuming the on-and-off relationship that began in Chicago when Sal Broglio had introduced her to Joe at his club. It continued for more than four years. Rose had forgiven him for the few other dalliances she knew about. She knew, however, that Lydia was a real threat. Rose knew that Joe did not want a divorce either, but she would punish him until he had to give up and live by her and her father's rules.

When Joe and Rose had begun to date, Rose had felt stifled by her preacher's kid, hyper-Calvinist upbringing. She latched onto the free-living Joe as her way out. Even though she tried to keep him from self-destructing and taking their marriage with him, his free-living did not moderate after they were married. He had blown many chances. Joe was afraid that she might let Lydia have him this time.

The problem with Lydia was minor compared to the catastrophe with Joe's financial issues. The previous day, his partners at Dordrecht ChairWorks, where he was a partner and head of marketing, had uncovered discrepancies in his department.

Joe had been losing consistently for several years at the Monday night club in Dordrecht and the backroom game at the Triandos Bar and Grill in Chicago. Triandos was a hangout for the office furniture crowd at McCormick Place's showrooms. Joe had not even known the backroom existed for the first few years he attended the annual market or used the multi-vendor gallery between shows to meet clients. Joe used McCormick Place to grow the commercial and hospitality divisions of ChairWorks. Chicago was more accessible for clients than having them take an extra flight before driving to Dordrecht from New Leiden.

Later, as the ChairWorks commercial business grew and expanded, the partners decided it would be advantageous for them to have a dedicated ChairWorks Showroom. As marketing director, Joe was put in charge. It was a simple arrangement. Two salespeople staffed it during the year. The regional manufacturers' reps from the country used it during commercial market events. Factory staff from ChairWorks designed the layout and updated it during market times. In addition to the semiannual market periods, Joe flew in for a day every other week to ensure operations ran smoothly. When called for, he would meet with large-volume customers for one-on-one presentations.

One of his friendlier competitors at the Chicago market had discovered that Joe liked to place a bet occasionally. He introduced him to Sal, who had worked his way up from doorman and bouncer to manager of the back room at Triandos. Joe had noticed Sal, who walked with a significant limp and seemed to have minimal movement in his left arm, but he had no idea what his position was. Sal had checked him out because Joe was warmly greeted and ushered in on his next Chicago visit. Things had started slowly, with Joe winning or losing on a cash basis. One night, Joe ran out of cash and asked Sal if he would take a check. Sal told him the room did not accept checks, but he could offer Joe a line of credit since he had become a regular. It would be a 'grand' to start. That night, Joe used the credit line and came out ahead. However, two years later, Joe was behind by over five thousand. On Joe's next visit to Triandos, Sal stopped him at the door and sat him down at the restaurant bar. Joe played the conversation over in his mind.

--Joe, the Boss says you got to catch up on the bill, at least half, before you can play again. And he's going to charge you the vig until it's paid.

--Vig?

--Yup, the vig—the interest.

--Oh…. How much is the interest?

--Five percent.

--Okay, that's not too bad.

--That's per week. And you're two weeks behind as of now. You owe five hundred. I need it now.

--That's unreal. How can he charge that much?

--Just because he can. Don't ask questions like that.

--Well, I only brought a hundred with me.

--Gimme the hundred. You better show up with at least four-fifty next week, or the Boss'll come looking for you.

--Who's the Boss? I want to talk to him.

--You don't want to talk to the Boss. And you sure don't want him looking for you. Get it?

--Ja, ja, I get it.

--You better get it. Also, if you want to keep playing, you are cash-only again.

Joe showed up the next week with the four-fifty and another hundred, hoping to recover his losses. He managed to win fifty and felt better. He returned to the hotel room that he could charge to the company because he had an appointment at the showroom the next day. As he was going to sleep, an idea came to him. The next day, he changed his flight back to New Leiden to the evening. After his appointment, he went to Triandos around noon and asked for Sal. They said he was not due in until four, but they would call him. They soon returned and told Joe that Sal wanted him to wait for him to arrive in an hour. He was there in forty-five minutes.

--Hey Joe, What's up?

--Sal, I need your help. I can clean this mess up, but I need to work with a good printer who won't ask questions. I need professional work.

--Not a problem. What do you have in mind?

--I need to set up a shell company so it can invoice my company for services and supplies for our showroom at McCormick Place. I can okay them. I can use the payments to cut down on what I owe you.

--So, how does that work?

--These invoices will be for extra supplies and services that don't exist.

--Great idea! That's what I call creative thinking. I'll set up the company and send you the bills.

--Ah, I don't think that will work. The invoices need to match purchase orders. I can approve the small ones, but larger ones require approval from a partner to sign off. That means that shipping and receiving paperwork needs to match as well. Work orders for services need to be okayed and checked, too. And I can't do too much at first. They'll get suspicious.

--Not a problem. I'll still set up the company. You can tell me what we need. Let's go see a guy I know who can do the printing. What shall we call our company?

Sal took Joe to the back office of a small printing shop in a rundown neighborhood. Joe noticed copies of driver's licenses and other official-looking documents. Broglio Business Services was activated, and Joe's financial rescue operation was underway. Joe and Sal split the proceeds after the printer took ten percent off the top. At first, Joe did not see the cash, but it paid his 'vig' and gradually reduced his balance with Sal. The McCormick Place fire in 1967 was both a disaster and an opportunity. As the new Merchandise Mart replaced it, a new ChairWorks 'NeoCon' showroom was planned and built, reopening in early 1969. More and larger 'invoices' became possible. Joe soon settled his debt with Sal.

A few weeks after Joe and Sal set up their arrangement, Joe received a call from George Bosch, the Dordrecht Chief of Police. George and Joe were friendly, but when George was in his 'chief' persona, he had a way of acting and sounding very pretentious for the chief of a department with only one sergeant, six uniformed officers, and four patrol cars.

--Hey Joe, I have learned that you have become involved with Sal, who hangs around the illegal card game at the Triandos restaurant.

--What? Where in the hell did you hear that?

--Never mind where I heard it. I need you to know that you need to be careful. Don't fool around with these guys.

--George, I'm just playing cards.

--I know it's more than that, Joe. Don't worry. I won't arrest you or ask you to give up information. I do some work with Sal's boss. You're lucky you know me because now Sal won't be able to mess with you. He's small potatoes. My guy, the Boss, talked with me. We have some things you can help us with, too.

--Like what?

--We'll get to that later. For now, do what you're doing. Let me know if Sal gets out of line with you. Just make sure you're paying the bills. And keep your bets small. If you ever get too far behind, I won't be able to help you.

George set up a lunch meeting with Joe and Sal at Triandos two weeks later. He told them about the Boss's plan to expand the reach of his gambling operation. His idea was to set up traveling games in medium-sized towns around Chicago. They would be small but high-class Vegas style, aimed at the country club set. Not only could they be profitable, but they would help feed the Chicago backroom network. George had told Sal about the Monday night card game in Dordrecht. The Boss wanted to use George to find a way to take over and expand the game. A club in Singapore was already running from Friday to Sunday nights. Monday should be a good fit. George suggested that he would need Joe to help sell the upgrade. He thought the Visser brothers from Middleburg and Harm Van

Arden, who had also had dealings with the Boss, could be brought on board to convince the rest of the group. Sal would be the go-between with Chicago.

Within a year, poker night became a real club. The bar was expanded, a blackjack table with a dealer was added, and a twenty-five-dollar minimum, hundred-dollar maximum poker game. Later, a storage room and two offices were torn down to make space for roulette and a catered buffet. Sal hired a staff of attractive young women to run the tables and serve the drinks and buffet. Most of them found the tips excellent and moonlighted from their jobs at other bars and restaurants. It did not take long for the word to spread. Men from Middleburg, New Leiden, and other West Michigan towns began to show up, reflecting the liberalized mood of the late sixties that had even made its way to Dordrecht. George was able to keep law enforcement from snooping around. The club was a success. After the Boss took his cut off the top, Sal, George, Harm, Joe, Dennis, and the Visser brothers all took their part of the profits. Joe's cut most often went to Sal to keep his balance down.

————————

But now Joe was in deeper trouble than ever before. The false invoices to ChairWorks and the override from the Monday night club no longer covered his continuing debt to Sal from the Triandos and Monday night gambling. The more he lost, the more he drank, starting an expanding spiral that never stopped. He was forced to turn in too many invoices, causing his partners, Matt and Mark DeVries, to question the expenses. They soon discovered the extent of the fraud and told Joe they would go to the authorities if he did not pay back in full. Joe had no way to do that.

Joe was immobilized, not seeing any way out as the three walls closed on him: Lydia, Sal, and the DeVries brothers. To do something, he called Peggy to have his tray picked up and then headed to the shower. At least it would temporarily ease the effects of the hangover. Fifteen minutes later, he came out of the shower and called the Dordrecht police station to try to reach George Bosch. He recognized the voice of Charley Vredevelde, the second in command. He heard Charley yell to George that Joe was on the line. George told Charley to transfer the call to the office. Joe listened to the door close before George picked up the phone again.

--Joe, I can't talk to you right now. Where are you?

--Hojo's. Rose kicked me out on Monday.

--What room?

--Uh, 114.

--Stay there! I'll come to see you in about forty-five minutes.

--Let me tell you what's going on.

--Not now. Just stay there. Don't talk to anyone until I get there. Okay?

--Okay, Okay. I'll wait for you.

Thirty-five minutes later, George knocked on the door. He was already talking as Joe let him in.

--Goddammit, Joe, you've fucked up this time. Just before you called, the PA from North Haven called me and said that Matt and Mark want him to file embezzlement charges against you. What the fuck is going on.

--George, you know I needed money. I padded my expense account and faked invoices for some services at the Chicago Showroom. Sal helped me. All the money went to him.

--Oh, shit. Now he's involved, too. That's even worse. It's downright dangerous. How much are we talking about?

--About thirty grand. It might be a little more.

--How much more?

--It might be closer to fifty.

--Probably?

--Hey, I didn't keep records.

--I guess that's a good thing. How are we going to get out of this? I'm going to get dragged into it with you, you know.

--That's why I called you.

--It was dumb to call the department. That damned Charley could stick his nose into this. But I can handle him. What's happened between you and Rose?

--She found out I had seen Lydia again. She says it's going to be permanent this time.

--That's not good. We need to get you back home. You'll look less guilty. Then we'll fight your other battles. Who's your lawyer?

--Adam Johnson in Middleburg.

--Well, he's a lightweight. Is he hooked up with Matt and Mark?

--I don't think so. His older partners worked with my dad. They helped us with the contracts when we joined ChairWorks.

--Okay. He'll be the best we can do for now. Call him. Tell him that Matt and Mark are accusing you of embezzlement. Tell him you're not guilty. Don't tell him we have talked, and for God's sake, don't tell him about Sal.

--Okay, I can do that. What else?

--Right now? Nothing. Stay here. Watch TV. Have the girls bring you lunch and dinner. No booze! I'll make a few calls as

I have time today when Charley is not in the office. He's like a Peeping Tom. I have an idea that will help get you back with Rose. I need to call the Boss and convince him and Sal that we'll keep them out of it. We need to slow down or stop Matt and Mark somehow. Adam might have some ideas. For now, stay here. Don't call anyone except Adam. I'll come back a little after eight.

Do you get it?

--Ja, I got it.

Joe sat down on the small lounge chair in his room, more dazed than before. He began to reflect on his life and how he had gotten mixed up in his situation.

Joe's father, Jan, had been raised as one of ten children on a farm fifteen miles south of Dordrecht. Joe's namesake grandfather, Johannes, had bought it for a dollar an acre when he arrived from the Netherlands in the 1880s. He settled among earlier immigrants from Overijssel in the Netherlands, becoming a small part of the Dutch-dominated area of southern Nederland and northern Singapore counties. Jan had left home at age fourteen as a boarder, laborer, and servant at a nearby farm. When he was eighteen, he moved to Dordrecht, still living with a local family, where he found a job in the local clock factory, making cabinets for both floor and large wall clocks. He met and married Maude van Draght, the niece of his landlord. They had four children: Benjamin (Ben), Jacomina (Minnie), Johannes (Joe), and Cornelia (Nelly). When Johannes passed away soon after Joe was born, the family sold the farm. Combining his share of the sale with his woodworking and cabinetmaking experience from the clock factory, Jan started a small workshop making custom caskets that he sold to local area funeral homes. He gradually expanded the shop into a manufacturing plant and marketed Berendts Premium Caskets throughout the Midwest.

Joe's mother, Maude, was raised on a fruit and vegetable farm outside Dordrecht. Her family had been pillars of the First Reformed Church for three generations, having arrived with the Dordrecht founders in 1849. Jan had attended church on and off since he left home, but he soon confessed his faith at First Reformed, where he and Maude continued the van Draght family tradition.

———————

Joe was always known, in his fun-loving way, for being disruptive in Sunday School, catechism classes, and other children's activities. Maude was often distressed that he was not taking religion seriously. However, he liked to sing and always joined the choir in school and church, continuing through college. However, singing in church choirs did not change his behavior. He was always in a bit of trouble but maintained a B average with little studying. Having fun was always his top priority.

At age nineteen, he first met Rosemary DeHaan while rehearsing for a Christmas Messiah performance with the Dordrecht Community Choir. He thought he knew all the girls around his age in Dordrecht, but she was someone new. Looking from his perch at the top of the tenor section to the altos diagonally across, he could tell she was blonde and pretty. Asking around during a break, he discovered she was a senior at Middleburg Christian High and the daughter of the new *domine* at First Christian Reformed. A week later, he executed his plan to lightly bump into her at the break, apologize, and introduce himself. The plan worked perfectly until he asked her out for a movie date. She politely and coolly said she did not go to movies or date public school boys. Joe's hopes were deflated, but he never got her out of his mind.

Two years later, just before he enlisted in the Army after Pearl Harbor, he was surprised to see her at a dance in New Leiden. This time, she accepted a dance invitation. He could remember the conversation.

--Wow, have you changed! I am surprised to see you here.

--I'm older now. I live in a co-op house on campus during the school year. Some of us like to have some fun, so we sneak out.

--Do you go to movies too?

--If they're nice ones.

--Like what?

--We saw *How Green Was the Valley* last week. I liked it.

--That's great. Is there another movie you'd like to see? We could have dinner and a movie.

--I don't think I'm ready for that. I still am not supposed to date public school guys. Especially someone with a reputation like yours.

--I have a reputation?

--You know you do. And I think you're proud of it.

--So why are you dancing with me?

--I love 'Stardust' and wanted to dance to it. We need to sneak just listening to it in our co-op. Plus, at least I know who you are. The other guys here are scary. We were about to leave to make our curfew, so I'll have to go when this song is done.

--Curfew at ten.

--Of course, it's Covenant College!

39

--Rose had been born in Oostburg, Wisconsin, where her father, Reverend Hendrick DeHaan, was the minister at his hometown Christian Reformed Church. He had returned after graduating from Covenant Seminary and serving as an assistant minister in New Leiden. His family had pioneered as farmers in the 1840s with a group of Dutch families in Sheboygan County. He had met and married a New Leiden girl named Catherine Beukema while a student. Their older children, Judy and Al, were born in New Leiden. Because Cathy disliked the small farming village community and church and his professional ambition, Hendrick accepted a call as minister to the Second Christian Reformed Church in Denver when Rose was nine years old. She was seventeen when he moved the family again to Dordrecht to be the minister at First Dordrecht Christian Reformed, one of the first five seceding churches of the 1850s.

Inside the Dutch Reformed community, Joe and Rose faced a massive wall of separation because of the minor but fierce doctrinal battles between the two denominations. Joe's infatuation gave him the necessary determination to overcome her defenses eventually, but there was not enough time before he went off to boot camp and on to England. After the war, when he returned home to Dordrecht and his job at the family casket factory, she was the one girl he could not forget. He found out she was still living at home, playing the organ at the Sunday evening service, and teaching sixth grade at Dordrecht Christian Schools. Once again, he met her at a community choir practice. She bravely accepted the dinner and movie date this time despite her parents' objections. She was older, more sophisticated, and ready to escape her restrictive preacher's kid existence. On their first date, they went to dinner at the

Middleburg Hotel and then to the Middleburg Theater to see *The Bells of Saint Mary's*. Joe was allowed a chaste kiss in the DeHaan driveway at the end of the evening. They were even more adventurous on the next date, featuring dinner and dancing at the Riverview Lodge in Singapore. Rose needed only a little encouragement to sip a cocktail and a glass of wine. This time, before they returned to the driveway, Joe stopped by the park a block from the DeHaan parsonage. The kisses were much more passionate.

The Reverend DeHaan was an obstacle, but the couple was just as much in love as he was against their marriage. They prevailed and were married less than a year later. To put a little space between them and their families, they joined the Dordrecht Second Reformed Church, which had a reputation for being more American and permissive.

Amy was born Amelia in 1947; Harry followed in 1949. His given name was Geerard, after Rose's grandfather. The nickname, Harry, easily flowed from the Dutch pronunciation of Geerard. When Jan made Joe the general manager of Berendts Caskets, they bought a Cape Cod starter house but soon moved to a Dutch Colonial-style home with more space. When Jan and Joe sold the casket company to a larger competitor a decade later, they could build an addition and a pool. Jan helped Joe buy into ChairWorks, in effect buying him the marketing manager position.

———————

Joe's reverie was interrupted by the shock of the phone ringing. He picked it up apprehensively.

--Hello.

--Joe, this is George.

--Oh, good. Hi, George. I was afraid someone else had found me.

--No, it's just me. But you are going to have to move. Have you called your lawyer yet?

--No, I've been thinking, trying to find a way out of this mess.

--That's good. But stop thinking and do what I tell you. First, your lawyer is too weak. I found a guy in New Leiden. He's tough. He can get the DeVrieses to back off. His name is Lenny Caputo. Get his number from information. Tell his office that Gordie Van Klompenberg referred you. They will take your call.

--Van Klompenberg? That junk dealer?

--Ja, don't ask, call. Don't give any info on the phone. Just get an appointment ASAP. Tell them it's an emergency. We need to slow down the PA.

--Next, we need you to go back home to Rose. We need her on your side. That means you've got to get off the booze. Call your friend Hank. Tell him the truth. You've hit bottom. You're ready to go to AA. Ask him to take you sometime tomorrow, not today. Can you do that?

--Ja, I need to do that.

--Good. Once you get started, we'll work on a plan for you to get back with Rose. As soon as you make those calls, check out of HoJo's. Do you have cash with you?

--I'll be under fifty after I pay for the room.

--Okay, check out and drive to John Visser's used car lot in Middleburg. He'll park your car in the back and give you a loaner and some cash. Then, drive to Singapore and check in to the Singapore River Motel on M-22 in Wakazoo. I want you

42

out of the county to keep you from being easily arrested until we can cool things down, okay? Got that?

--Ja, I got it.

--One last thing, get some change. Don't call anyone from the motel. Find a pay phone to call me at home at ten tonight. Don't call anyone else except to follow through with Hank or Caputo. Nobody! Got it?

--Ja, George, I got it.

--Okay. We'll be okay, George. Remember, I'm helping you because I don't want to go down with you. Talk to you at ten.

Joe followed the plan to the letter. Hank knew of a Thursday noon meeting at the Methodist church in Middleburg. He would go with Joe to sponsor him for the first few meetings. When he called Lenny Caputo's office, he was put on hold. After a five-minute wait, they told him they could see him late Thursday afternoon but to call back in the morning to confirm the time. He picked up five hundred in cash and a four-year-old Skylark from John Visser, who parked Joe's Riviera in the back of his lot. The motel was below Joe's standards, but at least he felt less exposed. George had made Joe even more aware of the danger he was in. He was not only concerned about the Nederland Prosecuting Attorney. Sal and the Boss were also not going to be happy about this. Once law enforcement started investigating Joe's embezzlement, they were also exposed. He stopped at a KFC for a box of chicken and picked up a bottle of wine and cigarettes at a convenience store before hiding in his room.

At ten, he went to the pay phone and called George, who picked up on the first ring. Joe confirmed that he had scheduled an AA meeting with Hank and would be at the Caputo law firm late afternoon the next day. George only made one change. Joe was also instructed to call Adam Johnson and have him work with the PA to head off any arrests or indictments. Sending Caputo to the PA might wave a red flag. Caputo would contact the Devrieses behind the scenes to pressure them to drop the charges. He told Joe to give any dirt he knew about his partners to Caputo and to profess his innocence to Adam. With George's help and advice, Joe managed to minimize the damage from his three predicaments.

After meeting Lenny Caputo on Thursday after five o'clock and Adam Johnson on Friday morning, Joe started to think that not all was lost. He had told Caputo that he could prove his partners' hands were not clean. He had seen indications that their IRS reporting was questionable. Caputo said he would work with that. Joe felt his share of the business, his only available asset after he had mortgaged the house to the maximum to pay for the addition and pool, was worth at least $150,000. He thought he should be able to use part of that to make restitution. Caputo agreed. Lenny also decided that his history with the Nederland County Prosecuting Attorney was not good. Hiring Adam to make that contact was wise. When Joe met Adam, he was also optimistic. He thought the DA would be willing to wait to see if the DeVrieses would drop the charges and accept part of Joe's equity as restitution.

The AA meeting did not go as smoothly. After he went to another meeting with Hank without standing up and acknowledging his alcoholism, Hank realized that Joe was buying time. He called Reverend James Scholten, who arranged a meeting with Rose. Rose was willing to try to get back together, but Joe would need to change his thinking and behavior. The three of them decided to set up an intervention. They enlisted the help of Rose's father, Reverend DeHaan, and two of Joe's three siblings, Ben and Mina. They also brought Harry back from WMU in Kalamazoo. Joe went to Hank's home, thinking he would just be meeting Rose with Hank and his wife, Karen. When he saw the group, he was angry and put up his defenses while the others tried to get him to admit that he could no longer continue to lie to himself and others about the wreck that his life had become. It was when the eighty-year-old Reverend DeHaan, who had managed to stay quiet, knelt before Joe while holding his hands. He softly told Joe that God would receive him back into the fold if he would kneel, pray, and ask him for forgiveness. Joe would feel God's boundless grace and Christ's unlimited forgiveness and atonement. The ideas were standard Reformed doctrine, but Joe internalized them for the first time. He and everyone else broke down, shedding as many tears as their stoic Dutch mentality allowed. It was decided that Reverend DeHaan, Hank, and Ben would rush him to the Christian Reformed Psychiatric Center in New Leiden for evaluation and probable admission into their addiction recovery residential program.

At first, George Bosch was upset when he heard about the intervention and resulting residential treatment, mainly trying to protect himself. As he worked through the problems Joe had created for everyone in the Monday night club, he realized that having Joe tucked away benefited him and Joe. Joe would be out of touch and unable to make mistakes. The PA would be less likely to arrest him. Only close family and his lawyers would be allowed to see him. After talking with Caputo, he called the Boss and bought some time for Joe to work out his debt.

Joe stayed in rehab for six weeks before he went home to Rose with only part of his penance paid. Rose's father insisted that he confess to the consistory of Second Reformed. Reverend Scholten set up his appearance for the next weekly meeting. Joe was embarrassed and ashamed, shed more tears, and obtained forgiveness and admonishment from the elders and deacons that made up the consistory.

Harry was not as forgiving. To him, divorce would have been the better choice for his mother. He had no faith that Joe would stick to any agreements. He told Joe that he could not forgive him and would never respect him as a man or his father again. Amy was more upset about the family's fiscal crisis than she was about Joe's behavior. The economic fallout kept her from being able to go back to the Chicago Art Institute the following semester. She treated Joe with sarcastic humor as if he were a boy caught with his hand in the cookie jar.

Although the terms were not in Joe's favor, Lenny Caputo successfully negotiated with the DeVries brothers. They agreed to drop the charges if Joe accepted their buyout agreement, which called for Joe to resign and pay restitution of $46,500. The buyout price would be $75,000, leaving Joe $28,500. It was a bitter pill for Joe. He thought the sale amount should have been at least $150,000. There would not be much left after he settled with Sal and the Boss and paid the lawyers. Lenny worked through Adam Johnson to bring the DA on board and close the case with no charges. Joe would not go to jail, and his bills would be covered.

But Joe, sobered up and safely in rehab, was already starting to think ahead. The DeVrieses, in their rush to make a profit and get rid of Joe, had neglected to include a non-compete clause in the agreement. Joe knew several competitors that he thought would be happy to hire him. He could get back with Rose, earn enough for a decent lifestyle, and live a proper life again, no alcohol, no gambling, no Lydia, and no mobsters to deal with. Joe's Riviera was back in the garage.

The no-mobsters part, however, was not to be. Hank had picked up Joe at the end of the six weeks and brought him home to Rose. The three of them sat, thanked God for Joe's return, and petitioned Jesus for the strength to avoid backsliding. After Hank left, Rose quietly acted pleased that their life was returning to normal, except for the absence of the well-stocked bar. She had just returned from the beauty parlor, trying to look her best. His favorite foods were on hand. She prepared his favorite roasted chicken meal for dinner. She was ready for something intimate, but Joe said he was tired and wanted to go to bed early. She was willing to wait.

When Rose went to her weekly Bible Study meeting the next day, Joe called George Bosch as instructed and was relieved that George picked up instead of Charley.

--Hey George, it's me, Joe.

--Joe! Welcome back! How does it feel to be free?

--Good. . . Great! Being home never felt so good. Free of all that crap.

--Well, Joe. We need to talk about that. You're not free of all of it.

--What do you mean? I'm done.

--Not quite. The Boss is pissed at Sal, so you don't need to worry about him. But he and John Visser did you a favor with the car. Now they want some help from you.

--What kind of help can I give them? I'm broke. And I need to keep my nose clean.

--They don't need the money and don't want much. The Boss and John have a deal going on with Van Klompenberg Salvage. It's actually a scam. They take late-model luxury cars with questionable titles from Chicago. They clean them up inside, out, and underneath. Do you know what I mean? Then, they return them to Chicago. Van Klompenberg flips clean papers from a destroyed car. They need another driver. You qualify because, somehow, you've avoided a DUI. Your license is clean. It'll be easy. John will show you the ropes. They even pay fifty bucks a trip.

--George. I don't want to be involved in that. It's too risky. I want to stay clean.

--You can never be completely clean, and it's only a little risky. What's dangerous is not helping the Boss. He has ways of expressing his disappointment.

Two weeks later, Joe and Jim Visser, John's brother, drove two cars to the Saturday Waukegan Car Auction. Jim accepted bids on both. They grabbed a sandwich at the onsite café and waited a block from the auction for two late model Camaros to pull up. They took the keys from the drivers and returned to the Van Klompenberg Salvage yard, just outside Middleburg. Jim Visser gave Joe his fifty dollars. Joe was returning to his alternate life, which now seemed like another dimension.

Chapter 4—Harry, First Monday, 1998

Harry woke up early Monday morning. He grabbed a coffee and a bagel from the breakfast buffet and brought it back to his room. Even though he was having breakfast with Allen later, he needed to eat something with the coffee to soothe the three-IPA mini-hangover resulting from his late dinner with Larry. As he sipped his coffee, he opened his briefcase. He reviewed the contracts he needed final approval for later in the week, looking for potential client objections and preparing effective responses. Realizing that there was nothing more he could do before the meetings, he showered, put on casual clothes, and headed to the Coffee Pot on North Street in downtown Dordrecht.

The Coffee Pot had been an institution in Dordrecht since the 1920s. Originally named DeKruyter's Restaurant, the founder's granddaughter recently upgraded and renamed it. Most natives still called it DeKruyter's. There was still a line at nine o'clock, but Harry spotted Allen at the front. He had a neatly trimmed ring of deep brown hair around his bald crown. His six-four frame was still slim and fit. They had time for only a handshake and a one-armed hug before they were seated.

By the time they had talked about their families and kids (Allen had five), their breakfast arrived: the Dutch sausage omelet for Harry and the low-cholesterol plate for Allen. Harry's mind flashed back to their childhood. He asked Allen about Jeff Klaasen, the third person in their neighborhood and Christian elementary school childhood trio. When Harry left for the public school for junior high, he had lost touch with Jeff. Allen had said that he and Jeff had also grown apart. Jeff was not into sports. Apart from being interested in music and art, he had become withdrawn and insular.

--I saw him at a reunion a few years ago. He has a men's clothing shop in Singapore that's only open in the summer. He seemed happier and more confident. He had a younger friend with him. I think bringing his friend was another step in his coming out.

--I remember hearing that he came out in high school. It was at graduation. Were you surprised?

--Of course. I was so naïve I didn't know what being homosexual meant.

--We all were naive back then. Amy told me they have become friends since they both have Singapore businesses.

--I guess he feels comfortable in Singapore. It has a reputation for being friendly to homosexuals and lesbians. I haven't been there for decades.

Harry realized he needed to change the subject. He mentioned that he had seen Larry at Der Kroeg the night before. Allen smiled, almost laughing.

--How is Big Larry? Whenever I think of him, I remember the last game against you guys in the tournament—the best game I ever played. I rang up twenty-two on him. He fouled out in frustration. Sweet revenge for all the times he was better than me at everything.

--You were a late developer!

--We beat you guys so badly that you even got in the game at mop-up time.

--Okay, that's enough rubbing it in now. I was only on the team because the coach begged me, not that he needed me as a six-one skinny reserve power forward. After football season, Larry didn't take basketball seriously. My job was to keep him focused and motivated. I failed that night. That game was on a Saturday. Friday was our party night.

--Excuses! Excuses! But enough of all that. It is good to see you for any reason, but I must discuss something. Confidentially, of course. I'm skirting professional standards only because you're a friend and have a need to know.

--Okay, hit me with it.

--Here's the condensed version. As you know, my dad was always Joe's accountant. I was not allowed near Joe's account when I joined the office. I remember his serious looks when Joe's name came up. Phone calls started with 'What are you up to now?' Gradually, I became more involved. My dad told me about when Joe was accused of embezzling from his partners at Dordrecht ChairWorks, the DeVries brothers. The charges were dropped for some reason, but he resigned and left with a reduced buyout. That was another time when your mom almost divorced him. It took him a couple of years while he worked for a company out of Vermont and later at DeJong, but surprisingly, ChairWorks took him back as a sales manager because he was good at it. He started making money again, but only as an employee.

--About five years ago, after your mom died, Amy came into the office with Joe after a second heart surgery. He wanted Amy to be familiar with his finances if the worst happened. After that, most phone calls we got were direct from Amy. When signatures were needed, she would pick up the documents, bring them to Joe to be signed, and then return them. Six months after my dad died three years ago, she called and said they wanted to go in a different direction. Everything was transferred to a guy named William Snyder in New Leiden. All I know about him is that his reputation and some of his clients are, shall we say, shady. Here is what I know and everything I can tell you. Joe's assets dropped sharply between when Amy became involved and when she dropped us for no apparent reason. This means my personal, not professional, advice to you is not to accept any settlement Amy offers at first glance. Enough money is involved, so you should get a lawyer specializing in probate to help you check it out.

--This does not sound good, but I am not surprised. Thank you. I appreciate your concern.

They finished their breakfast quickly and said their goodbyes. Allen was ready to leave, saying he had an appointment. Harry was disappointed that their relationship had become more formal and distant over the decades. The Dordrecht Reformed denomination divide was challenging to bridge.

Harry started to return to the Amsterdam Inn to prepare for the funeral, but he had time before he was due at the church, so he decided to loop around Dordrecht, something he hadn't found time for on his last two visits. DeKruyter's was in the middle of the three-block downtown on North Street, where two new stoplights had been added since Harry had left two and a half decades prior. Many of the same shops were still there. A new canopy covered the sidewalks on the center block. He quickly drove by the seven Dutch Reformed churches circling within four blocks of downtown. The old neighborhoods surrounding three downtown sides were still spotlessly kept. Even the modest homes had manicured lawns and updated facades. The houses on South Street, dating from the 1890s to the 1920s, were more extensive and impressive. Harry knew the names of the civic leaders whose families still lived in most of them. Harry perceived the town to still exist in a separate dimension, just as it had for the previous hundred and fifty years.

The high school he had attended was now a middle school with a new addition in place of the old bleachers at the football field. The field was still in the same place but was now outlined for soccer. He drove farther on North Street until he reached the DeJong factory, which had doubled in size since he had last visited the offices in the late eighties. He went north across the tracks to find that the original Berendts Premium Casket factory was still making caskets under its new name. Across the street, Dordrecht ChairWorks dominated the block. Going north, the new high school appeared, now twice the size of the original. Harry knew that the number of people in the town of Dordrecht was only slightly larger than in his day. The population growth that fed the school occurred in the township surrounding it. He returned to the Inn via the west side of the town where Jeff's grandparents once farmed. Harry, Allen, and Jeff had spent many summer days playing in and around the creek that crossed the farm and even catching sunfish in the small pond. The stream had been redirected and covered up. The pond was half the size and had a large sign that announced the entrance to Idlewild Acres, a senior living community. The loop had only taken twenty minutes of leisurely driving before Harry arrived back at the Amsterdam Inn.

———————

Wearing a medium gray suit, Harry arrived at Second Reformed at 1:30 as instructed by Amy. He found the side entrance and headed downstairs. He recognized Hank Plagmeyer, a friend of Joe's, about the same age, who always seemed to be at every church event. Today, he was an usher as well as Joe's friend. He greeted Harry warmly and pointed him to an open door down the hall, which Harry recognized as the consistory room. He always thought of it as the Holy of Holies of Second Reformed. He had been in it only when he had finished the catechism classes in tenth grade and made Confession of Faith. Not long after that, he considered it a weak moment, as he had already started on a path to purposeful agnosticism.

He was surprised that the mixed group he saw as he entered was allowed in. He had forgotten that the Reformed Church had opened the eldership to women soon after he had left Dordrecht in 1972. A few years later, women were allowed to be ordained as pastors. His mother, Rose, had quickly been asked to serve as an elder, but she refused because, under the influence of her Christian Reformed father, she did not feel that it was proper. He had also heard the Christian Reformed Church had finally followed suit decades later, shortly after Rose died. On the other hand, Joe had joined the church as a young man, but he had never been voted to be on the consistory, even as a deacon. The doubts about his character had consistently vetoed his election.

He saw Amy and Randy up front, ready for the pre-funeral meeting for family and participants. Amy was also dressed in a medium gray suit over a cream silk blouse, both expensive designer labels available at her store. Looking around, he was initially surprised at the lack of black-on-black clothing, although everyone was dressed conservatively. He remembered that Dutch Reformed tradition treated funerals not as a mournful event but as a celebration of the deceased person going to meet his Lord.

Amy and Randy gave him a look of relief that he had arrived on time, but Harry could feel them wondering why he could not have been ten minutes early. He recognized his Uncle Ben, Joe's older brother, in a wheelchair with a woman attendant on one side of him and a Labrador service dog on the other. Ben had dementia. Harry knew that the dog helped keep him calm. The Veenstras and DeHaans were there. He also recognized Randy's wife, Joanne, Reverend Scholten, and another Second Reformed man, a perennial elder whose name he could not remember. In the back corner, he saw Amy's live-in boyfriend, Doug Mason, and a mystical-looking man whom Harry assumed was Amy's guru, Gerrit Gerritson, Neither wore a coat or a tie. Next to them was a country music-looking couple, outfitted in country dress-up. There was also a well-dressed, thin, older man. Harry assumed he was the organist.

Randy greeted everyone before the prayers commenced. Randy and Reverend Scholten took their turn. Randy reviewed the itinerary, including the reception in the fellowship room after the service, where the Ladies Aid Society would serve sandwiches, dessert, and coffee. Harry was glad for the sandwiches because his late breakfast had caused him to skip lunch.

As the close family group filed into the church ten minutes early, the organist played two chorales (Bach, Harry guessed) and then a medley of Dutch Psalms. Harry could not remember which psalms they were or the words. At first, he was surprised that the church was filling up, but then he remembered that Joe had lived his whole life in the same small town where not only family and close friends attended funerals. It was also a time for community bonding.

The service was a clash of cultures. After Randy opened with a joyful prayer, Amy, with her guitar and the other two musicians on the piano and bass, changed the musical mood from the traditional reverence of the organist to a mélange medley of new-age praise band songs that Harry had never heard but had the younger members of the crowd clapping and singing along. A Bluegrass versions of 'Will the Circle be Unbroken?' was followed by 'Precious Lord' before 'Sweet Chariot' finished the session. Harry thought Amy's voice was more mellow and mature than he remembered from their high school days.

After the music, Randy, walking around the platform, painted a picture of Joe in heaven with Jesus, dancing and singing with the angels, having found his faith again in his later years. Several of Joe's old friends gave short eulogies: He was a good friend when one needed a friend (Hank); he had a contagious sense of humor and was the life of any party (Jim Visser); he gave people jobs when no one else would (Matt Devries); he supported philanthropic organizations with his time and money (Herm Den Arden). The band played a praise hymn, with most of the congregation singing the words printed in the program.

The mood suddenly shifted. The congregation, accompanied by the organ, sang a more somber psalm from the traditional hymnal while Reverend Scholten moved slowly behind the pulpit to give the sermon. He was even more grave than the organ, reminding the audience that 'From man came death' but 'From man came also the resurrection from the dead.' He left unsaid exactly where Joe and his soul were at present, but the Reverend assured them that Joe would be raised from the dead with the rest of those who believed when the last trumpet sounded on Judgment Day. Amy's group played one more praise-band hymn as the congregation sang along. Completing the musical circle, the organist returned to play the 'Hallelujah Chorus' as people were ushered out.

Harry spent the next forty-five minutes greeting and being greeted by old acquaintances and friends of the family, working his way to the rear exit of the sanctuary. Just as he reached his goal, a man of Harry's age and size approached him. He was noticeably tan and dressed trendier than the other men in attendance. His hair was a darker blond than Harry's but longer and professionally styled.

--Hello, Harry. It's been a long time!

Harry drew a blank before his recognition set in. He reached out both hands to shake.

--Oh, my God! Jeff! It took me a second. It has been a long time. I guess it's typical of Dutch folk to meet only at weddings and funerals. It's great to see you!

--You too, Harry. I was hoping to catch you here, although I came as a friend of your sister.

--She mentioned you to me a few times. You two have much in common, including living and working in Singapore.

--Ja. I have a men's shop. We spend time together now and then. We have some of the same customers.

--This is ironic. I had breakfast with Allen Zuverink this morning. We reminisced about the three of us in grade school. He said he saw you at a reunion.

--He did. I caused a real stir.

--I can imagine. It's still Dordrecht, after all. I drove by your grandpa's farm this morning. We had a lot of fun there. We can return to our childhood in a few years by retiring to the new senior living facility.

--We are getting there, aren't we? But I don't see myself in Dordrecht. I bought a bed and breakfast home in Singapore with a friend with my share of the farm sale proceeds. We also have a condo in Key West. How about you? Are you still in Denver?

--Yes, but things are changing. I'm divorced and selling my business. I'll be rudderless for a while.

--I've always felt bad about losing contact with you. My parents didn't want me to be friends with a kid from the public school.

--I've felt guilty, too. I thought you would blame me for leaving. Especially when I heard that you came out. That must not have been an easy time for you.

--It was tough at first, but it prepared me for what's become a good life.

--It also helped me to accept my son being gay. He was about the same age you were when he made his announcement. Knowing someone in my past gave me some perspective on what he was going through.

--It seems like we have a lot to talk about. How long will you be here? We could get together with Amy.

--Only if you want to referee. I'm leaving tonight, but I'll be back next week. I'll call you. Are you in the book?

--Yes, but I'll be in my shop most of the time. Here's the card. And one for the B&B. My friend, Rob, runs it. I'm the de facto social director.

They shook hands, and Harry watched Jeff leave. When he finally found the way to the new community hall in the new wing, he ran into Ben Berendts with his aide and Hank Plagmeyer. Hank, enunciating clearly, told Ben that this was Harry, Joe's son. Ben momentarily looked lost, but then he purposefully began kicking his foot.

--How's the leg?

Harry hesitated but then chuckled.

--Hey, Uncle Ben. I'm not kicking anymore. My leg is too old. How do you feel about outlasting your brother?

Ben seemed to contemplate before he lost the thread.

Hank smiled wryly and jumped back into the conversation.

--He goes in and out these days.

The aide was a tall woman who looked to be in her late thirties, dressed in slacks and a tunic top, less aide-like than usual for the funeral. Her hair and complexion, darker than most Dutch folk, caught Harry's attention. The rest of her appearance was attractive in a way that left him a bit speechless when she quickly added her comment.

--Mostly out.

She held out her hand to Harry.

--Hi, I'm Irma Schroeder, Hank's niece. I'm also a nurse at the assisted living unit at Covenant Gardens. I try to keep our clients involved in life to not slip completely inside themselves.

Up until last month, Ben would talk about Joe. I wanted him to be here, even though they didn't always get along.

With Harry still hesitating, Hank quickly replied.

--They were hugely different. Ben was a successful optometrist who was always on the straight and narrow, nose to the grindstone, always attending the Sunday services. He was one of the last holdouts on the consistory when they finally dropped the evening service. Joe was…well, Joe…Joe was Joe, as we know.

Irma interjected again.

--Ben used to say Joe was lucky he wasn't in jail.

--Harry chuckled and finally was able to reply.

--I guess we should give Joe a break since he's no longer with us. Hank, you were friends with Joe.

--We were almost best friends when we were young. We enlisted together. I was a mechanic and never got into front-line combat. Joe talked himself into a clerical slot for a supply colonel and stayed within England. I'm still not sure how he pulled that off. We had a falling out when those Monday night card games got out of hand, and my life with them. I went to AA and stayed as far away from Joe as possible. Ben and I became friends. He was a tremendous help to me.

They talked more about their families until Irma said it was time to get Ben a piece of pie. After they said their goodbyes, Harry glanced around. He was surprised to see Marilyn Bosch coming toward him. She looked more at ease than the day before, still dressed conservatively in a gray silk blouse and straight skirt. She had kept her strawberry blonde hair and the same shapely, slightly heavier-than-average figure that she had when they dated in high school. Harry felt his defensiveness toward her weakening.

--Hello again, Marilyn. Thanks for coming again.

She stepped to a corner of the room and almost whispered.

--I thought things were tense yesterday. It wasn't how I wanted it to go with you. Seeing you in person again was different than the memories. They had faded over time.

--How did you want it to go?

--Friendlier for sure.

Harry paused a few moments, letting his feelings settle.

--I'm not sure what that means.

--It means that seeing you jolted something inside me. Probably regret and guilt. I made the wrong choice. In the long run, it hurt me more than you.

--I'm glad you didn't say the short run, although that was good for me too. It allowed me to move on from Dordrecht. At first, you were the only thing I missed, until I finally let it go—meaning you.

--We need to talk some. I am out of sorts, not knowing what to do. Butch has been more difficult than ever. Plus, I think he has a new girlfriend. At least it isn't your sister like two years ago.

--Really? That news didn't get to me.

--I knew it wouldn't last, given their history. The new affair might be the one that will last. Anyway, you know me and can help me find myself again. Plus, you're not a part of the gossip circle. My last counseling session with a pastor was soon news all over Dordrecht and Middleburg.

--Was that with Randy?

--No, I wouldn't be comfortable with him. We used to be friends. Plus, I hear he's too hands-on, if you know what I mean.

--I think I do.

--Are you staying around for a while? Do you think we could meet?

--I am flying out late today but returning on Saturday. Larry and I will be duck hunting on Sunday morning, and I'm meeting with Amy on Monday.

--We could meet late Saturday afternoon. Butch is having a weekend golf and card game at Gun Lake with his friends. At least, that is what he's telling me. I know they like to go to that illegal casino there, too.

--Okay. I'm willing to talk. Choose a safe place. I don't know what flight I'm taking yet. I can call you when I know.

--What do you mean by a safe place?

--Away from the gossip circles, I guess.

--Speaking of which. We better break this off. Do you want my phone number?

--Yeah, I'll put it into my Nokia after you leave. Just give me the last four. I know the first six numbers—Middleburg, right?

She gave her number quietly. Harry watched her turn to leave before realizing he had been watching too long.

Amy came up behind him.

--I see you're stirring up old friendships. Be careful. This is still Dordrecht. Everyone is always watching.

--You must know. I hear you're still part of the triangle. Or quadrangle, I should say.

--Not for a while now. They say you can't go home again, or like Gerrit always says: 'We cannot step into the same river twice.'

--Who did he steal that from? One of the Greeks, I think. I do agree, though. I find that out every time I come back. We can't go home because it's not there anymore. Everything changes.

--You should be careful. I think she may be more interested in getting back at Butch than she is in rekindling the past with you.

--Thanks for the advice. You have personal experience, knowing how these things go.

--Believe me, I do. But now I want you to meet the people who helped me with Dad. Come on over, I'll introduce you.

As they walked to the serving table for the reception food, Harry realized they were the trio he had noticed at the funeral home. Amy introduced the tall man with the ponytail as Harv Nielson. The shorter, darker man was Nick Montez, and the woman was Lupe Rios.

--These guys were lifesavers, Harry. Because of them, Dad could stay home in our house and didn't have to go to assisted living or senior care. He was afraid of that. They work at Covenant Gardens Rehab Center across from the hospital. They took care of Joe there for six weeks when there were complications after his heart surgery. As you know, it took him longer than expected to recover. Dad had difficulty trusting healthcare workers, but he got to know these guys and liked them. When Dad had his stroke, I was thrilled when they agreed to help me care for him at home as a side job. Harv is a nurse's aide. Either he or I stopped in to check Dad's meds and ensure he was healthy. Lupe and Nick were personal care orderlies. She was there most days, picking things up and checking on his food. Their mother had been cleaning and doing laundry since Joanna left after Mom died. We filled his fridge with healthy stuff that he could make himself. Nick was the only person Dad allowed to help with a shower and other personal issues. He also drove Dad to his appointments and grocery-shopped when I couldn't.

--Wow, I didn't realize he needed that much help. Thank you for your work. I thought Joanna was still cleaning the house for him.

--Dad let her go after Mom died. He never felt comfortable with her. Too nosy, he said.

Until he saw her up close, Harry had not realized how attractive Lupe was. Not only did her bronze skin tone and medium-length black hair with natural-looking auburn streaks set her apart from all the Dutch women, but her shocking pink top showed more than a bit of cleavage. Harry thought that was a big reason that Joe was happy to have her around. She now spoke for the group in a slight Spanish accent, with her dark eyes focusing on Harry.

--You are welcome. We all liked Joe. He was a lot of fun. When he got crabby, we knew how to cheer him up. And the extra pay helped. It kept my daughter in nice school clothes. Are you staying in town for a while?

--I need to fly out tonight for work. But I'll return on Saturday for a few days.

--Well, we will let you go. Let's get together next week. I want to talk some more about Joe.

After she and the others said goodbye to him and Amy and turned to leave, Harry was glad to see some remaining sandwiches and desserts.

--I am starving, and I'll have to go after I eat.

--Go for it. It would be best to leave before any other girls come over and flirt with you. I noticed you've had three in a row.

--Was she flirting?

--As if you didn't know. I have some things to wrap up here. We'll see you on Monday.

Harry sat down to eat his sandwich and the last available piece of apple cobbler. He found a chair at a table where his Uncle Ben sat with his dog and his children, Harry's cousins, Jon and Mary, and their spouses, Martha and Con Bulthuis. As they reminisced while he slowly ate his cobbler, Hank came to sit close to him.

--Harry, I think you and I had a similar relationship with Joe, and I would like to discuss it with you. I'm still a bit unsettled by him and his life. Amy mentioned you were coming back to town this weekend. Do you have some time we could spend together?

--I would like that, too. My calendar is filling up, but I have some time late Sunday afternoon and evening. Do you want to meet for dinner?

--Why don't you come to my place? Most restaurants I like here are closed on Sundays, and I don't go where booze is served. Irma and her daughter are living with me now. She can help me whip up a Sunday supper. I'm still in the same house north of town on Park Street. I get home from the late afternoon service I usually attend at Bethel Christian Reformed around six.

--Okay, Hank, I'll see you a little after six.

--I look forward to it. Have a safe trip. I need to get Ben to the elevator. Irma is bringing the van to the accessible entrance.

Harry rushed through the last bites of his cobbler, wanting to help Hank manage Ben's wheelchair and his dog onto the elevator. He enjoyed seeing Irma one more time as he continued to help Ben until he was safely in the van. He watched them leave the parking lot before heading to the New Leiden airport.

Chapter 5—Amy, First Tuesday, 1998

Amy woke up at dawn on Tuesday morning. It had become her favorite time of the day after she purchased her condo eleven years earlier. This morning, the eastern sunrise created a bronze mirror as it reflected on a calm Lake Michigan, showing just one of its many moods. She brought her tea out to the deck, wearing her long down coat to fight the almost freezing temperature, knowing this could be one of the few days left in the year that the early morning air would be endurable. The store was closed Tuesday through Thursday in the fall season. As usual, Doug had stayed up late and was sleeping in. he slept in the loft bedroom, to which he was relegated supposedly because of his snoring but also because Amy preferred sleeping alone. More often, she found herself not missing Doug's presence. She was looking forward to three days away from him while attending the weekend retreat on Burt Lake. She hoped the retreat would resolve some of her doubts about Doug. She realized she hoped to find the courage to separate herself from him.

Her retreat would take place at a camp created and led by a 'teacher' named Gerrit Gerritson. Amy had been with him for almost two decades. She regarded him as her lifesaver. When Joe's financial setback forced her to leave art school, she insisted on not living at home. Joe helped her get a job in the new DeJong showroom in McCormick Place. She promptly lost that job after her dating a married client became known. She quickly found a bartending job at the Beeline Bar and Grill three miles north of Dordrecht. Soon, she sang one song each set with the weekend band, primarily covers she knew from her high school days with a folk band that had grown into folk rock. She found an apartment in Middleburg, hoping to do her art and fashion work on the side.

One night, Joe entered the Beeline with Theo Bolinyk, whose good looks and sophisticated manner immediately attracted Amy. She could tell that he was attracted to her as well. She was used to that reaction from men of all ages. They began to date, and she soon moved in with him in one half of the New Leiden duplex that he owned. Two years later, they were married. Amy wanted the marriage to end her mother's attempts to persuade Amy to leave her 'life of sin' and return home. She now had a life that felt like a thousand miles away from Dordrecht, even though it was only a twenty-mile drive on the state highway.

Wanting to get her out of evening work at the bar, Theo talked his sister, Stephanie, who owned an innovative clothing boutique called Mode du Jour in downtown New Leiden, into hiring Amy to help in her store. She turned out to have natural abilities. Her personality was like her father's, giving her sales skills that could not be taught. Her artistic and fashion design background was quickly translated into women's designer retail. Soon, she had built a following, clients who trusted her to find the perfect look. Amy joined Theo and Stephanie in the seventies party scene in New Leiden, often including pot, cocaine, and free-flowing alcohol. Theo had unlimited funds, more than his job as a Polaroid marketing rep would provide. Amy chose not to worry. They were having too much fun and felt invincible.

When the store was closed on a Sunday, Stephanie, feeling they both needed a 'cleanse,' took Amy to a yoga class. Amy experienced a peaceful feeling in her mind and body, leading her to become an acolyte, which included daily sessions at home. She realized it was replacing her childhood church, which she had ignored since high school. Yoga gave her a spiritual connection that she had been missing, without the baggage of Calvinist doctrine and the forced social conformity of small-town churches. She also had begun to tire of the party life with Theo. A few drinks and occasional pot use were fine. But the loss of control from coke and heavy drinking bothered her. Theo was still heavily into alcohol and coke, often not coming home at night, leaving Amy constantly wondering who he was with and how long their marriage could last. She knew he was also selling cocaine when he was short on cash, which had begun to occur more often. With her mind calmed by the meditation aspect of her Hatha Yoga classes and practice, Amy could limit herself to wine and some marijuana, avoiding hard drugs and excessive alcohol.

One day, she was intrigued by a flyer in the coffee shop near the store announcing a 'Christian Yoga' retreat weekend in the resort town of Singapore, a river harbor town close to Lake

Michigan about fifteen miles south of Middleburg. She cleared her schedule with Stephanie and called the number on the flyer. She got an answering machine that announced the retreat hours and asked for her name and phone number to sign up. She did not know what to expect but wanted a few days away from Theo and work. The next day, she received a return call on her answering machine. A woman named Angela acknowledged her reservation and looked forward to meeting her.

She left the store early on Friday to catch the introductory evening session for new attendees. She was familiar with Singapore. During her senior year in high school, she already had a false ID and was enjoying the bar scene in the village. In the summer months, her high school band was able to pick up some weekend gigs. Later, she and Theo often overnighted for a day at the beach and an evening of entertainment. He introduced her to the boat and mini-yacht crowd, including the wealthy set from as far away as Chicago and Detroit. The town would be comparatively quiet this weekend since it was late September. A light rain was falling, which would keep many regular weekenders away. More than half the stores had closed for the winter. Others would stay open to manage to find enough business to pay expenses and rent through the off-season.

Amy left around five, took the state highway past Middleburg, and turned into Singapore about ten minutes late. She found the small, old, wooden church where the retreat would be held a few blocks from the river, where businesses, restaurants, and bars lined the main street and the riverwalk area. The church appeared a little rundown, needing paint and some repairs. A new sign read 'The New Awakening--A

Christian Meditative Community.' Walking inside, she noticed some repairs were underway before she saw Gerrit Gerritson for the first time. At first, she was not impressed. He seemed average: fortyish with medium height and build, medium starting-to-bald hair, and dressed in rumpled khakis and a denim shirt. His voice was neither soft nor harsh, and his diction was relaxed but precise as he slowly approached her with a gentle smile and an extended hand.

--Hi. Welcome. I'm Gerrit. You must be Amy.

--I am. Thank you.

His handshake was warm, with the proper pressure, but Amy was surprised and slightly uncomfortable with the one-on-one meeting. She had expected more people. Gerrit could sense her hesitance.

--I'm sure you were expecting more people. There will be more tomorrow. We are a new group, and only a few Friends could distribute flyers. Please come into the office. I want to learn a little about you. I'm sure you have questions about us—and me. I have some tea ready. Would you like some?

--Yes, that sounds good.

Gerrit slowly led her into the office, showed her a worn but comfortable wing chair, offered her sugar or milk, and then slowly poured the tea into chipped coffee cups.

--Let me ask first. What attracted you to us when you saw the flyer?

--Well, I guess it was the 'Christian' yoga. I've been practicing yoga for three years, but I was raised Christian. The thought of blending the two was new to me. Besides, I needed a weekend getaway, and I like Singapore.

--What type of yoga do you practice? How often?

--Hatha. I go to a group once a week and do some most days at home.

--And what type of Christianity?

--Reformed.

--Ha! I was a childhood Calvinist myself. Ohhh, the misery! My best deeds were filthy rags.

--Tell me about it!

--Which branch were you in?

--Regular Dutch Reformed. But my mother was very much Christian Reformed. Her dad is retired minister.

--Ohhh! Hyper-Calvinism! Well. This is good. It will be easy for you to understand my concept of Christian yoga. First, let me ask you. Do you think there is more than one path to the knowledge of God?

--Yes. No doubt about that.

--My views on that are more complicated. But we can get into that later. Let's agree that there are many starting paths.

--What is the starting path of your retreat?

--Excellent question that requires a longer answer than I can give tonight. Like many Dutch people, you go right to the essential matters. As I said, I am also Dutch and was raised a Calvinist. In my case, my father followed his career to San Diego and had to settle for a conservative Presbyterian church. We have certain traits in common. I will jump ahead a little. From yoga, we bring breathing, posing, and meditation, allowing us to be in touch with our center as we travel the path. For now, we do not do some of the more complicated cleansing rituals you may have heard about.

--Thanks for that. I have heard of those. They seem gross to me.

--Of course, they do. You are from the West. As we progress, we plan to add a simple cleansing program of ritual bathing, eating, and massage.

--That sounds okay—more than okay. But why do you call it Christian?

--Jesus Christ is our example. We are finite beings who are trying somehow to connect with the infinite. Christ, the infinite Son of God, became Jesus, the finite son of man. He is our guide on the path.

--What about the church and the doctrine and the rules?

--What about them? They are not our concern on this path.

--I think I can deal with that.

--Excellent. Ron and Angela will be here in a few minutes. Would you like to join us for a short session of breathing and posing? We can talk more tomorrow between sessions.

--Yes, I would like that. How do you pay for the retreat, the church, and the rest?

--We call people who join us Friends. I've always liked the Quakers. I appropriated the term from them. Friends give what they can. I have a few longtime Friends who can help fund my work and set up a stipend. One bought this church and is renting it to us for a dollar a month while he sits on his investment. That means I don't walk around with an alms bowl or twist the arms of less well-off people.

--I should give you something for this weekend. Would two hundred be fair?

--More than fair, I think.

———

The weekend was enlightening for Amy. The yoga and meditations were more penetrating than she had previously experienced. Gerrit's short lectures helped raise her consciousness and confidence to new levels. His ordinary appearance was enhanced by a powerful presence in his eyes, which seemed to gleam with extra light and grow stronger during the yoga sessions. As she felt a change in her core being, she realized that she could no longer live with Theo and had no fear of leaving and living apart from him. An even more meaningful change began when she took one last walk around Singapore, seeing everything with new eyes. She saw a house a block off the main street with an apartment upstairs and an empty storefront space with a For Lease sign. In a vision that seemed possible, she saw herself living and working there. She did not doubt that it would happen.

After she returned to New Leiden, Amy still felt the same about that weekend and her vision. Within a few months, it soon became real, if not without obstacles. Theo agreed to a separation, but after several reconciliation attempts failed, he eventually had no objections to the divorce. But he was difficult about the settlement. A friend recommended a New Leiden lawyer named Carl Zandstra. Amy wanted a cash settlement because she did not trust Theo to stick to an alimony plan. Theo always spent more than he had, although Amy suspected he had hidden assets out of her reach. It took Carl over a year to negotiate a compromise whereby Theo signed over fifty percent ownership of the rundown duplex, half of which he had been leasing to an elderly couple. Theo thought he had made a good bargain but underestimated the duplex's value and potential. Carl explained to Amy that the neighborhood was transitioning and that the duplex would be a profitable investment. Amy relied on her vision to take the risk.

Because Amy needed to possess assets or experience to qualify for the lease, build the improvements, or purchase inventory independently, she needed to convince Stephanie to buy into her plan for the Singapore store. Stephanie was at first doubtful but intrigued. With the power of her vision behind her, Amy performed her best sales job ever. Stephanie agreed to sign the lease and supply the inventory. Amy would rent the upstairs apartment and manage the store for the same salary and commission she had previously received in New Leiden. The first ten percent of sales would go to Stephanie. Any profits would be split fifty-fifty. At first, Amy continued working in the New Leiden store during the off-season until the Singapore store had enough weekend business and private appointments with regular clients to focus only on what she thought of as 'her store.'

Seven years after the divorce and ten years after the opening of the Mode du Jour satellite store in Singapore, Theo sold the duplex. Carl had been right. Amy's share was close to $125,000. She told Stephanie that she wanted to buy her out for the price of the inventory in the Singapore Mode de Jour. If she disagreed, Amy would go on her own anyway and open a competitive store, taking her clients and ten-year personal reputation with her. Stephanie had no choice but to agree. The store could not have succeeded without Amy. She accepted $10,000 more for using the name, and 'Amy's Mode du Jour' was a reality.

Amy had more to accomplish. The ten-year lease on the store building was up for renewal. Since she had enough cash left over to make a down payment, she made a land contract offer to the owner. Once again, she threatened to move unless he agreed, which he did. She was now on her way to ownership for only a slight monthly increase over her earlier lease payments.

Throughout those years, she was a regular at the yoga and meditation meetings at The New Awakening. She also had monthly counseling sessions with Gerrit. From the first weekend retreat, she found more peace within herself and the world around her. She credited Gerrit with helping her find the confidence that led to her business and financial success. Although some of the people, both regular and casual Friends, seemed to attribute mystical powers to him, he called himself a guide and never claimed or denied any special abilities.

Rumors also abounded about his sexual relationships with both sexes. At first, Amy was not sexually attracted to him; neither did he hint at the possibility of a relationship. He taught that everyone was naturally bisexual and free to choose their partners. Amy took his words to heart and regarded him as a guide. Several years later, when it seemed proper, he guided her along a sexual path. Throughout those years, she contributed to him and the group more as a reasonable fee for service than a charitable gift–although she did take the tax deduction.

––––––––––

Ending her reverie, Amy came back in from the balcony and heard Doug begin his shower. She pictured his naked body and felt the familiar urge. She was not sure she was ever in love with him, but she did love his body and the sex. Doug played defensive back in football and placed at state as a 175-pound wrestler at Hamtramck High School, which earned him a football and wrestling scholarship to Central Michigan. In his second year of only playing on special teams, he tore his ACL. He struggled through recovery and eventually dropped out, knowing he could never keep his scholarship. After he had regained most of his strength through a vigorous fitness program and prescription painkillers, he joined UPS and became a driver. He found the challenge of the grueling daily schedule fulfilling. He also became a part-time fitness trainer.

When he met Amy at the Goose and Gander Pub in Singapore, however, he was unemployable due to two accidents at UPS and a failed drug test. His being a part-time bartender at the G & G did not deter Amy. He was thirty-four and still Adonis-like, with his super-fit frame, movie star features, and long blonde hair in a ponytail most of the time. Amy had not been in a meaningful relationship since her separation from Theo. Theo had been a slick and outwardly sophisticated, prosperous man-about-town, but physically, he was thin and unimposing. Doug was different and exciting, especially since he was nine years younger than Amy. She felt she was still attractive in her mid-forties; his obvious attraction to her was ego-confirming. She found him a place as a trainer and assistant manager at a Middleburg gym, a branch of a New Leiden gym owned by a client. Two years later, he moved in with her at the condo.

Doug came out of the shower, showing off his body in his tight boxers while he opened the fridge to search for breakfast.

--Are you still planning on that damn retreat this week?

--If you are talking about the well-deserved rejuvenating yoga and meditation seminar, I am.

--You could rejuvenate here, you know. It's been a while since we had any fun together. The funeral is finished. Our harvest is so bad that Nick and Manuel can handle the rest of the work. We could fly to Vegas or something.

--Forget it. But we must figure out how to make the farm worthwhile next year.

--Or how about Chicago? The Blackhawks have a pre-season match against the Red Wings this weekend.

Doug grabbed the orange juice and drank from the bottle.

--Just what I need. Thousands of people, hoping for a fight to break out. Forget it. I know where I want to be. Just go with one of your buddies. You'll have more fun.

--I didn't think you'd trust me.

--I don't.

--I get it. You're over me. Looking for an excuse to get me gone.

--Are you wallowing in self-pity now?

--I remember what you told me about Theo. You decided to divorce him after a retreat focused your mind.

--This might be the time. You can hook up permanently with one of those clients who get extra attention from you. Why do you want to hang around with an old fifty-year-old woman like me?

--Now, who is wallowing? You're still foxy. I wonder what your minister friend thinks about your weekend with your guru.

--It's none of his business. The two of them are on different paths, as Gerrit says. And he is not my guru. He's just a guide.

--I think they're both jealous of each other. Not for spiritual reasons, either. When it comes to you, their physical interest overrides the spiritual. But what do I know? I haven't been to mass since my confirmation. No priest would have time for my confession.

--Well. Let's say it's both. But good luck to them on the physical part. They're not my type.

--Just what is your type these days?

--He asks as he shows off his body in his underwear.

He put down the juice and took a step towards her side.

--I know what my type is.

Amy turned a little more away from him.

--And what is that?

--A fifty-year-old babe who feels uptight and needs a massage from a forty-year-old kid.

Amy felt his hands smoothly touch her in the right places. Her body relaxed and came alive with desire at the same time. Doug brought his breakfast with them as they returned to her bedroom for the rest of the morning.

Just before Amy and Doug had met, a megadonor had deeded an eighty-acre tract of land to The New Awakening, thinking they could use it as a natural headquarters for group retreats and individual rejuvenations. Gerrit tried to devise a plan, but there needed to be more money to make it work. He lost interest and moved on to other projects. Amy had half of the money left over from the divorce settlement and pictured an eventual peaceful, casual country estate where she could find peace away from her business. She used some to give Gerrit a cash deposit he could use elsewhere. They agreed on a fair interest rate for the balance plus flexible balloon principal payments, both to be paid once a year after her busy summer at the store.

When Doug joined her, he saw other possibilities—specifically, a pot farm. Amy told him he was dreaming, but he inspected the acreage. The things he knew about growing marijuana plants were that sunlight was needed, that it took surprisingly little area to produce enough pot to start a business, and that only a few varieties would do well in the Michigan climate. Although it had several small, shallow ponds and other areas that turned into swampland after the winter snowmelt, he found some hidden, sunny areas with good drainage where cannabis could be cultivated away from the view of anyone who passed. When he reported back to Amy, she had warmed to the idea. She also knew someone who could help.

———————

Jonnie Van Orden was a high school classmate who had gone to Vietnam and came home with a missing lower right leg and a severe case of PTSD. Even Dordrecht was too busy and disturbing for him. He moved in with his mother's parents on their farm four miles northeast of Dordrecht and settled into a quiet, rural life. He helped with the household and farm chores he could manage with his prosthesis. Jonnie took over the business details after his grandmother died and his grandfather could no longer manage the farm. He leased out most of the acreage and kept just enough to grow his necessary medicine. He had discovered pot in Vietnam and found that it not only helped with the pain but also kept the PTSD at bay most of the time.

With the family farm in the back of his mind, he brought back enough Vietnamese seeds to start a garden that would supply his needs. After a small start, he quickly found several semi-hidden areas near the farmhouse where he thought a larger plot of marijuana plants could be cultivated. He bought a small John Deere tractor, which he could manage to use, even with his damaged leg. Along with an improvised one-armed walker, it allowed him at first to work the small farm himself. Within the first year, he had harvested enough to supply his needs. There was a shed behind the barn that he cleaned out and used as a drying room. When his grandfather died and left Jonnie ten acres, including the house and the outbuildings, he saw the opportunity to expand. Manuel and Rosa Montez had helped his grandfather in his later years. Jonnie arranged to have a used mobile home on the edge of his property, where they could live with their two high school-aged children, Lupe and Nick. That allowed them to work for him through the winter. With their help, he expanded and soon had enough to experiment with varieties until he found and cloned a crop that was compatible with the Michigan climate and contained the potency of his original Vietnamese starter seed.

Living alone suited Jonnie to the extent that he only socialized twice weekly. On Sunday, he attended the morning service at the nearby Crossroads Reformed Church, where he slipped into a back pew for the service. He would grab a coffee and two homemade cookies at the after-service gathering before sneaking away as quickly as possible. On Friday evenings, he went to the Beeline Bar and Grill to sit at the counter, ordering a Coke and the deluxe hamburger plate, known as the best burger in the area. After eating, he returned to his pickup, parked behind the bar, and waited for customers.

Word of mouth spread quickly. He sold as much as he could produce. He gradually improved yields and THC content through trial and error until his Friday night bags were in high demand. He was careful, only staying for an hour or less when the small supply he had brought with him was gone. He was sure to remind his customers that his product was pure and clean with no dangerous psychedelic or addictive additives they might find on the street. Only one bag per customer was allowed. One of his best clients was a Nederland County deputy sheriff, to whom he gave a special professional discount.

Amy had seen Jonnie several times when she worked at the Beeline just before she left for New Leiden and before he was in his new business. She knew of his PTSD and prosthesis and treated him kindly but carefully. Jonnie remembered her from high school. She realized he had a crush on her like most other boys. He appreciated her attention, even though his only response was a small smile and a nod. It was more than he gave to others.

A few years later, she and Theo stopped in at the Beeline on a Friday night for old times' sake on the way to Singapore for a weekend getaway. Theo had heard from some friends about the excellent pot available. As they left, they went to the back parking lot to make a purchase. They were third in line, but Jonnie perked up when he saw Amy. He smiled a little and even asked Amy where she had been. The conversation was short; they got their bag and headed to Singapore. Later, in the B & B where they stayed, Theo pronounced the pot 'primo.'

Theo tried several times to get Jonnie to sell to him in bulk. Theo was no longer with Polaroid and had taken on some German and Japanese camera accessory lines as an independent rep. Needing to add to his income, he built a growing business as an upscale pot, coke, and pills dealer. Jonnie had always refused, but on one occasion, he finally invited Theo to the farm to check out his excess inventory. After Theo, having been impressed with Jonnie's operation, made a substantial purchase, Jonnie told him that his current harvest in the drying room was the largest ever. Theo could come again in six months when it was properly aged.

As Doug and Amy thought about the possibility of starting their own marijuana farm, she was reluctant to call Theo to ask how she could contact Jonnie. She was unsure how he would react, so she would need to convince Theo that she did not intend to compete with him. She only needed Jonnie's advice to start growing her own. She decided to take the risk and called him. She was surprised that he picked up. Theo was pleasant and reasonable for a change after he heard the reason for her call. He told her the only thing to do would be to meet Jonnie on a Friday night and make her request in person.

She and Doug went to the Beeline the following Friday. They found Jonnie at the bar enjoying his hamburger. She introduced Doug and asked him if he was still in business. Jonnie once again recognized her, but he hesitated before he talked. He quietly said no, glanced around to see who might be listening, and said he was into wholesaling. Amy explained that they were not looking for the product, but they were willing to pay for his knowledge and advice to help them start growing their own in Wakazoo County. He asked how much. They bargained. He offered to give them advice and a tour of his farm for a thousand in cash. Doug didn't hesitate to agree before Amy could think about it.

The visit to the farm the following week exceeded Amy and Doug's expectations. There was nothing obvious about the farm to attract attention. The house, the barn, and one newer, rectangular building were well-maintained. The land sloped down behind the house and had several treed areas, irrigation ditches, and a pond. It looked a lot like Amy's Wakazoo acreage. Jonnie got around on his small John Deere tractor. He hooked up a trailer and drove them around the farm. Rows of sunflowers and sweet corn camouflaged five separate small areas of plants. The results of the thunderstorm early in the previous morning made everything glisten. When they returned to the barn, he pointed out a couple working in the drying room, separating the buds. He told them that Manuel had started by helping with the planting and harvest years earlier. Now, he was full-time. His wife, Rosa, helped when needed. He didn't have to pay them much. They got a nice bonus in a product they could sell and free rent in the mobile home on the edge of Jonnie's land.

He took them to a separate room and showed them shelves of bud jars, either already aging or empty, waiting for buds from the drying room. Next, he brought them to the newer building he called his pride and joy. The south-facing half of the peaked roof was translucent fabric, letting in natural light. The tiered shelves facing south were filled with more than a hundred pots with sprouting marijuana plants. Jonnie always looked at the ground towards Amy's feet when he talked, seeming to ignore Doug.

--I should have been able to harvest this crop in March. These are all clones of the best mother plants in the fields. Unfortunately, Amy, I'll be out of business by then.

--What? Why? Are you sick or something?

--No, it turns out that my best customer, who happens to be your ex-husband, was arrested for all kinds of drug dealing last month. He must have been seeking a plea bargain because he turned me in as his pot source.

--Are you telling me that Theo has been arrested?

--Oh, ja. Do you remember ol' Charley Vredevelde, the old Dordrecht Chief of Police?

--I do. He and my dad had a few run-ins.

--You know he retired and is now double-dipping as Chief Deputy to the Nederland County Sheriff.

--What about him?

--He came to see me. The state boys asked the sheriff to check me out. Well, they didn't have to check me out. At least two deputies and one assistant DA are customers of mine.

--So, do you have connections? You're protected?

--Not anymore. Charley told me he talked the Prosecuting Attorney and the Sheriff into going easy on me because I'm a disabled vet. He was also probing to get me to name names. I told him Theo was my only big buyer, which is true. Everyone else is small potatoes.

Doug had been listening and looking around, impressed with Jonnie's operation. He jumped into the conversation.

--So, where does that leave you?

--Out of business. Charley told me they won't prosecute me if I quit the business. They want to protect themselves as much as I do. That's why I wanted you to stop by to look. It could be your lucky day.

--How's that?

--Most of this harvest was going to Theo. Since you are new and out of the county, I'd be taking less risk if I gave you a deal on all of it. I've thought this through. You'll need supplies and equipment, too. This shed is prefabricated. It could be part of the package.

Amy and Doug looked at each other. This was more than they expected. Amy asked the pertinent question.

--I don't know if we're ready for that. How much would you need?

--Need is the right word. $95,000. Cash. That's less than half of what it's worth. Added to what I've been saving and my disability payments, I can retire. And I need to retire. My leg pain is getting worse, and my other hip is getting to be as bad. I couldn't work much longer, even if this legal BS didn't force me to quit.

--Well, we don't have that kind of cash. We would need terms of some sort.

--Nope. No deal. I already have piecemeal and promises-to-pay offers. It's not like I could sue if someone didn't pay me. Plus, you could make half that back immediately by selling the product at retail.

Amy and Doug left feeling both surprised and deflated. They had not expected this kind of opportunity and were disappointed by their inability to take advantage of it. They daydreamed about how good a deal it could be on their return home. Amy was entirely out of cash, having just made the first balloon payment in several years to Gerrit, whose financial advisors had threatened to take back the Wakazoo acreage. Her equity in the condo would need to be more, even if she could qualify for a second mortgage. Her income was just enough to support her lifestyle, which was already below her lofty expectations. They went to bed that night, thinking about the negatives and forgetting about the temporary dream.

Chapter 6—Joe, Fall, 1992

Joe woke up the morning after Rose's funeral alone in the Dordrecht house, where he had lived with her for over forty years. From the front view, it was still a medium-sized Dutch Colonial. But they had added a two-story addition to the back side, including a kitchen expansion and a large gathering room on the first level below a large primary bedroom suite on the second. Combined with the pool in the backyard, the house always gave Joe a sense of accomplishment and satisfaction. There were more extensive and more elaborate homes in Dordrecht. However, Rose's hosting skills and Joe's entertaining personality had made it a favorite gathering spot of the upper echelon of Dordrecht's small-town society.

It was after ten o'clock. He had gone to bed late, needing a few extra Johnny Walkers to make up for the stress of the alcohol-free day. He had not slept well. This morning, he felt the house's emptiness for the first time after Harry and his family had left the night before. Joe had been surprised that they would stay with him. Harry had broken off their relationship years earlier, only interacting with Joe when necessary. It was perfunctory at best, even at those times, mainly because Rose asked him to try. Harry's wife Monica was just as distant. Joe had wanted to win her over from the time she married Harry, but there was a barrier he could not overcome. At least he could still joke and have fun with Dave and Jen. They were not too grown up as young teens to respond to him. He realized that they would soon be adults and beyond his reach. Luckily, Amy had been present much of the time the last week, acting as his partner and a buffer between him and Harry and Monica. That had made the visit bearable.

———————

Rose had been diagnosed three years earlier with breast cancer. She first had a lumpectomy with follow-up chemo. When the cancer returned, she had a complete mastectomy and more chemo. When it returned once more, she decided to end treatment. She was 'ready to meet Jesus.'

Joe had returned to work after his first heart attack in 1986, promising to cut back on his travel. He had even talked Rose into buying a 'vacation condo' in Miami that Theo wanted to sell quickly and cheaply. He had some money from his parents that they could use for the down payment. Renting it out when they were not using it would cover the mortgage payments. At first, Rose had enjoyed spending a few weeks away from the Michigan winter but soon missed her life with her friends and relatives in Dordrecht. She also could not get used to the Presbyterian church that she insisted on attending with Joe on Sundays in Miami. After the diagnosis, she had no desire to go south for even a few weeks. She had been there only six weeks during two winters before her cancer first appeared. When Rose was first diagnosed, Joe had decided to retire, but when her treatment seemed to work, he postponed it. He valued the personal freedom that its travel requirements provided.

When the cancer returned the last time, Joe became a more devoted husband. He was with her on her office visits. He worried along with her over her test results. He suffered with her during the final chemo treatments as Rose's illness progressed. When Rose decided to die while receiving hospice care at home, he helped administer palliative care and was alone with her when she passed away early in the morning of her final day. He could not admit to himself that he was merely assuaging his guilt, having a natural feeling of grief, but he could not forget Lydia and the second life he had always lived outside of Dordrecht. That life made him feel free and not ridden with the guilt he was dealing with at home.

When Rose first became ill, she told Joe he should sell the condo since they could not use it. Joe responded that he had checked with realtors, who said that selling now would be the wrong time. He assured her that he would be able to rent the condo for the season, which would net them a nice profit. He kept secret that he had given Lydia the keys and let her move in. He had enough stashed in a personal fund, unknown to Rose or their CPA, Allen Zuverink, to make the payments. He routinely found several reasons to fly to Miami to 'check on the condo.' Sitting quietly now, replaying his conflicted motivations, his guilt feelings were temporarily magnified.

———————

Just as his coffee was ready, the phone rang. After the second ring, it stopped. He sighed and dialed the number of his condo in Miami.

--Hi, Joe. Are you awake?

89

--I just woke up. I got in late. The family is gone, so you don't need to signal. I don't think that fooled anyone anyway.

--I realize that. I just never wanted to hear a voice that wasn't you. Besides, I didn't do it all that often.

--Too often for some people. Even when Harry still lived at home, he used to say I had a call from Lydia whenever the phone only rang twice.

--That was a long time ago.

--More than twenty-five years.

--If we've lasted that long, we must be made for each other. When are you coming down? I want to enjoy finally being number one in your life.

--You know you were always number one when I was with you.

--You were always a sweet talker.

--I will come as soon as I tie up some things here. It's getting cold, and I'm already lonely. Maybe at the end of next week.

--Does tying things up mean selling the house so we can be full-time?

--I've told you. The house is in a trust. The grandkids are the beneficiaries. I get to live here free now that I finally paid the mortgage. We can come here in the summer. It's too damn hot down there in Florida.

--Like I'm going to live in Dordrecht. Those Dutch Calvinists would try to burn me at the stake.

--After a year or so, no one will care.

--I will. Which also reminds me. Remember you promised me that you would add me to the title for this place? That would be one of the things you could tie up.

--I also took that back. It's almost paid for, too. Outside of my retirement programs, it's the only equity I have.

90

--What about me? I need equity, too.

--You made out like a bandit on your divorces. You're probably still blackmailing both of your exes. Plus, your dad is loaded.

--And also, a tightwad. A girl needs a little pin money. I never get much from you.

--Just free rent for the last three years. Like I said before, now that Rose is gone, I can put you in my will.

--You don't seem sad about Rose being gone.

--I was sad about her cancer. She suffered a lot. She was happy to go at the end. Now I'm seventy-one. My heart is holding up. I plan to enjoy the next few years. That includes enjoying them with you if you don't bitch about money every day.

--It won't be every day. Just enough to make you treat me right.

--You don't have to worry about that.

--So, when are you coming?

--I'm planning to take today and tomorrow to get organized. I'll call you tomorrow night.

Joe hung up and went back to the kitchen to find something for breakfast. He boiled two eggs, toasted two slices of raisin bread, grabbed a banana, and went to the sunroom on the south side of the kitchen, wanting to enjoy the backyard before all the leaves fell and winter set in. Thinking about Lydia, the guilt faded as his mind floated back to when he first met her.

He was arriving at the Triandos Bar when the bouncer, Sal Broglio, stopped him. He was talking to a dark-haired woman with the face and body of an Italian movie star. When Sal introduced Lydia Triandos, Joe was uncharacteristically tongue-tied for a long moment. He soon recovered.

--I am pleased to meet you, finally. I've been waiting to meet you for a long time.

--Really? How do you know me?

--I've been seeing you in my dreams for years.

--Oh! You're one of those smooth talkers. Are you all talk?

--Why don't I buy you a drink and we'll find out. Or how about dinner?

--Do you know what? I'll take you up on that. But not here; I'm sick of this place.

--You name it! Judging by your name, you must be one of the owners.

--Just a daughter-in-law. My papa is an investor, so I do have some influence. But right now, my husband is temporarily working in Florida, so I'm free tonight.

--So am I. Please tell me where you want to go, and I'll take you there.

As they left to catch a cab to Alexander's, Joe winked at Sal, who was watching with wide eyes and who silently mouthed, 'Be careful.'

Their dinner date eventually brought them to Joe's hotel room. Joe was not inexperienced in first-night sexual relationships, but he had never known anyone with Lydia's combination of passion and beauty. He was used to doing most of the work; with Lydia, it was a fifty-fifty partnership. He knew immediately that this would not be their last time together. They saw more of each other as Joe spent more time in Chicago, keeping the ChairWorks showroom open more often for smaller events, not just the winter and summer shows. The guilt he always felt when he returned to Dordrecht was quickly put aside as soon as he saw Lydia. He could not find the will to avoid succumbing to their desires.

Two years after their first encounter, Rose had somehow heard that Joe had a girlfriend in Chicago. Caught by surprise, he could not convince her that what she heard was untrue. He finally broke down and tearfully confessed. After he promised that it was over, she forgave him. At first, she insisted that he change jobs at ChairWorks and not return to the showroom. Joe successfully protested that it would not be financially possible.

The next time he went to Chicago, Lydia was furious at first when Joe announced that he needed to end their relationship.

--You're a fucking coward! A ball-less wimp!

--I know it seems that way, but I can't live in Dordrecht if I don't stay with Rose and my family. I don't have a choice. She would take me to the cleaners financially. My kids would disown me. I'd lose my job.

--What are you talking about? You're an owner.

--Minority. Matt and Mark could force me out.

Lydia changed her tune to sarcasm.

--You're such a weak little shit. Big talker. Fast talker. But you've got nothing behind it. You'll soon come crawling back to me.

--Don't count on it!

--Oh, I am counting on it. You can't get what you need from li'l ol' Rosie. I can't wait. You'll cry and beg, and I'll laugh when I turn you down.

Joe was wrong. It took six weeks until Lydia entered Sal's back room at Triandos. She was dressed to show off her best assets. Joe looked at her and could not turn away, feeling a stronger longing than he had known. She looked him in the eye and walked back out. Joe folded his hand at the poker table, rushing to catch up with her outside the restaurant. They rushed to his hotel.

Two years later, Lydia's drunken call to Rose had exacerbated Joe's problems with Dordrecht ChairWorks. She had been desperate because her husband, Lorenzo Triandos, insisted that she move with him to Miami, where he had opened a restaurant with her father. She tried again to get a commitment from Joe, even if it meant going behind his back to Rose. This time, when Joe confronted her and explained the seriousness of his legal and financial issues, she realized he was a lost cause. She was not about to go down with his ship. She made the best of it and moved to Florida to become the front manager at the Triandos Miami Chophouse. It would be five years before she and Joe reconnected.

———————

As he continued to sit and reflect, Joe was amazed that he had pulled things together after his legal and marital troubles. At first, he was diligent in his AA attendance. It helped that Lydia had escaped to Miami. She was too far away to be a temptation for him, just as he was too poor to be attractive to her.

As he expected, he found a company that needed a person with his contacts and marketing ability. The New England Chair Company had a solid reputation and business making wood dining furniture and occasional chairs for the residential market. Most of their business was supplying other residential brands with chairs. They could make them better and cheaper. Their private brand was only about twenty-five percent of their volume. They developed a new line of chairs for the office and hospitality market. Joe became the marketing manager. He convinced them he could work out of his home, find space in a co-op showroom in the new Merchandise Mart for the essential market weeks, and bring experienced reps on board to cover the rest of the country. It was what he had been doing for ChairWorks. It was easy. Plus, he could continue to fulfill his driving obligation for John Visser and the Boss without questions being asked. He was successful for two years until the company was sold to a furniture conglomerate. The new company offered him a manager's job in Connecticut at less pay or a straight commission sales job for which he would have to live in Chicago. He was once again at a crossroads.

This time, it was Hank Plagmeyer to the rescue. He was happy to be able to pay Joe back. Five years previously, when Hank had lost his job at the casket factory after reaching the bottom of his alcohol addiction, Joe found a place for him at ChairWorks. Hank soon became a lifelong AA member and a valued supervisor in the chair plant. When Joe began to attend AA meetings seriously, he and Hank reconnected with Vernon DeJong, who, like them, was also a recovering alcoholic. He was the second oldest son of Herbert DeJong, the founder of DeJong Systems, which had become a national leader in the new and rapidly growing open office workstation market. Hank knew that DeJong was planning to start an in-house chair program. He convinced Vern that Joe was rehabilitated and would be the perfect person to manage the marketing for the new division. After a series of interviews and a national search that found no one with Joe's knowledge and experience, Joe had a new position in Dordrecht with an increased pay package.

However, the downside of the new job was that driving for the Boss and John Visser became a problem. DeJong had a large, dedicated showroom in the Merchandise Mart, and several other employees would be making regular trips with Joe back and forth from Dordrecht. It would be difficult for him to escape scrutiny. Joe reached out to George Bosch, hoping to be released from his driving. George had sounded doubtful, but he had agreed to check with the Chicago people. When he called Joe back several days later, he only instructed Joe to be at the Monday night club on Monday afternoon before it opened.

Since joining AA, Joe had been sporadically going to the club. He kept his appearance of sobriety by never drinking alcohol in public in Dordrecht. He also was only allowed to gamble with cash, which he rarely had access to. Even though it kept him from getting in trouble at the no-limit tables, small pots and club sodas had little attraction for him. Not only did he miss the thrill of taking risks, but he also missed the ego boost of being seen as one of the big hitters. When he walked in, he saw Sal Broglio sitting at a table with a younger man dressed in an expensive three-piece suit. Sal called him over to sit down with them.

--Hi Joe, I want you to meet a friend of mine, Theo Bolinyk.

--Nice to meet you, Theo. I'm Joe Berendts.

--Sal has been telling me about you. He wants to see if we can work together.

--Is that right? What do you have up your sleeve, Sal?

--Well, Joe. I've been told you are unhappy with your present arrangement with our company.

--Your company? I don't know your company, but my situation has changed, and I won't be free to drive for you. Too many eyes will be on me. Too many questions will be asked.

--We appreciate the work you've done for us. We appreciate it so much that we want to offer you a promotion.

--A promotion?

--Yeah. You'll still be delivering for us. Just smaller packages.

--Like what?

--You don't need to know. Theo and I need to do some business together. We need a delivery man. I'll give you a package that fits in your briefcase. You bring it to Theo. He gives you a package. You bring it to me.

--Sounds dangerous. I don't think I can do it.

--What you're doing is already risky. This is less work and more reward.

--How much more is the reward?

--Add a zero to your current trip payment.

--A zero? Five hundred? I can't pass up an opportunity like this, even if I wanted to.

--I knew you would see it our way.

That meeting was the last time Joe saw Sal or George alive. His business arrangement with Theo continued and blossomed into a friendship.

———————

Joe heard the phone ring. Like his first call of the day, he was still tired of interacting with people, so he let the machine answer. The condolences and reminiscences had begun to fog together. He was not ready for more. As he heard Amy leaving a message, however, he picked up.

--Hi, Dad. How are you doing this morning?

--I'm tired. Ready for some peace.

--It was a huge funeral. Where did they all come from?

--She had a large family with fifteen cousins, spouses, and kids still living in the area. My family showed up, too, but not as many. Plus, she had friends from the CR and Reformed sides of the divide. She lived in Dordrecht since she was eighteen. You even cleaned up Doug enough so he wouldn't embarrass us.

--I had to give him hell to get him to do it. I even heard from Theo. I told him to call you.

--I got a message on the machine, but he didn't leave a number. He said he would call back.

--He only called me because he thought Mom left me some money.

--No luck there. She had saved some in her name, and her parents left her some, but she was nice enough to leave most of that to me after a large donation to several of her religious favorites. It's less than $200,000, but I can use it.

--To entertain Lydia, I suppose. Is she still living in your condo?

--What makes you think that?

--Theo keeps me informed. He's in Florida, too, you know.

--Since we are talking about money, I may as well give you some news that won't make you happy.

--What now?

--The last time Rose caught me with Lydia, just before she got sick, the only way she would back off from divorcing me was if I would agree to put the house in her name, along with life insurance policies on each of us. She wanted financial security in case we ever split up.

--So, what does that mean for me? Don't you inherit them anyway?

--Behind my back, she put them in a trust. Guess who the beneficiaries are.

--Who? More church groups?

--Nope. Your wonderful niece and nephew, Jennifer and David.

--No fucking way. She can't do that!

--Evidently, she can. And she did!

--That fucking Harry! How did he make this happen? What's going to happen to you?

--As far as I know, Harry doesn't even know about it yet. The trust is set up so that it doesn't transfer to them until I die. I get to live rent-free and receive a stipend from the interest on one of the bonds the trust holds. Big deal, it's less than $5,000 a year. It's a good thing I was able to keep some of my money hidden from her and her buddy Allen Zuverink.

--Can't you fight it?

--I don't think I can afford to. Besides, I want nothing to do with lawyers.

--Well, you should check it out. Ask Theo about it when he calls you again. He might know someone who can help.

--Not this time. I'm hearing he is going straight after getting an early release. Next time, he'd have to do some serious time. Even Lenny Caputo couldn't help him.

--I have a tough time believing that he is going straight. We'll see. He will find a different scam. Since Doug is working tonight, why don't I come over later this afternoon to help with your grocery shopping? I'll even make dinner for you.

--That sounds great! Can you clean, too?

--No way. Where's Joanna?

--I'm going to fire that old busybody. She'll tell the whole town about my comings and goings. You can help me find someone new.

--I do know someone. I can have her meet us tomorrow.

--Perfect. Would you call Joanna and give her the sad news?

--You're a chicken shit. But I might enjoy doing that for you.

Joe brought his breakfast dishes back to the sink and went to the shower. Unlike many men his age, he was still fastidious about his hygiene and appearance. Rose had always insisted on it. He also knew that it attracted Lydia.

———————

He recalled a phone call five years after their breakup when Lydia had moved to Florida. It was the same two rings and a hang-up on his office phone at DeJong. He had to dig into his Rolodex to find her Florida number under L. Martino, her maiden name. She picked up on the first ring.

--That didn't take long.

--I'm always happy to hear from old friends.

--An old friend? Is that the best you can do?

--I didn't want to make any presumptions.

--Go ahead and presume. I am an available woman now.

--Really? Why now? You've always said you can't stand Lorenzo.

--I finally caught him with the wrong woman. Someone whom he would not want to be linked with, and vice versa, if our divorce was contested in court. I am in an excellent position to get a quiet, amicable deal with a generous settlement.

--Where are you going to go?

--I'll stay here. I can stop at the restaurant occasionally and collect a check. Papa is still an investor. I'll be more of a consultant than an employee. With a five-year contract.

--Did you get the house?

--Oh, hell no. He has it mortgaged to the hilt. He is cashing me out using some of his money-from-nowhere accounts. Now it will be my money-from-nowhere. Tony and I will find something nice to rent.

--Tony? Your son. Are you still supporting his lazy ass?

--Not anymore. He's making some big money working for his grandfather.

--Scamming. You mean.

--He's doing important work. I think he is finally getting married next year. Plus, I have new friends here, too.

--Male or female?

--Depends on my mood. How about you? Is Rosie keeping you happy and satisfied? Or do you have side deals going on?

--To tell you the truth, I'm in between side deals right now.

--How convenient. I'm going to be in Chicago for a week next month. I could come and see you. Papa has conveniently moored his yacht in Singapore for the summer.

--Does he have a yacht? Is it big enough for both of us?

--It's a small yacht. It sleeps six.

--That'll work!

The affair soon rekindled.

Joe's thoughts returned to Rose's trust arrangements as he finished his shower. He had spent more time with Harry and his family in the past three days before the funeral than ever. For over two decades, he alternated between guilt and anger over Harry's refusal to forgive him for the problems that Joe's behavior had brought to the family. Joe realized that he had deserved Harry's rejection, but he was hurt that there was no give in Harry's position. Even Rose had forgiven him.

Joe's guilt diminished as his anger toward Harry grew as time passed. They had had a real blowup the winter before when Harry told him that he and Monica did not want him to take Dave and Jennifer on a Vail ski weekend.

--What do you mean? Why can't I spend some time with my grandkids?

--Are you serious? Do you not understand?

--No. You want to hurt me. You're penalizing your children.

--Okay. Here are three reasons: Drinking, gambling, and women. You haven't changed since the first time I became aware of them.

--You're just a self-righteous prig, like your mother and her whole family.

--No. I'm worse. They cave into you. They give you one more chance time and time again. I could forgive you if I saw evidence that you were sorry and wanted to change. But what you call remorse is regret that you got caught.

--Well, fuck you, too. As if I never did anything for you.

--You never did anything you didn't expect to get the credit for. That's why we didn't want you around the kids. Your attitude is always 'fuck you' unless you benefit.

That was the last time he and Harry had talked until the funeral. As far as Joe knew, Harry was not aware of the trust. Rose had kept that to herself. She told Joe that she wanted to keep the possibility of changing it open. Joe wasn't about to let anyone know. He had hoped to get it changed. Now, it was too late.

Unlike Harry, Amy had become closer to Joe. After he had taken Theo to the Beeline, where Amy was tending bar, and introduced them to each other, they became an alliance against Harry and the DeHaan family. Rose was constantly worried and upset about Amy and her life. Two years after the introduction, she had tried unsuccessfully to keep Amy from marrying Theo, which drove Amy closer to Joe. Joe was the opposite. When he could escape Rose and the conservative staff at DeJong, he enjoyed hanging out with Theo, even after his delivery obligations had ended. Joe was again lucky to avoid any legal consequences for participating in the car scheme or Theo's drug sideline. When a multistate and federal investigation had uncovered the Van Klompenberg Salvage operation, Joe was no longer driving and was not caught up in the sweep. The Boss also had escaped with only his lower-level henchmen, having been arrested and serving time. John Visser was not indicted, but Gordie Van Klompenberg received a two-year sentence. They knew enough, however, not to implicate the Boss. To avoid further scrutiny, the Boss had shut down all his operations in Nederland County, which meant that Joe's job as a mule between Theo and the Boss was also eliminated.

At first, Joe was relieved to no longer be an active criminal, but Theo kept him on his payroll, often needing him for 'odd jobs.' He still socialized with Amy and Theo, mostly at happy hours in New Leiden, which he could pass as late meetings with clients and suppliers to Rose. Theo had found a Miami source for his product, which allowed him and Amy to continue their expensive lifestyle one more year before they divorced. It also provided Joe with an occasional delivery trip to Miami, including visits with Lydia.

After Joe dressed, he went to the drop lid desk in the gathering room wall system to plan his next few days. He called Allen Zuverink's office and made an appointment on Friday to review his financials. He pulled out his medical records and remembered he had missed a meeting with his heart surgeon a month before when he was too involved with Rose and her care to worry about what was a routine follow-up. He called his cardiologist, Joe Westenbroek, at his office in New Leiden. Refusing to accept an appointment more than a month later, he insisted on talking to Jan Beltkamp, the office manager whose father had worked for Joe at ChairWorks. The appointment clerk said that Jan would need to call him back in the afternoon. He recalled his close call with death and the following heart surgery with an ironic smile.

Rose had always been disappointed that Joe did not want to travel out of the country on the typical touristy trips and cruises their friends had taken. They had gone on two short cruises, which Joe had enjoyed only because the ships had a casino and Rose allowed him to have wine with dinner. He was not interested in sightseeing and did not have an appreciation for culture. She was left on her own most of the time while he gambled. The dinners usually revolved around his stories that got longer and louder after he was on his third glass of heavily poured wine. She eventually lost her desire to travel at all with him.

She decided to join a women's Christian travel group consisting primarily of widows, which led to experiences such as a color tour in New England, a train trip through the Canadian Rockies, and a national park excursion in Utah and Arizona. These trips allowed Joe to spend more time with Lydia. Except for the annual ten-day NeoCon market in Chicago, Joe had been limited to a night here and there when Rose was home. He and Lydia had even broken off the affair again five years after she divorced Lorenzo.

This time, it was Lydia who called, using the two-ring code. She broke his heart when Joe called her back after closing his office door.

--Hi, this is an inconvenient time. Why are you calling? Can't it wait for this weekend?

--That's why I had to call. I won't be able to make it. I need to stay in Miami.

--Why's that? What's going on?

--Number one, it's cold up there. Also, I have some good news for me but bad for you.

--What would that be?

--Instead of coming to see you, I'm getting married again.

--What are you talking about? Who to?

--A nice man that I've known for a while. You met him once when you came down here. Jacob Epstein.

--That old Jew? Why do you want to marry him?

--He treats me right. Plus, he's pretty rich.

--Are you in love with him?

--No.

--How long have you been dating him?

--Since I divorced Lorenzo.

--Are you kidding me? Are you even fucking him?

--Such as it is. Like you said, he's old.

--Is he sharing his money with you?

--That's why we haven't married before. Everything goes to his kids. He's finally agreed to a prenup that I can live with.

--How much is that?

--None of your business. But I must be a good girl to collect the settlement, if you know what I mean.

--So, this is it for us?

--Not necessarily. He is old. But I did negotiate two weeks a year to travel on my own. You could be a part of those plans.

--That's only a little less than we see each other now. I could work something out.

Working it out was more manageable than Joe thought it would be. Lydia's new marriage coincided with Rose's new travel plans. Joe could not always get away for the entire two weeks, but Lydia found Jacob to be flexible if her dalliances were discreet and took place outside of Miami. He was also very understanding when she had to visit her ailing Aunt Estella in Chicago. Joe and Lydia were able to arrange meetings at least once a month in Chicago or on the yacht in Singapore in the summers, as well as having weekend getaways in Las Vegas when Rose was on a trip. Rose seemed uninterested in checking on Joe's made-up 'fishing with some of the guys' stories that he would use as his excuse for not being at home.

Joe's open-heart surgery had occurred six years prior while Rose was on her most extended getaway, a ten-day tour of the Holy Land, following the 'Steps of Jesus.' Joe and Lydia took advantage of her absence to spend four days at the new Mirage Resort in Las Vegas. In the middle of the second night, Joe woke up with tightness in his chest and feeling dizzy. Lydia was aware of Joe's first heart attack and his prescriptions to control his blood pressure and cholesterol. She also knew from Jacob's heart issues that the symptoms could be the sign of another heart attack, which meant that Joe needed to be examined and treated. She called 911 for an ambulance to take Joe to the emergency room at University Medical Center. Joe was diagnosed with a damaged atrial valve that would need to be replaced. Their holiday was over. Lydia flew back with Joe, who had been given blood thinners and instructions to return home immediately to see a cardiologist. On their arrival in New Leiden after an O'Hare transfer, Lydia sent Joe ahead to meet Amy at the gate. She waited until she could be the last passenger to deplane and walked over to the next gate to return to O'Hare and back to Miami. A month later, Joe was home with Rose, recovering from open-heart valve replacement surgery.

Joe returned to his desk and made a list of everything that needed to be done before he flew to Miami. Both Hank Plagmeyer and Amy could check on the house. Hank lived closer and would be more reliable. Otherwise, Amy's housekeeping prospect could replace Hank. She could also water Rose's indoor plants that he wanted to keep. It would be better if Hank were not snooping. Before he got further, the phone rang again.

--Hello.

--Hey, Joe! I'm glad I finally reached you.

--Hey back, Theo. I would have called you if you had left a number.

--My number is hidden for a reason. It's better for you if you don't have it.

--I thought you paid your debt to society and would be enjoying life on the outside. Are you still hiding out?

--Not from the law. Some other people would like to know where I am.

--What are you doing for a living? Something legal, I hope.

--I would like that, but I don't like being poor.

--Aren't they looking at you? You can't avoid scrutiny anymore.

--I am changing with the times. Different suppliers. Different customers. The law is behind the times.

--Like what kind of stuff?

--Steroids for bodybuilders, performance enhancement hormones, opioids for injury recovery. The pros are all using them. There's an untapped market for wannabes. Do you want in?

--Hell, no. You already gave me one heart attack.

--I thought that it was Lydia who overworked you.

--You both get the blame.

--I wasn't serious about you. I need someone younger. What do you think about Amy's gigolo?

--Do you mean Doug? He's not too bright, but he would be willing to do anything besides real work.

--Just the kind of guy I need. I want to keep Amy out of it, however. How would I contact him?

--I know he works as a part-time trainer out of a gym in Middleburg. I think it's called The Big Dutchman. He also bartends at the Goose and Gander Pub in Singapore.

--He sounds perfect for the job. I'll contact him. How are you doing without Rose? Who's going to keep you on the straight and narrow? Certainly not Lydia.

--I'm too old to get in trouble anymore. I am feeling more alone than I thought I would. I'll be going down to Miami next week. It will feel good to get back on the golf course.

--No waiting period between Rose and Lydia?

--I feel like the last years of Rose's illness were my waiting period. I need to get some fresh air after being cooped up. Will I see you in Miami?

--No way. I'm deep underground. Speaking of which, it's time to hang up

---

The first time Theo had gone 'underground' was when George Bosch was found dead at the DFG Club. Joe and George were supposed to meet with the caretaker to check the ponds for an algae outbreak similar to those plaguing other areas in Singapore County. Theo had called Joe the night before.

--Joe, I've heard you're meeting with George at the club tomorrow.

--Ja, we're on the maintenance committee. He said we need to check the ponds for algae.

--You need to find an excuse to back out. Let George go alone.

--Why? What's going on?

--Some people want to talk to George alone.

--Who are they?

--You don't want to know. Just make sure you're not there but that he is.

Joe met George as planned for breakfast at Boersma's, where he told him that something had come up at work. George was initially upset, but Joe persisted, saying he would be in the way because he didn't know anything about algae. George finally accepted his excuses and left the table quickly, as usual, without chipping in for the check.

When Joe returned to his car, he didn't recognize the man talking to George. He soon realized it was Theo, slovenly dressed in fishing clothes: old baggy khaki pants and a faded flannel shirt topped with a floppy hat.

--Change of plans, Joe. We need to go with George.

--What the fuck's going on, Theo? I didn't know you fished.

--I don't. This is my alter-ego costume. They're my dad's old fishing getup.

--Why do you need to be in disguise?

--I don't want anyone to spot me. We need to go with George to the club. Something is going down, and I want us to see what it is.

--What if they spot me?

--There's an old jacket and another hat in the cab. Grab it, and we'll go.

--What do you think, George?

--I think I'm glad to have the backup. You two can hang back when we get there.

--At least this coat is warm. It's going to be cold and windy out there. Thank God it's not raining yet.

As they drove to the DFG, Theo said he needed to take care of something out of town for a few weeks. He told Joe that it would be dangerous to divulge to anyone that they were at the club, especially if law enforcement investigators questioned him.

--You are making me nervous, Theo.

--You should be.

Joe's thoughts were interrupted by another phone call.

--Hi, Dad.

--What's up?

--I called Joanna and told her she was no longer needed. She cried a little. I told her that she would remind you too much of Mom. Rosa is a better cleaner than Joanna ever was. She'll even make tacos and burritos for you.

--Does she speak English?

--Enough to get by. I'll be there in about an hour.

Joe's memory went back to the time after George Bosch's death. He recalled when Charley Vredevelde showed up to interview him two days later at his new office at DeJong. A deputy from Singapore County was with him. Joe's heart skipped a beat. He remembered Theo's warning and put on a stern but surprised face.

--What can I do for you, Charley?

--Joe, this is Pete McAdams. Pete is the deputy who found George at the Fish and Game Club. We have some questions for you.

--Okay, but I don't know what I can help with.

--George told me the night before he died that he was meeting you for breakfast before the two of you needed to go the club to check on algae in the ponds. Is that right?

--We did meet for breakfast. I had an issue here that I needed to work on, so I couldn't go with him to the club.

--Did you notice any warning signs that he might be suicidal?

--No. He was on edge, but then he was always that way. He didn't seem like a guy who would kill himself. He was more likely to kill someone else.

--Pete, do you have any questions?

--Yes, I do. Joe, did the Chief own any weapons?

--Of course. He's…I mean, he was a cop.

--Any personal weapons? For hunting, perhaps?

--He always kept his hunting shotgun in his car.

--Do you know the model?

--It was a Remington—an older model. A classic, he always called it. He had a matching pair.

--You're sure he had two?

--Ja. He would carry both on weekend hunts up north.

--Charley, did your team find another Remington?

--No. We searched his house and only found a .45. It looked like a military pistol. It could be a souvenir from his time in the war. He always left his department weapon in his office desk drawer at the station. That was against policy, of course. Typical for him.

--That might mean something. The pistol would have been much easier than the shotgun if he were planning to kill himself. Joe, I've been wondering what was so important at work that caused you not to go with him to the club.

--We had a parts issue that was delaying a shipment of chairs for one of my best clients. I had to calm him down and push out the parts shipment on our end.

--Did you succeed?

--Ja, that's what I do. I found some in stock that I could flip from another client who wasn't ready for them.

--Were you planning to meet anyone at the club?

--Ja, Buck, the caretaker. Buck Johnson.

--Why is he telling us he knew nothing about a meeting or algae? The ponds had been inspected the week before and passed.

--I don't know. I only know what George told me.

--Do you know anyone who would want to harm Chief Bosch?

--Ask Charley. Maybe someone he arrested. I thought this was suicide.

--Most everyone does, except me.

At that point, Charley stood up and ended the interview.

--I think that's enough for now, Pete. If you find anything concrete, we can talk some more.

At the time, Joe felt he would not be let off that easily. The deputy looked to him like a 'dog with a bone.' He had recently heard about an investigation into illegal gambling rooms in Singapore County. He suspected that McAdams was involved. After twenty years of gradually reduced anxiety, he was again waiting for 'another shoe to drop.'

Chapter 7—Amy, First Tuesday PM, 1998

After their liaison Tuesday morning, which included an impromptu brunch and prime cannabis, Amy and Doug had forgotten their squabble. They sat down to review the backup business plan they had hoped would make them rich and made some adjustments to keep them solvent until a good harvest the following year would make them profitable again. Amy even consented to a modest expansion on the rear acreage of the farm. They reminded themselves how far they had come from that day when they thought they had missed a golden opportunity. Jonnie Van Orden had raised their hopes and then dashed them. That was before Theo came to their rescue.

The morning after Amy and Doug returned from their first visit to Jonnie's farm, she was surprised to get a call from Lenny Caputo, Joe's New Leiden lawyer. He was now representing Theo after his arrest. Theo, who was out on bail, needed her help with some information that required an in-person meeting. Could she come to a meeting in their office by the end of the day? It was essential to meet in person. Amy, full of curiosity, agreed to come at four.

On arrival, she was given a cup of coffee and ushered into a back office, where she waited for at least fifteen minutes. Looking as put together as always, Theo walked in with Lenny. Lenny did not sit down as he greeted Amy.

--It's good to see you again, Amy. Theo has some personal matters that he needs some help with. I thought this would be the safest place to meet—away from prying eyes. I'll bow out and allow you two to work out the details.

--My God, Theo. What's going on?

--Nice to see you, too. You are looking good, as always. A whole lot of bullshit is going on, that's what. With me hip deep into it.

--You look good, too, for a jailbird, anyway. How does this bullshit involve me?

--Profitably, I hope—and I'm not a jailbird yet.

--Okay, I'm listening. Although I usually don't come out ahead in your schemes.

--You did all right on the divorce. This could be even better for you.

--We'll see. What is it?

--It's simple. Every somewhat legal dollar I have has gone to my bail deposit and Lenny's outrageous retainer. But he should be worth it. He's the best. I need some cash to live on. My credit cards are maxed. As an indicted felon, loans are out of the question for me.

--I'm afraid I'm cash-poor too, Theo.

--I know. That's why you'll want to help me. I do have assets set aside. But I can't get to them, so I'm finding creative ways to turn them into a steady legal income. I'm assuming that I'm being watched. The feds and the state guys are now looking into me. I have business partners in Chicago and Miami, which makes all this shit federal. You can free up some of my cash and get it to me.

--And…what's in it for me? And why me? And where do I find the cash?

--You will remember the $95,000 borrowed for your business two years ago.

--What $95,000?

--The $95,000 you need to pay Jonnie Van Orden for purchasing his equipment and inventory. I'll give you copies of the 1985 signed loan agreement calling for a ten-year loan with annual 6% interest-only payments. There will also be receipts for the first two payments. That will give you ten years to use part of your new agriculture profits to pay me back.

Amy looked away to concentrate and think through the proposal.

--How did you know about Jonnie's offer?

--I planned it out for him after you called.

--I should have known. He was too prepared. Where do I find your cash?

--It's not cash. The documents will give me the cash. Remember the safety deposit box I had us open at First National Bank in South Bend just before we divorced? The papers I need are in two locked cash bags. Just get them and bring them here. Do you still have the key?

Amy paused, remembering Theo had set up this emergency response plan years before. She had accepted her part in it as the way a path to a better, much-deserved lifestyle was being opened for her. She understood that Theo was pulling her back into his schemes.

--And now I know why me.

———————

As Doug looked on six months later, Manuel and Nick planted the first clones of Jonnie's unique varieties. Jonnie had told them that Manuel and Rosa were in danger because they were undocumented and had drawn the attention of Charley Vredevelde, who was a known harasser of non-citizens. Nick and his sister, Lupe, were born in Texas, but their parents risked deportation if they stayed on Jonnie's farm. Amy offered them the old farmhouse on her acreage if they would work for her under the same terms they had with Jonnie. The house was in disrepair, but Gerrit had at least had the electrical and plumbing inspected and repaired when he thought he would live in it. The old coal furnace also worked, and there was still coal in the bin. Later, when Amy saw how well Rosa took care of the house and how many repairs Manuel had made with his time and money, she expressed her surprise and approval to Nick. He shook his head.

--Amy, to them, this is a mansion. You should see what they had to live in back in Parral.

The plantings and harvests gradually grew. Doug and Nick used their separate social networks to build markets for the finished product. Adding her share from the farm to her income from the store finally allowed Amy to afford the lifestyle she regarded as her right.

———————

Now, after years of success, the cannabis harvest on Amy's farm had been less than half their expectations for the third year in a row. Too much rain in the spring one year had flooded out half the plants. The following year, an August hailstorm ruined the buds just as they started to grow. Too much late summer rain and clouds limited the bud growth this year. Their limited profits would be gone after they paid the interest to Gerrit for the land contract and Theo for his startup loan. Their financial situation was a big part of Amy's decision that the time had come to separate from Doug. She paid all the bills; he spent his earnings from the farm and other jobs on personal expenses.

As they discussed, Doug disagreed with Amy's thought that they could raise their prices since harvests all over the state were down. He reminded her that their main competition was no longer domestic pot but cheaper and more potent Mexican buds. Even Nick was beginning to add them to the Montez family's share of the harvest for his retail business. Doug again brought up his plan to expand. He wanted to start to grow Mexican varieties on the unused back acres of the farm. Nick knew where they could get seeds and clones. They could add some greenhouses and be less affected by the weather. Amy was against it even though it would be profitable. It was too scary and made her feel like a real drug dealer instead of a counterculture organic farmer. They compromised on a tentative plan to add a greenhouse to extend the growing season and protect the plants from the weather—but only with Jonnie's varieties on the currently cultivated acres. It was settled that Doug and Nick would start working together to get the new plan going.

———————

After Doug went to the G & G for a fill-in shift behind the bar, Amy called Randy Veltmaan to tell him she would not attend Thursday's choir practice. She had the direct line to his office, but he did not answer. She left a message without mentioning the retreat. Ten minutes later, he called back and asked her to come in to talk over some things the following morning. She said she would stop by in the morning on her way to Burt Lake, where she was meeting some friends. He said those friends were what he wanted to talk about.

For the rest of the day, Amy caught up on some backed-up paperwork at the store and tracked some orders due later in the fall to appeal to holiday shoppers. She called Judy Marsden to confirm that she could cover the store on Friday before Amy returned to cover the weekend. Judy was a single schoolteacher she had met at The Great Awakening sessions at the old church. She soon became Amy's summertime and backup staffer at the store.

She checked the weather to ensure there was no early snow forecast for northern Michigan. When she was finally caught up and ready for the peace of the retreat, she returned home just as the phone rang. She did not feel like picking it up and let it go to the answering machine. Her heart skipped a beat when she heard Theo's voice telling her to call back immediately. She recognized the area code as the same Florida code she used to reach Joe when he could still go south for the winter months. She knew Theo had been released from prison with parole restrictions. She called him back rather than having it hang over her for the weekend.

--That was quick.

--How'd you know it was me?

--Keep up with the times. There's this new thing called Caller ID.

--You always have the latest. What do you want?

--What do you think?

--I don't think. I know. I don't have any money right now. Our harvest sucked.

--But you are now an heir.

--Really? My dad's ashes aren't even buried yet. Besides, he spent most of his money. He didn't even own the house he lived in for forty years. It's in a trust.

Amy told Theo about her parents' reconciliation after one of Joe's flings when Rose insisted he take his name off the deed to protect her from financial ruin if they divorced. She established an irrevocable trust for Harry's children when she became sick. By then, she was as upset with Harry's atheism and Amy's lifestyle as she was with Joe. She put the house and paid-up life insurance policies she owned for her and Joe into the trust. Amy had checked with her attorney, Carl Zandstra. The assets in the trust were untouchable, waiting for David and Jennifer to reach their twenty-fifth birthdays.

--Aren't you the trustee now? Break the trust.

--No. Harry's friend Allen Zuverink is still the trustee. Carl and his brother-in-law, who specializes in trusts, are trying to break it. No luck so far. Besides, I've already paid you $15,000.

--That was three years ago. You're six months behind on the interest payments, meaning the principal can be demanded immediately. Read the contract.

--Good luck enforcing that contract. Any court would start to wonder where you got the money.

--As you know, my friends get paid to enforce contracts.

--Look, Dad did have a little money left over and his Florida condo, for which I also will need to fight Lydia for ownership. Probate will take at least two months. When it's completed, I can catch up on the interest and give you a sizable chunk of the principal.

--Make sure I'm first in line, or I'll take your condo, your business, and your fucking pot farm.

--It was nice talking to you, too.

With her mood shattered, Amy slammed down the receiver. She went to her wine cooler, grabbed an open bottle of Gallo white, reached into her top cupboard for her Shake and Bake kit, and went out to her deck. She had stopped smoking cigarettes a decade before after having her teeth whitened. When a friend brought her the Shake and Bake inhaler from Amsterdam, she could also replace her pot smoking.

Amy reminded herself how far she had come since her breakup with Theo. The final straw occurred when she found out she was pregnant shortly after their first separation. They had just reconciled, giving Amy hope that they could have a life together. Theo's reaction dashed her hopes.

--You're not thinking of keeping it, are you?

--Of course, I am. This could be my only chance. I'm thirty-two, you know.

--Count me out. I don't want to have a kid getting in my way. Having a wife is bad enough. You'll never get any child support from me.

--Fuck you! Why can't we live like other people? Everybody has kids.

--Not me. You need to get rid of it. I'll find someone to take care of it. I'll even pay for it.

Amy went into her bedroom, locking the door. For the first time in her life, she cried herself to sleep. She woke up early in the morning with a feeling of desperation. Theo was still sleeping on the sofa. She kicked him in his butt, which was facing the outside of the couch.

--Get up, asshole! Let's get this done before it's too late. Then I can get you out of my life forever.

Theo made several phone calls that morning. They were on their way to Detroit before noon. They found the clinic a block away from the corner of Woodward and Grand. Two hours later, they were on the way back to New Leiden. Amy felt better after three days, but then a more widespread pain began to return. Two days later, Stephanie took her to the emergency room. After finding a severe infection, the doctors sent her to surgery for an emergency hysterectomy. Amy was not surprised. She already felt that this was her last chance. There would be no more reconciliations with Theo. It took five years before their divorce was final and five more before Amy finally received her settlement from Theo.

After the settlement, Amy drove up to the three-year-old condominium development on the dune north of the state park where the Singapore River flowed into Lake Michigan. When she attended a party years earlier in a client's unit, it became her dream to live there one day. Two weeks before the settlement, as she delivered a custom order formal dress to one of her best clients, she noticed a For Sale by Owner sign on the front door window of one of the units. Seeing that the sign was still there, she knocked on the door. The owner was happy to give her a tour.

The complex, comprised of eight two-story gabled duplexes around a cul de sac, sat atop a dune protected from the lake by another lower dune. Amazingly, the dune had built up on the original site of the port of Singapore, a company town of the same name built to ship out timbers from the surrounding forest. When there were no more trees, the sand took over the harbor. Singapore moved inland on the river. The dune eventually buried the original port.

The unit for sale was the northernmost unit facing the lake. The open living room and the dining/kitchen area had a perfect panoramic lake view across the lower dune. The garage was on the north side, set back from the central part of the home. There was a flex room in one corner of the downstairs. The main bedroom suite was upstairs next to a loft bedroom above the garage. They both had views through their gabled windows. The unit was beyond Amy's expectations. The growing success of her store after seven years and her settlement qualified her for the mortgage. After two weeks of negotiations and two months to close, she was able to move in.

An hour later, after two Shake and Bake bowls, she finished the wine. Feeling much better, she found one of Doug's frozen vegetarian lasagna dinners, quickly ate it, and packed a larger-than-necessary suitcase for her three-day trip. The following morning, she stopped at Randy's church and told him she would no longer attend. He took it poorly and accused her of being a fake Christian. Amy burned his ears with words he was unfamiliar with hearing and left quickly. Shortly after noon on Wednesday, she arrived at Gerrit's 'New Awakening Resort.'

Calling it a resort was a stretch, but it gave him the platform he wanted. When he sold Amy the farm, he had taken her deposit, borrowed more from some other well-off Friends, and bought a run-down group of cabins close to a nature preserve on Burns Lake east of Harbor Springs. He gradually upgraded them as his following and contributions grew. As each of the twelve two-bedroom cabins was upgraded and insulated, he could charge more for in-season rentals to the public. They were comfortable with queen or two twin options and a sitting area, but they had no plumbing. He changed half of the larger, lodge-style building, called the bunkhouse, into an all-purpose room for group yoga, meditation, and socializing. Along one side, he added three mini kitchens that renters and Friends could reserve for preparing meals. They also could be used to cook community meals during retreats. He solved the problem of adding plumbing to each cabin by adding a bathhouse behind the kitchen, complete with public men's and women's showers and saunas, plus unisex lockable rooms with a sink and commode.

Most of his help in the summer came from his Friends, including some who were paid, like teachers and college-age children of older Friends. Others were volunteers, encouraged to meditate when not working on menial tasks, receiving discounts for the retreats or other off-season stays. Some of them lived in a 'worker's village,' a run-down roadside motel a mile up the road, which one of his investor Friends had contributed to the cause. Improvements were on hold until the cabins' renovations were completed.

Amy was not one of those volunteers. She paid her way. Neither was she one of the major donors on Gerrit's nonprofit board, who received the first choice of accommodations and much of Gerrit's focus. Gerrit did not give her as much attention as he did when she first attended the Singapore and Burns Lake retreats. Amy sensed that he was disappointed that their relationship had not become intimate more often. Also, she had never become an official Friend because she had not attended enough of his 'courses' that entailed 'Deep Thinking and Feeling' instruction and practice, nor had she contributed enough volunteer time. Still, she regarded him as her guide to a higher consciousness. He once told her that her spiritual growth would always be limited if she continued perceiving all aspects of life as transactional. That was okay with Amy because she saw being transactional as ordinary and necessary. She also preferred keeping some distance from the other Friends.

Amy always felt comfortable with the New Awakening program and with Gerrit. She respected him for not taking complete advantage of his psychological power over many of his followers, a power he could have easily abused. After her years with him, she took him at his word that he was just a guide, unlike others who were beginning to speak of him as a prophet and teacher in his own right. She knew his biography well: a Presbyterian childhood, a philosophy/psychology degree at San Diego State, a year at Van Raalte Seminary in Middleburg (from which he claims to have run away screaming to save himself from insanity), and a three-year pilgrimage to India, Tibet, and Japan to find the true path to spiritual enlightenment. Not receiving the answers he had hoped for, he realized that he would need to start at the beginning—his Christian upbringing.

He returned to Michigan where, during his time at Van Raalte, he had met some Christians delving into the new mysticism of Thomas Merton and Thomas Keating. They were also resurrecting the ideas of Geert Groot, a pre-Reformation Dutch teacher from the original Dordrecht in the Netherlands. He had started the 'Brethren of the Common Life,' a movement that returned to early Christians' authentic communal and ascetic lives. Gerrit attended winter retreats with Ram Das at the Lama Foundation near Questa, New Mexico. Later, in 1984, he studied there with Thomas Keating, who taught him a deeper understanding of contemplative prayer. Forming his unique blend of religious teachings, he gradually attracted a following among those he called 'thirsty rejects of traditional Christianity,' mainly from an area that stretched from Chicago to Detroit. In addition to his Singapore Church and Burt Lake Resort, he created a touring seminar that he offered on select weekends to anywhere a Friend would sponsor an event, find a venue, and attract an audience.

The retreat did not disappoint Amy. There were only nine attendees, all of whom were more experienced than Amy in the 'Deep Feeling and Thinking' course. It was only her second time. The spartan accommodations, simple food, short enlightening seminars with Gerrit and the rest of the group., and long and quiet walks along trails in the nearby state forest had focused her mind on reaching a more profound peace during her yoga, meditation, and contemplative prayer sessions. The fall weather was cold and cloudy but dry most of the day. Overnight showers magnified the fall colors and aromas of forests.

She had a fifteen-minute counseling session with Gerrit before she left. The tone of the meeting was the opposite of her confrontational meeting with Randy Veltmaan on her way to the retreat. Gerrit had started the session by asking,

--Are you still involved with the preacher and his prosperity church? What's it called?

--Joyful Spirit. I suspect I'm over it.

--Really?

--Yeah, I met with Randy on the way up here. He got too personal and too pushy. He was upset that I was skipping his service to attend a non-Christian retreat.

--The last time we talked, you liked his church because it was non-judgmental.

--I know I did! But the mood changes if you don't buy into the whole born-again thing and offer up your time and money. He was over the top this time, pressuring me to fully commit to him and his church, without which I wouldn't 'prosper spiritually or financially in this world or the next.' He put his hands on me, asking me to pray with him. It didn't feel like he was interested in prayer.

--You are wise to recognize the situation. He uses emotion to control vulnerable people.

--I will miss singing, just as I got back into it. Am I being too transactional if I leave if things don't go my way?

--There is nothing inherently wrong with being transactional if one is aware. It's part of living in society. However, bringing expectations of specific benefits to one's spiritual path, whether physical, financial, or psychological, can slow the process and temporarily block the way.

--You've told me that before. I want to find peace. I feel much better after this weekend.

--Ahh, that's the transaction. You are trying to exchange your yoga and meditation efforts for peace of mind. That's achievable, but just like expecting money, love, or fame, it limits the ultimate discoveries that lie further along the path.

--At least I'm not expecting riches or power.

--That may be true in a narrow sense. We talk about greed being the source of evil. But greed is wanting more of, better than, or different from anything and everything, including peace and enlightenment. But don't worry. You are where you are supposed to be right now.

--Where is that?

--You are looking for some peace and finding it. Accept the gift and enjoy it. So many people, including me, sometimes want to rush on further, trying to find God and enlightenment before they are ready for the journey.

--Am I not ready for the journey? I've been doing this for a while.

--You'll know when you are ready for another level of self-knowing. A path will appear. For now, do what you are doing. This is not a competition. No one is keeping score.

As Amy drove home late Friday afternoon, she resolved to make three changes in her life. She was now sure that she needed to split from Doug, feeling him a weight holding her back from the life she wanted to lead. She intended to use her meditation and yoga practice to bring inner peace to her daily life instead of being a temporary respite from the turmoil that came as baggage with her attraction to him. She felt the same about Randy and his church. It was a wrong turn in her life path that she needed to undo. The farm also had to go. Doug was trying to take it over and change it from a calming hobby into a business that was becoming more dangerous. She was irritated with Gerrit for seeming to limit her to wannabe status among his motley group of followers. At least, however, he had said:

--For now, getting rid of some baggage would add to your opportunity for spiritual growth.

A light rain had been falling during the last hour of her trip back to Singapore. As she pulled into her garage from the cul de sac, she casually noticed a sheriff's squad car near the entrance but let it pass from her mind. The doorbell rang just as she was placing her luggage near the stairs. When she opened the door, a man in street clothes, backed up by two Singapore county deputies, showed his badge.

--Are you Amy Bolinyk?

--That was my married name. I'm back to Amy Berendts now.

--I'm Detective Grover Lukasen. We have a warrant to search your home and for your arrest.

--What for? What's going on?

Amy saw a van pulling up with more officers and another what looked like an unmarked government car. She recognized Sheriff Pete McAdams from campaign posters. Grover read from a notepad.

--Intent to manufacture and distribute controlled substances under penal code 33.7401. Please turn around. We need to handcuff you. You have the right to…

--You can't do this! I'm calling my attorney!

--You have the right to remain silent and refuse to answer questions. Anything you say may be used against you in a court of law. You have the right to consult an attorney before speaking to the police and to have an attorney present during questioning now or in the future. If you cannot afford an attorney, one will be appointed for you. You can make a phone call from the jail after we book you.

Pete McAdams walked in like he belonged in her condo. Other deputies followed, eager to tear it apart.

--Hello, Amy, I'm Sheriff McAdams. I hope you can cooperate with us. Can you tell us where we can find Doug Mason?

--You know I'm going to sue you for false arrest. No, I haven't seen Doug since Friday. I just got back in town from a retreat.

--Can you tell us where we can find Nick Montez?

--I haven't seen him for weeks. I assume you checked his apartment in Middleburg.

--The Nederland Sheriff is helping us with that. How about Theodore Bolinyk?

--Theo? I haven't seen him for months.

--When and where did you see him?

--Ask my lawyer. I'm done talking.

--Do you know who lives in the house on the acreage you own north of Wakazoo?

--How do you know about my farm?

--We find out about things. That's what we do. Does anyone else live in the house?

--I told you. I'm done talking.

Pete turned to Grover.

--Okay, bring her in, book her, and take her across the street to the jail. She'll be assigned to our VIP lockup cell. Meanwhile, we'll check this place out.

Chapter 8—Harry, Second Saturday, 1998

Harry arrived back at the Amsterdam Inn around 3:30 on Saturday afternoon. There were better places in the revitalized Middleburg downtown area, but the Inn was new and convenient. His week was as successful as he had hoped. He had closed a three-step deal that was the largest and most profitable he had ever brought into the company. All that remained were the final negotiations with his partner, which would free him from a job that had become burdensome. Not that he was without apprehensions. He would be a divorced, unemployed fifty-year-old male without a new life plan or direction. He would have a chance to find out what he wanted to do with the rest of his life. What would happen if nothing of interest appeared? He could play more golf and go to more of the Broncos, Nuggets, and Rockies games for which he had never had the time. That could get old after a while. He would have more time for Jennifer and David. Would they have time for him?

He put those worries aside and dialed Larry, who did not pick up. He left a message on the machine letting him know he had arrived back in Dordrecht and would be ready early in the morning. He took a few deep breaths and called Marilyn. She did pick up.

--Hi, it's Harry.

--Harry. I'm so glad you caught me. I was about to go to the church for a meeting. Are you back in town?

--Ja, I just got in. Do you still want to meet and talk?

--I do.

--Okay, where should we go?

--I've been thinking about that. I think the safest thing is to come here to my place. I could pick you up around five after my meeting. We could zip in the garage. No one would see. I have some leftover lasagna. You must be starving.

--Umm... I guess that would work. It certainly would be private.

--Good. I'll call you when I get there. What's your cell phone number? I just got a Nokia like yours this week. I can call from the car.

--Hold on a second. I'm rethinking this. Why don't I drive over? You can open the garage when I get there. Do you have an open space?

--Yes, Butch took his car. It could work better. No one can easily see our driveway. Plus, it'll be dark when you leave. Our house is on the third cul de sac on the right, just past the Odawa Lake Yacht Club. Do you know where that is?

--Ja.

--Call me from the gate. I'll buzz you in and open the garage door. We are the third house on the right.

--Six o'clock?

--Yes.

Harry drove to the south side of Odawa Lake, surprised by the new mansion-sized homes that had replaced smaller cottages along the shore. They were styled in various traditional architectural motifs, sometimes more than one represented in the same house. He passed the yacht club he was familiar with, except it was now twice the size with new docks, boathouses, and a restaurant. Not knowing what to expect and having some apprehensions, he had showered and dressed in his best business casual shirt and blazer. He turned into the cul de sac and called from the gate. Marilyn answered and buzzed the gate open. The houses in the complex were smaller than others on the shore drive, but they were new and looked expensive. He saw the open garage door on the third house and pulled in next to a Lincoln SUV. He saw Marilyn waiting at the inside door to buzz the door closed.

She wore a maxi dress that showed off her curves without being too suggestive. Her strawberry blonde hair was down and looked freshly styled. He walked up to her, not knowing what to do, so he leaned down to touch her shoulder and kiss her cheek. She made sure that their lips met and hers were parted. He responded the same, automatically adding a more than friendly hug. As their breathing became heavier, she separated and guided him past the kitchen onto a slim sectional sofa in an informal eating/sitting area, where their kissing continued along with hands exploring and bodies squirming against each other. As he reached under the folds of her dress, Marilyn pulled away.

--Are you sure you want to do this?

--I am now!

--I mean, should we?

--Absolutely! We've been waiting thirty years.

--Let's go to the guestroom.

Later, she jumped from the bed and said she would be right back. As he slowly began to dress, she came back in wearing a velvet robe and tossed a pinstriped velour robe to him that was more masculine.

--I have a bottle of wine opened that we were supposed to have an hour ago. Come into the kitchen. I'll heat the lasagna and make a salad.

--I feel weird wearing Butch's robe.

--Don't worry. It was a Christmas present that he never wore. He hates robes.

--My lucky day, I guess. In more ways than an unused robe.

The kitchen, which Harry had hardly noticed on the way in, could have been a showroom from a House Beautiful ad with all the latest appliances and finishes.

--Your house is spectacular. You need to show me the rest of it.

--I'll show you later, but let's eat first. I'm hungry now. I was too nervous to eat lunch. I hope you like the wine. Butch has a well-stocked bar if you'd like something more potent. He makes excellent cocktails.

--I think wine is perfect. This bottle looks expensive.

--Why don't you pour us some?

Harry poured, gave her a glass, and held his up to toast. She tipped the glasses and leaned in to kiss him again. He kissed her back again. Slowly, she pulled away.

--I didn't expect this to be so special.

--I wasn't sure what to expect.

--Did you expect anything?

--I took my second shower of the day. Just in case.

--What do you think now?

--You're even sexier than you were in high school. I hope I was not as stumbling and bumbling as I was back then.

--You weren't bumbling back then. You always had the touch. But you're even more sensitive now. Plus, your body is not so boyish.

--Thanks. I think. I was out of shape about five years ago. My bad knees kept me from exercising. Monica got me into Pilates. I only attended a few sessions, but I'm keeping it up. I don't know how great I look, but I feel better.

--Speaking of being out of shape, I was desperate to lose twenty pounds in the days since we made our date for today.

--Is this a date?

--It's turning out to be.

--If you have an extra twenty pounds, they are in the right places.

She kissed him again until the beeper on the convection oven announced that the lasagna was ready. They ate quickly and returned to the guest room with a second glass of wine. Their bodies and touches moved more slowly, taking advantage of thirty years of experience since their high school explorations. An hour later, Marilyn was making Harry, now fully clothed, a coffee for the road.

--Are you and Larry still planning to hunt at the DFG tomorrow?

--Ja. It's like what you and I are doing. We'll replay our younger years.

--I hope this is better! Did you know Butch didn't return to the club for years after his dad was killed there? He finally relented when George, our son, wanted to go fishing.

--Was he killed, or was it a suicide?

--Butch is sure it was murder. He thinks his dad was investigating criminal activity. He thinks it was related to the Van Klompenberg scandal a few years later. He thinks the Chicago syndicate killed him.

--Really? What was that scandal?

--Van Klompenberg used his junkyard to 'clean cars' for Chicago car theft rings. He pled guilty but refused to implicate anyone else. Butch thinks that saved his life. His sentence lasted less than two years.

--Does he have any evidence about his dad?

--Nothing definite. But that Indian deputy, now the sheriff in Singapore County, agreed with Butch. But the Singapore sheriff back then disagreed. The county people called it suicide.

--Amazing story! So Butch isn't over it yet?

--Oh, no! I made him go to the funeral home since we had many mutual friends. He always had bad feelings about Joe. He thought he knew more than he would admit. Did you know Joe was the last person to see George alive?

--No.

--He and George were supposed to meet for breakfast before hunting at the club. Joe was having breakfast at Boersma's when people saw them, but he always said he had to cancel the club because he had to work that day. He claimed that George left Boersma's parking lot in his Jeep to go hunting alone. Butch knows his dad never went hunting by himself.

--I don't see Joe as a killer.

--That's not it. He knew more than he dared to tell.

--I guess we'll never know now.

--Speaking of people on Butch's shit list, your buddy Larry is on it.

--Why is that?

--Do you remember the girl found nude and murdered on the side of the state highway south of town?

--Vaguely.

--Larry was one of the state investigators. He went public, blaming some Middleburg people for covering up evidence. Some of them were Butch's buddies.

--What ever happened?

--Nothing. It's unsolved. But Larry ruffled feathers.

--Sounds like him. I'll get him to update me.

The coffee was done. Marilyn walked him to the door with an arm around his waist.

--How long will you be in town? Can we do this again?

--I don't know where I'll be until I meet with Amy on Monday. But I'm a free man. You're still married, so you need to decide.

--I may also be free soon. I think Butch is seeing someone again. But I don't want to think about that. I want to enjoy us today. I haven't felt this good in a long time.

--Me, too. But you do need to think about it. You can call me anytime to talk.

The goodbye kiss lingered. She opened the garage door, and Harry drove off.

————————

The next afternoon, Harry returned to his room at the Inn, where Larry had dropped him off following their hunt at the DFG. The hunting could have been more successful and enjoyable. There was a slow fall drizzle most of the time. The ducks did not cooperate, even though the hunters tried two blinds on different ponds. They missed when they finally got a shot at a pair after patiently waiting for three hours. Larry blamed the drizzle that dripped in his eyes. Harry was out of practice and got his shots off too late. He was content to avoid messing with a dead duck. Even Buster, a black lab belonging to Larry's son, seemed disinterested, as if he knew how hapless the two hunters were. Larry's daughter-in-law had packed a lunch, so they quit early and headed to the relative warmth of the rustic clubhouse. Mostly, they reminisced about their high school days. Larry only smirked when Harry told him about Allen Zuverink still savoring Middleburg Christian's victory over Dordrecht High. Because of Marilyn's comments about Butch's feeling about his dad's death, Harry brought up the subject with Larry.

--What do you think? Was it suicide?

--I'm fifty-fifty on that. I learned about George being hooked up with the Monday night club and Joe's financial issues with the DeVries brothers. Some people also suspected him and Joe of knowing about the Van Klompenberg deal. But officially, it was declared a suicide by the old sheriff here in

Singapore County. They figured remorse and guilt drove him to it.

---But what do you think?

--Chances are that he knew too much, and someone didn't trust him to keep quiet.

--I heard that Butch and the new sheriff share that theory.

Harry saw an accusatory grin grow on Larry's face.

--I wonder who you've been talking to?

--Never mind that. I also heard you burned some bridges over a dead girl found off the old highway to Singapore.

--That's another unsolved case. I was transferred to help for a few weeks, but the town fathers wanted it hushed up. It was written off as a rogue killer/rapist. She was made out to be an innocent Christian girl, but the motel she worked at had a reputation for catering to rough characters, including union busters and drug pushers. McAdams and I agree on that case, too. We think she may have seen something she wasn't supposed to and paid for it with her life—and worse. She was beaten badly.

--As long as we discuss inside info from your working years, what do you know about Theo Bolinyk, Amy's ex?

--I worked on a Detroit case where he was peripherally involved, so I know a little. His is a sad story. He started as a fast-talking but well-liked sales rep and man about town. He always spent more than he made and abused all the party drugs of that time. He had to become a dealer to support his habits, which, as they usually do, gradually grew into addictions. He had a good lawyer who kept him out of jail for a while, but he finally was out of tricks. He pled guilty but kept his mouth shut, which might have kept him alive. I think he got out a little while ago.

--I heard that too. He and Joe were buddies before he married my sister. Were they involved in stuff together?

--Not that anyone could prove. They mostly hit the bars and underground gambling joints together. Theo's connections with the Chicago groups happened later and involved drugs, not gambling and car theft.

--I know Amy and Doug smoke pot. He went through a rehab stint for coke, too. Have they been involved with Chicago people?

--Not that I've heard. If they sell and use, it would be low volume—friends and family stuff.

--Well. We better get back. I need to rest up for my visit with ol' Hank.

--Okay, let's go.

Driving back to the hotel, Larry decided to quiz Harry.

--Tell me more about what's happening to you. Especially your family. I never thought you would get divorced. What happened?

--Hey, that sounds like a professional interrogator's question.

--It's a habit. So, what happened?

--I blamed her at first, but then I blamed myself–Reformed Church guilt, you know. I was too busy and out of touch. Monica hooked up with another teacher. I don't know if they fell in love with each other or with the lifestyle they could share. Both were teachers with an empty nest and time on their hands. She was a true Colorado mountain girl. He was a mountain boy. They ski both downhill and cross-country. They camp. They hike. I mean week-long hikes in the summer. They fly fish! He offered her something I was neither willing nor able to give. Once the kids were in high school and out of the house most of the time, we found we had little left in common.

--I hope you are ready for some lonely times if you don't make a good career switch.

--I can't say I'm not concerned. But I'll make something work out.

--How did the kids take it?

--It seemed like they were the adults throughout the divorce process. So far, they're doing great.

--Don't jump into anything too fast—with either work or women. That doesn't mean you can't enjoy your freedom. Just don't get tied up with old friends.

———————

Harry had about three hours before he needed to be at Hank's place for Sunday supper. He was not excited about going. Hank tended to sound like a preacher, and there probably would be no alcohol to smooth things over. To cope with his early morning start, he took a quick shower before he fell on the bed, hoping for a nap.

His mind swirled with the emotions of the last week. Joe's death brought back feelings he thought he had settled years before. He wished he could have had a better relationship with his family. He thought that he might have judged Joe too harshly even though he felt justified in doing so because of the many ways Joe had betrayed and hurt Rose. He had avoided closeness with his mother as she gravitated back to her family's conservative religiosity. Perhaps he could have been more open to a positive connection with her despite rejecting any connection to the church. He was also beginning to realize that his opinion that Amy was self-centered to the point of being narcissistic could be an exaggeration.

Now, he was beginning to think that his rejection of them made all three feel as betrayed and hurt as he did. If he could have found a way to be less judgmental and keep communication with them alive, they might have responded in a way that would keep them together as something more than a broken family. Then again, as he continued to think through it, a closer relationship never had a chance. Joe and Amy were just too toxic.

As he continued to try to catch up on his sleep, more guilt feelings crept up from his own family in Colorado. Why was he now willing to extricate himself from the demands of the business? Would it have made a difference with Monica if he had done it five years earlier, or had they also grown apart for other reasons? He was thankful that David and Jennifer had taken a neutral position and accepted the grown-apart explanation, not blaming Harry or Monica. He realized they had friends whose parents had gone through combative divorces and knew the damage that breakups could cause. A feeling of dread and self-doubt settled in as he asked himself whether he had missed signs from David that would have alerted him to his homosexuality.

He asked himself, 'What am I doing? I let my wife go. My kids are on their own. My parents are gone. I can't trust my sister. Now, I'm walking away from my business. I don't have any close friends except Larry. No wonder I let myself have a night of passion that I didn't realize I had in me, opening a thirty-year-old wound with a woman who was mostly getting back at her husband.'

He managed to reassure himself that he would figure it all out later and dozed off for half an hour before the alarm woke him in time for the visit to Hank's.

Hank lived on the north side of Dordrecht in a two-story farmhouse that his maternal grandfather had built with what was known as 'Dordrecht Brick,' which had been formed from a distinctive red color of clay found in a low swampy area west of the town. Hank was born in 1918 after his father was killed in the Great War. He and his mother lived with the grandparents, who were ready to retire. After Dordrecht annexed the farm and several others, zoning them residential, the family could develop the farm into single-family houses. As the town grew, they sold one lot at a time, as moderately priced homes were needed. They kept a few acres around the farmhouse, which eventually supplied land for the homes of five of Hank's uncles and aunts. When the grandparents passed away, Hank and his mother stayed in the house, living on their share of the proceeds of the land sales, which carried them through the Depression. After serving in World War II, Hank married Dena Wiersma and lived in the same home with her and his mother.

Harry knew the house well and drove into the driveway right on time. Irma had seen him arrive. She opened the side door and waved him into the kitchen. Harry was surprised that it had looked recently remodeled with up-to-date finishes and mid-range appliances. She was dressed in jeans and a tee under a loose-fitting flannel shirt. Her thick, dark hair was pulled into a ponytail. Somehow, she made it all look feminine.

--Hank still wears his suit for the second service. He may be the only one left who does. He's upstairs changing. Thanks for coming to see him. He's been looking forward to it.

--No thanks necessary. Hank was the only one of Joe's friends who noticed me. He was more like a favorite uncle. Speaking of which, I didn't realize he had a niece. I thought he was an only child.

--That's right. My father was his cousin. I'm his grandniece. I grew up two doors down–part of the family complex. As you know, Hank and Dena didn't have children. They always treated me like a granddaughter.

--Sounds like them. Hank said you have a daughter.

--Yes, I do. Janice is fourteen. She's at a social with the church group tonight. Can I get you an iced tea or a glass of wine?

--I better stick with the tea. I'm surprised Hank has alcohol in the house.

--He didn't until I came back into his life. Five years ago, he picked Julie and me up from a shelter in New Leiden and told us we could stay until we were on our feet. Dena had passed away less than a year before. After a while, he asked us to stay permanently. I agreed but insisted that wine be allowed. I had gone back to nursing and had a job at Dordrecht Hospital. The schools and church were great for Janice. I was glad to stay.

--Were you at the shelter to avoid a husband?

--Ja. That's another story, but he's out of state and out of our lives now.

Hank walked into the room with a slight smile and shook Harry's hand firmly, squeezing his shoulder with the other hand.

--I see you two have gotten acquainted. Have you offered Harry some of your wine?

--He opted for iced tea. You too?

--Of course.

--Okay. Why don't you two sit in the den while I prepare supper? I hope you like lasagna, Harry. It's Hank's regular Sunday night after-church meal.

--Great! I could eat lasagna every day. Although, I was looking forward to having liverwurst and boiled potatoes.

--That's enough sarcasm! Go sit down. I'll bring your tea. Our supper will be ready in a little while.

Hank led Harry around the corner to another updated, heavily windowed sitting room that Harry realized had been the back porch when he was a grade schooler and spent time with other neighborhood Plagmeyers while Rose visited Dena with women from the church during Ladies Aid meetings.

--The house is looking good, Hank.

--I wanted Irma and Julie not to feel like they were in a mausoleum, and I've been enjoying it. I wanted to do it years ago, but Dena said she was comfortable with the way it was. She was afraid that making it new wouldn't feel like home. I planned the restructure, hired the subs, and did some work myself. Irma did the decorating.

Irma walked in with the tea.

--Don't be too critical, Harry. I know that in your job, you're used to fancier things.

--Not really. What I do is functional, commercial, and technical stuff. Just putting pieces of a puzzle together, both conceptually and physically. This is comfortable and inviting.

--That's nice of you to say. Thank you. Keep on with your visit. I'll call you when supper's ready.

--Harry, I'm glad you've come. It would do both of us good to talk about your dad.

--I think you're right. This week has made me think about things differently.

--How is that?

--I guess I've felt sad about my parents and how I treated them. I was young and arrogant. My mother's fixation on religion put me off. I could've worked around it, but I wasn't willing to put in the effort. It was easier to avoid her. Joe was not trustworthy. I believed he only cared about what he wanted at any moment. That was true, but I was judgmental. You notice I started calling him 'Joe.' I didn't like to acknowledge him as 'Dad.'

--I'm glad that you are being introspective. However, it's important not to go too far down the guilt road. They were adults. You were a young man.

--I've been telling myself that, too. Then I think of my sister and my ex-wife. We were equals. I could have been more flexible and had a better relationship with them all these years. I might have been better off if I hadn't left Dordrecht.

--Is that what you think?

--No, not really. But I need to acknowledge what I left behind.

--You know, Joe earned most of your negative feelings. I tried to help him whenever he hit bottom. That's the only time he would listen to me. Every few years, he would get back in trouble. Sometimes, it would be booze, other times gambling. The worst was the involvement with women or just with one woman. It was usually Lydia.

--I don't know the details as well as you. Just the general overall picture. I don't know why my mom put up with it all those years. That soured my relationship with her, too.

--Dena and I spent more time helping Rose than Joe. She was terrified of a divorce and was always looking for a way to bring him back and get over his self-destruction. One of the last times, we worked out a deal in which he gave up interest in the house so she would never be on the street. When her cancer was diagnosed, we suggested she put it in a trust for your kids. Another time, he borrowed twenty-five thousand from an almost paid-up hundred-thousand-dollar whole life insurance policy on him, which he claimed to need for gambling debts. I knew he had no gambling debts because no one would give him any credit. At first, I thought he would use it as a cash stash to gamble with. Later, I found out he set Lydia up in a condo in Florida. Anyway, Rose kept up the payments on the insurance and put them in the trust. Your kids have a nice nest egg.

--I had no idea it might be worth that much. I guess that's one of the reasons my friend Allen Zuverink, whose father you knew well, warned me to get help with the will and probate. He thinks Amy has been moving money and assets from Joe to herself over the last few years. She's after the trust, too. I felt uncomfortable about not trusting her, but now—not so much.

--I know Allen and worked with his dad on some civic committees. Despite being on opposite sides of the great Reformed Church divide, we got along. He told me his great-great-grandfather was fined and arrested with the seceders Budding and Vander Muelen back in the 1830s in the Netherlands. Almost two hundred years later, we still haven't settled it.

--Weren't your ancestors on the first boatloads to come to Dordrecht?

--Of course. Allen's were, too. As well as your mother's on her mother's side. Their families were seceders both in the Netherlands and here. Our churches were physically one block apart but, religiously, two centuries.

--The battles continue, don't they? Some are new. Women elders, gays no longer in the closet, public money for Christian schools. The Covenant/Van Raalte basketball games are also football after Covenant finally caved and added the sport.

--There is always something to fight about. Let's not get off the subject, however. We were talking about Amy. She doesn't deserve any leeway. She has always been first and only for herself. They call it narcissism today. In his last years, she had entirely controlled Joe's life and his finances.

--We have a meeting tomorrow to discuss things with her accountant. She got Joe to replace Allen after his dad died, which raises a red flag for me. If I have a suspicious feeling, I'll need a lawyer.

--Plan on it. Today, I wanted to tell you how difficult it was for Rose to deal with your dad and his problems in the years after you left. It was like the ebb and flow of the tides. There were many times he fell off the wagon. The first time you were still here was the worst, but it reoccurred every few years. I mentioned some of them earlier. Lydia was always involved. The pressure would build up inside him until it needed to be released. I could never reject him, not only because we shared the disease of alcoholism but also because he rescued me several times by not letting me get fired from my job or finding me a new one. Without that help, I would not have eventually been able to stay sober.

--I know what you mean. He also helped me build my confidence until I could survive alone. My grandpa DeHaan told me once that Joe was like me as a kid—a late developer. In high school, he learned that being the life of the party gained him the popularity he craved. He never got over it. Grandpa thought Joe needed that fix of attention and approval as much or more than the booze and gambling.

Irma came around the corner and called them to the table. The talk turned away from Joe to a more mundane Sunday evening talk. Hank lamented the poorly attended second service, even in the Christian Reformed church that he attended in place of the canceled Second Reformed evening service. Harry complimented Irma on her lasagna. He did think it was better than Marilyn's the night before. She queried him about his kids and his life in Denver. He discovered she was now an administrator, the head of nursing for the assisted living wing at Covenant Gardens, the rehab center, and the skilled nursing facility in Middleburg. Hank and Irma filled Harry in on the latest Dordrecht gossip. Just after post-dinner coffee was poured, Harry's Nokia rang. Surprised, He jumped up and went to his jacket to grab the phone and answer. Hank and Irma were wide-eyed and wondered what the sound of a cell phone meant. Harry answered, hoping it wasn't Marilyn. It was Larry.

--Are you sitting down?

--Not anymore. What do you need? Roaming calls are expensive.

--You won't be going to the appointment with Amy tomorrow.

--Why? What's going on?

--She was arrested Friday. She's in the Singapore County Jail.

--What for? How did you find out?

--It's a drug charge. One of my former state police supervisors, Alex Vega, was called into the case since it will involve more than one county. He remembered that I was from Dordrecht and wanted to get some background.

--What did you tell him?

--As little as I could.

--Oh, God. This is going to be a mess. Can we meet for breakfast tomorrow?

--I'm meeting a client in the morning. Yes, I have an actual client. How about lunch at Boersma's?

--Ja, that will work. It's still in downtown Middleburg, right?

--Yup. Make it 11:45. We'll beat most of the crowd.

--Okay. Is the jail in Wakazoo?

--That's right.

--Should I call them?

--Sure, get the number from information. See what you can find out. You should also call her lawyer in the morning. They can tell you who it is.

--Good idea. I'll see you tomorrow.

Harry passed the news on to Hank and Irma, apologized, and drove back to the Amsterdam Inn.

Chapter 9–Pete, Second Sunday, 1998

Pete McAdams guided the sixteen-foot-long birch bark canoe up a large tributary of the Singapore River about twelve miles, as the crow flies, from its Lake Michigan mouth. It quickly narrowed down to a much smaller stream with just enough water width and depth to accommodate his canoe and two others of the same design that followed in a single file. He went around two bends, struggling to see through the shadows of the early evening dusk, before coming to a dock just before the river narrowed to a waterway that could only qualify as a creek. He was relieved that the brewing storm to the west had waited until the weekend trip was complete.

The creek had no official name, but Pete had learned to call it Toussaint Creek after his mother's family that had once, in the 1820s, owned an entire 64-acre section of Singapore County land on both sides of the creek. That land had dwindled to less than fifty acres as branches of the family had sold their portions. Pete's maternal grandfather, Pierre Toussaint, owned the last acres belonging to the Toussaint family. After his death, Pete and his mother bought two adjoining plots that raised their portion to over one hundred acres, including some Singapore River frontage. Their dream was to work with the Odawa tribe to procure more acreage that had been part of the tribe's winter hunting and fishing territory, hoping to create a historical site that would turn the land back to the way it was when the first Pierre Toussaint, the son of a French trapper and an Odawa mother, had purchased it. They were one of the few Native families who could remain along the Singapore River, named after the company that established a logging lakeport at the mouth of the river. The 'Indian' treaties with the United States had relegated most of their tribe to reservations further north in Michigan or as far away as Kansas and Oklahoma.

The small flotilla of handmade reproduction canoes was returning from a two-day round-trip journey into Lake Michigan that, as far as Pete had been able to research, had not been made in over a century. The last remnant band of the Odawa tribe had left the area for the northern reservation in 1849, and the custom of traveling south for the winter to hunt and fish seemed to have ended around 1870.

This new group had made the rugged transition from the river into the lake with little difficulty, happy that the waves were mild. After they camped around two miles north on a county campground beach, they began the more difficult return trip against the current of the river. It took all the experience and expertise of Frank Abair, the Ojibwe who had trucked his canoe down from Sault Ste. Marie in a small flatbed to help them make their journey. The most dangerous obstacle was leading them through that crosscurrent. Pete's children, Star and Mike, were with Frank in his canoe while Pete and his wife, Flo, paddled theirs. Pete's 'uncle' John Aishike, his mother's cousin, followed in the third canoe he had towed down with his son George from the Grand Traverse Ottawa band.

Pete, Flo, Star, and Mike had been planning this trip for three years. For several years, the kids had attended an Ojibwe summer camp close to Flo's family, who were part of the Ojibwe clan in Sault Ste. Marie. While there, they learned how to master handling large canoes in rough waters and build a native birch bark canoe from scratch. Pete was an experienced canoer but only with smaller manufactured canoes. The following summer, he and Flo went with them to Sault Ste. Marie to spend a week with an Ojibwe club, which was recovering the art of canoe building and taking them into Lake Superior. The kids, being Ojibwe tribal members through their mother, were accepted into the club. Pete was initiated as an associate member because he was a member of both the Odawa and Potawatomi tribes, who, along with the Ojibwe, considered themselves to be the 'Three Fires' people of the Anishinaabe Algonquin nation. They spent the week both canoeing and building. When the week was over, they convinced Frank and other club members to help bring the canoe-building culture back to the Singapore River area.

The McAdams family drove up four weekends to help harvest the materials needed for the canoes: the cedar in the winter, the birch bark in June, the spruce roots in late summer, and the spruce gum pitch in the fall. Frank came down several weekends to supervise the project and correct some errors as the canoes took shape and the spruce paddles were carved. John and George, who had always lived on the Grand Traverse Ottawa Band reservation, quickly joined to build their birchbarks. When the last of the material was collected, the group rented a van and brought the supplies back, first to Little Traverse Bay and then to the Toussaint acreage on the Singapore River.

Flo McAdams was born into the Ojibwe culture in Sault Ste. Marie, where her family lived near the Ojibwe reservation. She was fiercely proud of her native heritage. Her given English name was Florence Bearheart, but her Ojibwe name-giver had called her *Wabigwan* (Flower). Pete met her at Northern Michigan University, the only school that had offered him a football scholarship. They were married as seniors and began their careers in Escanaba, he with the Escanaba police department, and she as a middle and high school social studies teacher. Pete was soon drafted and was steered into the military police. He was sent to Vietnam shortly before Star was born. Star was named Nancy after Pete's grandmother when she was born in Escanaba. During Pete's Vietnamese tour, when Flo returned to Sault Ste. Marie, Nancy was welcomed into Ojibwe tribal membership with her naming ceremony. The name-giver called her *Namid* (Star Dancing). As she grew older, Nancy always preferred and was always called Star. Similarly, Mike was named Pierre Jr. but always liked Mike, short for his Ojibwe name– *Migiz* (Eagle). His ceremony also took place in Sault Ste. Marie during a vacation trip to see Flo's family. Having been conceived when Pete returned to stateside duty at Ft. Knox, Mike was born in Wakazoo. The family had moved there to care for Pete's mother, Lily, after his father, Gordon McAdams, died. Pete was hired as a deputy sheriff while Flo added coaching girls basketball to her teaching duties at Wakazoo High School, Pete's alma mater.

The group was elated and exhausted from the grueling and, at times, hazardous two-day canoe trip. Pete felt something inside him change. After taking his indigenous ancestry for granted until he met Flo, the encouragement from her and Lily raised his interest. He had gone through the ceremony of becoming an official member of his father's Potawatomie tribe at Gun Lake, where his grandmother had raised Pete's father after the first Gordon McAdams had deserted them. He was also accepted by the Ottawa band at Grand Traverse, where his mother had been born before her family returned to their land along the Singapore River. But this was different. For the first time, he felt an emotional and existential connection to the people who lived in Michigan before the first Europeans arrived. He now knew that he was not just a hanger-on in the white man's world. He belonged here, deep in his roots.

Flo invited John, George, and Frank to crash in the family's basement in Wakazoo, which had a bed and cots available, but they insisted they could make the almost four-hour trip back to Grand Traverse. Frank would stay overnight with a friend and head home across the bridge in the morning. Everyone helped load the canoes and said their goodbyes, sad that the thrill of the weekend was over but full of satisfaction from the effort and success of their journey. Pete sent the kids home with Flo in her CRV, checked the canoe ties, and ensured the new shed was locked. He went to his ten-year-old Bronco, knowing he would need to use its sheriff's department radio to call headquarters to find out what he had missed the last two days. Since he was elected, this was the longest time he could remember being out of touch with dispatch and his staff. He also had left his beeper in his truck. When he checked it, he found twenty-two numbers to call back when he turned it on.

He recognized that ten of the numbers were the home number of Brian Chatfield, his chief deputy. He would need to call him from home. He then called dispatch on the radio and got Benny Ramirez, a younger deputy usually assigned to a patrol car but who was filling in for someone. Benny had been in a backup car at the Friday arrest of Amy Berendts.

--Hey Benny, this is Pete. I'm back in civilization. Is there anything going on I need to know about?

--Lots, I think. What do you want first?

--Let's see. How are things with our lady pot dealer?

--She's not happy. She is still in our luxury suite in the jail across the street. Her lawyer is not willing to post her bail deposit. He said she still owes him money.

--She only needs $5,000 cash. Seems like she could get that.

--We've heard her and the lawyer yelling at each other. Having assets is one thing. Five grand in cash is another.

--What about the live-in boyfriend?

--She can't find him. We can't find him. Same for her ex, who is still involved with her. We just had a call from her brother. He said he'll come down tomorrow afternoon with her lawyer to take care of the bail and pick her up.

--Is he involved in this?

--Nah, we don't think so. He's from Denver. He happens to be in town. Their father's funeral was a week ago.

--You seem to be up to speed on all this.

--I'm just helping at Gossip Central, getting some overtime.

--I've been there–and not that long ago. What else?

--We also can't find Nick Montez, the boyfriend's wingman. Or his parents, who lived in the house on the farm. But we did pick up two Hispanic males snooping around the property.

--Who the hell are they?

--We don't know. No papers. *No habla* English. We are holding them temporarily. *La Migra* will come by tomorrow to deal with them.

--Okay, I guess I can't do much now. I'll see you in the morning. How long are you on?

--About an hour. Julie is coming in early for her usual graveyard shift. Also, Brian's wife, Betty, called to let you know he would return from a youth group meeting with their kids in about an hour.

Pete finally went home with the euphoria of the canoe trip lessened by the return to his sheriff duties. The Amy Berendts case brought back memories of his first case as a deputy. He took the call when George Bosch, the Dordrecht Police Chief, was found dead on the property of the Dordrecht Fish and Game Club in Singapore County. Over the years since then, he had often recalled his suspicions about Amy's dad, Joe Berendts. Joe had been with Bosch in the early morning and was supposed to have been hunting with him. Pete had never believed Joe's story that he had backed out at the last minute, but he could not prove otherwise. When Pete had confronted him before Sam Morgan and Jimmy Dickerson ordered him to drop the case, Joe did not bend under pressure, refusing to be questioned unless his lawyer was present. Now, Pete was dealing with Joe's daughter, who seemed obstinate and hard to believe. On the other hand, he could not imagine she was the instigator of a large drug operation. Getting her to cooperate would be the key to shutting down the organization and finding those who had gone underground. He would need to get in early in the morning to see if he could convince her to cooperate before she made bail. He was hoping that the weekend in jail would soften her up.

When he arrived home, the kids were eating one of Flo's homemade frozen pizzas. Flo was in the shower. He grabbed a beer and went to the small basement shower. After the two days of canoe travel and camping, it felt like a luxury spa. When he returned upstairs, Flo took another pizza out of the oven.

--Wow! What a woman I married. Canoeing, camping, and a gourmet meal at the end.

--It's called planning. You should try it sometime.

--I'd rather react and improvise. It's more exciting.

--And you'd be eating peanut butter tonight. How's work?

--I just talked to dispatch. Our Dutch princess is still sitting in our jail. She can't find anyone to help her put up the bail deposit. That means Sally and I can interview her again before her lawyer arrives tomorrow. Or her brother. I guess he's arranging the bail. But we'll stretch that out. Bureaucracy is like justice, you know. It grinds slowly. Did the kids hit the sack already?

--I made them clean up first. They couldn't wait to eat. We should have a family conference to see how we feel about the weekend.

--Let's let them sleep. Let it all sink in. We can take our time with it tomorrow night.

--That would be next Sunday. Every night this week has something on the schedule for at least one of us.

--I think that's okay. Let's say good night and tell them to gather thoughts and feelings throughout the week.

--Okay, Sigmund. You are the psych expert. I suppose you need to make another call.

--Yeah. Brian will be home at nine. It won't take long. I think our pizza is cooled, and I'm ready to eat.

They quickly finished the pizza and went upstairs to see the kids. They sat down and quietly shared the feelings they had experienced during the canoe trip. They agreed it was beyond an ordinary weekend vacation. It had bonded them with each other and the people who had gone before them. They vowed to take a more extended trip the following year. Flo went to their bedroom while Pete went downstairs to the lower level of the tri-level home to call Brian from his home office, which consisted of a small desk, a phone, and a police band radio.

--Hi, Sheriff. What's up?

--You tell me. Benny filled me in a little bit.

--Well, Ms. Berendts is still with us and not saying much except complaining about the food and mattress and threatening lawsuits. She should know not to piss off her lawyer. He's letting her stew. Everyone else has gone underground.

--We'll find them this week, I suspect. Do you think she knew about the operation on the far side of the property?

--She is just playing dumb. Even if she wasn't directly involved, she must have been getting paid to overlook it.

--Is there anything new on the tip we got?

--No. The voice is recorded on your direct line answering machine, but no one can place the voice. We know it must be someone who knows the number belonging to that phone.

--I try to keep that number to the few that need it. As we go along, we might be able to figure it out. Or else someone just passed it on to the wrong person. But, back to Amy. This will be her chance to tell us who could be involved and take some pressure off her. It's surreal to have a case with another Berendts. You remember her father, Joe, and the suicide, which was something more than suicide.

--Yeah, we were both newbies then.

--I think I'll give ol' Jimmy Dickerson a call tomorrow. He might know something. He might know a lot. This setup started longer than three years ago when we took over.

--True. It could be part of his retirement program.

--Ok, I'll be in early tomorrow. I'll bring breakfast from the Main Street Diner for Amy. Improve her attitude.

--I want to be there to see that. I think she would want the vegan special if they had one.

--A meatless omelet will have to do. Or just a side of rice and beans. Or just grits. This is harder than I thought.

--Tell you what. I'll stop at the bakery for croissants and a quinoa and fruit bowl my wife loves.

--Perfect. See you then.

Pete returned upstairs and turned out the lights when he found Flo asleep. He crashed on the bed, tired but still wired. He thought back to the George Bosch case and how it had led twenty years later to Jimmy Dickerson's retirement and Pete's winning the election to replace him.

Pete had been surprised that Jimmy had called the death a suicide so quickly, seeming to ignore evidence that showed foul play, but he was a new patrol deputy and had no influence. He had taken his doubts to the Wakazoo County Prosecuting Attorney, Sam Morgan, and was told to return to his patrol car and do his job. Pete followed the order, realizing he was an inexperienced new guy who could not make waves and risk his career with just his opinions. It took more than a year, but he successfully switched to the state police, being given his request to work where he could commute to Wakazoo. He started as a patrol officer, headquartered in Plainway in eastern Singapore County. He was good at his job and gained the confidence of the captain of his region, earning small promotions and job security. However, he kept his eye on the Singapore sheriff's department, watching Jimmy and Sam continue to win elections. They consistently scored newsworthy arrests during the campaign season. At other times, investigations went along slowly or found dead ends. He did notice that Jimmy and Sam spent a lot of time in Singapore and South Wakazoo, resort towns near Lake Michigan, with a bar scene and questionable activity. Pete was often frustrated that he could not follow through on any investigation into their actions because he continued to be assigned east of Wakazoo.

Fifteen years into his state police career, things changed. Pete received a call from an investigator from the state prosecuting attorney's office. He asked Pete to come to Lansing for an interview. He was told it was confidential and that he should not talk to anyone about it. Pete agreed and did not tell anyone except Flo. The interview took place the following week in the offices of the state PA. Alex Vega, the investigator, was confrontational at first. He seemed to assume that Pete was involved in criminal activity and coverup, hinting at gambling and drug activity. Pete explained several times that he was uninvolved and had no direct knowledge of wrongdoing in the department. He tried to get Vega to tell him why he was being questioned. Vega finally began to ease up.

--Do you know Sally Conners?

--Yes. She was a state Assistant PA. She was involved in a theft and embezzlement investigation at the Wayland School District. I was investigating a petty theft and thought that the accused person was being railroaded and that much more was happening. I called the PA's office and told them what I had found. They sent an investigator like you. He found more than I knew. Sally prosecuted the corruption case. I was a witness.

--Why didn't you call the county PA?

--State money was involved.

--Is that all?

--I thought it was beyond Sam Morgan's capabilities.

--His capabilities or his intentions?

--He has been suspected of conveniently making cases go away. Especially where money is involved, mainly on the county's west side. I don't get there much.

--Sally thinks you're a straight shooter.

--Thank her for me.

--You can thank her yourself. Can you have lunch with us?

Pete stayed for lunch. After Sally joined them, Alex reviewed their evidence, confirming Pete's suspicions for two decades. They needed someone on the inside to build the case. With a feeling of apprehension but also relief, Pete agreed. He would be risking his career and more, but he would finally be ridding himself of the guilt that he was doing nothing to end the graft in his county.

Sally and Alex arranged for Pete to arrest Joey Whitehorse in the far eastern part of the county, where the same group running the clubs in Singapore and South Wakazoo had a gambling operation just over the county line in Barry County. This was close to the home of Pete's father's Gun Lake Potawatomi Band, which was about to receive federal recognition as an official tribe. It was part of his patrol team's responsibility. The payoffs to law enforcement were going to Barry County officials, so they were not on Sam and Jimmy's radar. Joey was a Pottawatomie bartender already working with the state investigation on a possession charge in Plainway. Pete brought him to the Singapore County jail in Wakazoo to be held until he could be transferred to Lansing. At this point, Pete could then confront Sam and Jimmy with the information he had received from Joey Whitehorse. His connection to the state investigation would stay covert. He remembered Jimmy's response.

--What are you trying to do, Pete? You need to stay out of this.

--Look, Jimmy. I'm tired of working my ass off and getting nowhere. I'm not a starry-eyed rookie anymore. I've got two kids that need to go to college soon. My house needs upgrading and repair. So does my Bronco.

--What do you want me to do about it?

--Let me in on a little bit of the bonus money. You're letting money go to the Barry County guys. Some of that should be going to me and a couple of my men. The shit is happening in our area. There's enough for us, too.

--I don't know what I can do.

--I know you got to go through Sam and whoever else is running the show. They're the same guys that shut down the George Bosch investigation when I was a rookie.

--Is that still a stick in your butt?

--Nope. I'm over it. But I want what's coming to me.

After Pete received his first cash payment, which he turned over to Sally and Alex, he went to see Jerry Blackbird, a Potawatomie friend of his father. Pete's father was named Gordon McAdams after his father, whom he had never seen after he was two. He was raised in his mother's Pottawatomie family and considered himself one hundred percent part of the tribe. Jerry and Gordon had been on the outside of the tribal power structure. Pete remembered his dad complaining about corruption at the top of the tribal council. Jerry told him all he knew. Most of it was typical money issues—large salaries and personal expenses paid by tribal funds. He was concerned that it would only worsen if the band achieved official recognition and followed through with their ready-to-go plans for a large casino. He also knew about two tribal members who had gotten behind at a backroom gambling spot. Pete got their names and arranged to see them at a Wayland restaurant, away from the reservation. Initially, the men were unwilling to cooperate, but because they knew Pete's dad, he gained their trust. He convinced them that they would be protected and could be part of the cleanup of tribal politics. He introduced them to Sally and Alex.

The men had been contacted and threatened by debt collectors who were pros who came from Chicago. On a suggestion from Alex, Pete contacted the collectors, shaking them down for a percentage of their collection fees. It took three years, with Pete feeding information to Alex and Sally. They gave him money for a late model used Bronco and several vacations so Sam and Jimmy could see him spending his cut. The hammer came down as part of a multi-state investigation including the BIA and the FBI. Pete's participation was kept concealed. Several organized crime figures from Chicago were arrested. Because they were not the prime target part of the more critical case, Sam and Jimmy were allowed to plead guilty to a reduced charge with an agreement to resign, for which they received a suspended two-year sentence. They were not about to offer more and admit their role in the bigger picture. At the time, they believed that Pete had gotten off for lack of evidence, so he was not suspected of being a plant. Neither was he needed as a witness. As soon as they resigned, Sally and Pete decided to run for their offices. At that point, it was leaked that Pete was part of the investigation. Sally had contacts who helped them run a professional campaign in a small county. With Pete's hands being clean, they won easily as anti-corruption candidates in a crowded field.

Pete now felt that with the Berendts family back in his life, the dead file case of George Bosch would be revived.

The following morning, after the canoe trip, Pete called Sally from home.

--You're up early, Pete, what's going on?

--I need to check in with you on Amy Berendts. Have you been updated?

--I'm surprised she is still with us. An aggressive attorney would have her out by now. What is the lawyer's name?

--Zandstra, from New Leiden, I think. I guess they had money conflicts. Her brother is supposed to take care of that this afternoon.

--If it's who I think it is, he's a divorce lawyer. He'll be looking for a criminal defense person to take over.

--I want to talk to her this morning. What am I allowed to ask?

--Name, rank, and serial # is the military expression.

--I thought I would bring her breakfast and ask how she likes her accommodations. Who knows? She might decide to help us.

--That's okay. Just be careful. Have someone with you and remind her that she does not have to say anything.

--I'll be good–her best friend. Are you going to be the lead on the case?

--No. I have other things going on. Politics, mostly. Donovan will take it. We got the arraignment scheduled for the late afternoon.

--Okay, wish me luck.

Anxious to get to the office and begin his day, he grabbed the thermos filled with Flo's smoothie mixture on his way out of the house. He hoped having something decent to eat would make Amy feel comfortable. He thought she would be anxious to proclaim her innocence and point some fingers that would speed up the investigation. Plus, he was intrigued by the opportunity to bring up Joe as a side conversation with her and her brother.

When he arrived at the sheriff's department, he went directly to his office, uncharacteristically skipping any interaction with his office staff. He took Brian's food and asked Mary Lu Bowling, his administrative assistant, to join him. They walked across the street to the jail interview room to wait for Amy. When she arrived, without makeup and with her clothes and light blonde hair disheveled, he thought she looked ten years older than three days earlier. They sat with her at a round conference table for small staff meetings.

--Good morning, Amy. I am a little surprised that you're still here.

--That's bullshit, and you know it. You waited until the weekend to arrest me to make me sweat it out.

--I brought some breakfast for you from the outside. The staff said you weren't eating. This should be edible. There is an organic vegan smoothie that my wife makes in the thermos. My coffee pot makes a decent cup, or would you like tea?

--I'll take the tea. Herbal, please. So now you're being the good cop?

--Mary Lu, would you ask for some herbal tea for Ms. Berendts? She can get started with breakfast.

Amy fiddled with the croissant and the veggie bowl, opened the thermos, and poured the contents into a glass from the tray. Pete continued calmly as she sipped. When Mary Lu returned and sat down, Pete started the tape recording.

--This is Sheriff Pete McAdams interviewing Amy Berendts. Amy, we are recording this conversation both for your protection and ours. Mary Lu Bowling is also in the room. Amy, you've been advised of your rights and don't have to talk to me. As to the timing of your arrest, we received a tip on Wednesday. We went to your property and saw signs of suspicious activity. On Thursday, we got the search warrant for your property and completed the search. You did not get home until late Friday. We arrested you at once when you arrived home.

Pete looked at Amy, who stared back at him with no emotion. He continued:

--I have two other reasons to have this meeting. One is to make sure you are okay physically and mentally and have not been mistreated. I only see one arrest with no charges filed on your record, so I assume you've not spent a weekend in

171

custody before. Jail can be disturbing the first time someone experiences it. How's the smoothie?

--Quite good, thank your wife for me.

--My second reason is to let you know what you are up against because of what we found on the property. It would be best if you shared it with your attorney. Have you found a lawyer, or do you want the court to appoint one for you?

Amy took a bite of the croissant, then another, and reached again for a sip of the smoothie.

--I called my attorney. He is looking for an experienced defense attorney to join my team.

--That's good. I think you'd be surprised at what we found. The house is on the narrower south side of the property, where the river cuts the corner. We found a marijuana growing and drying operation, which I am sure you know about.

A female guard came in with the tea and set it on the table. As she left, Pete continued the interview.

--As you know, your property's large northern section is separated from the south by a stand of trees and a swampy area with several small ponds. Our search in the north section found a more extensive marijuana operation with grow houses and temporary storage sheds with packages of buds ready for sale. We are still figuring out the crop's exact size and potential street value in each section. We also found the beginnings of a meth lab—equipment and supplies. The property to the northeast of yours is vacant. There was evidence of heavy traffic along an old tractor trail on the back section of the property. Except for a 220 electrical hook-up going along the east side of your property from your storage shed, there was no evidence of traffic from the front to the back of the property.

Pete stopped talking to see if Amy would respond. She finished the croissant and smoothie. She slowly added a sugar packet to her tea, pulled the veggie bowl over, and took a sample bite. She sipped the tea and finally responded.

--I have nothing to say about any of that.

--I didn't think you would. We also still have not found Nick Montez or his parents. Or Theo Bolinyk. Or Doug Mason. We have already talked to Lupe Rios. She claims ignorance.

--I do, too. What's next?

--You'll be arraigned this afternoon. Your brother called in last night and said he would call your lawyer and arrange bail. We have a shower that you could use before the arraignment. Can your brother bring some clothes?

--I haven't figured out why you're being nice to me, but I'll take advantage. Have Harry call Judy Marsden. She helps me in my store. She has a key to my condo. Have him tell her to pick out something that would look good in front of a judge—conservative but not expensive-looking. Bring my shampoo and body soap—and my travel makeup kit, too.

--I'm being nice because I want you and your attorney to decide that it is in your best interest to cooperate with us.

--By the way. Who tipped you about my farm?

--Mr. Anonymous. Someone out to get you or your boyfriend, I would guess. Unfortunately for you, it turned out to be true. Amy took several more bites from the bowl, finished the tea, and gave Pete Judy's contact information. As the guard came in to take her back to her cell, she turned and asked.

--What's for lunch?

--How about a salad from the deli at the grocery store?

--Make sure it's vegan.

_____

Pete turned off the recorder before checking his beeper, which had vibrated in his pocket. It was Benny Ramirez, who was still at Amy's property with a search crew. He returned across the street to use his office radio to contact him, hoping he was close to the patrol car.

--Hi, Sheriff.

--What's up?

--We found something here.

--Okay. What did you find?

--It was behind the old barn. A denim jacket, just lying there. It has what looks like blood stains.

--I'll be there in twenty minutes. Don't touch anything. And keep it under wraps until we know what we're dealing with.

Before he left, Pete called Alex Vega in Lansing. He managed to convince the operator to put him through to Alex.

--What's so critical, Pete?

--I need one of your crime site teams to check out a farm for me. My staff doesn't have the ability I'm looking for.

--Tell me more.

Pete told him about the marijuana operation and the fresh, bloody denim jacket.

--Okay, but I can't get anyone there until Thursday.

--I can work with that.

--I'll put John Newsome's team on it. He'll give you a call about the particulars.

Chapter 10—Harry, Second Monday, 1998

Harry woke up on Monday with the phone ringing instead of his alarm, which he had set for seven. He got up to go to the desk to answer, wondering who could be calling him. It was too early for the ringing phone to be from a law office.

When he arrived at the Amsterdam Inn the night before, he decided to see if he could reach anyone at the Wakazoo jail. A deputy named Ramirez answered and seemed familiar with Amy's arrest. He told Harry that her lawyer had contacted her but could give no additional details except that she would have an arraignment and bail hearing on Monday afternoon. When Harry asked for the lawyer's name and contact information, Ramirez could only give him the name Carl Zandstra, and that he thought he was from New Leiden. Harry told the deputy that he would come to the jail before the hearing and be prepared to post bail. He tried to call Zandstra but only got the answering machine. He left a message asking for a call back first thing on Monday.

The ringing phone was Larry.

--I couldn't sleep until I remembered the guy's name.

--Which guy?

--A lawyer. I finally remembered his name and went back to sleep.

--What's his name? And why is it so important?

--Reggie Robinson. You know him. He played basketball against us at Wakazoo and then at MSU.

--Ja, I remember. He made you look bad when he was only a sophomore.

--He made me look bad again on the witness stand a few years ago. He was one of the few guys that got the better of me on offense and defense.

--And why is this important?

--You need to get him for Amy. Reggie would be the best if you couldn't have Caputo, who's involved with Theo Bolinyk. No one runs over him.

--Does he practice in Wakazoo?

--No, he has an office in New Leiden and Lansing, but he's still a hero in Wakazoo. I wanted to catch you before you talked to Zandstra. If he doesn't go along with Reggie, fire him.

--Got it.

--By the way, when you talk to either of them, let them know I'm now an investigation consultant who would love to work with him.

--Okay. See you at lunch.

--Ja. See you there.

———————

Harry showered and went to the restaurant at the Inn for breakfast while he planned his morning. He needed to find out if the court would take a check for the bail. He also remembered a mailer from his Visa card that they were offering no-fee cash advances. Zandstra would know the details. Reggie

Robinson would know for sure. He decided to find Reggie's number and call his office immediately after breakfast. Why involve two lawyers if one could do the job, he thought.

As he drank his coffee, waiting for his order, he wondered why he was jumping in to help Amy. Their relationship had never been close. Although she was only two years older, the gap seemed larger. As they grew up, she was socially precocious, while he was trailing most of his peers. She was unimpressed as he finally began to catch up in high school. Even now, he could still feel her scorn for her very uncool little brother. On the other hand, he felt himself being drawn back into his childhood existence. She was the only close family he had left. He could also feel the similarities between them. They both had left the Dordrecht Dutch family culture and their religion. They both had complicated relationships with their parents because of it. To be accurate, Joe also had his issues with the culture, but they were more a tugging against the moral chains that kept him from what he called 'having a good time.' The roots of his character were still deep in the culture and the church.

He remembered Amy's battles with her parents. They had tried to prevent her from dating older boys, but she attracted high school boys while she was still in junior high and college men while she was in high school. She would either sneak out or throw fits until she got her way. She was caught drinking several times, which shocked Rose. By the time she was a high school senior, Joe and Harry knew it was a regular occurrence. Twice, Joe had taken calls from George Bosch to come and get her before she was brought in on charges for drinking in one of the Singapore County parks on the beach. George and the Singapore sheriff, Jimmy Dickerson, had a deal to send juveniles back to their county of residence if the charges were minor. Amy also refused her mother's wish to attend Covenant College in New Leiden. She was allowed to go to a more liberal Reformed college, Van Raalte in Middleburg. As a freshman, she did not pass any of her courses except art.

Seeing her excel in art since primary school, Joe and Rose paid for private tutoring and summer art camps to get her to focus on something that would reduce her rebellious behavior. Using the same reasoning, they gave in to her long-held wish and allowed her to enroll at the Chicago School of Art. She finally found success in both fashion design and graphic commercial art. However, she was forced to leave the school when Joe could no longer afford the tuition. Retaliating, she doubled down on her rebelliousness. After she moved out from home, she found work waitressing and bartending while she took part in the party culture of the late 1960s. Perceiving her as wholly self-centered and self-serving, Harry lost what little respect and care he had for her.

He asked himself: What changed? Why do I care now? Why am I jumping into the middle of her mess? Before he could answer his questions, the server brought his breakfast. He thought again about the lawyers and realized that Larry could get carried away and he could be making Harry move too quickly. He should meet with Amy before making any changes. He decided to work with Zandstra.

He finished breakfast, returned to his room, heard the phone ring, and answered.

--This is Harry Berendts.

--Hello, Harry. This is Carl Zandstra. I got your message. I'm glad you want to help Amy out. She's in a tough spot.

--I know. I've always thought she could dodge bullets, but she might not this time.

--You're right. What do you know so far?

--Just that the charges are serious. The arraignment will be this afternoon. How are you handling bail money?

--We have an issue with that. It took three years to collect from her after I handled her divorce. My partners will not put any funds or guarantees upfront. I've already called down there this morning. I talked to a deputy who said you were ready to help with bail. Is that right?

--Ja. I can do that. She'll get a substantial amount from our dad's estate, so I know I can get it back. What do I have to do?

--Nothing, except to write a check to us for the bail deposit amount. We'll hold it in escrow as a guarantee and work the bail through the firm. I should ask why you are still willing to work with her.

--Let's say that our relationship was more than professional for a while. She dumped me, but I don't want to leave her hanging.

--I'm not surprised. I guess I feel the same way. Should we be looking for a criminal defense attorney at this point?

--We need to think about it. I know a couple of people that might be good.

--A friend of mine is insisting that I try Reggie Robinson.

--I hadn't thought of that. Reggie would be the best if we could get him to take the case and if she can afford him.

--How do we get him?

--As we're talking, I remember knowing someone who could get him to talk to us. I'll try to set something up. Where can I reach you?

--I'll be running around. Call my beeper. Leave a number. I'll call you back.

Harry suddenly realized he had forgotten that he would need to reschedule a meeting with Amy's accountant. She was to let him know the location. Not recalling a name besides Bill, he called Allen Zuverink at his office. Allen was out, but his assistant was familiar with the situation and found the number for WPS, CPA, and its principal, William Snyder. He called and discovered the meeting was set for ten o'clock, less than an hour away. He explained to the receptionist that Amy was unable to attend the meeting. He suggested that Snyder return his call at ten instead so they could review details over the phone and reschedule the appointment.

Harry needed to call his office in Denver, but they would not open until ten o'clock, Michigan time. He turned on the TV to find local news while waiting for Snyder's call.

It was 10:20 when the phone rang. It was a secretary asking for him to hold for Mr. Snyder. Another minute went by. Finally, a voice came across the line.

--Bill Snyder.

--Uhh. Bill, this is Amy Berendts' brother, Harry. We were supposed to meet in your office this morning. Amy has had some difficulty.

--Difficulty?

--Ja. She is being detained in the Singapore County jail

--Jesus Christ. What's she done now? DUI?

--Nope. Worse than that. The sheriff found a drug operation on some land she owns just north of Wakazoo.

--Oh, God. Yeah, I know that property. She has never done anything with it. I've told her to sell it several times. There is no potential for either appreciation or investment. That's about all I can discuss with you, however. She would need to be in the room or authorize me.

--I get that. She had a concept to make it sort of an ashram. I just wanted to explain why we will not be at the meeting. Also, she needs you to think of ways to free up some cash for bail and attorney fees. I'm sure she will talk to you as soon as we can arrange her release.

--You're right. I know some excellent defense attorneys if she needs a reference.

--Carl Zandstra, her divorce guy, is working on it. He thinks he may be able to get Reggie Robinson.

--Wow! It would be great if he could get him. Better than the guys I know. He won't be cheap, however. And he will want financial references. Tell Zandstra to call me if he needs information. I can talk to her attorney.

--Thanks, I'm glad you're willing to help.

--Amy and I go way back before I was her accountant. Before I married, I hung out with Theo, her ex. I consoled her through the divorce.

--Not you, too!

--Oops. Well, that was a long time ago.

--It always is. Okay, I'll be in touch.

--Better yet, have her call me as soon as possible. Besides her lawyer, I'll be the most important person in her life.

Harry hung up and took a few deep breaths, telling himself that he was working in a milieu that was not familiar to him. He would need to be aware and step carefully. Before calling his Denver office, he went to the restaurant for a coffee to take back to his room and think. Many details about the buy-out would need to be resolved. He talked to Craig Klein and his partner, updating the other on their different views of the new contract's details and the buyout's completion. Harry agreed to be in Denver on Thursday to move both projects along.

He then called the sheriff's office to arrange a meeting time with Amy. The receptionist put him on hold for several minutes. She finally returned and said Amy could see him between one and two. She added that Amy wanted him to contact Judy Marsden so he could pick up clothes, toiletries, and makeup from her Singapore condominium. Harry confirmed that he would and said he would get to the jail by 1:30.

————————

Shortly after 11:30, Harry arrived at Boersma's to meet Larry. As he had driven on the sunny morning through the downtown blocks of Middleburg along Main Street, he was surprised by the renovated commercial area. New restaurants, upscaled pubs, refurbished and newly built boutique hotels, trendy art galleries, and upscale, fashionable retail shops signaled the growing success of the Dutch entrepreneurial spirit and the marketing of Middleburg as a resort town. The traditional throwback establishments like Boersma's were mixed in, lending a mix of Dutch heritage and midcentury authenticity to the atmosphere. The inside of Boersma's seemed unchanged from Harry's memory, with vinyl-covered booths, chairs, and counter stools. New laminate tops covered the tables and counters. The dispensers, various appliances, and other equipment behind the counter appeared to be post-war vintage. All of it, however, was obviously brand new or refurbished.

Harry picked a booth and sat down to wait for Larry. He soon came in, walking briskly and creating a wake behind him, which the server followed. Asking for a large Coke, he barely left Harry time to ask for iced tea with lemon, no sugar.

--Can you believe it? I'm in business! I've signed my first account, and it's a beauty!

--Congratulations! You told me last night. What is it?

--I can't say, of course. But it's a corporate malfeasance case. Right up my alley. It could take up half my available time for a year or more. Which is perfect.

--That's great. Which means you're buying.

--Hey! I haven't been paid yet.

--I'm ordering the luncheon steak if it's still on the menu.

--Go for it. I'll find a way to expense it.

--Watch it! Or they'll be investigating you.

--I didn't spend twenty-five years with the state cops by not being careful. So, what's happening with your case?

--Well, let's review. My loving, that's literally loving, sister has had affairs with both her lawyer and accountant. That's an excellent way to get a discount. They still have a thing for her and want to help.

--What's your excuse?

--I don't know if I'm feeling guilty or lonely. It's a family thing. I feel a need to help.

--Are you working on getting Reggie?

--We are. Zandstra knows someone who he thinks could get us an interview. Her CPA, Snyder, says he can find cash to pay for it. I'm waiting to hear what is happening on that front and in Wakazoo.

--What's your next step?

--I need to go to Singapore to pick up some things for Amy from her condo and then to Wakazoo and meet with her at 1:30. Do you want to come along?

--I wouldn't miss it. I might find another client.

--I appreciate your support.

They were halfway through their luncheon steaks when Harry's beeper phone rang. It was Carl Zandstra's number. He called him back on his Nokia.

--Hey, Carl. What did you find out?

--The arraignment is at 3:30. I am meeting with Amy at three at the courthouse. A defense attorney will be with me.

--Who did you get? Did Reggie not work out?

--Actually, he did. He is sending one of his assistants to meet with Amy and me to check the situation and decide if we should work together.

--That sounds like progress. I'm meeting Amy at the jail at 1:30. Larry Vandevoss is with me. We'll see you at the arraignment.

--Okay, Wish us luck.

Harry and Larry arrived at the Singapore County jail in Wakazoo just before 1:30. The visit to Amy's condo had gone smoothly. He was bringing a carry-on with her change of clothes and necessities. The guard behind the front counter put the case behind her desk before guiding them to a small room, which Harry guessed was an interrogation room, based on the movies and TV shows he had seen. After they waited several minutes, a dark-skinned, well-built man with Native American features walked into the room. He was halfway

between Harry and Larry's height and carried himself with easy confidence. Looking at Harry, he said,

--Hi, I'm Sheriff McAdams. You must be Amy's brother.

--My name is Harry, Harry Berendts. This is Larry Vandevoss.

--I know Larry a little from our days in the state police. I remember you, too.

--I'm remembering you, as well. You were Wakazoo's all-state quarterback when we were sophomores.

--You were the skinny little kid who kicked two field goals and an extra point to beat us 13-12. We didn't even have a kicker. I had to try to run for the PAT.

--And I can still feel where we met.

Larry was rubbing his shoulder.

--Whatever happened to your quarterback? George Bosch's son, Butch Bosch. He was in my class.

Larry answered quickly with a smirk before Harry had a chance to reply.

--That's a touchy subject. He's a big-time real estate guy in Middleburg. He stole Harry's girlfriend. Now Harry's trying to steal her back.

Harry made an exaggerated grimace and roll of the eyes. Pete ignored the comment and continued.

--What's your position here, Larry? I can only let relatives and attorneys in the meeting.

--I became a consulting private investigator after I retired.

--That's right. I heard you had retired. I haven't seen you since we were on the team investigating that motel murder case.

--I was assigned primarily to the northeast division. I ended up in Lansing working with Alex Vega. I think you left just before I got there.

--If you worked with Alex, you'll be okay. I'll be back with Amy in just a few minutes.

Harry held up a hand to slow the sheriff down.

--Actually, I should meet Amy alone at first. We don't want to intimidate her. If we have any questions for you, Larry, we can bring you in.

--Good idea. Just make sure you get directions to her property. I still want to get a look at it. Is it barricaded, Sheriff?

--No, I have a deputy stationed there. I'll tell him to let you look. But don't try to touch or disturb anything. I have a crime scene team from Lansing scheduled to come in on Thursday.

--I know the drill.

A deputy led Amy in after Sheriff McAdams and Larry stepped out of the room. Harry was shocked by her appearance.

--Hi. Are you okay? You don't look so good.

--Thanks a fucking lot. How would you look if you had spent your weekend in jail?

--Sorry. I was expressing concern. I brought your stuff. Do you want to change?

--Not now. I'm supposed to have a chance to clean up before I need to be in court.

--The receptionist has your overnight case. Have you eaten? Can I get you something?

-Sheriff Pete is my new best friend. He's been bribing me today with a gourmet breakfast and lunch.

--Okay. It sounds like you are in a real mess. I spent the morning on the phone for you, talking to Zandstra and Bill Snyder. Larry is with me. He had the idea of getting Reggie Robinson to help with your defense. Have you heard of him?

--Ja, I have. But why not Lenny Caputo?

--It would be a conflict. He's tied up with Theo.

--I don't know if I can afford someone like Robinson.

--Snyder says you can. I guess you're seeing Carl next. He's bringing Reggie's assistant. You can meet with them and decide what to do. Bill and I have offered guarantees and convinced Carl to work out the bail situation. You'll be out late today, I think.

Amy was quiet and took what Harry recognized as several cleansing breaths.

--I'm relieved that that help is available. I've been feeling desperate. Thanks for helping. I'm surprised. I know it's a cliché, but I didn't think you cared.

--The past few weeks have influenced me. I've been distant and sometimes antagonistic, but suddenly, family means more to me. Except for my kids, you are all that's left. Soon, I won't even have a career to worry about.

--I get it. I'm changing, too. I haven't been a model citizen, but I've been trying to stay legal lately. If it weren't for that damn Doug, I wouldn't be here.

--Okay, that's as much as you should tell me. Save it for your lawyers. When you see them, you should nudge them to hire Larry as the private investigator for your case. He's competent, a bulldog, and would be on your side.

--Ja, I can see that. Say 'hi' to him for me. I think he always did like me a little.

--I don't want to think about that.

There was a knock on the door. A deputy came in to tell Amy that the bailiff was ready for her. Harry and Amy got up. Harry stepped over and gave her a brotherly hug. It was the first since Rose's funeral.

--Here's my cliché for the day: See you in court.

Harry and Larry took two wrong turns before finding Amy's property off River Road. The sunny morning sky had changed to clouds in the afternoon, with chilly rain in the forecast. The two-track driveway ran almost fifty yards to the farmhouse, which was rundown outside but seemed livable. A small unpainted barn and another small shed stood another hundred feet behind it, looking like potential barnwood tear-down projects. Behind a row of trees, they spotted a new, arched greenhouse at least fifty feet in length. Standing close to the greenhouse, the deputy waved at them to stop close to the barn. They got out and visually surveyed the area as they walked to meet him.

--I assume you are Amy's brother. I'm Deputy Ramirez. Sheriff McAdams said you could look. There is not much to look at. Most of the marijuana crop is drying in the barn, ready to strip and package. This part is just a part of the operation. There is a more extensive outdoor plot around and past the turn in the tractor path that leads to the west.

Larry was already looking around intensely, noticing the yellow police tape around all three of the buildings, while Harry was not sure what he should be looking for.

--I'm Larry Vandevoss, retired state police. This doesn't look like much. Why is everyone so excited?

--There is a lot more that way. I guess it's what they call the back forty.

--How do we get there?

--You can drive around and use the neighboring driveway on the back side or walk along the footpath that zigzags between the two ponds.

--We have time to walk. Can we get into the house and the barn?

--Sure, I'll let you in and come with you. You must know the drill. Don't disturb anything.

They walked into the barn first and moved to the small shed before examining the house. Harry thought Larry was unusually quiet. He was in work mode, taking everything in. After they went through the buildings, Harry noticed a small circle of tape around an eight-foot diameter circle of empty ground. He poked Larry and pointed to it. Larry crouched down on one knee and inspected it closely. He looked up at Ramirez as if he were going to ask him about something, but he got up and turned away. He did not ask questions, as if he didn't want Ramirez to know his thoughts. They headed past the outdoor plot and found the path to the back forty. They went past the river and the ponds. Harry was surprised at how much this section looked like the Dordrecht Fish and Game Club. They suddenly came to a clearing filled with a much larger operation. There were three greenhouses the same size as the first and a taller, enclosed metal building that served as a barn. Two open fields of plants filled most of the rest of the clearing. Yellow tape surrounded each of the buildings and the fields. He looked over the entire area and finally asked where the neighbor's driveway was. Ramirez pointed northwest, where they walked about a hundred yards. Because of the angles of the properties and the curve in the road, it was short, less than a hundred feet. It was an easy access to Amy's back forty.

Larry looked at Harry and said he had seen all he needed to for now, although he stopped several times on the way back as if he needed to double-check something. He also noticed the above-ground conduit bringing power from the main house. It took up more of his attention. Harry prodded him to move on so they would not be late for the hearing.

———————

They arrived ten minutes early at the courthouse next to the jail and found the proper courtroom between two options. It was smaller than they expected. They chose the side they hoped would be the defense and sat in the front spectator row. When a dark-suited man who seemed to be at least in his late fifties came in with a younger woman, also dressed in a dark suit, and sat in front of them, they assumed they were the prosecutors and moved to the other side. The man and woman both turned around and looked at them. It was always difficult for a man of Larry's size to avoid drawing attention. They then noticed Pete McAdams and a deputy filling the seats they had left.

Less than two minutes later, Carl Zandstra came in accompanied by a large, imposing Black woman who looked very fit. Her short heels made her taller than Harry. Her navy coat dress added a tailored, professional look. Her hair, trimmed into a medium-length natural Afro, was accented by oversized burgundy eyeglasses. Her posture and calm facial appearance let everyone know she was serious and confident. Zandstra turned around and introduced her to Harry.

--Harry, this is Juanita Jones. She agreed to act as Amy's attorney at this hearing. Harry is Amy's brother, Juanita.

--I am pleased to meet you. Thank you for helping Amy.

--I am pleased to meet you, too.

Her voice matched her appearance. It reminded Harry of Barbara Jordan's, oozing with seriousness.

--Are you going to be Amy's lawyer beyond today?

--We will see. Amy and I are on the same page, at least for the little time we had to meet this afternoon.

--This is Larry Vandevoss, a friend and security consultant. He's holding my hand through all this. It's all new to me.

Just then, a deputy led Amy into the courtroom. Harry was shocked at the transformation in Amy's appearance. The shower and makeup, the tied-back hair, and the conservative black blazer with tailored taupe pants projected an image precisely the opposite of a pot farmer. As soon as she found a seat with Carl and Juanita, the judge, a surprisingly young fortyish man, obviously fit and vain about his appearance, took his seat on the platform and nodded to a clerk, who announced the charges and the case, presided by Judge Dennis Eubanks. The judge looked at the prosecutor.

--Good afternoon, Mr. Evenson. Do you have any details to add to the list of charges?

--Good morning, Your Honor. Let me just add that the size and complexity of the cannabis farm found on the defendant's property were extensive. This is a significant and severe violation of the laws of the state of Michigan.

--Thank you. I see we have a defense team that is new to this court. Would you please introduce yourselves?

--I am Carl Zandstra from New Leiden. I have represented Ms. Berendts in civil matters for more than a decade. My co-counsel is Juanita Jones, from New Leiden and Lansing. She will be taking the lead in this criminal matter.

--Welcome to our court. We received your *bona fides* by fax, Ms. Jones. Do you have any comments on the case?

--Thank you, Your Honor. I agree with the prosecution that this is a serious matter. Since the consequences could be severe, we must proceed deliberately and judiciously with no rush to judgment, especially this early in the process. We stipulate that Ms. Berendts owns the property in question. Still, the prosecution has supplied no evidence that she has been directly involved in the criminal activity found on that property. Neither have they provided evidence that the small amount of banned substance in her residence belonged to her and not her guest resident. We ask that the charges be dropped so law enforcement can conduct a proper investigation and present a complete set of facts to a grand jury.

--The court finds that the evidence presented is sufficient to remand the defendant into custody. Mr. Evanson, do you have a recommendation for bail?

--Yes, Your Honor. The defendant's involvement in the ongoing crimes committed on her property is evident, as is the seriousness of the charges and the fact that she has the assets to flee the district. A bail amount of $250,000 would be justified.

Amy was ready to jump up and protest, but Juanita put her hand firmly on her leg.

--Ms. Jones?

--Thank you, Your Honor. I find several points of contention in the prosecution's statement. First, the prosecution has only a presumption of Ms. Berendts' involvement. These charges are premature. They cannot find other suspects and witnesses who do not wish to be found. They are trying to intimidate her into giving evidence and information that she does not have. Next, I must point out that most of Ms. Berendts' assets are tied up in three properties and a successful business in Singapore County. For her to flee would be abandoning a lifetime of hard work and sound investments. Most importantly, the Singapore County sheriff and his deputies have abused her civil rights while she has been in his custody, including an unnecessary three days in the sheriff's lockup without legal representation. Once again, intimidation was their motive. Just before she was first able to see her brother and her lawyer, Sheriff Pierre McAdams told her: 'We just want you to cooperate.' Finally, the search warrant for Ms. Berendts' home in Singapore was issued improperly. We will be moving to find any results of that search to be inadmissible if this case ever gets to trial. We submit that the only just and fair outcome of this hearing would be that Amy Berendts be remanded within the borders of Singapore County, with permitted visits to Lansing and New Leiden to consult with her attorneys and her CPA.

The courtroom was silent while Judge Eubanks stared at Juanita Jones and Amy. He turned to look at the prosecution table and the sheriff behind them. Next, he looked down at his paperwork. After an extended, awkward silence, he finally spoke.

--The defendant is remanded as requested by counsel. She is to physically report to the clerk of this court every Monday morning until this order may be revised. She may not visit the rural property in question. She will notify the court of any contact with, or knowledge of the whereabouts of, suspects, witnesses, or other persons of interest that the court will provide to her. Failure to do so will be considered a violation of her bail terms. The court is adjourned.

Harry was not sure whether to be shocked or relieved. He looked at the prosecution table, saw the shock on their faces, and assumed that Juanita had scored a real coup. Amy had a relieved smile and hugged Juanita before she turned and hugged Harry. Larry had an ironic grin on his face. Carl Zandstra seemed mystified.

--What happens now, Juanita?

--Not a lot. Amy will need to do some paperwork and be free to go until a grand jury reaches a formal accusation or refuses the charges. That could take a while.

--How did you pull that off?

--I'm as surprised as you are. I pride myself on my bail hearings, but usually, I can only get bail reduced. Most of my clients, however, are Black or Brown and economically challenged. I guess being a rich, beautiful white lady makes a difference.

Amy grimaced.

--I don't care. I'll take it. Can you wait for me, Harry?

--Absolutely. Okay with you, Larry?

--Ja. Let's grab a beer. There's a restaurant with a bar across the street.

--I'll stick with iced tea. The whole sheriff department would love to stop me for a DUI. Amy, call my beeper if we're not back in the lobby when you're ready.

Juanita jumped back into the conversation.

--Carl and I will want to meet with you, Amy, after you are released. We will be conferring while you are being processed. It may take longer than Harry would want to wait. Carl could take you home. Singapore is pretty close. We could get something to eat while we review some things. What do you think, Carl?

--My pleasure. No trouble at all.

Amy avoided eye contact with Carl.

--Works for me too. Have you got my keys, Harry?

--Here you are. The Sheriff should have your other set. I'll call you in the morning.

--Not too early. I'll be sleeping in.

Everyone went in their separate directions while noticing the prosecution and Pete McAdams still conferencing at the front of the courtroom.

———————

Harry arrived back at his hotel room after dropping Larry off in Middleburg. Larry had finally told him what he was thinking regarding their inspection of Amy's farm and the results of the hearing. He wondered whether Amy knew the extent of the operation. He suspected that Doug Mason was the instigator, but Doug would have needed help to set it up and find buyers for the product. They would be higher-level additions to Nick Montez and his family. The sheriff was on the right track, looking for Theo or someone else with his contacts. Also, that small, circular area marked off on Amy's farm had a blotchy stain that could have been blood. Something significant had been found there.

Larry had snickered that the sheriff was caught grooming a witness. Pete McAdams knew better but had not planned to come up against an aggressive defense attorney like Juanita Jones. Even the judge was in awe of her. Larry had begun the day thinking that Amy was in serious trouble. After the hearing, he thought she would have a chance at eventually pleading guilty to heavily reduced charges and avoiding jail time. Larry's take on the case allowed Harry to feel some relief.

A light on his room phone meant he should call the front desk. The desk clerk gave him a name and a number to call. It was Lupe Rios; she said it was urgent. Harry dialed the number.

--Hello. This is Lupe.

--Hi, Lupe. This is Harry Berendts. What's up? What's urgent?

--Harry, I'm sorry to bother you, but I've been trying desperately to get a hold of Doug or Amy. Do you know how I can reach them?

--Not Doug, but Amy should be reachable by tonight. She's been out of touch.

--Can you get her to call me? My brother Nick is in trouble, and we need help.

-- What kind of trouble?

--He missed his night shift at Covenant Rehab, where we both work. I was trying to find him when I finally got a call. He's been shot.

--What happened? How bad is he hurt? Where is he?

--We are at Jonnie Van Orden's farm. Jonnie called me last night. Nick has been there since Saturday night. He was shot in the shoulder. Jonnie was trying to treat him, but it's become infected. It's serious. We need to take him to a hospital.

--Jonnie Van Orden, didn't he attend high school in Dordrecht? In Amy's class? How is he involved?

--Nick and my parents used to work for him. After he was shot, he didn't know where else to go.

--Why not go to the emergency room? Oh, I get it. He's part of the pot operation on Amy's Farm. He wants to avoid law enforcement.

--Yes, but now he's going to the ER, and it will be reported. We will cross the county line to the closest ER in New Leiden. Hopefully, they will accept it as a random drive-by or something.

--What is Amy supposed to do to help?

--Nick will not give them up. He'll keep quiet. But he'll need money for medical expenses, plus enough to drop out of sight if he doesn't get arrested.

--That's sounds like extortion.

--They're all in this together. They owe him. Harv Nielson, too. He's part of all this. If he gets picked up, he will talk. He needs to disappear like everyone else.

--Harv Nielson, the ponytail nurse? Is he involved, too?

--Kind of. He's an aide, not a nurse. He does have access to the drug closet at Covenant Rehab. He trades opioids for pot from Doug and Nick. He started a personal business.

--Okay. I'll call Amy later. Will you call me in the morning? Let me know what happens at the ER. It would be best not to talk to Amy directly. She needs to assume that she is under observation by various law enforcement agencies.

--So, you know more than I do about all this?

--I'm learning fast.

Chapter 11—Amy, Second Tuesday, 1998

Amy woke up earlier than she hoped on Tuesday morning. She was still wound up tight from the trauma of the weekend. Her release had gone smoothly. The meeting with Carl and Juanita on Monday was both disturbing and hopeful. Juanita had started with the worst-case scenario. Prison time was still a real possibility. The expense would use most of her assets if the case went to trial. Amy would need to agree to cooperate to secure a deal that would keep her out of jail. The good news was that the prosecution had made some mistakes. That could be used as bargaining power. Amy's job was to follow the terms of her release, go about her regular life, and refuse to talk to anyone about the case without the presence of her lawyers. Any deviation could reduce their ability to negotiate favorable terms for her. Amy agreed with the plan and asked Juanita to continue representing her, hoping to stay out of jail and avoid a trial.

The morning was cool and breezy, so she sat at the kitchen counter with her coffee. She fought a strong need to find some cannabis. Instead, she decided to take the opportunity to continue the three days of abstinence that her jail stay had forced on her. When Carl had dropped her at her condominium, he offered to come in and share a pipe. He also announced that he had finally gotten a divorce the year before and would be available to renew their relationship. Amy ended both offers quickly and firmly.

She realized that separating herself from Doug, without turning him against her, would be a top priority. She had not told Juanita the full extent of her involvement at the beginning of the marijuana operation. She wished she had ended it all before Doug started to get greedy and tried to expand. She was genuinely shocked at the size and scope of his expansion on the back section of the farm. She knew that he could not have accomplished it without receiving money and connections from Theo, which meant that she would eventually need to deal with Theo's issues. But for now, he would need to be avoided. She wondered where they were hiding but was relieved she did not know. That was one less thing she needed to hide from the prosecution. She was startled out of her reverie by her ringing phone, which she did not want to answer, wishing she had the Caller Identification that Theo used. She answered because she was afraid not to.

--Hello.

--Amy, it's Harry.

--What now?

--We need to talk.

--Okay. Tell me.

--It would be best in person. I need to show you something.

--Why so secretive?

--You'll know why.

--You'll need to come and see me.

--I can be there around noon.

--Come to the store. I have some work to do.

--Perfect, see you then.

Amy was mystified. Harry was not acting like his usual straightforward self. Now, she added him to the men in her life who were no longer meeting her expectations. Doug was missing. Ordinarily, he could not act independently, needing her approval for anything out of the routine. Theo was panicking, unlike the super cool, under-control image he always tried to project. Now, according to the sheriff, he was missing too. She was glad she had a new female lawyer interested only in her legal situation. She was prepared for Carl and Bill Snyder to try to reignite a relationship with her after she thought she had pushed them aside for good.

She tried Theo's numbers in New Leiden and Miami. Both rang on and on. Not even an answering machine message. She called the Goose & Gander Pub to talk to Dick Fillmore, Doug's manager. He was not in yet, but the person answering said that Dick was upset that Doug had missed his shifts on the weekend and that he was not able to contact him. She called Bill Snyder and left a message for him to call her back. She was anxious to rearrange her finances to deal with her legal expenses. Finally, she left a message for Judy Marsden to set up a time to help her get caught up at Mode du Jour. She would need to expand her holiday plans to generate more winter income. She thought a private event or two would attract some attention. Realizing she had skipped breakfast, she stopped at her regular coffee shop for a take-out vegan breakfast bowl on the way to her store.

When she arrived, she first went to the back stockroom, where she found and opened two shipments of new merchandise, one with a new line of tops and the other with leather accessories. The process helped her take her mind off her legal problems, but it did not give her the enthusiasm boost that she usually felt when things she had fallen in love with at the market arrived at the store. She then opened the mail in the back office, stacked the general correspondence on her desk, and put the invoices needing to be paid on a second desk where her bookkeeper, Shirley Venema, worked twice a week, doing the basic bookkeeping. Bored with the desk, she rearranged two feature racks in the showroom with the new tops and created a focused display of the leather goods on an accessory shelf, more out of a need to do something than to make a significant improvement. They would need to be changed again when more of her fall shipments arrived.

She was surprised when Harry knocked on the front entrance door fifteen minutes early. She went to open the door for him.

--Wow, you must be worried. Tell me what's going on.

--I will. It's a beautiful day, let's go for a walk.

--Really? Why not just sit here? It's cold and windy outside.

-- It's not that bad. I need some air.

--Okay, okay. Let me lock the door. We'll go out the back so I can set the alarm.

--Wow, this is nice! It's the first time I've seen your store.

--What did you expect? That I had a shitty t-shirt and jeans shop?

--No, but this is top-notch. It could be on Rodeo Drive. You should be proud of it.

--It's not Rodeo, but I do have some clients that shop there. I usually am proud of it, but I have other worries to think about right now.

They walked out the back after Amy had found her heavy jacket in the stockroom while she set the alarm. They headed toward the boardwalk along the river.

--No more mystery. Tell me what's going on.

--I am sorry about all the intrigue. Larry has spooked me. He's convinced that the feds could be involved and that they see you as a link to bigger fish. He thinks you may be bugged at home and the store.

--That sounds paranoid to me.

--That could be, but why not be careful? If I were you, I would only talk about ordinary stuff unrelated to the investigation, whether at home, in the store, or on the phone— even in your car. Or email. Do you use email?

--I've started with my suppliers. I'm planning to set up a client database. I could send promotional and new-arrival announcements without paying the printer or the post office.

--That's great. Just assume that they are watching that, too.

--Is that what you wanted to tell me?

--No, that's the prelude. Now, the sad news.

--Let me have it!

--Nick has been shot!

--What? When? Where? Who shot him? Is he dead?

--No, he took a bullet to his shoulder last Thursday. We think it happened on your property. The Sheriff has an area marked off on the ground that Larry says has blood stains. Nick went to Jonnie Van Orden for help. Jonnie treated him as best he could, but it became infected. They had to take him to the ER last night. They took him to New Leiden, hoping to avoid scrutiny from the Singapore Sheriff that would link him to the shooting of Doug and his drug operation. Nick could be in deep trouble.

--How did you find out?

--Lupe called me at the hotel. She was trying to reach you. I told her that was not something she should do. How did Jonnie get involved with this?

--He used to have an extensive pot farm. He would deal mostly behind the Beeline. His leg was getting worse, so he needed to close his business. Doug, financed by Theo, bought his stock, including starters and seeds. He brought it all to my farm. Nick and his parents worked for Jonnie before they worked with Doug. Jonnie learned a lot about pot in Vietnam.

--Okay. Don't tell me anymore. If anyone asks, all I know is that it happened on your farm. I don't want to know about the extent of your involvement. The Nick problem gets worse, however.

--How?

--Lupe and Nick expect you to help them in exchange for him staying lost.

--Help them how?

--Medical and living expenses until he can get settled out of state and across the border in Texas.

--Fuck! I don't know how I will pay for my problems, let alone his. I left a message for Bill Snyder. He's supposed to call me, so we should get back.

--Don't tell him anything. Just make an appointment ASAP. Clear it with the court and meet with him. Even in person, tell him only what you need to get operating cash for your legal needs. Build it up to have some left over for Nick. Five–make it ten thousand. That should take care of it if there are no more medical complications.

--Listen to you. How do you know all this stuff?

--It's all about Larry. I spent all day yesterday and more than an hour on the phone this morning with him. He's turned me into a new person. I don't recognize myself.

--Okay, I'll meet with Bill, hopefully, tomorrow. I'm going to New Leiden in the morning to see Juanita anyway. What about Lupe and Nick?

--I'll call Lupe. I'll tell her we talked and that you're working on it.

--Are you sticking around?

--I'm still here tomorrow. I need to be back in Denver on Thursday and Friday. I'll see what happens after that.

--By the way, no one seems to know who called the Sheriff Department about my farm. I can't figure it out either. I know some people who don't like me, but none of them would know what Doug was doing at the farm.

--It could have been just a curious neighbor. Or someone out to get Doug.

--You could be right. Okay, wish me luck.

--I think you may need more than that. You better do lots of yoga and meditation to find karma.

--It's not karma, it's nirvana. But that doesn't work either. Like Gerrit says, 'If it's transactional, it doesn't work.' We need to talk some more tomorrow. Why don't you come back tomorrow night and buy me dinner so we can review what we learn?

--That's transactional.

--Ja. It is, but it's not yoga.

Harry pointed to his car and said goodbye. Amy headed back to her store.

The following day, Amy was soon on her way to appointments with Juanita Jones and Bill Snyder. Tuesday afternoon in her store had been both productive and therapeutic. She had put the new worries about Nick and Lupe aside and delved into her work. She contacted the designer for the tops she had just displayed and arranged a trunk show for her summer line in early June. She then added another event with the lead designer from her favorite label the following week. She was already planning her first email campaign, a save-the-date announcement for both events, which would follow a direct mail piece promoting more new accessory lines like the leather goods she had just received, which would arrive in the spring. A group of vendors had joined to offer the full-color brochure to small, exclusive stores nationwide at volume pricing. She and Stephanie both signed up. Not only was she adding a new merchandise category, but she was raising the level of her marketing. She also knew she could add a website to her AOL account but would need help. She remembered meeting a young man at Gerrit's spring retreat who was starting an internet website business. She would need to get his contact information from Gerrit.

Energized by her latest ideas for the store, Amy then called Juanita and Bill and was able to set up the times for the following day. She called the court clerk in Wakazoo to get approval for the trip to New Leiden. Realizing that she had time in between, she decided that she would stop at Lenny Caputo's office to try to find out anything about Theo and his whereabouts. The court did not need to know. Finally, she called Gerrit at the resort office and left a message. After she locked up, she returned to her condo, where he called her back in the evening. After getting the information for Todd Barrington, the website designer, she broke down in tears and gave Gerrit a summary of her troubles since she left the resort.

Gerrit, as always, reacted calmly and without judgment, implicitly reminding Amy that 'there is no emergency.' He offered little advice except to remind her to find the quiet place within herself. He then said he needed to check on a few things at his Singapore church building, which was now used more often as a rented event center than for New Awakening Yoga and Meditation sessions. He would come down to Singapore on Thursday and could meet with Amy in the afternoon. Amy felt immediate relief and found enough courage to continue her efforts to extricate herself from her predicament. She insisted that he stay overnight in her condo. After an hour of meditation, she could sleep soundly for the first time since she had left the resort.

———————

Amy arrived near the Reginald Robinson Law Offices in downtown New Leiden fifteen minutes early before taking ten minutes to find the closest parking garage entrance. Using five more minutes to get to the entry and take the elevator to the thirteenth floor brought her to the reception desk on time. The receptionist with a light brown complexion asked her to take a seat, where she waited fifteen minutes until a Black man who looked like a young Harry Belafonte introduced himself as 'Brian Michaels, Ms. Jones' legal intern.' He escorted her to Juanita Jones' office, where Juanita greeted her warmly.

--Good morning, Amy. I hope you are coping with everything. I know this is not easy.

--I'm doing better than I thought I would. I was able to lose myself at work yesterday, and yoga helps.

--Excellent. Before I start, is there anything you want to ask me? Or something new that you thought of that you want to tell me?

--No, I want to understand better what will happen and when.

--As do I. This case is still very fluid. We need to go ahead with the idea that the sheriff and the PA are most interested in the unknown parties behind the operation.

--Unknown parties?

Just then, a tall, very dark-complexioned man with short natural afro hair forming a U around the bald oval crown covering his scalp and forehead stepped into the office. Juanita stood up.

--Amy, this is our senior partner, Reginald Robinson.

--I am pleased to meet you, Ms. Berendts. Please call me Reggie.

--Okay, then you should call me Amy.

--Thank you, I will. Before we go further, I need to bring up some business. Specifically, we need to talk about our fees. We will bill Monday's hearing through the Zandstra Law Group, but we need an agreement and a retainer to continue with the next phase. I wanted to discuss this with you in person to assure you that our entire firm, not just Juanita, will be at your service.

--What's included in the next phase? How much is the retainer?

--Let's say our goal is to avoid a formal accusation. That would be the next phase for which we would need $5,000. If you are indicted, it would be at least another $10,000, depending on the charges. More if it goes to trial.

--That's a lot of fucking money, but what choice do I have? I could find someone cheaper, but they would just get paid to have me convicted.

--That is good thinking. Can you get the money?

--I think so. I am seeing my accountant next. He's told me he can free up the cash I need. Unless you'd like to trade. I have a farm with some equipment I could throw in.

--I think we will pass. Can you come back on Friday? We will have the agreement ready and be able to complete everything.

--I will be here. The afternoon would be best.

--Excellent.

Reggie walked over and shook Amy's hand.

--We will give you our absolute best effort. Please continue, Juanita; I'll interject if I have anything to add.

--We were discussing the unknown parties behind the drug operation on Amy's property. We know about Doug Mason and Nick Montez. We agree with the prosecution that they are just lower-level actors. This operation has all the markings of organized crime. It may not be as large as many others, but it is just getting started at this stage.

--Organized crime? Like the mafia?

--Well, mafia is not the term we use today, Amy. We suspect big-city criminal groups or groups with connections to Mexican cartels may be involved.

Reggie added:

--Or they might be cooperating or competing.

Juanita continued:

--Property ownership of the farm makes you the first step of the operation and the only person they could find and arrest. That puts you under a lot of pressure. Some of that pressure will be relieved once they reach the next level. Our job is to protect you until they focus elsewhere.

--How do we do that?

--As I said initially, that's still a fluid situation. We did well at the hearing. Sheriff McAdams will not give us another gift. We are lucky that the County Prosecuting Attorney, Sally Conners, did not take the hearing herself. She would not have allowed me to sway the judge on bail. She is an excellent prosecutor. We have defended cases before when she was on the state PA's staff. I'm sure she wants to wait until more prominent figures become involved before she steps in and takes over.

--Am I indicted at this point?

--Not yet. They will bring the case before a grand jury. Their best answer is that they will impanel a grand jury in the first week of December. There could be another bail hearing if they bring a formal accusation.

--How can I get a deal if I'm uninvolved and have nothing to tell them?

--You are involved. You own the property. Your live-in boyfriend is a prime suspect. You are a target witness who, in their mind, is not cooperating.

--I don't know how much I should tell you.

--You should tell us everything that would help your case. First, it would be good to know exactly what you do know about what was happening at your farm. It will be hard to hide any of that from the prosecution. It would be best for us to get ahead of it and frame it in your favor.

--Okay, I knew that Doug and Nick were growing pot. I was okay with it because I wanted to get free, homegrown pot for myself. They were supposed to sell only to friends and family, keeping it small. We only started because my ex, Theo, helped finance the startup. I had no idea the size of the front part and certainly no knowledge of the 'back forty,' as they call it.

--Would you be willing to testify to all that—to name Theo, Doug, and Nick?

--I've been thinking about that. I can't do jail. I don't want a felony on my record. They need to give me that before I'll testify.

--Let's work with that for now. I'll feel out the prosecutors. Do you have anything to add, Boss?

--Does Amy have anything to add—like the whereabouts of Theo, who we now know is at least financially involved? Or Doug? Or Nick?

--My brother told me yesterday that Nick Montez has been shot. He heard from Lupe, Nick's sister. She said he was going to an ER in New Leiden. She would not say which one. She wants me to help him out with 'expenses.'

After a silent moment, Juanita responded.

--We might be able to use this. It's hearsay two steps removed, so you are not under any obligation to give the information to the prosecution. However, it could buy us some goodwill.

--What if Nick turns on me to help himself?

--He could do that. Can he prove that you have been directly involved in all the facets of the operation?

--No. After the small beginning, I was not involved.

Reggie didn't hesitate to jump in.

--I like it, Juanita. Let's probe carefully with Sally. Don't give her anything too easily or too soon. We'll see how much we can get by cooperating with them. Do you agree?

Yes, let's make that our goal. Is there anything else we can help with this morning, Amy?

--What else do I need to do?

--Follow the terms of your bail carefully. They won't hesitate to use any excuse to put more pressure on you.

Amy made an appointment with the receptionist for 2:00 on Friday before walking around the corner to Lenny Caputo's office. He was out, but when Amy asked the receptionist, Rebecca, if the office had heard from Theo, she looked knowingly at Amy but said she didn't know. But when Amy told her that she needed to repay Theo for a loan he had given her, the tactic worked. Rebecca showed more concern than a casual business contact would merit. Amy assumed that she was another of Theo's conquests. Rebecca said she had heard that Theo was vacationing out of the country, somewhere in the Caribbean. After asking her to give her repayment message to Lenny so he could pass it on to Theo, Amy also asked to borrow a phone for a local call. Rebecca took her to a small conference room behind her desk.

Carl Zandstra was in and took her call.

--Hi, Amy, how does it feel to be free?

--It doesn't feel like freedom. It feels like I am on a leash that only lets me go so far.

--Beats a kennel. What can I do for you?

--We were so involved in my troubles and the hearing that I forgot to ask about progress on my mother's trust and the Florida condo.

--Well. Zero progress. We must flip the trust matter over to my brother-in-law, Peter Van Velsen. He's the probate and real estate expert. He needs a $10,000 retainer to start on it. You also know that my partners will not put any money upfront.

--You mean you won't. Tell you what. Set the trust aside for now. The condo case is simpler and easier to win. Plus, I don't want that bitch, Lydia, to have it. Let's find a Florida lawyer to start looking into it. I'm seeing Bill Snyder next. I can get $2,500 for a retainer so they can begin. Do you know someone?

--I always know someone who knows someone. I'll let you know what I find out. How do I contact you?

--Call me at my condo or the store. I don't care if anyone listens when we are not discussing the court case.

--Okay, it sounds like you are properly paranoid.

--I need to be.

Amy ended the call and walked three blocks to Bill Snyder's office. The receptionist had her wait in a large conference room and offered to bring her coffee. Amy asked hopefully for herbal tea, which drew a sad-faced response. She was surprised when Bill walked in immediately, not following his usual pattern of making people wait at least fifteen minutes. He brought her to his office.

--Hey, you look great after what you've been through the last few days.

--Thanks. I'm not feeling normal, but I hope to put everything behind me.

--I'm here to help. What can I do?

--Right now, I need cash.

--You have some bonds we can cash in. This isn't the best timing, but this is the definition of an emergency. How much?

--I have enough to live on and keep the store going for a while, at least through the rest of the year, but I won't see any profits till late spring. Right now, I need about ten grand for legal retainers. More later, depending on what happens.

--I can get that. But I should do more than that, at least $25,000. I'll have to dip into your 401K for more. That could have tax consequences and penalties. Your income was good this summer. You could get a second mortgage on your condominium. Better yet, sell the damn farm.

--Like anyone would want it now.

--True. I'll have the money ready by Friday.

--That'll work. I'm seeing Juanita Jones on Friday afternoon.

--Juanita Jones? I hear she is something else in the courtroom. Just like her boss, Reggie.

--She saved my ass Monday. Are you buying me lunch?

--Absolutely. Where would you like to go?

--There is a new vegan place close to the old Covenant campus.

--Oh… Okay, I guess you are the client. I'll have a steak and a half tonight.

Amy returned to Singapore just after four. She felt that she was beginning to get her life under control. Lunch with Bill went quickly. She used the tried-and-true rationalizations to fend off his casual attempt to restart their relationship: It would be a possibility later, but not now; there were too many complications. At least he had managed her money issues, just as Reggie and Juanita seemed to have temporarily moderated her legal matters.

She had stopped to see Stephanie and her store, which she was preparing for the winter season. As always, it looked up-to-date and well-put-together, although Amy always thought it lacked a special touch of creativity that she had a knack for adding to her Singapore store, whether it was an out-of-the-mainstream accessory line or an artistic touch to the displays. She was jealous that Stephanie's busy season was coming up soon, while she would need to wait until late spring for her business to pick up. She did notice a group of coats from a new designer that she had passed on at the market. Amy decided to try to bring some in for her weekend winter business.

She and Stephanie discussed the preparations for the direct mail campaign. Amy agreed to use the same agency to design the back page copy and layout and use their mailing company. All Amy would need to do would be to clean up and enhance her client mailing list. She pressed Stephanie about what she knew about Theo and where he had gone, but Stephanie was convincing when she pled ignorance.

When Amy walked into her kitchen from the garage, she checked her machine. Harry had left a message on her phone that he would come around 5:30 to take her out for dinner. She thought they could drive to South Wakazoo to a new restaurant on the inlet that she had heard good things about. It was the only decent place in the county she had not tried. After a long day of meeting and travel, she showered again to feel fresh, changed into casual clothes, poured a Chardonnay, and waited for Harry.

When he arrived, Harry was not excited about driving twenty miles to eat, but Amy was in the mood to go and even insisted that they take her Lexus with the top down. It was warm for an October night but still cold enough that Harry was even less enthused.

--Come on, Harry. It'll feel good. We'll turn the heat up. I'll even let you drive. Besides, your rental sucks.

After Amy grabbed a coat and one of Doug's ski jackets for Harry, they climbed into the Lexus and drove to Annie's Garden Restaurant. It was fun, and it was cold. They both were surprised at the restaurant's quality. The menu and atmosphere were trendier than most resort town restaurants, which were usually upgraded diners or steakhouses added onto bars. Harry was still shivering when their drinks came as he sipped his Old-Fashioned.

--Next time I'll know to pack all my ski clothes. I didn't think I would need them in October.

--Don't be such a baby. You had fun.

--Do you know you've told me that since I was born

--And you deserved it.

--Speaking of ski clothes, I remember the trips with Joe to Boyne Mountain and that trip of a lifetime when we went to Vail.

--Those were special. Although, you were a real wuss at first.

--Hey, give me a break. I was only ten. By the time we went to Colorado, you were trying to keep up with me.

--There is something about male hormones kicking in.

--They were some of the best times with Joe, though. They tend to get buried under everything that pissed me off about him.

--They were fun. But I always had the feeling that he was showing off about what he could afford to do for us. In a way, he always made it all about him.

--He called once before Mom died because he wanted to come and take Jen and Dave to Vail. It was after Mom was sick and forgave him for one of his flings. She believed him that it wasn't with Lydia. I almost let it happen, but Monica wasn't having it. She got to know him during our wedding week. He tried to make that all about him, too.

--That damn Lydia! I never understood why he kept going back to her.

--She made him feel important. He always felt inadequate around Mom, especially her family.

--No doubt! I know how he felt. I was never accepted, either. They were all incredibly self-righteous.

--Well, from their point of view, you and I are headed for hell. I am sure they prayed that Joe would be in a state of grace when he died.

--Let's change the subject. Did you hear from Lupe or Nick?

--Ja. A message awaited me at the hotel at noon after I dropped off Larry. It turned out to be Jonnie's number. She was still there when I called back. She can't find Nick. Jonnie said he was patched up and given antibiotics at the New Leiden Hospital, but he sneaked out of the ER before the police arrived to check out his gunshot wound.

--Are you keeping Lupe away from Marilyn?

--Do you have a spy checking me out?

--No, I don't need one. I noticed there was something you didn't want to tell me. How is Marilyn?

--No comment.

Their orders arrived. Amy had the chef's green salad with chickpeas. Harry had roast chicken. They talked more about their childhood. Amy was surprised that they were almost bonding. Harry remembered that he wanted to ask her about Jeff Klaasen.

--I was shocked to see Jeff at the funeral. Did you see him?

--Just for a minute. We'll get together soon in Singapore.

--He is doing well. He was pleasant to me. Since we stopped hanging out together in junior high, I thought he might have some bad feelings. He blamed it on his dad, who didn't like me because I switched to public school.

--More likely, you weren't one of the bullies who made his life miserable, even before he came out. I know he resented

Allen Zuverink for abandoning him when he should have defended him, considering our three mothers were friends.

--Allen is still conservative, even narrow-minded. Have you seen Jeff's B & B?

--Yes, it's getting excellent reviews. His friend Rob has done a fantastic job on the refurbishing. It's almost done. Rob is a lot younger than Jeff and an absolute stud. He's a real catch for Jeff.

--Like I said, he's landed on his feet. I'm thinking of getting out of the Inn on my next trip. I would be more comfortable at River Haven.

--Are you coming back right away?

--Ja, I'll be back this weekend. We still need to bury Joe's ashes. Plus, we can settle his financial stuff when you're ready after your tough week.

--We do. I'll be ready next week.

They finished the meal. Amy drove back in a warm car with the top up.

When they drove into the entry of her condo complex, Amy felt her heart skip a beat as she saw two police cars and a Bronco near her garage door. She pulled up and asked Harry to find out what was happening. As Harry got out and walked over, she noticed that one was a local police car and the other was a deputy sheriff. She also saw Pete McAdams standing by a Bronco. Harry walked up to him. They talked briefly, and then Harry turned to Amy and waved her over. Feeling her anger take over, she almost ran to confront the Sheriff.

--What the fuck do you want now? Can't you leave me alone?

--Calm down, Amy. Take a deep breath. Can we go inside and sit down? I have some very bad news for you.

Amy felt her anger turn to dread.

--Tell me now. Get it over with.

--I found Doug today. He'd been shot. He's dead.

Amy felt her body crumble. Harry grabbed her around her back and led everyone inside. He remembered the security code and sat Amy down at the dining table. While he went to the refrigerator to find a drink for Amy, Amy had recovered enough to speak.

--Tell me more. What happened? How did you find him?

--He was at the DFG Club. I had a personal reason to be at the club. Buck Johnson, the caretaker, came with me, and while he went to the shed to get some tools he needed, I started to look around. Doug was not hard to find. He was shot with a shotgun.

--Who the hell would do that? Just like Nick.

--We don't know who. What's this about Nick?

Harry gave Amy a double shot of cold Smirnoff and answered Pete.

--Nick's sister called me last night. Nick had been shot on Amy's property last weekend. On Monday night, he went to an ER in New Leiden to get patched up. Now he is missing again.

--When did you plan to tell me?

--When Amy wasn't present, or her lawyers were. Once again, it would be best if you weren't questioning her. The conversation about Nick is over. Tell us more about Doug.

--It was deja vu for me. I found him near the spot where I found George Bosch twenty-five years ago. Both died from a close-range shotgun blast to the face. A Remington shotgun was on the ground close by. It was made to look like a suicide, which any professional would doubt. In both cases, I think they were shot elsewhere and moved.

--Could it be the same person?

--I guess, but in my mind, it is more likely to be a copycat sending a message. There were some differences. We won't be publishing those.

--Is Amy in any danger?

--That's why the local police are here. There's been a break-in at your store, Amy. It looks like they broke in through a window, broke open the cash register, and got some cash out before the local police could respond to the alarm. Your motion alarm did go off. How much was in there?

Amy put her vodka glass on the table and gathered herself with a deep breath.

--Just the $250 bank. There is a floor safe hidden in the back. My jewelry on display is not cheap, but there are no precious stones.

--There was no other obvious evidence of damage or anything missing. You'll have to make a report on precisely what's missing. We don't have enough patrol officers to keep someone here all night. Keep your alarm on.

Pete called over the Singapore Chief of Police, Cory Epperson, who was standing off to the side. He gave Amy the number of a window company that would board up the broken window. He asked Harry and Amy to follow him to the store to assess the loss and finish the report. Against Amy's objections that it was not necessary, Harry insisted that he would sleep over and cancel his trip to Denver. Amy gave in on the sleepover but remembered that Gerrit was coming the next day and could stay with her the next few nights. Harry relented. Pete had one more question.

--Did Doug have a gun or a rifle?

--Not a rifle. He did have a pistol. He usually kept it in his truck. Pete nodded his head.

--We haven't found his truck yet.

With that, he stood up and told Amy he would like to talk was legally protected. Everyone went to their cars. Harry called the glass company's emergency response line before he and Amy headed to the store. They went through the motions of inspecting the store and waiting for Cory to finish his preliminary report. Amy could not find anything else missing. Cory gave her his card and told her to call him personally if she needed anything. Amy got the feeling that he meant the personal part literally.

They returned to the condominium, still not believing what had happened. They talked for an hour before they were ready to sleep. Amy told Harry more about her life with Theo and Doug, plus something he did not know about Joe. Finally, feeling able to sleep, Amy showed Harry how to open the sofa bed before he returned to the store to watch the repair company board up the window.

Chapter 12—Harry, Second Saturday, 1998

Early Saturday afternoon, Harry again drove his rental Accord into the Amsterdam Inn parking lot. He was glad this would be the last night. While in Denver, he had decided to do something different. Taking out the card Jeff Klaasen gave him, he called the River Haven Inn in Singapore. Jeff's partner, Rob Miller, answered. Because it was the slow season, Rob offered Harry a discount and an open-ended stay. He suggested one of the large, renovated rooms over the carriage house, which were also the most private. Rob also apologized that he would be cooking breakfast himself on weekdays during the off-season, but he offered Harry access to the kitchen if he wanted to make lunch or dinner. Harry accepted and arranged to check in on Sunday morning.

Harry's life in Denver seemed to be coming to an end. The closing of the sale of his share of the business went more smoothly than he expected. More than a half million new dollars had been transferred to his T. Rowe Price cash account. There would be another annual quarter million plus for each of the next five years. Combined with his company retirement and personal IRA, he was as rich as he ever hoped. He was unsure of the state and federal tax implications but assumed he could keep at least two-thirds of the total. He had already decided to work with Allen Zuverink as his financial advisor. He could think of no one more trustworthy. He was free of work and free of worrying about money, but he did not know which direction the rest of his life would take.

When he, Jennifer, and Dave met in Boulder for dinner the night before, he felt a growing contentment among them now that the shock of the divorce had worn off. The kids could tell that Monica was happier and that Harry had recovered with minor permanent psychological damage. He felt relief and satisfaction that they had chosen their next steps. Jennifer was transferring from a bio-chemistry major into pre-med for her fifth year, planning to specialize in contagious disease research. She had her mother's scientific brain. David's homosexuality had become a fact, accepted by all without the initial anxiety. He had settled on a computer science degree. He chose it because it would keep his career options open. Every business, non-profit, and government organization would soon need people with his expertise.

Harry decided to tell them about their grandmother's trust. Even though it would not make them wealthy, money worries would not force them to cut their education short or make other short-range choices that would limit their long-range goals. He said goodbye, telling them he did not know when he would return to Colorado. He was on a mission to keep his sister out of jail.

Three callback messages were waiting for him as he checked in. Lupe, Larry, and Hank had called. He went to his room and called Hank first. Irma picked up.

--Hi, Irma. Hank called, but I can talk to you first. I want to take you and Hank out to dinner tomorrow night to return the favor of last week's supper.

--Let me check with Hank.

There was a pause.

--Hank is begging off. He doesn't want to go out after the five o'clock church service.

--Then it's just you and me. Where would you like to go?

Irma's voice brightened.

--There's a new restaurant on the lake in Middleburg by the yacht club that I've been hoping to try. It's getting great reviews. It's also pricey.

--Not a problem. My ship has come in. You'll be doing me a favor by helping me celebrate.

He didn't say that it was uncomfortably close to Marilyn's house.

--If you can pick me up at 6:00, I'll make the reservations for 6:30.

Harry imagined an approving smile forming on Hank's face. She told Harry Hank had called to let him know that his Uncle Ben had experienced another stroke and was in critical condition in Middleburg Hospital. She filled him in when he asked about the details before asking about Amy. He replied only with what he dared to reveal. He mentioned his move to the B & B. They kept talking. Fifteen minutes later, Harry remembered his other messages.

--I'm sorry to break this off; I need to call Larry. Plus, I'm due at Amy's soon. When do you think I could see Uncle Ben?

--I'm going tomorrow after church. You could come with me.

--To church? No. To the hospital? Yes.

She laughed.

--Meet me at the hospital around twelve. I want to check on another of my patients while I'm there.

Next, he tried Lupe. There was no answer, either in person or by a machine. When he called Larry, he did pick up. He and Harry had quickly touched base the day after Doug's body was found, but neither had any added information. Larry's work had kept him busy. His analysis of the new client's case required him to inspect several locations on the Lake Michigan coast.

--How does it feel to be working again?

--I'm not sure yet. I don't have a state badge to hide behind. Which is just as well since I am not announcing myself. I won't be strictly undercover, just checking out the situation without getting in anyone's face.

--At least you have something to do. I feel a bit lost.

--Enjoy the vacation. We can do something tomorrow. Yesterday, I was thinking about what you had heard about Jonnie Van Orden. Last night, I went to Der Kroeg to see if he was still there on Friday nights like he used be when it was the Beeline. He was there just as Amy had said. He was not doing well at all. He was using a walker in the bar, and when he left, I saw him get into a converted van with a wheelchair lift.

--What did you find out?

--Nothing yet. He was a little on edge and seemed afraid to talk. We didn't know each other that well back at Dordrecht High. He loosened up a little when I mentioned that I was working with you to help Amy. He said we could come out to his farm this weekend.

--That sounds like it might be worth the trip. It's too late today. How about tomorrow afternoon?

--That's good for me. What time? I'll pick you up at the Inn.

--I forgot to tell you. I'm moving to the River Haven B & B in Singapore tomorrow morning. It will feel less commercial, and I'll be closer to Amy. But I will be seeing my Uncle Ben at Middleburg Hospital around noon. He's had another stroke. I can pick you up around 1:30.

--See you then. Say hello to Marilyn for me.

--She's not in my long-term plans.

Harry and Marilyn had talked on the phone several times since their reunion the previous Saturday night. Harry tried halfheartedly to convince her that that night should be a one-time rendezvous. He was feeling guilty about interfering in the lives of a married couple. She was not easily swayed. She talked him into picking her up in the Meijer parking lot at three o'clock on Saturday afternoon. They could go back to his room and talk.

Harry had time for a shower and wardrobe change. He arrived on time before driving around the parking lot twice to find her white Lincoln SUV hidden between an RV and an extended cab pickup. They nervously exchanged small talk on the ride back to the Amsterdam Inn. As he closed the door to the suite, she tossed her coat on the sofa and turned to press against him.

--I've missed you terribly.

--It's only been a week. The last time, it was thirty years.

--Don't tease me.

She pulled away, walked to the bed, and smoothed her navy silk dress.

--I'm not teasing you. You're a married woman. I'm being realistic. I'm afraid we're only causing ourselves trouble.

--Butch has broken our marriage vows. We can't break what's already broken.

--That could be true. But we could destroy it. That's one reason I think I'm hesitant and uncomfortable.

--Uncomfortable? I think it's just your Calvinist guilt. We think we've outgrown it. But we never do.

--I'll buy that. But the other thing that makes me uncomfortable is being your revenge lover. She stood up, clutched his arm, and guided them both down on the bed.

--I don't think that's true. I think we're both getting the comfort we deserve.

Harry's defenses evaporated.

———————

By 5:30, after Marilyn had left, Harry headed to Singapore to have dinner with Amy. When he arrived, Gerrit answered the door. Harry could not resist focusing on his eyes. They were a light gray, almost colorless. Harry felt them piercing directly into his mind from somewhere deep in Gerrit's consciousness. The effect unsettled him.

--Hi. You must be Harry, the long-lost brother.

--I am Harry, but I didn't know I was lost.

--Just a figure of speech. I'm Gerrit Gerritson.

--Yes, I know. I saw you at the funeral. Is Amy around?

--She went to the store to check on the repair work. They finally replaced the window today.

--Have they found anything new about the break-in? I haven't talked to her since Thursday morning.

--Not that I've heard. The upstairs tenants were out of town. The police checked the neighbors. No one heard or saw anything. They didn't find any useable fingerprints.

--Anything new on Doug?

--No. The sheriff is being secretive. He'll only say they are searching the DFG Club and Amy's farm for clues. 'Meticulously searching' is the phrase he used. They are also trying to find out where Doug was between the last time Amy saw him and his death.

--And they haven't found Nick?

--Not that we've heard.

They could hear the garage door open as Amy drove in. They returned to the kitchen to meet her as she walked into the condo from the garage entrance.

--Hello, Harry. I see you've met Gerrit. Are you two getting along? I hope you're not talking about religion.

--Absolutely not! I just got here. Gerrit is updating me on the crime wave you're involved in.

--Don't exaggerate. Let's sit down and do some more updating. I need a glass of wine. How about you, Harry?

--Do you have a beer?

--Of course. Gerrit?

--I have some tea left in the pot. I'll reheat it.

They took their drinks to the living area bay window with a lake view. The sky was gray, making the lake take on a dark, mysterious cast. Amy said that Juanita had sent a man to check for 'bugs.' He found none but warned her there could be electronic surveillance on her line. They also advised that being

229

near a window was the safest area to talk. Harry started the conversation by quizzing Amy.

--What's happening with Doug's arrangements? Has his family been in touch? Where are they living now?

--I called his mother in Hamtramck on Thursday. His dad died about five years ago. I didn't give her the whole story. I called it a hunting accident. When she called back this noon, she said his two sisters, who still live in the Detroit area, wanted to have the funeral there. I had to tell her his face was disfigured, and the sheriff was not releasing the body until he could rule out foul play. I suggested that they have a memorial service without the body. Being Catholic, that didn't sit well with them. What do you think I should do, Gerrit?

--You told me he hadn't been to confession or mass in years. In their mind, that means his soul will, at best, exist in the lower levels of purgatory. You don't care about any of that. I would urge them to contact the local Catholic parish and mortuary for help. They might give the family some comfort. Do you agree, Harry?

--Sounds good to me. But what do you think, Amy?

--I can't believe the mystical monk and the atheist agree. I tend to lean toward the burning of the body like the Hindus. It should be done in a public viewing so we know the spirit has left it. You are right, though. I should let them have his body so they can find comfort in their rituals.

--Okay, let me know if I can help arrange that. By the way, I am not an atheist. No one raised like us can ever be rid of the idea of God.

--What are you, then?

--I am nothing, I guess. Or maybe a sort of pantheist. A confirmed atheist is just like a true believer. Just guessing at answers to questions that only have answers beyond our capability to understand. We don't even know what questions to ask.

--Gerrit says we don't have answers either. We are on a path, just searching. Is that right, Gerrit?

--That's the most straightforward metaphor. Harry might have an objection to that.

--Just the fact that you think you are on a path is an illusion. You have no idea where any of the paths might lead. For most people, they lead to a reliance on idols. Or they get lost in the woods, walking in circles, just like me and everyone else.

Amy looked at Harry with frustration.

--What do you mean by idols, Harry?

--The list is endless. The Church, the Bible, revered figures like Jesus and Gautama.

Amy and Gerrit did not reply at first before smiling knowingly at each other. Gerrit replied quietly.

--It's as if we speak a different language on opposite sides of a mountain.

Harry spoke just as quietly.

--So it seems. But I'm not here to argue about religion. As you know, Amy, we both did enough of that with Mom and Grandpa. What progress has Juanita made to get your charges reduced?

--None yet. Sheriff McAdams and Sally Conners think I'm holding back. That I know more than I do. Juanita said they won't make a better deal until I give up more.

--Is she right? Are they right?

--There may be some things they don't need to know. But it's all changed now. Doug's shooting has raised the stakes., even though they know I had nothing to do with that.

Gerrit looked calmly at Amy.

--You know, Amy, we can't assume that. Even though they know you didn't pull the trigger, they may believe you had a strong motive if Doug would be willing and able to attest to your significant involvement in the entirety of the drug operation. You could have had someone else involved do the actual killing.

--Who might that be?

--They seem highly interested in Theo.

--Theo is long gone.

--I don't think they believe that.

Harry let out a sigh.

--Well, all you can do now is stand your ground until they indict you.

Gerrit stood up.

--That's correct. There is nothing more to do now. I'm hungry. I made a bean salad while you were gone, Amy. We still have a big bowl of the brown rice risotto you made yesterday. Are you staying, Harry? We have plenty.

--Uh, I would like to return to the hotel and crash. I need to pack up what little I have. I'm moving to Jeff's B & B tomorrow. I can't stand another motel night. I'll pick up something on the way. Junk food takeout sounds good to me right now.

———————

Harry was in his room on Saturday night, wondering whether to save the three slices of pizza he had left over. Although he suspected he would not eat the rest, he wrapped it up as best he could and put it in the small refrigerator with three leftover cans from a Blue Ribbon six-pack, which he had also picked up in his frenzy of nostalgia. A rare, televised game between Western and Central Michigan enhanced the mood. Thirty years prior, Harry had gotten into the rivalry game as a sophomore—four plays as the holder for three extra points and a field goal. Each was successful and helped the Broncos to a 24-0 victory. After the winter quarter that year, he had dropped out and went to work for DeJong Office Systems.

He toyed with the idea of changing his mind about attending a church service at Second Reformed in the morning but decided that it would be a nostalgic step too far. The weather forecast for the morning looked good, so a drive to the lakeshore and a long walk on the beach would be more inspiring.

With all the events of the last two weeks swirling in his mind, he took the pen and notepad from the desk, intending to jot down some notes to organize his thoughts. Before he finished two bullet points, the phone rang.

--Hi, Harry. This is Lupe.

--Hi. I called earlier.

--I was still working. I just came off a double shift. We need to talk.

--When can we meet?

--How about now? I'm too wired to crash. We could meet for a drink.

--I've already had my limit tonight. How about coffee?

--I need a drink or two. There's a new pub on the interstate, two exits from where you are. You can have a Coke. I'll be there in ten minutes.

--Okay, I'm on my way.

Harry found Lupe sitting in a booth toward the back when he arrived. As he sat down, the waiter brought a cocktail in a tall glass for Lupe and a glass of beer to the table.

--I thought you could nurse one. I hope you like IPAs.

--I'll force myself. It'll be better than the Blue Ribbons I just had. They weren't as good as I remembered. I'm sorry you had a tough day.

--It's part of what I want to talk about. I covered the overnight shift for Harv Nielsen. He still hasn't shown up.

--How involved is he with Amy's farm?

--Somewhat. He didn't help with the pot but was one of Doug's pill suppliers. Now they are suspecting him of stealing drugs. He has access to the pharmacy supplies at Covenant's rehabilitation wing.

--What kind of pills?

--Xanax, oxy, various uppers. Whatever he could sneak out.

--It seems you know all about it, but you're not involved.

--Not actively involved. I'm passing on what I've heard.

--You better be careful. This is a murder investigation now.

--I'm all too aware of that. Sheriff McAdams asked me to come in for questioning next week.

--Are you going?

--I'm going to Legal Aid on Monday. I won't talk to him without a lawyer.

--Good move.

The waiter came by with a burger and fries. Lupe dove in.

--Want some fries?

--No, I'm good. They would fight with the pizza I just ate.

As Lupe ate half the burger and half the fries, she changed the subject.

--Did you talk to Amy? Is she producing what we need?

--Ja. I told her what you told me. She's willing to help. But she's being carefully watched. I don't know if her funds are accessible.

--She needs to get us something so Nick can stay underground. Harv, too, if we can find him before the law does. He could take down everyone if he would start to cooperate.

--I'll tell Amy again, but I won't be the bagman. I'm already more involved than I want to be.

--Keep giving her the message. She can find me.

--Where are you living?

--Believe it or not, I'm sitting in your dad's house. Amy asked me to move there for security reasons when Joe was admitted to the nursing home for his last few days. My apartment lease was up, so I grabbed the opportunity.

--Enjoy it while you can. As soon as probate is completed, it will be owned by my kids.

--Amy told me all about that just before Joe died. She is going to fight it.

--Good luck with that. She's tied up with more pressing legal issues.

--Maybe I should invite you back to your house. You could be my new landlord--with privileges. But I'm too damn tired, and I look like shit after twenty hours on the job.

--I don't think you could ever look bad. But I don't need privileges right now.

--Yeah. I know. I hear you're enjoying a high school reunion.

--Hearing from who?

--It doesn't matter. I may be Mexican, but this is still Dordrecht. It's hard to hide from prying eyes.

That's one reason I have a new home starting tomorrow. I'll be at the River Haven Inn in Singapore. Here's the number.

She got up, taking the card from Harry with a knowing smile while squeezing his shoulder as she left. Harry followed after paying the bill.

On Sunday afternoon, after seeing his uncle Ben with Irma in the nursing home, he met Larry at his son's house, waiting for him in the driveway, leaning against a new GMC Suburban. Larry directed Harry to the passenger seat as he jumped into the cab. They headed northeast of Middleburg and Dordrecht toward Jonnie's farm.

--Nice ride! Business must be good. At least you're driving something that fits you.

--It's like buying clothes my size. I don't have a lot of choice. I was in Ludington and saw this as I passed the dealership. It spoke to me, telling me it was time for a new image. I leased it under the business name. Doesn't it make me look successful? Plus, it makes tracking my expenses easier. I only need to keep track of my personal miles.

--I'm sure you'll track them diligently. What do you think Jonnie will be able to tell us?

--I'm not sure, but we know he is connected to several people involved. Doug's shooting has changed everything. Murder moves everything up a notch in the minds of law enforcement folks.

--He did help Doug and Amy set up their pot farm.

--And he's close to the Montez family–Nick, Lupe, and their parents.

--He's a link to Theo, too.

--Ja. He sure is.

--By the way, there is another person in the mix. Lupe told me last night that Harv Nielson, who worked with her and Nick at the rehab center, is now missing. She said he was pilfering pills from the nursing supply. Doug was a customer.

--Okay. One more name on the whiteboard. What were you doing with Lupe last night?

--Paying for her dinner.

--Can you juggle all these women? How was Irma today? Did she take you to church?

--No way. I went for a long walk on the beach before I checked in to my new home away from home. It helped clear my head before Irma and I saw my Uncle Ben in the hospital with Hank. He had another stroke.

--How is he doing?

--Not well. My cousins are talking about hospice care.

--Did any of your lady friends get cleared away?

--I plan to keep them all at arm's length.

--Good luck with that.

--To continue with the Harv Nielson story, I asked Irma how well she knows him. She is the head of the skilled nursing unit at Covenant Rehab. She does have some contact with him. She also knows there is an investigation into missing drugs in the rehab division and that Harv is a suspect.

--Ah, maybe his going missing is unrelated to Doug's shooting.

--Or he could become a prime suspect.

--Absolutely. Hey, you're getting good at this detective stuff.

--I never missed an episode of *Magnum PI*. I'm even taping the reruns.

They pulled into the long driveway at Jonnie Van Orden's farmhouse ten minutes later. Jonnie opened the door and came onto the front porch to greet them as they exited the Suburban. He moved slowly using his walker. Harry went up the porch steps and held out his hand.

--Hi, Jonnie. I'm Harry Berendts. It's been a while since we were in Dordrecht High.

--Hello, Harry. Good to see you. You too, Larry. Come inside, guys. You're a lot bigger than the little sophomore I remember, Harry.

--And a lot older. How is your leg? Amy told me about your Vietnam injuries.

--Not good. But I'm living with it.

--That's got to be hard to live with. I can't imagine how difficult it must be. That was an awful war.

--I volunteered for it. Three times. I lost the lower half of my leg on my third tour.

--That may be, but sometimes I feel guilty–that's not the right word. I feel relieved that I got into the Guard. I feel guilty about feeling relieved.

--There's no need to feel guilty. At least you didn't dodge your duty.

--I initially believed in what you all were trying to do. Later, it was politics that got in the way. We wound up in the middle of a corrupt power struggle in the South.

--You could be right. We grunts didn't know what was happening at the top. How is Amy? It sounds like she is in some real trouble.

--She is. I'm trying to help her stay out of prison. It's beginning to look like she's only a part of a much larger crime ring. The question is how much she knows and how much she dares to say. Doug is dead, and Nick's been shot. It's getting dangerous.

--I hope I'm not in the same situation. Charley Vredevelde called yesterday. He wants me to meet with the Singapore County Sheriff next week.

As they sat down at the kitchen table, on which Jonnie had put several Cokes, a bowl of potato chips, and some dip, Larry grabbed a Coke and a handful of chips and then joined the conversation.

--Don't go without a lawyer. This thing is about to blow up. My state police friends will soon be involved. The feds, too. Pete McAdams is tough enough, but he can't be compared to the big boys.

--I've been out of it for quite a while. I don't think I can help them.

--You know some of the players. Who knows what they will dredge up to put pressure on you?

--Doug is dead. They have Amy. Do you know where Nick is, Harry? I don't.

--No, I don't. Lupe says he went to Texas and over the border. Do you know if that's where his parents are?

--I know that's where they were planning to go. They still have family in Chihuahua. They saved a lot of money over the years—enough to retire there, which they always planned to do. Do you think they could be extradited, Larry?

--They could be, but I don't think the feds would want to go through the trouble. Nick might be another story. Harry, we should try to talk to the sheriff as soon as possible. We could offer him a little bit of what we know and see if he'll reciprocate with some info of his own.

--Okay, I guess. You know how law enforcement thinks. I'm available all week.

--I'll drop a few names of friends of mine and see if he'll see us. I'll tell him you can squeeze us in between your lady friends.

Harry turned to Jonnie, ignoring Larry's last comment.

--Did you also have some dealings with Theo Bolinyk?

--I wish I had never met him. If not for him, I wouldn't have known Doug. I wouldn't have any involvement with this mess.

--Do you have any idea where he is?

--No, and I don't want to know.

--I understand why. Who could've told the Sheriff Department what was happening at Amy's farm?

--I've been wondering about that, too. I don't know anyone who had something to gain.

--How about Lupe? Is she involved or just trying to help Nick and her parents?

--I think she must have known what we were doing here and what Doug and Nick were doing at Amy's Farm. How much was she into it? I don't know.

--She told me Sheriff McAdams wanted to talk to her too. She said she was contacting Legal Aid to get advice. You should, too.

--You guys are right. I do need to find a lawyer. But I have enough money to hire a real one. I don't need charity.

--That's good. Larry, you found Amy a great lawyer. Any recommendations?

--Ja, I know a competent guy in North Haven. I'll call you with his name and number after I check with him and tell him the situation. I think he's also had some dealings with our mutual buddy, Charley Vredevelde.

They spent another half-hour reliving some of their high school days before Harry and Larry left to return to Middleburg, where Harry transferred to his rental. When he returned to River Haven, he called Amy to see if she needed anything. She was glad he asked and gave him a list of things she could not get in Singapore: specialty hair products from her regular hair salon, several makeup necessities from an exclusive store, a list of fruit and vegetables from an organic grocery, and a case each of her favorite white and red wines. Shopping for them would require a trip to New Leiden.

--There goes my morning.

--As if you have anything else to do.

--Actually, I have a more extensive social life here than I had in Denver. I lived for my work.

--A little trip to help me out will keep you out of trouble with all your lady friends.

--Speaking of trouble, what do you know about Harv Nielson? Seems he's missing. He's also in trouble at work. He's suspected of raiding the pharmacy stockroom.

--That's not a surprise. He helped Joe after his heart surgery and then at home after his stroke. That was the total of my involvement with him.

--I hear Lupe also helped and still lives in our house.

--She lived there once before for several months when Dad needed someone around to help. She didn't charge for her time, and I didn't charge her rent. Her mother's been cleaning for Joe since Mom died.

--That worked out. Speaking of the house, when do we get to meet with the lawyers and accountants? We need to get the trust figured out, as well as other aspects of the will.

--As you know, I can't leave Singapore. It'll be a while before we make any progress on that.

--Don't BS me. That's precisely the kind of exception the court will approve.

--I don't even know where to start.

--I'm sure you do, but you want to delay. That's okay. I'll get with Allen Zuverink. We'll hire a lawyer and get the ball rolling.

--Allen's not involved anymore.

--He's my advisor and will know where the bodies are buried. Oops, that's too literal a comparison for this situation. I was talking about financial, not human, bodies.

--Do what you must. I won't slow you down. I need whatever is left that I can cash out.

--I'll get your stuff. Can you email the shopping list? I can use the internet hookup in the office at River Haven. I'll see you sometime in the afternoon tomorrow.

Harry changed his shirt, picked out his tan blazer, and left for Dordrecht to pick up Irma. When they arrived at the Golden Age Brasserie with its Dutch East Indies motif, the host seated them at a table with a lake view. Harry ordered a medium-priced Napa Valley merlot from the wine list after Irma told the waiter she would like a glass of their house red. They were making pleasant small talk when the wine came. While Irma was hesitating over the menu, Harry suggested steak and lobster. Irma wondered whether she was that hungry, prompting Harry to ignore her doubt and order the steak and lobster for her. He picked out the prime rib for himself. Irma gave him a look, the meaning of which he could not decipher, but she didn't protest. They decided to skip appetizers. Harry restarted the conversation.

--I'd like to know more about your life. How and why did you come back to Dordrecht to live with Hank?

--That's a serious question for a first date if that's what this is.

--Let's not call this a date. That way, we can get to know each other without expectations and Hank and Uncle Ben as chaperones. The reality is that I'm in a place right now where I need to take a serious look at myself and what the rest of my life will turn out to be. You might be able to help. You've had a successful transition.

--Sometimes I wonder how successful it's been. Giving Janice a safe home has been my priority. That has worked out well, even though I am finding that raising teenagers is not easy. My job is also okay. I'm lucky to have it even though I've had to put aside the dreams of my younger self.

--Tell me about those dreams.

--I went into pre-med at U of M. Since elementary school, I had always wanted to be a pediatrician. I met my first husband, Richard, when I was a junior when he was in medical school. I was in love. We married, and I changed to nursing so I could make enough money for us to live on while he completed his medical training.

--He wasn't Julie's father?

--No. Richard found a better wife during his residency. I was no longer needed. I married Gordon too soon on the rebound. Another doc.

--Did he move on, too?

--No. He was a good guy, except when he drank. Which eventually became most of the time when he wasn't working.

--This time you left him?

--Ja. But not until the third time he hit me and the first time he threatened Janice. I put my tail between my legs and came back to Dordrecht.

--I'm sure that wasn't easy. I'm glad I didn't have to do it.

--I didn't have any choice. My mom was sick, so my dad sold the house and moved with her into assisted living. I wanted to help them. Hank was my salvation. He made no judgments. He gave Janice and me a home. Then he acted like we were doing him a favor by staying there. He knew what alcoholism could do to a person and the damage it caused to those living with him. The bottom line is that I'm thankful for my life's direction, even if I sometimes wonder what might have been.

--You're still young enough to try again.

--Not until Janice is through college. Then I will be too old.

The waiter brought their dinner.

--But that's enough about me. Tell me about your exciting life in the Rocky Mountains.

--Nothing was exciting about it. I was a decent student, but I had no career ambitions. Nothing caught my fancy. I cared more about sports and worked at it to keep my scholarship. After my sophomore year, when I hoped to become the first-string kicker, Western brought in an Argentine transfer from Purdue. He had a lot more length than I did. He later kicked for the Bears. As a third-year benchwarmer, I lost my scholarship. I dropped out to do six months of active duty in the National Guard and never went back to school. Joe got me a job with DeJong. Their open office system was beginning to launch, so there were opportunities for advancement. I quickly became the leader of the installation crew and was able to design layouts as well. My specialty was correcting the errors of architects and interior designers. After supervising a large installation in Denver, the Denver dealer offered me a job. I was happy to have a lifeline out of Dordrecht, away from Joe.

--Was Joe that bad?

--He wasn't quite like your second husband. Gordon, was it?

--Ja.

--He was always functional and not more violent than the average Dutch father of his generation. There was no way, though, that I could forgive him for the way he hurt my mom. I could never respect him or trust him. I was also angry with her for living with his behavior and always forgiving him. I needed to be somewhere else. When I moved to Denver, I felt like a giant weight was off my shoulders.

--What did he do, exactly?

--That's too long a story for now. Let's just say drinking, women, and gambling. Not to mention embezzling and connections to the Chicago mob.

--Really. Is that all? I want to hear the details someday. How did you meet your wife?

--We started dating two weeks after I got to Colorado. Some friends introduced me to Monica when she was a student at the University of Denver. I took courses at the CU-Denver campus part-time until I got too busy with work. Three years later, she was a middle school teacher, and we got married. The kids followed. Our lives followed the typical template of the era.

--How did your breakup happen?

--I changed. My partner, Craig Klein, was the office manager at DBP. We decided we could do better on our own. We formed a marketing company focused only on reselling office system components. He did the operations and finances. I did the design specifications and sales. We struggled at first, but our timing was perfect. We grew every year. We worked harder every year. I had no life except home and work. Even vacations were short. I was no longer the man she married, and she no longer had the life she wanted. She found it with someone else who valued her more than his career.

--Is that why you decided to sell?

--Yes and no. I recognized that the obsession with work had turned my life out of control, like riding a bike down a mountain road without brakes. I hadn't chosen it. It just happened to me. Craig and his son Eric wanted to go even faster and more extensive. I realized I wanted to get off. It was good timing. We worked a deal that, if I'm careful, takes care of my financial needs for the rest of my life, assuming Craig and Eric continue to be successful. I don't doubt that they will be.

--It sounds like you got off the bike without crashing.

--Ja. Now, I'm on a mountain road without knowing where I am or where I want to go.

Their meals arrived. They reverted to lighter conversation until the plates were empty except for half of the mashed potatoes on Irma's.

--I knew you could eat the whole thing.

--There is some left that I am not eating.

--We'll ask them to hold half the potatoes next time.

--Don't think I'm not thankful. This was a real treat. I owe you some more home cooking.

--You don't owe me a thing, but I won't turn it down. You do owe me some advice, though. Back to where we were. I was lost and directionless on a mountain road. What do I do?

--I can't answer that question., but I do have an idea. I attended Al-Anon meetings regularly for a couple of years. The best thing I took with me that proved helpful is an old, overused phrase in every other self-help book on the market. When you start working with it, you'll see it can work. It is: Be your own best friend.

--That's it?

--I know it sounds simplistic, but it has helped me. Think about it. Your best friend knows you. He likes you. He will tell you the truth about yourself and others. He has your best interests at heart, short- and long-term. He'll help you make decisions. You can be a friend to yourself better than anyone else can.

--Being a stoic, introverted Dutch guy, I could work with that. How do I start?

--You might want to start by walking down the mountain road until you come to a village where you find a place to eat and stay overnight.

--Like Dordrecht? Or Singapore?

--Either would work.

--Could my best friend be a 'she' instead of a 'he?'"

--Absolutely.

--And then?

--Sometimes you just *be*. It's like AA, one day at a time.

--Hey, this is good. It's better than Amy's guru, from my point of view. One day at a time. You've been waiting a while. Are you still just existing?

--Pretty much. That might be all there is for me. But I am open to more.

After Harry paid the bill and took Irma home, he asked if good friends could hug instead of shaking hands. They hugged, said good night, and wished each other a good Monday.

Chapter 13—Pete, Third Monday, 1998

Pete McAdams arrived on time Monday morning for a meeting at the courthouse with Sally Conners. When the receptionist said she was on her way into the office, he stood in the lobby waiting for her. He needed to meet with Sally to begin the process of impaneling a grand jury to investigate the killing of Doug Mason and his marijuana operation. He was expecting a report from John Newsome and Laura Denison later in the day, providing sufficient evidence. His meeting at dawn earlier on Monday morning at the DFG with Tim Harvison, the Michigan conservation agent for Singapore County, had provided more information, and the previous several days had given him an understanding of how events spanning twenty-five years could be interrelated.

———————

Late on the previous Wednesday afternoon, Pete had called Alex Vega again. He was anxious to get an expert examination of the Doug Mason shooting scene at the DFG in addition to his previous request to investigate Amy Berendts' farm. He also would need his help with a medical examiner since it would be a weeklong wait in a non-emergency case. He hoped that Alex could add the DFG and a medical examiner to the team scheduled for the next day on Thursday morning.

Pete and Alex had bonded during Pete's years in the state police because they shared their partial Indigenous heritage. Alex, however, traced his mother's family to the Pueblo people in Taos. His father's family considered themselves Spanish, having arrived in Sante Fe with the earliest settlers. He had come to Michigan after he met his wife, Sarah, when they were both stationed in Korea. She was an Army nurse who was born and raised in Lansing. Like Pete, Alex was in the military police. After finishing his criminology degree at Michigan State, he started a career in the state police, where he eventually rose to the rank of Captain.

Alex listened to his description of the shooting and thought it should be a priority. Fifteen minutes later, he called Pete back and said that John Newsome would be in Wakazoo around noon on Thursday with a medical investigator added to his team.

John arrived at Pete's office as scheduled late Thursday morning with Laura Denison, the medical examiner who would inspect the body on-site before it was brought to the county morgue. Their first stop was at McDonald's for double quarter-pounders at John's request. John was a fiftyish heavy-set man with red cheeks and a creative combover. He told Pete that this was his only chance for junk food without his wife and coworkers looking over his shoulder as he looked guiltily at Laura. While Pete gave them the background information about the situation at the DFG, John finished his burger before Pete started on his. Laura was a tall, slim, auburn-haired woman in her thirties. She finished half of her chicken tenders. Pete put his burger back in the wrapper. John and Laura followed him to the DFG, where they were greeted by Benny Ramirez, who had been protecting the site since midnight. He was taking an extra shift for overtime as usual. Benny carefully took off the tarp that was covering the body.

John and Laura unpacked their equipment and efficiently went to work. Pete watched while he finished his quarter-pounder. About half an hour later, the hearse arrived. At the same time, John called Pete over to point out highlights of what they found. Laura carefully guided him behind Doug's head, lying against the tree. Leaning to one side and turning his neck, Pete saw what they wanted him to see. A quarter inch of the narrow point of a rifle bullet sticking out of the back of Doug's skull. It was clear that Doug had been shot twice: once in the face with a shotgun and once through the brain with a rifle. John and Laura took another fifteen minutes to finish up. Laura planned to return on Monday for the official autopsy in the morgue. John would send a report to him the following week. When Pete asked John if the ponds should be drained to look for the rifle, John shrugged.

--It would be a lot of work. But you never know what you might find.

———————

On Saturday morning, while cleaning some brush on his mother's riverfront property, Pete found a blockage on Toussaint Creek, creating a new pond that could threaten the outbuildings. The jam was too big for muskrats. Looking more closely, he was only slightly surprised to spot a family of beavers. He had heard that they were beginning to return to their old habitat in southwestern Michigan. He realized he would need to do something about the beaver dam, but he was unsure what the wetlands regulations allowed. He radioed the office and asked Julie, the weekend dispatcher, to check his Rolodex for Tim Harvison's number. Pete had worked with him previously on several investigations involving water issues. Now, he had two new problems to discuss with him. He returned home and called Tim.

--Hi, Tim. This is Pete McAdams. I'm sorry to bother you on Saturday, but I want to ask you some questions.

--Hi, Pete. It's no problem if I don't have to get out of my pajamas. I'm waiting for Brenda to wake up and cook my Saturday breakfast.

--Say hi to Brenda for me. One of the questions is professional, and one is personal.

--Okay. Let me have them.

--First, I have a crime scene at the Dordrecht Fish and Game Club along the Singapore northwest of town. I've been trying to avoid draining the ponds to look for evidence, mainly a murder weapon, but I've decided that at least two must be drained. I will get a court order on Monday, but I wanted your input on the best way.

--I'm afraid I can't tell you anything without looking. It will be complicated.

--I assume that. Can you meet me early on Monday? This is a murder case. Time matters.

--Yeah, I can do that. I know where that property is. Seven-thirty?

--Great. Now, the next question. Unbelievably, I found a beaver dam on the creek on my mother's property. Have you seen beavers around here?

--No, but I've been expecting them. There have been quite a few sightings in this part of the state. It's the first one in our county that I have heard about.

--The problem is that the dam creates a pond threatening our outbuildings.

--The easy answer is that you are allowed to disturb the dam to restore the creek's flow. But you must preserve at least part of the dam so the beavers can rebuild. You will probably need to do that several times before they settle down. If they multiply, most will move on to a new home.

--It sounds like I have my work cut out for me.

--I'll stop and look after we meet at the club.

--I see this as a cool thing. We're trying to let our property revert to nature, the way it was before the French and English came to the area. But I'm conflicted because one of my ancestors was a French trapper who helped eliminate the beavers from the county.

--That's great. A county conservation and preservation group is working in some other areas. They would be a helpful resource.

--I'll take any help I can get. Why don't you bring their information with you on Monday?

--Will do. See you then.

———————

The early Monday morning meeting with Tim had gone smoothly. If Pete obtained a court order, the conservation department would not stand in the way of draining the ponds if a plan were in place to restore them as they exist. Tim thought they could use a cleanup. He also recommended a hydrology firm that could properly drain and restore the ponds. Now, Pete needed to convince Sally to get the court order and the Board of Supervisors to authorize the expense from county contingency funds. He had no room in his budget.

Sally arrived with an extra black coffee and bagel for Pete. They sat down as Sally started the conversation.

--What's up? You called this meeting.

--I have a few things. First, how was your weekend?

--Fabulous. Cynthia and I went to have dinner and see *Les Mis* in Chicago. Both were outstanding. It's like being in a different country.

--Welcome back to the boondocks. I've started a war with a beaver family trying to block our creek.

--For real beavers?

--Yup. And I'm not allowed to destroy their lodge. It looks like a long war. But back to business. What is the progress on the grand jury?

--Let's talk about that. What potential crime would we present? What's the evidence going to be? What witnesses can we call?

--The crime is murder. The state crime team and I agree that Doug Mason did not kill himself. We know he was involved with drugs. We use that as a motive. Some witnesses must be found, but we have Amy Berendts. Jonnie Van Orden is also available.

--Who is he?

--He set up Doug and Amy in business. He's also worked with Theo Bolinyk and the Montez family.

--Who are we looking to indict?

--All of them for various drug offenses unless they cooperate. We can indict a guy like Bolinyk, even if we haven't found him yet. The plan would be to work toward indicting someone for the murders.

--What else?

--We know this is a copycat of the George Bosch murder two decades ago. Some of the players are still around. We need to include the Bosch case in the investigation.

--That seems like an overreach.

--That's why I want to drain two ponds near the site where both bodies were found. We need to get a court order.

--More overreach.

--I don't think so. According to Laura Denison, the Lansing medical specialist who came to the site for the forensic examination, the shotgun found near Doug was not the weapon that killed him. Keep this detail confidential: she found a rifle bullet lodged in the back of his skull. That was the kill shot. The rifle it came from could be in one of the ponds. We found tracks on a direct line from the body to the pond. We should have a complete report later this week. Let me repeat. This information is confidential–me, you, and the judge. We can use it to test witnesses' knowledge and truthfulness.

--Okay, but we may need more than that for a court order.

--Yes, I know. I also went back over my notes for the Bosch shooting. Bernie Kerchovsky was our medical examiner back then. He wouldn't give an opinion on whether the rifle on Bosch's lap was the one that killed him. I found shotgun damage to a tree beyond the body. So, there were at least two shots. I also found areas around both ponds with recent heavy foot traffic.

--That is something. I'll run all this by the judge. Can you put this in a report? If I can get the okay to impanel the grand jury, then we should be able to get the order to drain the ponds to look for the disposed weapons.

--I already have a draft. Is tomorrow at noon soon enough?

--Yes. I'll schedule some time with Judge Eubanks for the afternoon.

--One more thing. I read over my 1972 interview with Joe Berendts that I was able to complete before Sam and Jimmy forced me off the case. At one point, Joe dared me by suggesting I look in the ponds for more bodies. I took it as sarcasm, trying to send me down to a dead end. Rereading it now, I can see that he was trying to tell me something without incriminating himself with us or exposing himself to retaliation from his mob bosses. If he were innocent, he wouldn't have been so secretive. He was afraid of something or someone.

--That's an interesting angle. I'll have to think about how we could use it. How will you pay for the draining and refilling?

--I'm going to the state first. They are part of the investigation. Otherwise, I'll need to go to the board. I have no air left in my budget.

--Good luck with that.

--My next worry is my meeting with Amy Berendts and Juanita. I want to break her down so she will cooperate with me. They're both tough nuts. What can I offer her?

--Goodwill at this point. You could hint about a grand jury investigation they could get ahead of, but don't make it definite.

--Okay, that's something. I'll get that report to you. I know you can work your magic with the judge.

———————

Pete returned to his office with an hour to spare before meeting with Amy and Juanita. He brought his draft report that he had printed the night before from his desktop at home and gave it to his office manager, Priscilla Morrison, asking her to clean it up and put it in the proper format for Sally to give to Judge Eubanks. On the way to his office, he checked in with Brian Chatfield to see if there were any pressing issues he needed to deal with. Brian said it was a quiet day with nothing he could not handle himself. He did remind Pete about his four o'clock interview with a new patrol squad candidate. Pete acknowledged the reminder with a nod, said his good mornings to the office staff, and took his messages from Mary Lu Bowling while asking her to hold his calls before closing the door and sitting down to plan his interview with Amy and his approach to the investigation of the DFG shootings.

Brian, Priscilla, and Mary Lu, along with the Manager of Corrections, Lt. Neil Lamont, formed Pete's core management team. When he took over the department almost three years earlier, he soon replaced or demoted eight senior staff members Jimmy Dickerson had left behind. He brought Brian back as Captain and Chief Deputy to supervise all uniformed deputies. Brian returned from Plaintown, where he had become the Chief of Police after leaving the Singapore Sheriff's Department at the same time that Pete had left more than twenty years earlier. Pete recruited Priscilla and Mary Lu, both administrative supervisors whom he had worked with in the Lansing headquarters of the Michigan State Police. Neil, who had been in management at the Michigan State Prison in Jackson, was Pete's fellow student and teammate at Wakazoo

High School. All four were eager to return to their hometown to work for Pete. It helped that they were able to double dip after taking early retirement from their earlier positions.

Grover Richards, the head of the five-person detective bureau, was the only supervisor connected to the old regime. Thus far, he had not given Pete a reason to fire him with cause, but neither had he earned Pete's trust. Having good reason to believe that Grover still had connections to Jimmy and Sam, Pete kept Grover under his direct supervision. Pete kept the current investigation into the Dordrecht shootings in his own hands. Grover and his crew could continue to deal with lesser crime in other parts of the county.

Pete realized he would need to talk with Charley Vredevelde about his progress in scheduling interviews with Jonnie Van Orden and Lupe Rios, Nick Montez's sister. He called Charley at the Middleburg branch office of the Nederland County Sheriff.

--Hi, Pete. How was your weekend?

--It's a long story involving beavers.

--For real beavers?

--Yup. I'm pressed for time here. I'm meeting with Amy Berendts and her lawyer in a few minutes.

--I hear she has a hotshot girl who works with Reggie Robinson.

--Yup. I hoped you had something to tell me about Lupe Rios and Jonnie Van Orden.

--Nothing of note. I've already called them again this morning. They are both willing to talk with us but want to lawyer up. I asked them to do that quickly so we could talk. This is a murder investigation, after all.

--Okay. I'm busy this week, but my schedule can be flexible. Any morning would work.

--I've had another person of interest come up.

--Who would that be?

--A nurse at the rehab center here named Harv Nielson. He is under investigation for raiding the medicine cabinet there. Along with Nick and Lupe, he helped Amy take care of Joe. Like a lot of other folks in this case, he has disappeared.

--Thanks for the heads up. I could use that to get Amy to loosen up and tell us something.

--I'm glad to help. I'll call you when I hear from Jonnie or Lupe.

When he hung up the phone, Mary Lu knocked on his door to tell him that Amy and Juanita had arrived.

As he walked into the small conference room, Pete felt the glare of Juanita Jones as she shifted the coffee mug that Mary Lu had just brought her.

--Sheriff McAdams, I want to start by expressing my reservations about the direction of your investigation, specifically about my client. We have tried cooperating with the investigation, but here we are again. If we are here to give you the same answers to the same questions we previously answered to the best of our abilities, it will begin to feel like harassment. I hope you have a different line of questioning.

Pete took a sip from his mug. Juanita's use of the British pronunciation of 'harassment' seemed to give extra weight to her objection.

--I will ask some follow-up questions related to earlier interviews. I am also open to any suggestions you have for a new direction for the investigation. I assure you that I have no intent to harass her.

--Thank you. What can Amy help with today?

--First, a question for you, Amy. Have you learned anything new about the whereabouts of Theo Bolynik?

--No.

--Nick Montez?

--No.

--We have a new person of interest who I believe you know: Harv Nielson. Would you describe your relationship?

--My brother told me about Harv stealing pills where he works. I know him because he helped care for my dad in the rehab center and later at home.

--He is wanted for questioning about missing medications at the Middleburg facility where he was working. Do you have any knowledge of his involvement in the missing medications?

Amy looked at Juanita, who stood up and guided her to a corner of the room, where they whispered for less than a minute and returned to the table.

--The only thing I know is what Doug told me. He said several times that he was trading pot for pills with Harv. He didn't say where Harv was getting the pills.

--Do you know where he might be hiding out?

--Not really. Saginaw is his hometown. He might have gone back there.

--Thank you for that information. I'll pass it on to the Nederland County Sheriff's office. They are handling the investigation in Middleburg. They may want to talk to you.

--They know where to find me. I can't go anywhere.

--Juanita, you questioned the direction of our investigation. What direction are you objecting to?

--You keep putting Amy at the center of it. She is on the periphery. It's time you focus elsewhere.

--Like where?

--I've been looking at the old case files. George Bosch was thought to be tied up with Chicago organized crime figures. Currently, so is Theo Bolynik. That direction needs to be looked at.

--Do you know anything about that, Amy?

--I know my dad had gambling debts owed to what he called 'the mob.' Years ago, they were rumored to run games in Dordrecht above Van Heitsma's bowling alley. I think Van Heitsma has dementia. But John Visser is still around. He's the Honda dealer in Middleburg now. An offhand remark my dad made while we were talking about a year ago came back to me. He said that he and Visser were damn lucky they didn't get caught up in the Van Klompenberg deal because they had stopped driving cars for him a few months before he got caught.

--That was the stolen car scam back in the seventies.

--Ja. I remember, too, that Joe was involved with Theo in some suspicious deals when we first met. Theo routinely hinted at his connections to people he was afraid of. Theo and Doug must have been getting money and support from somewhere.

--That's true. What else?

--I've just had a thought. You should check out Lydia, Dad's girlfriend. He said several times that his relationship with her kept the mob from killing him. She had connections.

--Now, that's something new. What's her last name? Where is she now?

--She's in Miami. Her first husband's family owns a restaurant there and in Chicago. Triandos was their name. They have a son named Tony. He's bad news. I can't remember her second husband's last name, though. But she'll be easy to find.

I have her info at home because she is still living in what is now my condominium in Miami. She's contesting my dad's will, claiming he left it to her. She also comes to Singapore sometimes. She stays in her dad's boat, which my dad described as a large cabin cruiser. He used to meet her there. It is more like a small yacht. I bet she'll be coming soon to make her case.

--Okay. Get whatever you have to me, and I'll look at that angle.

Juanita stood up to leave but then sat back down.

--I think it's time to get the restrictions lifted on Amy's freedom to travel. If she is cooperating and not a suspect in the more serious charges in this case, they seem harsh.

--I'll talk to Sally, but I think she and the judge will stick with them. Amy has plenty of freedom if she gets the court's permission.

--And one more thing, another direction that needs to be checked out. What about the two unidentified Mexicans who were picked up? Were they part of the picture?

--We are working on them. ICE has them on hold and is trying to find connections for us, but it's been a dead end.

--Good luck with all that. I must let you know that this meeting was a complete waste of time. You're lucky we are due to meet next with the court clerk. Otherwise, I would be charging your department my time and travel.

Pete went back to his office after Amy and Juanita left. The first person he wanted to talk to was Jimmy Dickerson. He called the assisted living facility near the county hospital, where Pete knew he was now living. Jimmy developed emphysema while still the sheriff before Pete forced him to retire. It was now complicated by a severe stroke that partially paralyzed his left extremities. The operator connected him with Jimmy's on-site caseworker, who suggested that Pete stop by between three and four when Jimmy usually went to the lounge after his afternoon nap.

Needing to get back to his everyday issues, he called Brian, Priscilla, and Mary Lu into his office to go over the duty rosters for the week and issues that he would need to deal with himself. Wanting to free himself to concentrate on what he was now calling the DFG cases, he delegated everything, giving the administrative issues to Priscilla, adding the detective bureau to Brian's responsibilities, and asking Mary Lu to cancel or postpone anything on his calendar that was not essential.

Mary Lu reminded him that Mike had an invitational cross-country meet at Middleburg Christian High on Tuesday and that Star's next volleyball match was Thursday at the Wakazoo High gym. Pete figured he could still make those while making the travel time pay by scheduling early afternoon meetings in Middleburg with the people involved in the DFG cases. She also reminded him that he would be expected to attend a County Board of Supervisors budget committee meeting on Tuesday night. Pete had forgotten but realized it would be one thing he would not want to miss.

When the meeting was nearly finished, Pete looked at his security camera monitor behind his desk. He noticed Harry Berendts and Larry Vandevoss approaching the reception counter. Pete waited for reception to call Mary Lu's desk. He told her to go to her desk, pick up the call, and reply with instructions for Harry and Larry to wait fifteen minutes. He reviewed some final details with Brian on scheduling and asked

Priscilla to get with accounting to prepare the latest year-to-date, actual-versus-plan budget report for him, hoping it was good news. He would need it when he brought up the extra expense to drain the ponds at the Dordrecht property. When they left, he busied himself with minutiae. Remembering a detail that he had forgotten, he went into Brian's office to remind him to check for any response to the stolen vehicle alert they had sent for Doug's pickup. Deciding that he had made them wait long enough, he finally went to reception to meet Harry and Larry.

--Good morning, gentlemen. What brings you here today? Good news, I hope.

Harry shook hands and answered while Larry gave a casual salute behind him.

--We do have some news. Some of it may even be good news. We also have questions. We want to buy you lunch and update each other.

--I have some questions for you, too. Lunch sounds good. There's a decent place around the corner, but my policy is to go Dutch...uh, if you pardon the expression.

Harry shook his head and replied.

--Not a problem. It's a myth created by an English king—both the name and the implication. It's our contribution to the English language.

While walking to the Wakazoo Grill during a dry spell in a morning of intermittent light rain, Pete pointed out a historic brick building next to the Sheriff Department.

--That's where the old Sheriff's office and jail used to be. It was built in 1904. Our historical society is working to turn it into a museum. Too bad it became too small. Our building is now thirty years old and is already getting crowded. I doubt anyone will want to bother preserving it when we grow out of it. The new jail and the courthouse are over there across the street.

--You should show me your offices, Sheriff. I could design a layout using refurbished components that would allow you to use your space better.

--Get in line. The guys from DeJong have already been working on it. They built a new plant just outside of town, you know. The county gave them a big tax write-off to bring jobs here.

--Better here than Mexico or off-shore.

As they walked further, Peter pointed out the downtown area, parts of which looked no different than they had appeared in the 1930s.

--I know it's not been maintained or updated like Middleburg or Dordrecht, but we are working on it. We don't have the tax revenue that Nederland County has.

Larry smirked and commented.

--We Dutch like our cows—beef, dairy, or cash.

Harry and Pete shook their heads in disgust as they entered the grill. They each ordered the King Burger Platter on Pete's recommendation.

Harry replied when Pete asked:

--Well, what do you have for me?

--I want you to know that I've involved myself in this for only one reason: to keep my sister out of jail. I'm not even sure why it's important to me. I could make the case that she deserves it, I guess. However, she might have made different choices if I had not chosen to be the absentee little brother. Juanita called me on my Nokia just as we arrived. We met in the parking lot in the next block. She said that she and Amy had taken the approach of encouraging you to look in different directions. Larry has some information about that. Larry?

--We've heard you plan to interview Jonnie Van Orden and Lupe Rios. We talked to Jonnie yesterday. Harry has also spoken with Lupe. You will value their input. Both are on the fringe of your investigation. Both could be indicted for something, so they have reasons to cooperate. However, considering Doug's death, they have reasons not to be seen working with you. You'll need to decide how to make them feel safe.

--You're right about that. I may alter my approach to them. What else?

--I've been thinking about Joe, George Bosch's death, and the influential Dordrecht guys involved in the Monday night club in Dordrecht. The rumor was that an Italian guy from Chicago had taken over, expanding the games, the alcohol, the girls, and the clientele. Amy just confirmed that for me. She bartended sometimes during the transition. There was a guy named Sal. When George was killed, this Sal guy disappeared, and the Monday night club was shut down.

--Sal? Last name?

--Don't know.

Larry gathered his thoughts and continued.

--This morning, I went to see Gordie Van Klompenburg. He still spends time at the salvage yard, which his sons run now. I asked him what he knew about the Chicago mob types involved in his stolen car deals. He looked at me as if I were ridiculous. He is still too scared to talk. But he did have an axe to grind. Joe's death triggered his anger again at being the only one who served time. He pled guilty to shorten his sentence but passed up the opportunity to avoid jail entirely. He valued his life too much to give up his Chicago partners. He claimed not to know where the cars came from or where they went. Nameless and varied drivers dropped them off and picked them up. He claims that he never even saw them. He got paid with a cash bag stashed in the cars. But we know three guys who drove: Joe and the Visser brothers, John and Jim.

--The Honda dealers?

--Ja. John was in used cars back then, and Jim, who had been friends with Joe since grade school, sold Honda motorcycles. Jim died of colon cancer two years ago. John still runs the dealership with his son and two nephews.

--I need to shop for a Honda.

--I already did. He told me to go to hell. That was not nice for a CR elder.

--CR?

--Christian Reformed Church. Big supporter of Middleburg Christian Schools. He paid for the field and bleachers when they added football a few years ago.

--My son is running in a cross-country invitational there tomorrow. It starts and ends on the field. I'll have to thank him for his contribution.

--Anything else?

--Nah, that's all for now.

--Harry?

--I have something just as interesting to tell you. But please tell me first what you can do to help Amy.

--It's what she can do to help herself. Just help us find Theo. That might be enough for Sally to not press for jail time.

--Okay, that sounds fair. I got a call this morning from Hank Plagmeyer, an old friend of Joe's. His daughter works at the Middleburg rehab and nursing facility. Are you looking for Harv Nielsen?

--Yes. Does Hank know where he is?

--No. But he does know who he is.

--And who would that be?

--The grandson of George Bosch. His mother was George Bosch's daughter with his first wife. They lived and stayed in Saginaw. George came to Dordrecht after their divorce, along with his son, Butch. In my mind, that could explain the copycat suicide attempt.

--I need to find out more about this guy. He also worked for Amy, taking care of your dad. That's another connection she could help with. Do you think she knew about Nielson's family connection to George Bosch?

--I doubt it. Hank made the connection because he knows everybody and everything that has happened in Dordrecht over the last eighty years. But he doesn't gossip. He only told me because he knows it could be critical to the case.

--Okay, I appreciate your input, gentlemen. I am not focused on any single direction. There are a lot of questions and a lot of loose threads. I'm checking out every angle.

Larry looked at Pete with a suspicious expression.

--I'm glad to hear that. I've been concerned that you would try to score some points against the Dutch folk who took land from your ancestors.

Pete answered with a wry smile.

--They didn't take the land. They just bought stolen land for a dollar per acre from the US government that had already stolen it from us. So did Pierre Toussaint, my French three-greats-grandfather. He bought a whole section. That's why most of my family stayed here instead of going to the Leelanau with Chief Peter Wakazoo, my three-greats-grandfather on my mother's other side. If our oral history is correct, my Odawa ancestors stole western Michigan from another native tribe, the Mascoutan, after the Iroquois chased the Odawa out of Canada. With the help of my father's tribe, the Pottawatomi, and iron knives bought from the French, they killed most of them and chased a remnant to the western plains. My interest is in getting the whole story told. The Odawa tribe was fierce and significant. They helped the Ojibwe with their hunting ground fights against the Dakota Sioux. They traded from Montreal to Green Bay. Their warriors took their canoes to upstate New York to help win a battle for the French against the English. It took two centuries for the French, English, and Americans to beat us. We were and are again becoming a proud people, not the ragtag stragglers that the Dutch met when they arrived. It took them little time to send the last three hundred north to the reservation.

--Oops, I'm sorry, I think I hit a sore spot again.

--Not at all. I enjoy talking about it. I could go on for hours. But I still have a sore spot about that fake Indian chant your fans used to aim at me. I think I could still recite it. I took it personally.

Harry grimaced.

--That was inexcusable, but it was aimed at every opponent, not only you.

--I think they were more vehement when I was the target.

--That was mainly because you were the best we played against.

--That's a diplomatic answer. I'll accept it as an apology. My wife would not be as accommodating. You should listen to her talk about her Ojibwe nation and the abuse they lived through.

But back to Amy. I'll treat her like everyone else. I'll let the facts determine the outcome.

Harry cut back in.

--I'm glad you have an open mind. I'll talk to Amy again to see if she can give me any further details she may have forgotten or didn't think were important.

--Let me know if you come across anything new. I have a lot to work on. We'll know a lot more by the end of the week.

Their King Hamburger plates came. They shared stories about their high school and college sports memories. They exchanged information about their kids. After Harry and Larry said their goodbyes, Pete returned to the Sheriff Department, where Priscilla gave him the latest budget numbers. He took it into his office to examine the details. Halfway through, a few line items caught his attention. There was some good news for him to report to the board. He had postponed some purchases that were not needed until later, cutting his year-to-date deficit in half. He knew that would not be enough to get approval for the funds to drain the ponds, but it would help. He reviewed more of the report and found potential cuts that would bring him in line before the end of the year. It would be essential to show fiscal responsibility if he wanted the board to seriously consider the increase he planned to ask for in the budget for the next fiscal year.

A single line item jumped out at him. The Dive, Rescue, and Recovery team he was expanding and professionalizing had taken longer to come together than he had expected. The result was an almost $50,000 surplus, most of which would not be spent by the end of the year. His mind quickly made the connection. Draining the ponds could be made to fit in the Dive, Rescue, and Recovery category. At least it involved water. He called Tim Harvison and left a message when he got the machine, telling Tim that he had some funds that could pay for the draining and refilling. He asked Tim to get the bid as soon as possible and get the contractor to commit to completing the draining by the end of the week. He spent another hour making notes for a report to add to his budget presentation. He gave the copy and notes to Priscilla before heading out to meet Jimmy Dickerson.

Just as he was at the exit door, he heard Mary Lu call him. He stopped and went back in. She had Amy Berendts on the line. She had had another break-in at the store and caught the culprit—Nick Montez. Pete told her he would immediately send Brian Chatfield and a patrol car and follow as soon as possible. He had an appointment but would be back in the office around 5:00. He found Brian, updated him, and went to see Jimmy.

———————

The assisted living building where Jimmy was living was just a three-block walk from the sheriff's office. It was attached to a skilled nursing and memory care facility across a parking lot from an affordable senior independent living building. The whole complex was a three-year-old project funded by a HUD grant with matching state funds. It was not luxurious but supplied a clean and safe environment for more than two hundred of the county's less affluent senior citizens. The reception desk was ready for Pete and pointed to the dayroom where Jimmy was waiting. He was thinner and sitting less upright in his wheelchair than the last time Pete had seen him a few months prior when he was still living at home.

--Hey, Jimmy. How are you getting along? Are they treating you alright?

--I can't complain about the treatment. This is a much better place than where my wife Louisa stayed when she got sick a few years ago. It seems like everything is all downhill now, though. At my age and condition, things don't get better.

--I'm glad Wakazoo finally got a place like this. It was desperately needed.

--How about you? How do you like my old office?

--I wish I could spend less time sitting in it. I have a tough time seeing enough of my family. And I sometimes miss being out in the field.

--So, is this a social visit, or do I need a lawyer?

--It's business. But you don't need a lawyer. I'm looking for background.

--I hear you have another body at the DFG.

--Yeah. It looks like a copycat of the first one. This time, there are drugs involved.

--What makes you think I can help?

--We let you off easy last time to get you to retire. I need to know what you know about those underground social clubs you allowed to thrive. We shut them down, but the Chicago folks may be back, this time as marijuana farm financiers and who knows what else.

--Why would I help you now?

--You might like to even the score. You're sitting here being old, sick, and broke while the other guys took all the money.

--I made plenty. I liked to gamble. I lost most of the time. Is it their fault I only have Social Security and a crummy pension left?

--No, that's on you. But you could do the right thing.

--Look, Pete. I don't know as much as you think I do. If you tell me what you are looking for, I'll help if I can.

--I'm looking for organized crime types from out of town who may still be in our county.

--I'm out of the game. I don't know what's happening today. I was also kept in the dark about many things in the past.

--What about Sam Morgan? Is he still in the game? What does he know?

--He still has a hand in. He knows more than I do.

--How do I get him to talk to me?

--You'd need some heavy-duty leverage.

--I've decided to drain the ponds closest to where George Bosch's body was found. Would I find any leverage?

--It could be worth your time and money to try that.

--Someone told me that Joe Berendts, who I thought was holding back on what he knew back then, had a girlfriend connected to crime bosses. She has a boat in Singapore. Would she be worth my time?

--I know her. Lydia, her name was. She came to the clubs in Singapore and South Wakazoo now and then. Sometimes with Joe. The Chicago guys treated her with respect, so she had connections with someone important.

--Do you know Theo Bolynik? Was he ever around?

--Sure. He acted like he was someone important. It seemed to me he was all show.

--Do you know where he is now?

--No. He was from New Leiden. He talked a lot about going to Miami and the Caribbean.

--Were drugs available at the clubs? That's what Bolynik went to prison for.

--Not in the clubs. But connections were being made. The transactions took place somewhere else.

--Like where?

--That's a question for Sam and Theo. I didn't get involved with that.

--Were you involved in the stolen car deal with Van Klompenberg?

--Not directly. Some of the Chicago guys were complaining when it was exposed. They were worried that their clubs would be compromised. But after the threat died down, we continued until you shut us down.

--It wasn't me. It was the state police from the Lansing head office and the state PA.

--You were in the middle of it. I'm surprised you're still alive.

--They decided to cut their losses.

--Be careful. You're stirring things up again.

--I'm always careful. Has Grover been here to see you lately?

--Nah. Is he still the lead detective?

--So far. Do you know anything that would help me change that?

--Nah. He's a good guy. He'll do what you tell him.

After Pete said goodbye to Jimmy and returned to his office, he found that Nick Montez was already booked and waiting for his lawyer. He was just in time to join Brian for the interview with the traffic patrol prospect. He was a patrol officer from Decatur, a small town fifty miles south, who wanted to move to a more professional department. At the end of the interview, feeling like this prospect would work out, he let Brian discuss the rest of the hiring process.

Pete found the day shift getting ready to leave. He told Priscilla he would be in the office early the next morning but planned to be out most of the day and that he would call in for messages or be available on the radio. As soon as he got to his desk, he called Sally Conners. She had left for the day, but he left a message letting her know that the stakes were raised because of his interview with Jimmy, making the court order to drain the ponds a top priority. He then called John Baker, the sergeant in charge of the harbor patrol unit in Singapore. John answered quickly. When Pete asked if he was familiar with a miniyacht owned by a Chicago father and daughter, he said that there was one that he knew of that fit the description. It was the harbor's largest boat, which was docked at the yacht club in the summer. He thought it went to Florida in the winter. Pete asked John to meet him at the yacht club office at nine the following day.

As he hung up the phone with John, Brian returned to the office with another announcement. Doug Mason's pickup had been found in Saginaw.

--Saginaw? Isn't that where Harv Nielson is from?

--Is he?

--That's what Harry Berendts told me.

--What should we do now?

--I'll need you to handle it with the state police tomorrow. They'll need forensics to go over the pickup. They'll need to impound it and find a place to store it. We'll need them to help us find out more about this guy. Let me know if they will jump on this. If they drag their feet, we'll need to pull some strings in Lansing to get them to move. I'll call Harry's friend Larry. He's only been retired a little while. He may know someone there that would help us move things along.

--Okay. I'm on it.

--Hold on. Where are we with Montez?

--He's in for the night. His sister called. He has a Legal Aid lawyer coming to see him tomorrow. She didn't trust our public defenders. She said she would make bail tomorrow.

--We only have a simple B & E charge right now. But he could be a material witness to a drug conspiracy and murder, too. He's also a flight risk. The court may go along with a high bail amount. That may get him talking. It looks like we'll have a busy day tomorrow. I'm going home to clear my mind.

After a family supper, Pete watched the last half of Monday Night Football with Mike before going to his home office. He quickly listed his tasks already planned for the next day. He often wrote down a quick list before he turned in for the night. He found it helped him sleep better by putting it on paper so he would not worry about things during the night. He knew the list would be waiting for him in the morning.

<u>Tuesday:</u>

- Meet John Baker at the yacht club. Check out Lydia Triandos
- Interview Nick Montez with his lawyer
- Check on the pond draining
- Interview Jonnie Van Orden and Lupe Rios with Charlie in Middleburg
- Check out John Visser. Visit him in Middleburg
- Mike's cross-country meet
- Budget Meeting

Chapter 14—Amy, Third Monday, 1998

Amy walked back into her condo after Juanita had dropped her off following the meeting with the county clerk in Wakazoo. Juanita had encouraged her to come up with anything new that she could offer Sally and Pete to keep her from being indicted. Anything new about Theo would be helpful. Amy was unsure that disclosing everything she knew about Theo would be safe. He had often hinted that he had friends who would not appreciate someone who talked. During the past week, she had called him several times at the last number she had used the week before, but there was no answer. She kept hoping that he would call her.

Gerrit was not in the house. He was getting groceries while Amy went to the interview with Juanita. She was surprised at how domesticated they had become in just a few days. Gerrit closed the resort for the winter and planned to use the time as a sabbatical. That meant he would be free to stay with Amy until she no longer felt the fear of being alone. Even though they had known each other for two decades and had several periods of intimacy, they had never shared the same living space. Now, she realized that being with him full-time differed from being just a student or occasional lover. The peace and calm she felt when with him seemed less euphoric but more permanent. She found herself hoping that he would stay longer than planned.

She checked the machine for messages. There was still nothing from Theo. There was a message that Harry had left before they had met in the Wakazoo parking lot. One of his issues was the settlement of Joe's estate. They had not talked about it in front of Juanita and Larry. She knew that Harry was right about it being in her interest to get things settled soon. She would need cash, and if things went the wrong way with the grand jury, she would be free from other distractions if the estate issues were out of the way.

The following message was from Bill Snyder, asking her to make an appointment to see him on Wednesday or Thursday. He had some documents that needed her signature. Also, he wanted to share his latest ideas with her.

Before she called Bill back, she called Harry at River Haven and was patched to his room.

--This is Harry Berendts.

--Hi, Harry. It's Amy. I'm glad I got you.

--What's up?

--Bill Snyder can see us on Wednesday or Thursday so we can review Dad's finances. What would work for you?

--I can do Wednesday, anytime. Just let me know. Do you want to ride together?

--No, I want to tie in other appointments while there.

--Does that mean I don't need to get your stuff in New Leiden?

--Ja. I'll get Gerrit to go with me on Wednesday. He likes to shop for organic groceries. I can stop for the other stuff after my appointments.

--Okay. That's a relief. I was about to go. It sounds like you and Gerrit are becoming close. How long can he stay?

--We are getting along great. He has a break for a couple of weeks. He plans to go to a retreat in New Mexico next month. He says he needs to get rejuvenated. I wish I could go with him.

--If we could clean up this mess, you would be free to go anywhere.

--I doubt anything will happen that fast. How was your meeting with Pete McAdams?

--We opened his mind a little bit. At least he said he would investigate other possibilities. He's hung up on Theo, though. He's not ready to let you off the hook unless you can give him something. How did your meeting go?

--I don't have anything new. Theo has already been sent to prison once. I've had nothing to do with him since.

--Then all we can hope for is that Pete will find another direction that leads to something that will take the pressure off you.

--There's a lot for him to find, I think. I see Gerrit coming in, so I'll let you go. I'll call Bill and let you know the time on Wednesday.

Amy went to open the kitchen door from the garage to let Gerrit in.

--Did you find what you wanted?

--Just enough for a few days. There were almost no natural or organic options. The root vegetables looked okay. Anything green was questionable. I got some bulk beans we'll need to cook. I got lots of fruit. This is a difficult place to be vegan.

--Tell me about it. It's not so bad in the summer. There's lots of local produce. I'm going to New Leiden on Wednesday.

You could come along to fill up on stuff at the new organic and natural store that opened last year.

--That sounds necessary if you want me to stay for a while.

--I want you to stay for as long as you can. Can you postpone your stay at the retreat? I might be free when this bullshit is over with. Then I could go with you.

--I would like that. I'm surprised you'd want to go.

--I am, too. I guess I'm getting used to being with you. It feels good.

--In that case, I'll put it off until spring. It's a primitive place and too cold for me in the winter. I could still be back in Harbor Springs right after Easter.

--I thought you needed to rejuvenate.

--I'm doing some of that here with you.

--Okay, I'm glad our paths are joining. Let's enjoy it while it lasts.

--For now, let me put these things away. Then I'll make us some lunch.

--Thanks. I'm starving. I'll make some calls to set up my Wednesday in New Leiden.

Amy made her calls and made appointments with the various receptionists for Wednesday. She would repeat the schedule she had followed the previous Wednesday: Juanita, Lenny Caputo, Carl Zandstra, and Stephanie if she had time.

Gerrit's lunch was delicious, whether with organic ingredients or not. They followed with an hour-long yoga session and then made love for the first time since he had arrived in Singapore. It was not as physically passionate as Amy was used to with many of her partners, but it felt as if her spiritual essence became involved. Rather than feeling drained afterward, she was energized. Even the high she experienced in the kitchen, as they shared her inhaler with some tea on the side, was mellower, less an escape than a unique experience of the present. The phone ringing broke her mood. She went back to the bedroom to answer. She felt another jolt when she heard Theo's voice.

--So, how was your time in lockup?

--Wonderful. I had two days to work on my poses. It helped get me centered.

--What happened to Doug? Who killed him?

--They don't know. You're one of the suspects.

--I had nothing against him. Plus, I'm too far away.

--He knew stuff about you. He would have easily caved under the pressure.

--They need to look somewhere else. Doug knew what would happen if he turned on me. Did all that yoga help you find my money?

--Bill has twenty thousand freed up for you. But I don't know how I could get it to you.

--I don't know, either. I assume you're being watched, both physically and electronically. How about your brother? He could carry some cash.

--Harry? I don't think he would want to be involved. He's trying to help me but won't cross the line and do something illegal.

--I guess I'll need someone to get it to me. Just get the cash and be ready.

--I'll do that. I'm seeing Bill on Wednesday. I'll have it ready.

--When do I get the rest of my ninety thousand? How do I know you'll come through?

--I need to sell the farm, but that won't happen until this case ends. I'll also be in a fight with Lydia for the condominium in Miami. My lawyers tell me that my mom's trust, including the Dordrecht house, is unbreakable. It all goes to Harry's kids. I'm not trying to piss you off or renege on what I owe you. You need to be patient.

--I won't be patient forever. I need to cut this short. I'll call you back when I have found someone to pick up the payment.

Amy was surprised that Theo had stayed on the line and said as much as he had. She assumed her phone was being bugged for incoming and outgoing numbers, but he must be confident that his number and location were masked. She decided to ask Juanita if she should reveal Theo's call to Sheriff McAdams. He would know that she had an unidentifiable call and confront her with it. She would only need to say that he was asking her for money.

She called Juanita again. She was still not available. The receptionist said she would be back in the office at the end of the day. Carl Zandstra called as soon as she hung up.

--Hi, Amy. I wanted to let you know I found an attorney in Miami. His name is Grady Hutchinson. He did not ask for a retainer upfront. He quickly checked and found only Joe's name on the deed. There were no other claims. That means that unless Lydia has a signed document dated after Joe's last will that we have in our possession, she does not have a credible claim that the condo belongs to her.

--What does that mean? What is our next step?

--We sit pat until she does something official. At this point, she is just blowing smoke.

--When can I take possession?

--As Joe's appointed personal representative, you have management power now. You can't sell it until probate closes.

--How long does that take?

--That's the other reason I'm calling.

Peter just called me. The first hearing is scheduled for three weeks from tomorrow.

--Who is Peter?

--Peter Van Velzen. He's my brother-in-law, remember. The probate specialist. You'll be getting a notice and will need to attend. He'll be there with you. After that, it will be at least six months, assuming no one is contesting.

--Fuck that! Lydia gets to stay there while we sit and wait.

--Not necessarily. You are the de facto manager of the property. You can rent it to her or tell her to leave.

--How do I do that?

--Eviction is always tricky. Grady and I think it would be best to get her to lease it. We'll send her a lease agreement and give her a choice: Sign the lease and pay the deposit along with the first and last month's payment, or vacate within thirty days. If she chooses to do neither, we'll start eviction proceedings.

--Let's start doing that right away, okay? It will feel good to be doing something.

--I'm on it.

Amy had barely hung up when the phone rang again.

--This is Juanita, Amy. Did you call me?

--I did. Can we talk on the phone?

--It's okay. Since you were arrested, they can't listen in. If the grand jury is impaneled, they could get your records and see your calls and for how long and to which number you were connected.

--That's why I'm calling. Guess who called me?

--Must be Theo.

--How did you know?

--He's the only one you would call me about.

--Here's my question. Should I tell Sheriff McAdams about it? What if they find out later that I didn't inform them?

--It wouldn't look good, but it would not be anything they could use against you. From what I've learned about Theo, he probably disguised his number anyway. But maybe we can use this to gain some favor with Sally and Pete. What did you talk about?

--He wants some money he thinks I owe him. I told him I was broke. He threatened to send some goons to collect. I think I bought some time by telling him I would be selling the farm and my dad's condo and would be able to pay him.

--Okay. I want to run this by Reggie. We must ensure we will gain some favor and not just more trouble for you. I see you made an appointment for Wednesday. We'll talk more then.

Amy's answering machine had taken a call while she and Juanita were talking. The message was from the alarm company asking about an entry into her store, asking if they should notify the police. She dialed right back. They informed her that the back door had been opened and no entry code had been entered. Amy had reached them before they called the police. She told them that she was expecting a delivery and would be there shortly. Her employee could have failed to lock the back door. As she ran out, she told Gerrit something had come up at the store. She was not sure why she did not want the police to come. Her first feeling of fright was outweighed by the thought that she wanted to know who it was before the police arrived. She wished she had let Doug keep a gun in the house.

When she arrived at her store, Amy saw a strange pickup in the single rear parking spot. There was no damage to the door, but she noticed the whole handle assembly had been jimmied. Ignoring her apprehension, she pushed open the back door and shouted.

--Who's in here? I'm the owner. You need to leave.

A form came out of the shadow. At first, all she saw was a gun. Then she saw the face.

--Nick, you asshole! What the fuck are you doing here? Put that gun down!

--Hi, Amy. I need some money.

--Like the first time, you mean. It was you who broke the window and took the cash. Now, put the gun down. We'll figure this out. I need to call the alarm company back, or they'll notify the cops.

Nick lowered the gun and backed away.

--I'm sorry about the window. I'm desperate. This time, I had a crowbar with me.

--Okay, don't panic. I'm going to the phone to call the alarm company. You can listen to me telling them everything is okay.

Amy dialed and told the alarm company that a delivery man had found the back door unlocked. She reached out her hand for Nick to give her the gun.

--Nick, what are you doing? Everyone thinks you're in Texas or Mexico.

--Except Lupe. She wouldn't give me money, either. She wants me to turn myself in.

--She's right. Look at me. I'm free. I could avoid jail time. This is a murder case now. If we cooperate, the law will give us a break.

--So, what do I do?

--First, we hide this gun. Where the fuck did you get it? I'll put it in my car for now. You didn't shoot anybody with it, did you?

--No, I got it from a friend. We switched pickups, too.

--Let's call Lupe and figure this out.

Nick called Lupe and told her what was happening. Lupe said she would call her Legal Aid contact and call back. She called back five minutes later and said Nick should turn himself in at the Sheriff Department. She had contacted the Wakazoo Legal Aid office. They would send someone when Nick called after he was processed. They could represent him until he found another attorney or was assigned a public defender. After Nick listened to Lupe and agreed to turn himself in, Amy changed the plan slightly. She wanted credit for bringing Nick in. She called the Sheriff office and insisted on speaking directly to Sheriff McAdams. He was available to talk to her.

--Hi, Amy. What's going on?

--I have a gift for you, Sheriff.

--What's that?

--It's who's that. I have Nick Montez here in my store. He broke in so he could double dip on my cash box. I've talked him into turning himself in.

--We'll be right there.

--I need to tell you to go easy on him. His sister has a lawyer from Legal Aid standing by. Plus, he needs protection. We don't want him to wind up like Doug.

--Absolutely. Tell Lupe he'll be safer with us.

Amy waited for the deputies to come to the store, hoping Pete would also show up so she would gain maximum credit for finding Nick Montez. Instead, Captain Chatfield, whom Amy had only met in passing, had Nick handcuffed and taken away in quick order. The arrest was routine. Nick was passive.

Amy called Gerrit and updated him, wondering what to do about the broken door hardware. Gerrit said he could do a temporary fix until they could find a contractor to repair the door and install a new lock. He found a drill Doug had left in the garage and stopped at the hardware store for a padlock and latch kit. When he got to the store, he secured the hasp and latch on the outside door and tested the padlock.

An hour later, they were back at the condo, where Amy found a message on the machine. It simply said:

--I'll call you back at 6:00, your time.

She recognized Theo's voice. When he called back an hour later, she was fortified by a second glass of wine.

--I just talked to you. What do you want now?

--Change of plans. I need to go to South Bend to clean up some things. You can meet me there.

--I told you. I'm confined to Singapore.

--It's a straight shot down Highway 40. It's an hour and a half away. Borrow Gerrit's truck. No one will know you're coming.

--How do you know Gerrit is here?

--I told you. I have friends there.

--You're crazy if you think I will risk breaking my bail restrictions to pay you. You can drive up here. Find an old pickup and wear those same old farmer clothes you wore back when you wanted to go incognito.

--Too risky.

--Then wait for your money.

--What if I find out that you are not the one waiting for me to show up?

--Who else would it be?

--Your new best friend, Sheriff Pete.

--It would do me no good to squeal on you. You would take me down with you. You managed to involve me in just enough of your shit to leave your stink on me.

--I'm glad you see it that way. When can you have the cash ready?

--Wednesday.

--Okay. Be ready. It'll be Thursday or Friday. Remember, I've got eyes on you, just like your buddy, Sheriff Pete.

--I hope it's not Nick. He just turned himself in after he broke into my store again.

--What a dumbass! But he's only a minor problem. My friends are a lot smarter and more dangerous.

--That's what you told me a hundred times. Where do we meet?

--Plan on the Wakazoo Hilton unless I tell you differently.

--There's no Hil…. Oh, I get it. I don't even know if it's still open.

Theo hung up. The Hilton reference brought up her memories of twenty-five years ago.

Amy had just started working at Stephanie's boutique in New Leiden when she got a strange call from Joe. He was nervous and was speaking in a soft voice. He and Theo were stranded in a roadside motel just outside Wakazoo. They needed her to pick them up and return to Middleburg, where their cars were parked. Joe put Theo on the line when she suggested they call a cab.

--Don't ask any questions, Amy. This is a matter of life and death. No one can know that we are here or ever were here. You are the only one we can trust. Just pull up to room number 14 when you get here. Wait in the car. We'll come out if the coast is clear.

--Holy shit, Theo. What's going on?

--No questions, I said. We'll fill you in later.

--I can't leave until Stephanie gets back. She should be here in half an hour.

--That's okay. Make up another excuse for Stephanie, like your mom is sick or something like that. Don't tell her that I'm involved. Don't mention Joe, either.

--Okay, I guess. How do I find this place?

--Take Highway 121 south until you see CR 333. Take a right to Wakazoo. When you reach Wakazoo, take another right on Route 60 back towards Middleburg. It will be on the left side, just over a bridge, north of town.

--What's it called?

--The Singapore River Motel. It has a weird-looking fish on the sign.

When Amy arrived two hours later, she was shocked that Theo would stay in what was obviously a dump. Joe and Theo both walked quickly to the car. Joe was dressed in what looked like his office shirt and pants but with a casual jacket and no tie. His clothes were rumpled as if he had been doing hard labor somewhere. Theo was put together as always, wearing a suit and tie and carrying a small flight bag. Joe climbed into the back seat of Amy's two-door Skylark convertible, where Amy could see the distress on his face.

--Are you okay, Dad?

--I don't know. I think I'll be all right. I've never been through anything like this before.

--Relax. Take some deep breaths. Just focus on breathing. What the fuck is going on, Theo?

Theo sat in the passenger seat, looking much calmer as if he had gathered himself since she had talked to him on the phone.

--Drive toward Middleburg. Our cars are in the parking lot behind Boersma's. We'll get out one at a time if the coast is clear.

--The coast is clear? You're scaring me with all this crap. It sounds like a murder mystery.

--That's exactly what it will be if anyone discovers we were there. That's why we want to get away without being seen. I don't think that caretaker saw us. He was working on one of the back ponds, away from the shooting. We don't want it to be known that we could be witnesses.

--Witnesses to what?

--Okay, I'll tell you. But believe me when I say we are putting our lives in your hands. Some people I know don't want witnesses to what happened. I'll start at the beginning: George Bosch planned to meet Sal Broglio and some of his associates at the DFG. They chose the location because there's usually no one there on weekdays this time of year. George asked Joe to come with him so at least he wouldn't be alone. A contact of mine called me and told me to stop Joe from going along. I got hold of Joe and told him, so he planned to ditch George after they had breakfast at Boersma's. Later, the same person called me back and said that Joe and I should go with George. I went to Middleburg, where I caught them outside Boersma's. The three of us took George's car to the DFG. When we arrived, George parked the car by the main pavilion close to the first pond, telling us to stay there. He walked around the bend in the two-track road toward the second pond. A few minutes later, not even five minutes, we heard two shotgun blasts. While deciding whether to check them out, we heard one more. Joe was freaking out. I quieted him down as we sneaked away from the pavilion. We were walking off the road and the trails, bushwacking our way toward the sound of the shots. We stopped short of the next pond, trying to stay undercover. We were as close as we dared to get. We saw two bodies. One looked like George. The other could have been Sal. We also saw two figures heading back up the road to the pavilion.

--Are you kidding me? You could be dead! How did you get away?

--I was staying at that fleabag motel. I've stayed there several times when I needed to be in Singapore without being noticed. They take cash and don't ask for ID. I would rent a banged-up used car, dress for fishing, and give a fake name. No one would ever know that I was there. As the crow flies, the motel is about a mile from the Fish and Game Club. We stayed out of sight and worked our way back through the brush and trees, freezing from the cold and wind. That's why Joe is such a mess. I got myself cleaned up.

--Of course, you did. What are you going to do now?

--Absolutely nothing. If anyone asks, we were never there. I wasn't even in town. Joe had a problem at the office and could not go with George after breakfast. That's our story. And your story is that you know nothing about any of it. You went to check on your mother and went back to work.

--How is Dad going to explain his appearance?

--He'll go home to change and tell your mother he had a flat.

--Who was the contact that called you?

--Someone whose name you do not want to know.

Amy dropped them off in Middleburg and returned to New Leiden.

Gerrit came back into the kitchen to break up Amy's reverie.

--What's up with Theo now?

--He's coming on Thursday to pick up his money.

--That sounds risky for both of you. This might be your chance to let the police meet him.

--I've told you that Theo has stuff on me too. I don't know if I could get a decent deal with the court if they discover everything I've been involved with. I don't dare turn him in for that reason alone. Plus, he has threatened physical harm to me if I cooperate too much.

--I have a feeling that you haven't told me everything. It makes it hard for me to help you. I think you should get some things off your mind.

--Okay. I'll tell you what I was thinking about. It would make me an accessory to something.

Amy hesitated before taking a deep breath. She went on to tell Gerrit about the day of George Bosch's death and her rescue of Theo and George.

--I bet that was a frightening experience, but I don't think it would change things much. It doesn't seem like you knew what had happened.

--I know a lot more.

--That could help you. Did you ever commit a crime with Theo or your dad? Or did you only hear about what they did?

--The most serious thing I did was pick up and deliver some packages for Theo when Joe could not make his regular run to Chicago for some reason. I didn't ask what was in the packages, but Theo paid well, and I needed the money.

--When was this?

--It started before we were married and stopped when we divorced.

--That was a long time ago. There could be a statute of limitations that will protect you. Run it by Juanita. She could use it to your advantage. It seems to me that what you know is mostly hearsay. The sheriff could use it as a roadmap without charging you or making you testify.

--You're right. I know other stuff, too. In his last few years, Dad talked a lot. He had things to get off his chest. Like you're saying. It's all hearsay, but Pete McAdams and a grand jury would like to hear it.

--What did he have to say?

--For one, my dad never regarded himself as an addict. He claimed he liked to party and used the alcohol to liven things up. He never got drunk alone. He never gambled alone. It was always while people were watching him take risks. He needed the attention it brought him. When he went overboard and got in trouble, he could quit cold turkey on both without any withdrawal issues.

--Attention is a basic need for everybody. For some, it becomes a drug.

--That's what his AA sponsor, Hank Plagmeyer, told him. He said alcohol and gambling were secondary addictions.

--He sounds like a wise man. Many of the AA old-timers are expert psychologists. But being an addict of any kind is of no interest to the law.

--But Sal Broglio and his organized crime bunch are. He involved Joe in all kinds of things: driving for the Van Klompenberg stolen car ring, setting up the Monday night club with illegal booze sales, gambling, and girls for hire. Sal even tried to pimp me out when I was bartending. He said I would be his highest-priced girl. I wouldn't need to do it in Dordrecht. He had several other clubs I could work in.

--Did you go along with it?

--Fuck, no! And fuck you for asking.

--I only wanted that on the record.

--Oh, I almost forgot. Sal was Dad's partner in the scheme to embezzle from ChairWorks. Both almost went to jail for that.

--Oh, yes. You told me about Joe's financial troubles a while back.

--Sal was just a doorman and gofer for the big Chicago guys. If Theo and Dad are correct, he was murdered at the DFG, and George Bosch did not kill himself. There is no statute of limitation for murder. Someone could be getting nervous.

--Have you heard anything about the big guys? That would be valuable information.

--That brings us to Lydia.

--What does Lydia have to do with it? I thought she was his girlfriend.

--She was his great love for the last thirty years. Another addiction. She was born to the mob and married to it. When they first got together, Joe feared being attacked or killed by her husband's friends. Instead, Lydia saved his ass many times. When he got in trouble, she went to her father. He found a way to work things out and kept the goons and her husband away from him. Dad met her father several times. His name is Gus Martino. He doted on Lydia and seemed to like Dad just because Lydia liked him. He even offered to set Dad up in his own business again.

--Why didn't he take him up on it?

--He said it would break up his family. Joe said that Gus appreciated that. Family was important, but it was okay that he saw Lydia on the side.

--So that's Joe rebelling against Calvinist restrictions and then reeling himself back in to assuage his Calvinist guilt. That's common. Especially today. It seems that now, more than ever, the Dutch Reformed culture is dealing with those contradictions.

--Even me?

--Absolutely.

--Now I'm hungry, let's eat something.

--It's ready. While you were out, one of my key investors called. He wants to meet with me. I need to make a quick trip to New Mexico. Will you be okay if I leave tomorrow? I'll come back Wednesday night.

--Ja. I'll need to work on getting the door fixed at the store. I have some other things at the store that I need to catch up on, too. The sheriff and his merry men are a phone call away. Harry is meeting me in New Leiden on Wednesday to review Dad's financials.

--Those merry men belonged to Robin Hood. They did not like the Nottingham Sheriff.

--Whatever.

Amy and Gerrit ate their supper quickly. Gerrit said he needed some quiet time, meaning deep meditation, which could take hours and which he always did alone. She was ready for an early night and went to her bedroom, planning a short meditation of her own after a quick shower. But as she finished her shower, she sighed as the phone rang again.

--Hello.

--Amy, this is Lydia.

--What the fuck do you want?

--That's my question.

--What do you mean?

--I received a call from a lawyer threatening to evict me from MY home unless I agree to sign a lease and pay rent for MY home.

--What did you expect? It's not yours!

--It is. Joe gave it to me.

--You have no proof of that. Even if he told you he would, he never did. It was just another of his empty promises. His will, officially witnessed and filed with the court two years ago, specifically leaves it to me. You have no case.

--My lawyer tells me I have a weak case, but not an impossible one.

--You have a lousy lawyer.

--My papa's lawyer is quite good. We could tie you up in court. But he tells me it would be best to work something out with you.

--It's worked out. Sign the lease and pay the rent.

--He also tells me you are in a lot of trouble and don't need more. I want to buy the condominium. I expect you to give me a friendly price.

--Fuck you. If your lawyer were any good, he would know it's tied up in probate. I can't sell it. If the court sold it, they would need to have it appraised. They would not approve a bargain price for you.

--Appraisals can be bought like anything else. And don't forget. I know all about you and Theo and your past sins. I'm sure the law would be very interested in them.

--You wouldn't dare. Theo and his partners would take you out.

--Don't kid yourself. I try not to get personally involved, but my roots reach much deeper and wider than Theo's.

--Look. I'm not going to let you steal it from me. I'm meeting with my people tomorrow. They'll be in touch. Who do they call?

--Call me. I'll get my team ready.

Amy knew that she was too tense to meditate without some help. She knew Gerrit had brought some hashish with him from the resort. She decided she needed something extra to calm her down. She found his stash and her pipe in the kitchen. She felt her mood shift and went through several poses, after which she fell into a deep sleep.

Chapter 15—Harry, Third Tuesday, 1998

On Tuesday morning, Harry's River Haven room phone rang before his alarm awakened him. As he picked it up, still half asleep, Larry's excited voice woke him up the rest of the way.

--Are you ready to go to Saginaw?

--Why would I want to go to Saginaw?

--Doug's pickup showed up there.

--Really? How did you find out?

--Pete McAdams called me early this morning. He asked if I knew anyone in the Saginaw office who could speed up the process for him. He needs the car impounded and given a deep dive inspection by forensics. Eventually, he wants it shipped back to Wakazoo.

--Did you help him out?

--I know Barry Evans, the guy in charge of the Saginaw office, so I gave him the name. But I had to tell him not to bring up my name. Barry and I have had a couple of run-ins. He's a by-the-books guy.

--That doesn't explain why we want to go to Saginaw.

--Harv Nielson is from Saginaw, remember? Chances are that he drove Doug's pickup to Saginaw.

--Do you think that he killed Doug?

--That's one theory. Or else he was just a witness who managed to get away. Either would explain why he's missing. McAdams wanted Harv checked out, too. I told him we would snoop around.

--He was okay with that?

--Not officially. But he didn't tell me to stay out of it.

--What do we have to go on?

--I called a buddy in Lansing. He found a court record of Harv when he was eighteen. Reckless driving. The address listed might be his mother's. We'll start there.

--I may regret this, but I have nothing else to do. Pick me up in an hour. I'll still be eating breakfast in the dining room.

--Order me a Western omelet. I'll be there when it gets to the table.

They were on the road to Saginaw in Larry's new Suburban within an hour.

--Can we find another station?

--You don't like Garth Brooks?

--A little country goes a long way. Don't you have some oldies or something? Or find some local news. We need a weather report. It looks okay now, but who knows what it'll be like the rest of the day.

--I looked this morning. There is no rain in the forecast until tonight. This truck only has a CD player, so all my cassettes are obsolete. It's going to cost me a fortune to replace them.

--David is a geek and an audiophile. He's copied all my cassettes onto CDs. It only costs me a buck for a blank CD.

He will change my video tapes to DVDs as soon as the prices decrease. He says my VCR will be obsolete in five more years.

--Damn, I just bought a new one.

--Your new TV will be obsolete, too.

--No doubt. Go ahead and find some news or something on the radio. We'll be in Saginaw in less than an hour. We'll stop for gas and find a city map when we get closer.

The house listed as Harv's address was in a well-maintained, older section of Saginaw north of downtown, consisting of various craftsman and Cape Cod homes that looked like they were built in the 1920s. They pulled up in front of a brick bungalow that matched the address.

--Knock on the door and ask if they've seen Harv lately. Tell them you worked with him in Middleburg.

--Why me? You're an experienced lawman. Plus, he saw me at the funeral. We could spook him.

--He saw me, too. People remember me.

--I don't know what to say.

--I scare people, especially women. You look harmless. Tell them you are a friend of Butch and Marilyn. That's the truth, especially Marilyn. They knew you were coming here for a visit and asked you to check on Harv. This would be Butch's sister's house if she still lives here.

Harry walked up to the door and knocked. Larry watched as a woman, looking to be seventy or eighty, answered. He saw her talk to Harry briefly and then return into the house, leaving the door ajar. In another few minutes, a younger woman came to the door and spoke to Harry. After they talked for at least another five minutes, she turned back into the house for a moment and came back with a pen and pad. She wrote something on the pad. They nodded to each other, and Harry turned to come back to the Suburban with a satisfied smile on his face.

--This job is easy. They were very accommodating. They are worried about Harv and want me to tell them what I find out.

--Who were the two women?

--The older one was George Bosch's first wife, Butch's mother. The younger one is Butch's sister and Harv's mother.

--What did they tell you?

--That's not the best news.

--Because?

--He was here last weekend. On Wednesday, he borrowed their second car to go to London to see his ex-wife and daughter. He hasn't been back.

--London? He can't drive to London.

--London, Ontario, stupid.

--Oh yeah. How far away is it? Should we check it out?

--She said it's about a three-hour drive.

--What else do we have to do?

--Nothing that I can think of.

--What kind of car did he take?

--She said it was a five-year-old white VW Jetta. She gave me the license number, too.

--I'm up for it. What do you think?

--Okay. Let's do it. We'll need a Canadian map. I'll also need something to read. I saw a drugstore a few blocks away. I could get John Grisham's new book there. They could have maps, too.

--Who is John Grisham?

--Where have you been? He wrote that book, *The Firm,* a few years ago. Tom Cruise was in the movie. He's written about ten books already, all best-sellers about lawyers. I think I've read them all. His new one is called *The Street Lawyer.*

--It sounds like you know more about the law than I do. You could create a mystery novel about this case and our adventures. Or a screenplay. I'm thinking Tom Selleck could play me when they make the movie. He already has the Tiger hat.

--He'd need to put on some weight.

--Speaking of my weight, let's get some lunch before we take off for London.

An hour later, they crossed into Ontario via Port Huron at the southern tip of Lake Huron. They stopped for gas and another local map when they arrived in London. After getting lost twice, they parked across the street from a 1970s duplex in a neighborhood near the London city limits.

--Okay, Sherlock, use the skills you have been learning in that legal thriller you're reading. Let's find out what the ex-wife knows if she's home.

--She could be home. Harv's mother said she was a nurse.

--I hope so. I don't want to hang around the rest of the day.

--Why me? It's your turn. And why am I Sherlock? I'm more like Watson. You should be Sherlock. You both share an oversized ego.

--True. And deservedly so. But you are still less threatening. So, Watson, you'll be. Women trust you. Just tell her that you are Harv's Uncle Butch's best friend. Not to mention how

303

close you and his wife are. You did well last time. You can do it again.

Harry was shaking his head as he exited the Suburban and went to the door. Once again, a fifty-ish woman greeted him. This time, she let him inside. Ten minutes later, the door opened. Larry watched Harry saying goodbye to a younger woman with a handshake while she held a toddler's wrist with her other hand. Harry climbed back into the Suburban with a paper in his hand and a sly smile.

--You're right again, Sherlock. I am good at this.

--What did you find out?

--That was Harv's ex, Bethany, and his son Kris—with a 'K.' Named after Harv's father. We were lucky. She was about to leave for her shift. The other lady was her mother, Betsy Blanchard. She wanted me to stay for coffee and a snack.

--You draw them like flies to sweetcorn.

--It's the natural blond hair my mother gave me. You should try dying yours.

--Ja, right. Blond hair and dark freckles. That's a good look. Tell me more.

--Harv was there two days ago. He earned some visiting time with little Kris on Thursday and Friday by giving her a grand in cash, which she described as a down payment on child support he owes. He left on Saturday, saying he was going to Windsor to stay with a friend for a few days.

--And she happened to know the address?

--Ja. He uses it as his official Canadian address for the custody agreement.

--And Windsor is on our way home?

--According to the map, it's a shortcut compared to going back through Saginaw.

--Let's hustle. I want to be home before dark. We'll need another map.

Two and a half hours later, after stopping for Colonel Sander's nuggets for a snack and another map, they arrived at a three-story apartment complex of at least a hundred walkup units. Larry looked longingly at the last half of Harry's nuggets, but he forced himself to get out and walk around the buildings until he found the apartment number where they hoped to find Harv Nielsen. He returned to the Suburban and backed it into a spot in the second row of the parking lot, where they could see the stairway and entrance to the second-floor apartment. Dark clouds were accumulating, which allowed them to see a light inside. They talked between nuggets.

--What do you think, Watson? Are you up for knocking on the door?

--Do you think he's here?

--There's a white Jetta about four cars to the left.

--I don't know. This seems different. I don't think there are any ladies to charm. If he gets spooked, you should be the one to handle any violence.

--We could go together.

--Let's wait a little while. We might find out if anyone is with him.

While they finished the chicken, they saw two shadows moving in the apartment. When the lights went out, they saw two men standing on the landing, gesturing and talking. After a few minutes, one came down the stairs while the other returned to the apartment. As it began to rain, they watched as the first man walked toward them and then turned on the sidewalk to open the door of a blue Camry directly under a parking lot light turned on by the darkening sky, helping their visibility.

--Oh, my God, Larry.

--What now, Watson?

--Who do you think that is?

--I don't think anything. Who do you think it is?

--I know who it is. It's Theo Bolinyk.

--Oh, my God is right. What do we do now? We only have one car.

--We've got to follow Theo. He's the bigger fish.

--Okay. That's right. Harv might sit tight in this apartment. There's a pen in the glove compartment. When I drive past the Jetta, check the plate number. See if it matches what you got from Harv's mother.

--I see it. It matches.

--Can you see Theo's plate on the Camry?

--Ja, Thanks to the light. I got it, too.

--Damn. This is the worst possible vehicle to tail someone. I'll have to stay back and hope for the best.

--I thought you said it wasn't going to rain.

--I didn't check Canada.

They chased the Camry and then fell back when it turned on Highway 3. It became a straightaway so they could easily follow without being noticed. It soon became evident from the highway signage that Theo was headed to the international bridge. They were only three cars behind when they lined up to cross the bridge into Detroit. But the delay was long enough that they had lost him when they passed the checkpoint.

--As soon as we see a safe spot to gas up and find a phone, we need to call this in, Watson. We've done everything we can do.

--My heart is just starting to slow down. I'm not used to the excitement.

After losing Theo, Harry and Larry headed northwest on I-96 until they were out of metropolitan Detroit. They left the freeway near Twelve-Mile Road when Harry had a good connection for his Nokia. After deciding to pay the roaming charge, he called the Wakazoo Sheriff's Department. Pete McAdams was out, but he was connected to Brian Chatfield.

--This is Chief Deputy Captain Chatfield.

--Hello, Captain. This is Harry Berendts.

--What can I do for you?

--It's about what I can do for you.

--What do you have?

--Sheriff McAdams called my friend Larry Vandevoss last night to ask him for contacts in the state police office in Saginaw so he could ask them to prioritize the hunt for Harv Nielson and the recovery of Doug Mason's pickup.

--He told me he was going to do that.

--Larry gave him some names, but he didn't think they would jump right on it, so we decided to go to Saginaw and check things out ourselves.

--I would not recommend that.

--Too late. We've been there and are on our way back. We are legal now that Larry has his PI license. He's working with Juanita Jones.

--Did you find anything?

--Obviously, we did. That's why I'm paying extra roaming charges on my Nokia to call you. We went to Harv's last address Larry could find. It turned out to be his mother's house. His grandmother lived there, too. He had dumped Doug's pickup and borrowed their second car, a white VW Jetta. He said he wanted to go to London, Ontario, to see his ex and daughter.

--So, he's in Canada?

--Probably. We went to his ex's address and found he had been there for the weekend. She said he left Sunday night to go to a friend's place in Windsor.

--I suppose you went there, too.

--Of course. It was on the way home. Guess who we saw leave the apartment after waiting a while to decide what to do?

--I can't guess.

--Theo Bolinyk. We followed him to the border but lost him at the bridge into Detroit. We're calling you from Twelve-Mile Road and I-96.

--Holy shit! I hope you got the license number.

--If you're ready, I'll give you all the info we gathered.

Harry gave Brian the information he needed and then called Amy to bring her up to date. After no answer, he reached her at her store and told her the same story.

--Are you sure it was Theo?

--Definitely. We got a good look.

--That's a surprise. I wasn't expecting him until Thursday.

--What do you mean? Have you talked to him?

--Ja. He called yesterday. I don't know how he will contact me. He just told me to be ready.

--Now Pete McAdams knows he is coming too. You better stay away from him.

--You told him all this?

--I told his Chief Deputy. They'll be watching you.

--Why did you tell them?

--Because I'm trying to help you. You will get some of the credit. I told them Larry is working on your case for Juanita.

--Next time, call me first. We need to be on the same page.

--If you tell the whole truth for a change, we'll find ourselves on the same page.

--You don't know what you are getting into. Thanks for trying. Are you still meeting me in New Leiden tomorrow? At least I'll be gone if Theo shows up.

--What time?

--Our appointment with Bill is at eleven.

--Okay. My phone's about to lose power. See you then.

Harry and Larry drove back to Singapore, trying to fit all of what they had learned into the overall picture of the deaths at the DFG.

--Okay, Watson, who killed Doug Mason and why?

--It looks to me like it was Harv Nielson. Doug might have owed him money. Or he was afraid Doug would finger him to get a lighter sentence.

--Finger him? Is that a legal term?

--Rockford used it.

--The other possibility is that Doug and Harv were supposed to meet. Harv found Doug already dead, shot by someone else. Harv got away by taking off in Doug's truck.

Why was Doug's body set up to copy George Bosch, Harv's grandfather?

--The shooter might have thought that would be a clever way to set up Harv.

--How did Harv get to the club property?

--With Doug? They could have been there together, planning to meet someone who turned out to be the actual shooter.

--So, we have two possibilities. Or more, for all we know.

--Placing Doug into the bigger picture, we have three possibilities for the shooter or shooters other than Harv.

--I'm listening, Sherlock.

--We now know that Theo is involved.

--That's one.

--Mexican drug gangs are involved.

--That's true. And the third could be the Chicago organized crime figures, who we are no longer supposed to call The Mafia or La Cosa Nostra.

--Are we getting ahead of our skis here? My sister is warning me about poking into things we should be avoiding. Speaking of Amy, where does she fit in?

--Everywhere, unfortunately. It's her farm. She's Theo's ex. Joe was close friends with George Bosch. They were connected to the underground Chicago-run casinos. Doug and Nick were working with Mexicans.

--What do we do next?

--You are going with Amy to New Leiden tomorrow, right?

--Ja, we're meeting at her accountant's office to discuss Joe's finances. Calmly, I hope.

--See what you can get out of her. Rile her up a little bit. I always found I'd get two diverse responses if I pissed someone off in an interview. Either they clammed up and gave up nothing, or they would get so angry that they forgot what they were trying not to tell me and wound up giving me something I could use.

--What about you?

--I'm going to the courthouse in North Haven and next to Lansing if necessary. I want to get to the archives to check that old Van Klompenberg case. Some of the same characters seem to be involved in these cases.

When they arrived back at River Haven after six, Harry spotted Pete McAdams beside his Bronco. Larry parked nearby while Harry got out and met him between the two vehicles.

--Hello, Sheriff. It's surprising to see you here. What can we do for you?

--Captain Chatfield filled me in on your little adventure. I was in Middleburg to watch my son in a cross-country meet. He said you were on your way back. The timing was right, so I thought I would try to catch you and dig deeper into what you found.

--I just moved here. How did you know where to find me?

--I'm the Sheriff. It's what my team does.

Pete talked with them for almost half an hour, double-checking each detail and ensuring accuracy. Toward the end of the conversation, Larry mentioned his theory that there were three suspects in the murder of Doug Mason.

--Those are reasonable targets, but you're forgetting another group.

--Who's that?

--If you link the multiple town mini-casinos, George Bosch's death, the Van Klompenberg car theft ring, the Van Orden farm, Amy's farm, and Doug's murder, local politicians from at least three counties and the state were involved.

--Who are they?

--I'm not ready to tell you that. But I am telling you to be careful. I can't tell you what to do if you don't interfere with my investigation. But, Harry, your sister is not innocent. She's involved with dangerous people. The charges against her may be too severe to avoid prison time even if she cooperates. That means you are in danger, too.

--Point taken. Tell my partner here the same thing.

Larry looked unconcerned.

--I'm always careful. But I've just thought of another choice, Sheriff.

--What's that?

--Some, or all, of the above.

McAdams slowly nodded and said goodbye as he hopped into his Bronco.

Larry was starving after the conversation with Sheriff McAdams and wanted to go to the Goose and Gander, but Harry needed to check his messages. He found several, but only one from Lupe he wanted to reply in front of Larry. She wanted to update him about Nick's situation. He made Larry wait a little longer to be fed while he returned her call.

--Hi. This is Harry. What's up with Nick?

--It's a long story. You'll need to buy me dinner again.

--I already have a date. We're going to G & G. Are you ready for a three-way?

--Depends on who it is.

--It would be you, me, and Larry.

--Big Larry? I would be okay with that.

--I'll be there in half an hour.

--Harry and Larry walked to the pub to enjoy the crisp and clear fall evening. When they arrived, Lupe was already sitting at a table with a glass of whiskey and a cherry.

--I didn't think you were an Old-Fashioned girl.

312

--I'm not. I'm just bitter.

--You got me on that one. Do you know Larry?

--I know of him. But we've never actually met.

--Hi, Lupe. I'm Larry Vandevoss.

--Now we've met. You are indeed a big Dutchman. Do you fly, too?

--Sure, but not on my own anymore. I need a plane, a helicopter, or at least a balloon.

--That would be some balloon!

An infectious smile accompanied Lupe's banter. Larry replied with a bashful grin. The waiter came by. Lupe ordered another Old-Fashioned and the rotisserie half chicken. Harry said he would have the same—both the drink and the chicken. Larry ordered the full-pound T-bone, an order of wings, and an IPA to start. With a softer voice than usual, he asked Lupe about her brother.

--I would rather talk about it after another drink and with a full stomach.

--Start with the easy stuff and work your way up.

--It's not easy. You've been away today. Did you hear that Nick turned himself in last night? Amy caught him at her store again.

--That was him the first time?

--Yes. I got him a lawyer, so he's not talking.

--We know he has been in the agricultural business, growing and selling specialized products, first with Jonnie Van Orden and then with Doug.

--They started small. That's how Nick wanted to keep it, but Doug was getting greedy. Both Nick and my parents were looking for a way out. That's why Mom and Dad were able to get away so quickly. They had been making plans to get back to Chihuahua. They just left a little earlier than planned.

--Did they go back home?

--Yes. They had saved their money over the years. They left Mexico as paupers. Now, they've returned as part of the gentry.

--Do you think they will be extradited?

--That county attorney lady, Sally Conners, told Nick she wouldn't need to if he cooperated.

--That's a powerful incentive.

--Absolutely. His lawyer is holding him back, however. He wants to get a firm deal for him, as well as protection. He only told them about the shooting. He doesn't want to get shot again.

--What happened that day?

--Here's my drink. Let's take turns. Tell me about your day.

--What's to tell? Just some international intrigue, stakeouts, and car chases. Harry romanced some attractive women, who put us on the right track.

--I can believe that. He has skills.

Harry quietly sipped his drink and looked up at the ceiling.

--We did finally locate Harv Nielson in Windsor. We tracked him from Saginaw, where he had taken Doug's pickup. How well did Nick know Harv?

--We all worked at Covenant Rehab. Harv was in the clinic, so we never worked closely together except when we had a side job, helping Amy as the care team for Joe. Harv and Doug had a pill deal going on. Nick wasn't part of that.

--So, who shot Nick?

--I only know what Nick told me and Jonnie. He said Doug told him to meet two Mexican guys bringing in some product. Doug had a big deal pending and needed to supplement what he had ready to sell from the farm. Nick was supposed to receive cash in exchange for a bag of pills. Nick told me he met them at their van waiting at the farm, where they showed him the marijuana in the back. When he showed them the pills, they grabbed them and leaped back into the truck. He hung onto the door before the driver could close it. The passenger shot him in the shoulder. They just took off. He says that it was lucky they didn't want to take the time to kill him. They easily could have.

--The Sheriff Department picked up two Mexican men at the farm. Are they the same ones?

--Not according to Nick. They showed him pictures of the guys that were sent to ICE. Nick knew they were just looking for work. His mom and dad hired them now and then when they needed extra help. They're harmless.

--When was the last time Nick saw Doug?

--I don't know. He was supposed to put the marijuana in the shed and wait for Doug. He never showed up, so he removed his jacket, wrapped and taped his shoulder as best he could, and drove to see Jonnie. He thought Jonnie knew some first aid, which he did, but not enough.

--What does Jonnie think about everything? Why would he help Nick evade arrest?

--I hadn't thought of that. I don't think Nick is telling the whole story.

--Why did he break into Amy's store?

--He needed money. That was the fastest way he could get it quickly without exposing himself.

--How much of this does the sheriff know?

--Most of it. He grilled me this afternoon after he met with Jonnie in the morning. From his questions, I could tell Jonnie told him a lot. My lawyer tried to protect me, but I had to confirm some of what they already knew.

--They?

--Charley, what's-his-name, that old police chief from Dordrecht. He was there, plus a guy from the state police.

--Sounds serious.

--It was. They recorded it. They also reminded me of the penalty for lying under oath and told me to expect a grand jury summons.

When their dinners came, they ate hungrily. Lupe gave Larry the new potatoes and a section of her chicken, telling him that her barbecued chicken made with her father's recipe was better. Larry said he would like to try it. Relieved that her attention was focused on Larry, Harry told them he needed to return to his room to make one more call. Larry objected.

--I need dessert, Harry. What about you, Lupe?

--I want a brandy, Hennessy preferably, since Harry is paying.

--Not this time. This is a business meeting. Larry can put it on his LV Investigations expense account. I'm out of here. You two can party on.

Harry walked back to River Haven, mentally exhausted from his long day and knowing that he had two phone calls that he could not delay. He took a Coke from his mini-fridge and dialed the first number.

Marilyn answered using her Nokia. After she told him to wait, he could sense her moving.

--Okay. I'm in the kitchen now. The reception is good here. Butch is downstairs in his office. Where have you been? I've been calling you all day.

--Yes, I know. I've been busy trying to help Amy. Larry and I were all over the state and even went to Canada.

--I want to see you for sure tomorrow afternoon. Just tell me where we can meet.

--Tomorrow won't work. I'll be in New Leiden most of the day.

--If you cared, you could find the time.

--Marilyn, we both know our thing can't last.

--You seem to last very well when we are together, just like I do. I haven't responded that way for at least a decade.

--That's true for me, too. But it's physical and short term.

--How do you know that?

--It's the feeling that I've had an itch and finally scratched it. I think it's the same for you.

--Even if that's true, it doesn't mean we don't have other feelings for each other.

--To me, the problem is the feelings we don't have.

--Like what? You were never a romantic person. I don't see you looking for love like a teenager.

--You are right about that. But it's a matter of trust to me. The fact is that I don't trust you.

--Just because I made a mistake and broke up with you thirty years ago?

--And the belief I have that you would do it again.

--Now, you are just being cruel, getting back at me.

--I think I'm doing both of us a favor, saving time. Wasted time that would only lead to the same ending.

--You've hurt me enough that I'll save some of my pride and give up. You can't see past your decades-long hurt.

Harry heard the click with a sense of relief, but he was still concerned that this would not be the end. With a deep sigh, he reluctantly dialed the number for his last call of the day, another call he had no choice but to return.

--Hello.

--Is this Butch?

--Ja.

--This is Harry Berendts, returning your call.

--I wondered if you'd have the guts to call me back.

--What can I do for you?

--I've heard that you've been seeing my wife.

--That's true. We talked about old times.

--I've heard it wasn't just talk.

--Sometimes people think the worst. I've heard the same thing about you and my sister.

--Touché! But that's not why I called. My sister called me. She said you and Larry Vandevoss were looking for her son, Harv. She's worried he might be in trouble. Plus, he hasn't returned her car. I told her I would try to find out what was going on.

--You've heard that Amy is in trouble. Harv is part of that. Amy's boyfriend, Doug Mason, is dead. He and Harv were involved in some drug transactions. Harv drove Doug's pickup to Saginaw. That's why he needed his mother's car. We tracked him to London, where his ex-wife lives, and Windsor this afternoon. We left him and her car there at his friend's apartment. We found someone more interesting to track down.

--What kind of drugs?

--Doug grew marijuana on Amy's land in Singapore County. Harv is suspected of raiding the pharmacy supply vault at Covenant Rehab. He's AWOL from there. They met when Amy hired Harv to help with my dad's care in his last couple of years.

--So that's why I saw him at the funeral home. This is not good news.

--No. It's not. Amy has a big-time lawyer. We're trying to keep her out of jail by cooperating with the sheriff in Wakazoo, but he thinks she's holding back. If you find Harv, his best bet is to turn himself in and cooperate. This case is growing. The feds and state police are getting involved. Charley Vredevelde is working on the missing pills case if you want to know more. He's a Nederland deputy now, working out of the Middleburg office.

--Okay. I will check with him. Do you know where Harv's pickup is?

--No, but I suspect Charley may have found it by now. But let's get back to our first topic. Marilyn and I won't be talking over old times any longer. It's a dead end for me and for her too.

--I guess that's good news. Thanks for the info. The truth is she'll go back to her preacher friend for consolation.

--Randy Veltmaan?

--Ja.

--And here I thought she had good taste in men. First me and then you. Her choices keep getting worse.

The call with Butch had given Harry the resolve to continue his separation from Marilyn. Now he showered and crashed, wondering if his time tomorrow with Amy would be as surprising as today had turned out to be.

319

Chapter 16—Pete, 3rd Tuesday, 1998

Pete left Sam Morgan's house with just enough time to grab a sub from the Kroger deli to eat on the way to Middleburg for his interviews with Jonnie Van Orden and Lupe Rios. He had found Sam at home. Sam was cordial initially, asking him in and offering coffee, which Pete gladly accepted. They started talking while Sam's wife Eva prepared the Mr. Coffee.

--What can I do for you, Pete?

--Well, Sam, I need some help with several cases that reach back to your time in office. New evidence has caused us to take another look.

--Like what?

--It started again when Joe Berendts died two weeks ago. Do you remember him?

--Ah, yeah. He was one of those Dutch guys, a friend of the Dordrecht chief that shot himself. What was his name again?

--That's right. I'm not sure the chief was Dutch. He was a bit of an outsider. His name was George Bosch.

--So, he died. So what?

--Well, just after the funeral, we got a tip and found a substantial marijuana operation on some property owned by Joe's daughter just north of town, close to the DFG Club.

--Okay. Again. So what?

--It turns out that Amy, that's Joe's daughter's name, was unaware that her boyfriend had expanded what she thought was a little plot of cannabis plants for personal use into a commercial operation. Not only that. He was working with Amy's ex, Theo Bolinyk. Remember him?

--Yeah, a real slick sonofabitch. We couldn't pin anything on him.

--Eventually, the state did. He spent three years in prison for running a cocaine operation in New Leiden. He worked with some guys from Detroit.

--Huh. We thought he was hooked up with the Chicago gangs.

--You mean, you knew he was hooked up with them.

--We couldn't prove it.

--How hard did you try?

--What are you trying to prove now?

--I'm not proving anything yet. Things keep happening that I'm trying to pull together. Like Amy's boyfriend being killed by a shotgun and posed in the exact location and a similar position to George Bosch. Have you heard about that?

--I heard there was a shooting, not the details. Are you sure it wasn't another suicide?

--This time, I brought in the state crime scene staff. They decided that he was moved and posed. He could not have created the shotgun blast's angle or the damage that killed him. Too bad that you kept the George Bosch crime scene from getting the same professional treatment.

--Looks to me that you're right. You have a bunch of extraneous tidbits that don't link up, so you're grasping at straws.

--I checked out an interesting boat at the yacht club this morning.

--What about it?

--It belongs to a friend of yours.

--I don't like boats that go on the big lake. I fish in only small lakes and rivers.

--I don't think this one catches many fish, either. One more thing. Tomorrow morning, I'm having the ponds at the DFG Club drained. What do you think I'll find?

--Dead fish and a bunch of muck. You know, there is one thing I don't understand. When you got involved with all that state gambling and graft investigation, why did I get dirt thrown at me? They never proved a thing. It was all Jimmy. You could've just gone after him and earned your sheriff's badge. You and I would've made a good team. Instead, you helped that lesbian bitch beat me.

--I've always chosen my teammates carefully. Sally and I cleaned the whole house, not just the front room.

--You missed a lot. What about the county commissioners and all the shit they're into?

--I need something to do next year.

Sam stood up and said he had things to do. Pete took a second sip of coffee and left, knowing that his short visit had accomplished its purpose. Sam was rattled.

Pete's day had started early. He called Larry Vandevoss from home, hoping to catch him at his son's house. He wanted help from the state police office in Saginaw and thought Larry might know someone who could take possession of Doug Mason's pickup and locate Harv Nielson. Pete was familiar with the staff at the Lansing headquarters from his time on the force, but he didn't know anyone in Saginaw. Larry was still living with his son and answered immediately. He gave him the name of the number two person in the office. He also pressed Pete for more detailed information about Harv and the pickup. Pete gave him as little as he could without seeming ungrateful for his help.

He left home with his coffee thermos to meet John Baker two blocks from the yacht club entrance. Both drove their personal vehicles and dressed in civilian clothes. Pete did not want to alert anyone that law enforcement was interested in the largest of the boats docked at the club, one of three that could qualify as a yacht. John led the way as they walked, trying to look casual, to the end of the dock where there was enough room for the sixty-foot Viking yacht named Dorothea. Pete could not help but be impressed. They stood and looked like they were admiring the boat like any casual observers. They did not see any sign of activity. Two other yachts, just a little bit smaller, were docked nearby. A fifty-ish woman was standing on the top deck of one of them. Pete walked over casually and, as he looked up to her, caught her eye.

--Good morning. It's a beautiful day. And a beautiful boat. Are you taking her out today?

--Hi. No, not today. It's getting too cold this time of year. My son and a friend are taking her down to Florida next week. She'll be waiting when we fly down next month.

--I wish I could go with you. I think that the boat on the next dock might belong to a friend of a friend of mine. Do you know the people who own it?

--I don't know their name. I met his daughter once. She used to stay quite often a few years back. She's from Florida, but her dad is from Chicago. I think I've seen him a couple of times. But both kept to themselves.

--That sounds like the guy. Thank you. Enjoy Florida.

Pete and John walked away. They headed to the yacht club headquarters, where Pete saw a sign for the office. A woman sat at a desk, pecking at a keyboard and frowning at a monitor. Pete walked up to her desk, flashing his badge.

--Hi, I'm Sheriff Pete McAdams. This is Lieutenant John Baker. Is the manager in?

--Not for an hour or so. I thought you looked familiar. I voted for you. Thanks for getting rid of that crook, Jimmy Dickhead.

--Thanks for voting for me. I hope we are gradually making progress. I wondered who the owner of that big Viking yacht down at the end of the docks was. Do you know, by any chance?

--The lady, who used to stay there quite often, is named Lydia. She says she's the daughter of the owner. I can look up his name for you.

--That would be great. What was your name?

--Betty Fields.

--Thanks, Betty.

Pete and John waited patiently while Betty went into the manager's office. She took about five minutes and then walked back with a satisfied smile.

--Here it is. It's an LLC called GM Enterprises. A man named Gus Martino signed the dock space lease agreement.

--Hey, that's great, Betty. Do you know what else you could do for us?

--Just let me know.

--We would prefer you not to tell anyone we were here. I don't want Mr. Martino to know law enforcement is checking on him.

--You got it, Sheriff. I for sure won't tell my boss. He loves to gossip. He'd be telling the entire world.

--Thank you, Betty. Let me know if you ever need us to help you with anything–anything legal, that is. Make sure you pay for your parking tickets.

--I always obey the law, Sheriff. But I may call you if we have any problem, people show up around here. The last time, the response took too long.

--John oversees the river and the harbor. He'll make sure we do better next time, right, John?

--Yes, sir. Here's my card, Betty. Ask them to get me on the radio if I'm not in my office.

Betty looked at the card and seemed impressed, so Pete decided to go for more.

--You know, there is one more thing that could be helpful.

--Whatever I can do, Sheriff.

--If you see any activity at the boat in question, would you let me know? Confidentially, of course. Here is my card.

--You'll be the first to know.

Pete returned to his office, hoping Betty would keep their secret. He knew that most people liked to gossip, even if they promised not to. Sharing secrets gives one a sense of self-importance. When he arrived, he checked with Brian to see when Nick Montez's attorney was due. Brian had set up the interview for ten o'clock, allowing Pete to check his messages with Mary Lu and make phone calls. The messages were primarily routine and could wait. Two needed a return call and some follow-through. He asked Mary Lu to pass them on to Brian. She told him there was fresh coffee brewing in the lunchroom and that she would bring him a mug when it was ready. He gave her a thumbs-up and grateful grin.

His first call was to Jack Stevenson, a friend and classmate from Northern, who was also a criminology major and was now with the FBI in a mid-level operations job at the FBI Clarksburg, West Virginia location. After being put on hold and transferred twice, a receptionist said Special Agent Stevenson was unavailable and took Pete's phone number, giving him the impression that he would be lucky to get a callback. He tried to impress her by saying he was the Sheriff of Singapore County and that he and Jack had previously worked together. He hoped Jack would at least get the message.

While he was trying to focus on the upcoming interview and the direction he wanted to take with Nick Montez, Jack called back.

--Hi, Pete. Or should I call you Sheriff McAdams now?

--I'm happy you called me back. You must have gotten another promotion. There's a brick wall in front of you.

--That's just the way things are here. How are you and the family? Is Flo keeping you on the straight and narrow?

--We are fine. She still tries. I have great kids, thanks to her. How about you?

--Jill and I split up about two years ago, but everyone is okay. But you didn't call to reminisce. What can I do for you?

--We have a situation here involving drugs and murder. I suspect some involvement from Chicago-based organized crime. I was hoping you would know who I could contact to check for information about some who may be involved.

--How about me? That's my department now. My office is a clearinghouse. We keep a data bank focusing on nationwide and international connections among crime gangs. We have a big file on Chicago folks.

--I have a guy named Gus Martino. He has a yacht here but doesn't spend much time on it. His daughter is Lydia Epstein. She was previously married to a guy named Triandos, who has restaurants in Chicago and Miami. Then there is another guy from a few years ago named Sal Broglio. I haven't come across anything about him lately.

--Gus Martino already rings a bell. I'll get them checked out for you. Anything else?

--Just as background, there was a stolen car ring that the FBI broke up in Nederland County just north of us. That was back in the seventies. Some of the same local names are showing up again. Also, the former Sheriff and PA were implicated but not charged when I took over three years ago. We broke up some underground gambling rooms that we knew had Chicago connections. We shut them down but could only make charges stick against some lower-level local guys. The out-of-towners left incognito. Some could not be found or named. Others got off because of a lack of witnesses willing or able to testify.

--That's typical. Okay, I should be able to get something back to you in the morning.

--Outstanding! Thank you. When are you coming back to Michigan?

--In December, for the holidays. But remember, I'm from Escanaba long way from you.

--You should recall that Flo's family is from Sault Ste. Marie. We might be in the UP at the same time.

--Let me know. We could meet up somewhere.

--That would be great. Thanks again.

After thirty minutes of busy work, Mary Lu knocked on Pete's door and told him Brian was ready in the interview room with Nick Montez and his lawyer. After ensuring the tape recorder was set up, Pete introduced himself to Nick, whom he met in person for the first time. The lawyer, who appeared to be in his twenties, introduced himself as James Velez and began the conversation.

--I must insist that Mr. Montez be released at once. The charges against him are minor and lack concrete evidence. He is being used as a pawn and discriminated against because of his Mexican heritage. He is an American citizen from birth and needs medical attention.

--I appreciate your aggressive representation, Counselor, but drug trafficking is not a minor offense, and the evidence points to Nick's involvement. In addition, he is considered a material witness involving the possible murder of Doug Mason. Furthermore, he is a flight risk since his parents, who are also wanted for questioning and face some of the same charges, have fled to Mexico. I see from the intake form that Mr. Montez listed his place of birth as San Elizario, Texas. I suspect it is close to the Mexican border, and Mr. Montez is familiar enough with the territory to join his parents readily.

--San Elizario is just outside of El Paso in Texas, a state in the United States and not a territory.

--I am aware of that. I'm sorry if I misspoke. We just want to ask a few questions to give him a chance to clarify his involvement in Doug Mason's drug trafficking operation and his death.

--He will not answer any questions unless granted complete immunity.

--That's not going to be offered at this time.

--You do know that the court has granted our request to move up his bail hearing to two o'clock this afternoon. We know that Amy Berendts, who is more involved with these cases, was released without needing to post bail. We expect the same treatment.

--She was not considered a flight risk.

--As Mr. Montez should not be. He did not leave the state with his parents and has not been out of the state for more than two decades.

--Okay. Let's call that check for now. But not checkmate. We have already had a nurse examine Mr. Montez's shoulder. But out of caution, Captain Chatfield will arrange for Mr. Montez to be taken to the emergency room before the hearing for a more extensive examination. That's all I have for now.

--Thank you. I assure you that Mr. Montez has told me he is willing to cooperate. But I will not allow his civil rights as an American citizen to be abused.

--Neither will I nor my staff.

Pete excused himself and went back to eat his lunch of leftovers and review his afternoon schedule.

When Pete arrived at the Middleburg sheriff's branch office, Charley Vredevelde led him to a room set up for the interviews. Pete recognized Alex Vega.

--Hello, Captain. What brings you to our West Coast counties? I thought you would have bigger things to work on in Lansing.

--Hi, Pete. I didn't have a chance to tell you last week. I'm planning to be a neighbor when I retire next spring. My wife and I bought a cottage up near North Haven. I've served as a special advisor on organized crime to the new Michigan State Police Colonel for the last few months until I finally retire next spring. He asked me to check in with Sheriff Dillingham regarding this case. He referred me to Charley. You would be my next contact, so I thought I would sit in.

--I'm surprised we are that important to the people in Lansing.

--This case is growing by the day.

--Yes, it is. It's several cases that are connected. One refers to a suicide I investigated when I started as a deputy. These interviews are just the beginning. But let's see what happens.

--Charley was telling me about a police chief who died from a shotgun blast. He still doesn't think it was suicide.

--Neither do I.

Charley came back in with a lawyer that Pete did not recognize and a slim, bearded man with a walker, who he assumed was Jonnie Van Orden. Charley made the introductions in his typical ponderous tone, which Pete imagined he had copied from the old Reformed *dominies* in Dordrecht. The lawyer's name was Harrison Bennington. Pete thought the name fit his appearance and that the name, his medium-length full head of recently styled gray hair, his trim build, and his expensive suit had attracted many of his clients, regardless of his legal acumen. Charley then continued.

--It is stipulated that Mr. Van Orden is not a suspect and is here of his own volition. He is a longtime Nederland County resident and farmer. He is also a decorated veteran of the US Army. Mr. Bennington wants to make an opening statement.

--Thank you, Sergeant. Mr. Van Orden stipulates that in the past, he grew and harvested marijuana plants for his personal consumption to alleviate the pain from wounds he received while serving in Vietnam. He sometimes sold some of his excess harvests to supplement his income. The statute of limitations has expired on these actions and is not germane to this interview. Before this meeting, the Prosecuting Attorney and I agreed to an immunity agreement allowing Mr. Van Orden to speak freely. I will not allow any harassment or overly aggressive questioning. You can begin, Sergeant.

--Thank you, Jonnie. Is it okay to call you Jonnie?

--It's okay, Charley. We've known each other for a long time.

--Jonnie, do you know a man named Harv Nielson?

--Yes, I've met him.

--How did you meet him?

--He came to my farm one time with Amy Berendts. That was her maiden name before she married Theo. Nick and Doug were with them, also.

--That would be Nick Montez and Doug Mason, Amy's boyfriend?

--Ja.

--Thank you. We want to know more about all those people. Is there anything else you can tell us about Harv Nielson?

--He pissed me off. Amy, Doug, and Nick wanted advice on growing pot. I had sold them some starter plants when I stopped growing them myself. They weren't doing well. I told them that they were overwatering. Harv tried to sell me some pain pills. It seemed that was why he had come along with the others. I didn't need them. I was getting what I needed legally from my doctor. We worked hard to keep my dosage under control. I resented being tempted.

--Did he say where he had obtained the pills?

--He said he got them from work.

--Thank you. Do you want to go next, Pete?

--Yes, I do. Thank you for being here, Jonnie. And thanks for your service and sacrifice. I was in 'Nam too. Where were you stationed?

--All the fun places. In '67, I was in what I later learned was called Operation Cedar Falls, not too far from Saigon, which they now call Ho Chi Minh City. We were supposed to wipe out the Cong and NVA in the Iron Triangle. We mostly just chased them into Cambodia. My next tour was farther north in Khe Sanh, just in time for TET. As you might know, it was the biggest battle of the war. They call it a draw now, but it spelled the end for LBJ. My luck ran out on my third tour when we retook 'Hamburger Hill.' Nixon was in charge by that time. That's where I took two rounds in my hip and leg. They were hamburger meat. That ended what I thought would be an army career. I was E7 by then.

--I am embarrassed. I was an MP in Danang for a year in the middle of all that. Easy duty. Mostly GI drunks.

--Maybe I was one of them on R & R.

--I was gone just before TET.

--Don't apologize. I made my choice. I live with it.

--I respect that. Back to our matter. Let's start with Nick Montez. How did you meet him?

--He spent his teen years on our farm. His parents helped at harvest time for a few years. My parents gave them year-round work as they grew older and let them live in a mobile home on the farm. I was rehabbing most of the time and wasn't much help.

--Rehabbing from your injuries or your addictions?

Harrison Bennington raised his palm to stop the question, but Jonnie talked through it.

--I don't mind answering. Both.

--Thank you for your honesty. We won't be holding that against you. Your recovery is admirable. What happened to Nick and his parents when you closed your business?

--They went with it. They went to work for Amy and Doug.

--How about Theo Bolinyk? Do you know him?

--Ja.

--How did you meet him?

--Amy introduced him to me at the Beeline. He bought a lot from me. He was knowledgeable.

--Did he buy more later?

--Ja.

--How much? For what length of time?

--Several years. In some seasons, he bought all of it.

--What did he do when you retired?

--He financed the purchase of my inventory and equipment for Amy. Later, as I understand it, he helped them expand and worked with Doug to do more.

--How do you know he financed it?

--He told me in advance that she was coming to see me and told me how much to ask for.

--How much was that?

--Ninety thousand.

Pete looked questioningly at Charley and Alex and then continued.

--Can you tell us anything more about Theo?

--He's a scary guy. I only worked with him because of Amy.

--Were you asked to testify against him? He was eventually convicted and served a prison sentence.

--No, I was interviewed, but my lawyer at the time would not let me answer most of the questions. Then they said they didn't need me.

--Were you and Amy close?

--No. We went to high school together. Like every other guy, I had a teenage crush on her. I was flattered that she would work with me.

--When you were active, were any of your customers law enforcement officers?

Bennington raised both palms this time; Jonnie did not answer. Pete was quiet for a few seconds and then signaled he was finished while thinking that he would like to talk to Jonnie alone next time. He walked over and shook hands with Jonnie. As the others were filing out, he stepped aside with Alex.

--I don't know that we can do anything about it, but letting Jonnie entirely off the hook even though he was involved enough to collect almost six figures seems suspect.

--I've been checking on that. The unofficial information is that the former Nederland County Sheriff's son was a customer. So was one of his deputies. That's why the extent of

Jonnie's involvement was buried. We got Theo Bolinyk anyway, so the state didn't push it. We didn't need Jonnie.

--Still, we should pull Jonnie's military records to see if he is telling the truth about his service. You could get them faster than I could.

--Good idea. I'll take care of it and send you a copy.

--Let's keep our eye on Amy Berendts. She is trying the same play. She is way more involved than she will admit. A sum like ninety thousand is not small time.

--Agreed. I'm trying to set up an interview with her. Let's keep the pressure on. We might get Theo convicted a second time, along with some bigger fish.

--That's my plan. I may need some help from you.

--Just let me know. I've got six more months to work on it from my end.

A few minutes later, Charley was on his way back with Lupe Rios and a young woman who looked little more than college-aged. Charley introduced her as Lupe's attorney, Sandra Gillum. Before Charley could start the meeting, she beat him to it.

--I need to ask why we are here today. Is Ms. Rios under suspicion? Do you need to inform her of her rights? What do you want from her?

Charley appeared irritated but went ahead carefully.

--As far as Nederland County is concerned, we are investigating the theft of various drugs and medicines from the pharmacy at Covenant Rehabilitation Center. Ms. Rios has been employed there for more than a decade. We would like her to give us information relevant to our investigation.

--Can you be more specific?

--First, we want to ask her about her relationship with Harv Nielsen, who is a suspect in this case.

Lupe didn't allow her lawyer to stop her from replying.

--I have never had a relationship with Harv Nielsen!

--How is that possible? You've worked together for years. You both were on the team with a side job caring for Joe Berendts.

--Oh, you mean a relationship in general. Of course, I knew Harv. As I got to know him better, I tried to see as little of him as possible. I told Nick to stay away from him, too.

--Are you referring to your brother, Nick Montez?

--Yes.

--Can you be more specific? Why did you want to avoid him?

--He and Doug, Amy Berendts' boyfriend, were getting into other stuff, not just a little bit of pot. I told my parents, too. That's why they decided it was time to move back to Mexico. They didn't feel safe anymore, especially after Theo showed up again.

The law enforcement men looked wide-eyed at each other before Charley replied.

--You just mentioned a lot of people. Let's start with Harv Nielson. Did you know he was stealing from the dispensary?

--No. I had no access to it. I just gave the meds they gave me to my patients. How much could he steal anyway, without causing suspicion?

--We think that, at first, he only did take a little. Later, he and a person from the pharmaceutical supplier figured out a way to increase the size of the order coming into the rehab center. Most of it quickly left via Harv. Someone from accounting got suspicious and took an inventory. Harv disappeared at the same time.

--That's way beyond what I, or Nick for that matter, was aware of. But you can be sure that Doug and Theo were involved.

Alex spoke before Charley came up with more questions.

--So, you know Theo Bolinyk. How well did you know him?

--We dated for a while.

--When was that?

--After he and Amy divorced. Before he was arrested. That's when I dumped him.

--How long did you date?

--A few months. I was attracted to his money. He took me to Vegas a couple of times. A show in Chicago. Just before the end, he let me stay in his Miami condo with a girlfriend for my two-week vacation while he was busy hiding from the law.

--We were looking for him then. Why didn't we notice you?

--I don't know. I was hiding in plain sight. A neighbor at the condo told me there was an FBI search the week before we arrived. I didn't get involved in his shit. I was having fun enjoying his money.

--Do you know where he is now?

--No. Nick told me that Amy thinks he's out of the country.

At this point, Sandra Gillum did interrupt.

--Gentlemen, Ms. Rios has been helpful, but I think this interview has gone on long enough. We'll need a formal immunity agreement before we can go ahead.

Pete held up his hand.

--I have just one question. Do you know anything that would help us find the killer of Doug Mason?

338

--No. Theo would be my choice. But he wouldn't do it himself. He'd hire someone.

--Who would he hire?

--That's two questions. It's okay, though, because I have no idea.

Pete stood up, thanked Lupe and Sandra Gillum for their cooperation, told Charley and Alex he needed to get to another appointment, and hurried out the door. He thought he had a lot of information to process from the interviews, but he wanted to see John Visser at his Honda dealership before seeing Mike's cross-country meet at Middleburg Christian. He also wanted to talk more with Alex when Charley was not listening.

The Honda showroom was in the building Pete remembered as the Pontiac dealership on what had once been the primary state artery into Middleburg. When he parked and walked in, still dressed in civilian clothes, the man who greeted him looked doubtful when Pete asked to see Mr. Visser, the owner. Pete took out his badge and was pointed up a stairway. The same routine happened again when he stopped upstairs at what looked like the reception desk, which a stern fifty-year-old woman occupied. She also seemed impressed by the badge and the 'Sheriff' title. She went down a short hall, knocked on a door, and entered. She quickly came back out and asked Pete to go right in.

John Visser was a tall, slim man with rosy cheeks and a ring of neat white hair around a bald scalp, like a caricature of a Dutchman. He held out his hand and enthusiastically greeted Pete.

--Hello, Sheriff. I recognize you from the news. I remember that you played basketball against my nephew back in the day.

--I remember that we lost. We always lost to Middleburg Christian.

--We specialized in basketball back then before we added football. What can I do for you?

--I'd like to say that my wife needs a new car and likes the ratings that the Civic is getting. That's true, but we can talk about that another day. I am investigating the death of Doug Mason. You may have seen it on the news.

--I have seen it. I'm the President of the Board of the DFG Club, so I am interested in what happens on the property.

--I'm in town for interviews with some people who may have pertinent information. I'm working with Charley Vredevelde and Alex Vega, who is part of a state police organized crime task force. Your name came up. I'm on my way to watch my son run in a cross-country invitational at Middleburg Christian High, so I thought I would stop in. I'm looking for background information.

--I would like to help, but what would I know about all this?

--The investigation is looking back a few decades. Am I correct that you were a friend of Joe Berendts?

--I guess you could say that. Not really a close friend. What does Joe have to do with this? He just died.

--He did. Doug Mason was the live-in boyfriend of Joe's daughter, Amy.

--Okay, I guess that's a link.

--Were you and Joe gambling friends?

--I was once young and foolish.

--Young and foolish enough to drive stolen cars for Van Klompenberg?

--Do I need a lawyer?

--Nah. I'm only asking about things past the statute of limitations. Unless you were involved in the murder of George Bosch. There is no statute of limitations for that.

--Let me go back to the beginning. I learned to love the high of gambling in the dorm at Covenant College. By the time I transferred to Ferris for a business degree, I was setting up games. I even went to games at Michigan State and Western. The Army games in Korea put me over the edge. Over the years, I managed to quit several times for more than a year, but someone always lured me back into a game.

--When did you get involved with the Chicago-run games?

--A friend took me to the Singapore underground club, the same one you finally shut down. I went back on my own. Joe was there, too. He took me to Chicago once. I got behind. I had to drive to stay alive. So did Joe.

--How did you avoid arrest when the Van Klompenberg stolen car ring was exposed?

--Joe said he had protection. He said it would protect me, too.

--What happened then?

--My family and my pastor staged an intervention. I went to Gamblers Anonymous. It finally stuck. So far, anyway. My first prayer every day is to ask the Lord for the strength to abstain from the games. I don't even play Monopoly with the family. The old rush would come back as strong as ever.

--Who did you work with on the driving?

--A guy named Sal Baggio or something like that set it up the first time. I knew him from the gambling clubs. After that, I just got a call and a location. I would bring a car from Van Klompenberg, make the switch, and bring one back to him.

--Who paid you?

--I didn't get paid. Sal, at first, and the guy who took over after he disappeared, didn't charge the 'vig' as he called it. I still needed to pay back the principal, which I eventually did.

--Who was that guy?

--A younger guy named Tony Triandos. He was the restaurant owner's son who ran one of the Chicago backroom operations.

--Did you know Theo Bolinyk?

--Sure. He married Joe's daughter. He was always hanging around. The rumor was that he could supply your drug of choice out in the parking lots at various locations. He was finally arrested a few years ago.

--How were you able to walk away from the organization?

--After the Van Klompenberg case, everyone laid low. I know Tony went to Florida. I walked away quietly and kept my mouth shut. No one bothered me.

--What do you know about the death of George Bosch?

--I was hoping you wouldn't ask that.

--Why is that?

--I'll be very exposed if anyone finds out what I tell you, but I've wanted to get this off my mind for a long time. Tony was drunk one time when he was collecting from me. He wanted to impress me that it would be foolish to underestimate him. He said he became a 'made man' when Sal disappeared the same time George Bosch was shot. If you watch mafia films, you know what that means. That could send you in the right direction.

--I do know what that means. Was Tony the son of Lydia, Joe's longtime girlfriend?

--That's right. And I'm done talking now. I've given you enough. I want to go on living.

--One more thing now that I know your position on the board. I'm applying for a court order to drain the ponds at the DFG, looking for more evidence for both murders. Will the club oppose it?

--No, I'm for it. They should be cleaned up anyway. We've neglected maintenance because it's not being used much anymore. We are considering selling it and using the proceeds to add to some acreage we own up north. I'll call Buck Johnson and tell him to help you out.

--Thanks for that. It'll keep our investigation going. On a personal note, if you are serious about selling, let me know. I may know a buyer.

Pete said goodbye and headed for the football field that John had funded at Middleburg Christian High. When he arrived, he caught Mike's eye while stretching out with his teammates. The invitational was a non-league event with twelve Class A and B teams from regional schools with a reputation for good cross-country programs. Mike was only a sophomore but had been placing fourth or fifth with his Wakazoo High team. His reach goal in this meet was to squeeze into the top fifty percent of the ninety-six runners. He thought a 15:30 time for the slightly more than three-mile course would give him a chance. Pete started the stopwatch he used to help Mike train in the summer. He gave Mike two thumbs up as he watched the runners pass by. The course wound around the school property and then looped around the sizeable adjacent city park, with some small hills that gave the race an authentic cross-country feel.

Fifteen minutes later, the runners were coming across the finish line. Pete saw Wakazoo's top runner finish somewhere around the twentieth slot. He estimated that Mike was in the mid-sixties. But his stopwatch showed a time of 15:33, a personal best for Mike. He strode over to where Mike's team was assembling and showed him the stopwatch while congratulating him on a good run against stiff competition with a pat on the shoulder. After he told Mike he would see him after his evening budget meeting, Pete rushed back to the Sheriff's branch office in Middleburg. He needed to use their phone to make calls that could not wait until he returned to Wakazoo.

After Pete was given an office to use, his first call was back to his office. Brian gave him the news he had gotten from Harry and Larry. Not only had they located Harv Nielson in Windsor, but Theo was back in Michigan. They even had his plate number. Brian had already checked the plate. It was a Camry rented in Toledo to Thomas Bossly with an Indiana driver's license. When they checked, they found that Thomas Bossly and his license's address did not exist. The state police patrol division had been notified to look for the Camry.

With everything else in the office under control, Pete called Alex Vega at home. Alex was highly interested in the update on Theo. He told Pete he would follow up and ensure that Brian's information would receive top priority at headquarters. Pete then walked over to Charley's office to inform him that Harv Nielson had been found. Charley wasn't happy that Harv was in Canada. Extradition would be difficult and time-consuming since he was only a suspect and not indicted. Pete suggested that they produce a plan to lure him back to Michigan. He promised Charley that he would keep him updated.

Next, Pete called Jack Stevenson at the FBI office in Clarksburg. He knew he would not be in his office, but he now had his direct line. He left a message about Tony Triandos and the possibility that he was involved with Sal Broglio and George Bosch. He needed to be added to the gangsters-of-interest list.

He then reached Sally Conners in her office.

--Tell me some good news.

--What would you call good news? How was Mike's race?

Sally was a scholarship distance runner at U of M. She was not nationally ranked, but her athletic scholarship paid for her undergraduate degree. She had been helping the girls' cross-country team as an unofficial assistant coach who did more coaching than the head coach, who was the type that just did the paperwork and let the girls run. She also took an interest in Mike's progress.

--Very good. He missed his goal time by three seconds on a challenging course. He finished back in the pack, though. It was a strong bunch of runners. But back to my issues. How did it go with Judge Eubanks?

--You scored twice. We got the grand jury. You and I need to get together with a preliminary witness list. We can get impaneled in the first week of next month.

--I've been busy today. The witness list is expanding.

--Don't overextend it. Keep it local. The judge was on the verge of leaving it all to the feds because of the links to organized crime.

--That's okay. It may go to them eventually. But we must be ready if our local murder investigation gets buried in a fed case. What about my court order for the ponds?

--You got it if you can afford it. You'll need permission from the owners to go on the property.

--I have thought of that. I've talked to one of the club's bigwigs from Middleburg, who might be on your witness list. He has reason to keep us happy.

After clarifying some details with Sally, Pete took a side trip before returning to Wakazoo. He caught Harry and Larry in Singapore as they arrived at the River Haven B & B. He wanted to get a personal feel for the results of their day trip.

Knowing he would need his budget paperwork and notes for the evening budget meeting, he stopped at his office before going home. He had everything prepared with primarily good news for the committee. He wasn't expecting anything else of interest to occur, but when he arrived, he found a message on his office phone from Betty Fields asking him to call her back. He also found he had just missed a call from John Baker, saying he had received a call from Betty, asking Pete to call as soon as possible. Knowing that Betty must have some news, Pete returned her call, hoping she was working late. She was.

--What's up, Betty?

--Something interesting for you, I hope.

--Tell me.

--Lydia called me this afternoon. She'll be here this weekend to stay on the boat until it needs to go to drydock in Chicago. She wanted us to give it a safety check and a cleanup since it hasn't been out for a while. She said her dad would also be coming in for a few days.

--That's more than interesting. Does the cleanup mean you'll be inside the living quarters?

--Absolutely.

--Could you use some extra help with that? I know someone who needs some work.

--No, we've got it....um. Oh, I get it. I do think I could use some help.

--Good. I'll send him over to apply either tomorrow or Thursday.

Pete rushed home, knowing he would have just enough time to wolf down the bowl of Flo's special chili con carne that she had waiting for him before he put on his dress uniform and rushed to his budget meeting.

.

Chapter 17—Amy, Third Wednesday, 1998

It was close to four o'clock on Wednesday when Amy parked her Lexus in the condo garage after spending the day in New Leiden. She anxiously picked up her tote with the cash Bill had freed up for Theo and went directly to the safe in her bedroom. She had to look in her desk drawer to retrieve the combination from a label on the bottom of her stapler. Theo taught her to add one to each digit and write it on the label backward. When they separated, she had changed it to subtracting two from each number, hoping to slow him down if he ever tried to open it. She only used it for her best jewelry or a big cash day at the store.

She knew he would be upset that there were only fifteen thousand dollars. To get even that much, Bill had made her go to three different banks to avoid being even close to the federal ten-thousand-dollar limit on cash withdrawals without providing their social security number and other personal information.

She checked her machine and found several messages, but the one from Theo was the most important. He said he would be at the meeting place at five o'clock. With forty minutes to burn while waiting, she poured a large chardonnay as her thoughts returned to her day in New Leiden.

·————————

After being slowed down by driving through rain that ranged between a drizzle and a downpour, she was five minutes late for her appointment with Juanita Jones and Reggie Robinson. Neither of them was smiling when she was escorted into Reggie's office. This time, Reggie took the lead instead of following Juanita.

--Amy, we have two problems we need to discuss. One is minor, I hope. I'll address that first.

--What's that?

--We have almost used up your retainer. The pressure from Sally Conners and Sheriff McAdams has been unrelenting. This is no longer just a drug case. They are also considering you a suspect in Doug Mason's death. It's taken up a lot of Juanita's time. We will need another installment before we can go much further.

--You've kept me out of jail, so you're doing your job. I'm seeing my accountant next. He'll free up some funds for me. Just give me an invoice before I leave.

--It's ready for you at the front desk. The other issue is more serious. The sheriff has been against a negotiated plea deal for you because he feels you are holding back from telling the whole truth of what you know.

--Like what? He wants me to make his case for him. I don't know what he needs me to tell him.

--For instance, they interviewed others who portray you as a central figure in the marijuana operation, not just an innocent absentee landowner. Then, there is your ex-husband, a convicted felon whose name keeps appearing in this investigation. They think you are still working with him. They want you to help them find him. They are even looking into your relationship with your father, who they claim had worked for an organized crime group for decades.

--It's all guilt by association. Plus, I have given them some good stuff.

--That's our line when we talk to them. It seems that what you've told them has just whetted their appetite. But it would be wise of you to remember that they already have enough for a conviction on a felony charge. That would mean jail time. If others started talking first, we would be in a difficult position. You could be implicated in more felonies, including murder.

--Murder! Are they crazy? What do they want from me?

--They know you didn't pull the trigger, but they think you may have been involved in Doug's death. I think it's safe to say that they want Theo and whomever he is working with or for.

--Even if I wanted to, I couldn't. Theo is too careful. He doesn't trust me.

--But he does want money from you; perhaps that could be used as a lure.

Amy gulped the last half of her glass of wine. She felt a dread come into her mind that made her realize she was boxed in. Juanita had warned her as she left the law office that she was probably being watched, perhaps by more agencies than the Sheriff Department. Amy had noticed a squad car parked at the corner convenience store at the last turn before the road led to her condo entrance. She had to assume unmarked vehicles were waiting to follow her if she went to meet Theo.

He would know something was up if she didn't meet with him. She would become not only expendable but a problem to be eliminated. Her best chance was to help the law bring Theo into custody. She dialed Juanita. To get through to her, she told the receptionist that it was a matter of life and death.

--What's up, Amy?

--I know where Theo is going to be in twenty-five minutes. He'll be in Wakazoo.

--Stay by the phone.

She poured some more wine, waited, and agonized, hoping she had made the right choice. Ten minutes later, she answered the phone and was surprised to hear Pete McAdams' voice.

--Where is he, Amy?

--Where is who?

--Theo, of course. I just talked to Juanita. You are in a dangerous situation. We are watching you. Either we'll follow you, or you can tell us and stay safe. That's what Juanita wants you to do.

--What kind of deal am I getting?

--That's between Juanita and Sally. But there will be no deal if you don't work with us.

--Okay. What choice do I have? I'm supposed to meet him at the Singapore River Motel. He'll be dressed like he's going fishing. Probably driving an older car or pickup. I'm supposed to meet him in ten minutes.

--We are on our way there. Stay home. I'll send a car to protect you if he comes to your place.

--There is already one here.

--I need that one. I'll get Cory to send one of his local guys.

Amy waited for news, expecting Gerrit to return from Colorado in about an hour. She thought her meetings in New

Leiden with Harry had been tense, but they were nothing compared to what was happening as she waited. She knew from talking with Harry before the meetings that he and Larry had been playing detective on Tuesday and had seen Theo in Windsor. They had passed on a description and plate numbers of a rental car he was driving to the Sheriff Department. Her thoughts returned to the previous day of meetings in New Leiden.

———————

After she met with Juanita, she arrived at Bill's office to find Harry waiting in the building lobby, sitting next to Allen Zuverink, who had a large file box on the floor next to him.

--Hi, Harry. I see you have a friend with you. Hello, Allen. Nice to see you again.

--Good to see you too, Amy.

Allen's tone was pleasant, but Harry responded without a smile.

--I'm glad we're all getting along here. We'll see if it continues. You'll be happy that Larry and I saw your ex yesterday. He's on the move.

--Where was he?

--Windsor, Canada, unbelievably. He crossed over into Detroit when we lost him. We passed on the description and plate number of his rental Camry to law enforcement.

--Who knew? Never mind Theo, I thought this was a friendly meeting too, Harry. You can see I didn't bring any reinforcements. I thought we were getting along these few weeks.

--I thought so, too. However, I'm part of the away team here. The receptionist made us wait in the building lobby instead of welcoming us into their comfortable office. She didn't even offer us coffee and Danish. I want to make sure that what I'm shown today is on the up and up.

--Why wouldn't it be?

--I can think of many reasons. I've never known you, or Joe, to be a rule follower.

--I don't have to show you anything, you know.

--You do need to show us. We oversee Rose's trust. We need to be sure that its assets are intact. I also must be sure that Joe's true wishes were represented in the last will you filed. If there is any doubt, I'm not afraid of joining Lydia in contesting it. Showing me all the details in a friendly meeting could save us time and money.

Bill Snyder walked into the lobby and jumped into the conversation.

--It looks like Allen has a big file with him. Would he like to show it to us?

Allen smiled and replied quietly.

--You already have it. It's four years old. It shows the state of Joe's finances when you took over the accounts from my dad. Harry deserves an accounting of the management of his assets from that time to his death.

--Why would he? Amy was given power of attorney more than two years ago. Frankly, it's none of Harry's business.

--It would be Harry's business if Amy took advantage of a stroke victim. Also, Joe's financial situation could negatively influence the assets in Rose's trust. I have replaced my father as the trustee. The trust stipulates that Harry is the guardian of his children, who are the trust beneficiaries until they reach the age of twenty-five. Until then, funds can be drawn only for their post-high school education, not exceeding twenty thousand dollars each per annum. The administration fee is also limited.

Harry spoke up again, more quietly than Allen.

--We believe that Amy used Joe's assets for her personal benefit and that the trust assets may have been put forward as collateral on loans made to Joe. If you don't provide evidence that this is not the case, I will get a court order to obtain his financial records.

Bill and Amy both started to reply. Bill held up his hand; Amy waited with tight lips.

--Amy, since this is not the friendly meeting we expected, ending it would be in your best interest.

--Absolutely! Fuck you, Harry.

Harry was already standing up while Allen was grabbing his file.

--Don't get hostile, Sister. We have another meeting to get through. It's lunchtime. See you in an hour.

Amy glared as Harry left and turned to Bill.

--He can't do any of that, can he?

--Not easily. But if he is willing to spend his money, he could cause problems.

--Like what?

--It would not be easy to prove, but he could make a case that, after his stroke three years ago, Joe was bullied into giving you power of attorney. That gave me the ability to move his assets over to you gradually. Remember, your goal was to get them under $100,000 so Joe could qualify for Medicaid senior care payments if he ever needed to be placed in a facility. Your last step was to threaten to abandon him unless he changed his will to leave everything to you. It's not a good look.

--You helped with all that.

--I just gave you options.

--I thought they were recommendations.

--Whatever. We would not want to have anyone looking too closely at the records. Joe did well over the years after he recovered from his issues in the early seventies. He had almost a million dollars in assets. We had whittled that down to under two-fifty. We would not want to show anyone the increase in your assets during the same period.

--I worked hard for that.

--Yes, you did. Some of it was legitimate, but you would have been unable to build your real estate and portfolio the way you did without Joe's assets. It would be best if you found a way to compromise. Work a deal, buy him off. Just like Lydia.

--Speaking of Lydia. What do I do about her? How do I shut her up about the condo?

--Tell her to make you an offer and then negotiate. Be prepared to lose a couple of hundred, however.

--Christ! I'm bleeding money all over. Now, Reggie needs more because a murder charge is now a possibility.

--That's the problem you're up against. You're fighting for your freedom. If you walk away a free person with twenty-five to fifty percent of your assets intact, count yourself lucky.

Amy left Bill and walked over to Carl Zandstra's office. She arrived early for the appointment and was glad Carl could see her.

--Good morning, Amy. Have you had lunch?

--I think I'll skip it today. There's not much time. I've just had a nasty meeting with Harry, with another one coming up here.

--We do have time. I just canceled the meeting.

--Why? What happened?

356

--I received a call from Gerald Brooks.

--Who's he?

--One of the best, if not the best, probate attorneys in western Michigan. Harry retained him this morning. The battle over the estate will now be played out between attorneys instead of directly with Harry.

--One more expense to drain me. Do we need to hire a big hitter like this Brooks guy?

--We already have one. My brother-in-law, Peter. Remember? He's in the 'A' league, just like Brooks. But you are right. It won't be cheap. It would be faster and cheaper if you could find a way to compromise with your brother.

--Bill Snyder just told me the same thing. My freedom is going to cost me. What do we do next?

--Nothing. I'll tell Peter to let them know that you would prefer this negotiation to be non-adversarial without giving away too much in advance. We'll see what happens. Your main job is to work with Reggie and Juanita on the criminal side of things. Come on, I'll take you to the club for lunch. I think you need a drink.

––––––––––––

By the time Gerrit arrived just before eight o'clock, Amy still had not heard anything from the sheriff or his staff about Theo. She was left wondering if they had found him, if they arrested him, or if he slipped away again. She told Gerrit the story of her day as soon as she could get him to sit down with his tea and her wine. She described the meetings with Bill and Carl that did not go well. She then included a final New Leiden stop to see Stephanie. She wanted to feel her out about buying the Singapore store if Amy could not keep running it.

357

Stephanie was intrigued by the idea. She told Amy that she would be willing to purchase the inventory, 'not at full value, of course,' and sign a rental agreement for a season to see how it went. She could not risk more because Amy would no longer be there, and she was the store's biggest asset.

She took a deep breath before she told Gerrit about Theo and Pete McAdams. Gerrit had seen the squad car and suggested they could go down and ask if the patrol officer could get the Sheriff on the radio.

The police officer turned out to be the Singapore Chief, Cory Epperson.

--You should stay in your house, Amy. Theo is still at large.

--Fuck. They missed him! I'm not surprised. He's like a snake. He can slither away from anything.

--Either he's on foot, or he found another ride. They finally found the rental across town.

--What do we do now?

--Let me walk you back up to your unit. I wouldn't want anything to happen to you. The judge also released Nick Montez without bail. I wanted him to stay in custody on a B & E charge for the break-ins at your store, for your sake.

--Where is he now?

--He needed a place to stay in the county. A cousin near Wayland agreed to let him stay with him. Who knows how long he will stay put?

Gerrit gave Amy a questioning glance and then told Cory.

--I'll get her back inside. We'll wait to hear from the sheriff.

When they were safely back in the condo with all the doors locked, Gerrit insisted on turning the alarm on. He played around with it and figured out how to not arm zone three, which would have turned on the interior motion detectors.

--That chief seems a little too interested in you.

--I noticed that, too. I could use that to my advantage.

--I'd avoid him. This town is known for corruption. He could be playing for the wrong team.

--You might be correct, but I'm afraid of what Theo will do.

--Let's think about that. Of course, he's going to think that you turned him in. But think about it. The Sheriff knew about Theo's car. It must have been spotted. That lets you off the hook. You can tell him you were on the way and noticed you were being followed. You turned around and went back home to avoid exposing him.

--Do you know what? You're right. That could work.

Amy's phone rang again. It was Juanita.

--Sorry I'm calling so late. I have another case that's just blown up. What's happened so far?

Amy filled her in on the details and then summed up her situation.

--Theo slipped away. I'm going to be the bad guy on all sides. Pete McAdams thinks I tipped Theo off. Theo thinks I turned him in. Gerrit thinks I can explain my way out of it, but I'm unsure. Hopefully, Theo is going to be too occupied to worry about me.

--I hope so, too. I'm glad Gerrit is there with you. I would worry if you were alone for many reasons. Anyway, I also called because I have some news of my own.

--Bad or good?

--I'm not sure yet. I received a call from Alex Vega. He is a long-time state investigator assigned to an organized crime task force in Lansing. He wants to arrange an interview with you.

--What do I know about organized crime?

--That's what he wants to know. Theo and Doug are both on their radar. That's one degree of separation from you— twice. Also, the possible drug charges in Singapore shine a light directly on you.

--Fuck! They're both like a bag of rocks pulling me down.

--The other news is that Singapore County is no longer pursuing the investigation into your farm and your acquaintances. The state is taking that over.

--Is that bad or good?

--It might be good. It's a serious investigation, but you will be a small fish in a big pond. I think a deal with no prison time is possible if you cooperate. But Sheriff McAdams is following through with both the murder cases.

--Both?

--Yes. Doug's, of course. And that dead file case about that police chief. Once again, your connections make you at least a witness, and I know McAdams is thinking about you being part of a murder conspiracy.

--He's out of his mind.

--Perhaps, but he is not backing away.

After talking with Juanita, Amy felt light-headed from the events of her day. She asked Gerrit to make supper while she took another shower and went through a yoga routine to calm her anxiety. After one of Gerrit's vegan creations, another glass of wine, and a shared pipe, she regained control of her mind and body again. Then the phone rang one more time.

--Damn, do I need to answer that?

--Yes, you do.

It was Harry.

--Fuck you, Harry. Haven't you given me enough trouble today?

--Sorry, this is a different issue. It's about one of your partners in crime, Harv Nielson.

--He may be a criminal, but he's not my partner.

--Harv is why Larry and I went to Canada. We started looking for him in Saginaw and followed him into Canada.

--What are you? The Hardy Boys?

--We prefer Sherlock and Watson. Larry is a licensed PI, you know. That's why I'm alone today. He has an actual, paying case to work on.

--Oh, I'm sure. What case is that?

--Top secret, of course. What we want to do now is to get Harv to come back to Michigan, preferably somewhere around here. Lupe thinks that he could take some pressure off Nick. Especially for Doug's murder. Harv had more reason to kill Doug than Nick. More than you did, too. That's why you should help us.

--What am I supposed to do?

--Lupe told Larry you could reach him in Canada if you needed him for Joe. We know that he often spent time with his son and his ex. He sometimes stayed with a friend in Windsor. That's the number we're looking for. His mother has the ex-wife's number, but the number she had for Windsor is not working anymore.

--Okay. I've got two numbers. I'll get them for you. How do you know his mother? Is she willing to help?

--Did you know that Harv is your friend Butch Bosch's nephew? I met his mother in Saginaw. We hit it off. She wants Harv to stop running, return to Middleburg, and make a deal. She also wants her mom's car back, which she loaned to Harv. That's Harv's grandmother, George Bosch's ex-wife.

--It all sounds incestuous to me. You should also know that Singapore County has passed the drug investigation that started with my farm up to a state organized crime task force. I don't know if that would include Harv's pill theft in Nederland County.

--What does that mean for you?

--Who knows? Time will tell. Anyway, I wish you luck with Harv, I think.

Amy found the numbers in the card file beside the kitchen phone and gave them to Harry. Gerrit said he was ready for his evening meditation and sleep. Amy was also hoping to be able to sleep and recuperate. She went to her bedroom, hoping there would be no more calls. There was one more. She took a deep breath before picking up on the third ring.

--Hi, Amy, this is Tony.

--Tony! What the hell do you want? I hope your mother didn't make you call. I'm not giving in to her, so don't try to talk me into anything.

--No, no. I'm calling for me. I'm coming to help Grandpa Gus move his boat to a Chicago dry dock next week. We could reminisce. When I knew I would be coming, you were the first person I thought of. We had some good times.

--Christ, that was five or six years ago. It was a fling for a few weeks. I'm with someone right now.

--Already? I heard your last boyfriend was just killed. Was it you who did it?

--Fuck, no. An old friend is helping me with my grief, such as it is. It's working.

--Okay. I'll leave you alone for a while. How would you like to spend some time in sunny Florida this winter? Repeat the past.

--I think I'll pass. Where's Sandy?

--At home. She kicked me out.

--What a surprise. I'd invite you for a drink next week, but you and Gerrit are on different planets.

--Gerrit, the guru? I guess I can't compete with that. You must be in Pious Amy mode right now. If you change your mind, you can call when you're ready for a fun time. I'll get a room above the pub. My mom will be using the boat.

Amy remembered the winter when she and Tony were together for almost six weeks. Rose had died in the fall of 1992. Joe had talked Amy into coming to Miami with him after the holidays to stay in the two-bedroom condo he was renting from Theo. Joe wanted desperately to get out of the cold Dordrecht winter and the oppressive religious atmosphere created by Rose's funeral. Amy felt she needed a break after a successful but exhausting season in her Singapore store, followed by the final month of Rose's illness and death. She knew that Joe would mainly be with Lydia in the condo she was renting from him. That was fine with her. She also needed the alone time away from Doug, who was always in her life even before he moved in with her.

She tried to avoid Lydia, but one time, Joe insisted she go with him to Lydia's for drinks. Lydia wanted her to meet her son, Tony. Amy was not ready for him in one way, but he was exactly what she needed in another. He was a gregarious, six-foot-tall, light-haired Italian who lit up and dominated the scene wherever he went. Joe had only told her unflattering stories about him that questioned his character and intelligence. They were typical of Joe's complaints: Tony could never hold onto a job; his father and grandfather had to support him; he wasn't intelligent or ambitious enough to even be more than a greeter at one of the three Triandos restaurants in the Miami area. But, as she became involved with him, Amy saw something different. Although Tony played the irresponsible playboy role, she saw the respect and sometimes fear with which the restaurant employees treated him. Even his grandfather seemed to interact with him as an equal.

Since he was five years younger than she was, his attention surprised and flattered her. There was a hint of danger in his fearlessness, his having no bounds on his behavior, and his apparent connections to his grandfather's reputed criminal enterprises. That hint excited her, but it also made her cautious. She was sure he was having a fling while separated from his wife and two children. He even told Amy he would return to Sandy and the kids after she got over his latest escapade with a blonde model he met in Las Vegas. Amy let him know that she was okay with that. It was just a fling for her, too. In the meantime, in addition to the sexual intimacy, they explored the Miami nightlife and twice spent a weekend at a casino resort in the Bahamas. They were business trips for Tony. He had connections everywhere he went. After six weeks, Sandy was ready for him to come home, while Amy was ready to go back to Singapore.

Amy woke up early on Thursday morning with dread dominating her thoughts. Gerrit's door was closed, meaning he was sleeping or deep in meditation. The first thing that disturbed her was how she had let her ego take over when Tony called. She was flattered that he called, wanting to see her again. She knew that because of his grandfather, he still had connections to Chicago organized crime with tentacles that reached Michigan, especially along the Lake Michigan coast. She thought it possible that he could get caught up in the state police investigation–the same investigation that she was desperately trying to avoid.

She realized now that his call was a threat, letting her know he was watching her. She could see herself in a no-win situation. Even if she promised not to tell the sheriff everything she knew, Tony could decide to do away with her anyway. Dead people will never become witnesses. Cooperating and receiving protection would be her best chance to survive and avoid jail time. The same was true of Theo, but he wasn't as scary as Tony.

Another problem appeared as she thought through her situation. The investigation was now divided. She would need to get agreements from both Singapore County murder investigators and the more comprehensive state and federal drug team, which would mean that she would need something to offer both. That would mean giving information about Theo's drug operation and Tony's involvement in a murder.

Gerrit came from his bedroom as she was preparing her morning tea and breakfast. Unlike most people, his mental state was already in peak form when he woke up. She brought him up to date on Tony's late-night phone call.

--That does seem ominous. What is your response going to be?

--I'm thinking I need to cave. Tell everything I know to get protection and probation instead of jail time. It's the safest thing to do at this point.

--I agree with you. We should also consider moving somewhere safer. You are an easy target. You would need permission, of course, but it's something we could ask for.

--Where would we go?

--Let me think about that. You should call Juanita and get started on the negotiation.

Amy got a call back mid-morning after leaving an urgent message for Juanita before the office opened.

--What's up, Amy?

--I am ready to make any deal that would allow me to avoid jail. I won't hold anything back.

--Why the change of heart?

--I realize that I am a target whether I testify or not. My best bet is cooperating for a no-jailtime deal and protection from Theo and Tony.

--Who's Tony?

She gave Juanita a quick review of the previous day after she had left Juanita's office.

--Okay, we need to rework our strategy. I am entirely booked today and tomorrow but could work in a lunch meeting tomorrow.

--We'll be there. I want Gerrit to sit in with me.

--Be here at one and bring lunch. The seafood linguini from Giuseppe's would be good.

--You got it.

Amy found Gerrit at the desk in the office, writing cursive in a thick notebook.

--We're set with Juanita for tomorrow at one. I hope you can go with me.

--Absolutely! It would be best if you weren't traveling alone. I've also been thinking that we should get some private security. It seems like the sheriff doesn't have the will or the workforce to do what needs to be done. I don't know how to find someone in a small town like this.

--I like that idea. I'll bet Harry's friend Larry would know someone. I'll give Harry a call.

She tried to reach him at the B & B and left a message for Harry with Rob. Then she remembered his Nokia phone and dialed it.

--This better be important. I'm paying roaming rates. I'm surprised I have a connection. I'm north of Traverse City.

--It'll be quick. I want to talk to Larry. I want to add a private security service. I thought he would know someone.

--That's part of his service. I saw it on his business card. He's just starting but has many contacts from his state police career. He says he's full-service. He could put together a team for you. It sounds like things are getting scary.

--They are. It's not only Theo, either. How do I reach him?

--I have his beeper number on my phone. Here it is.

Amy thanked Harry and dialed the beeper number. Within a minute, her phone rang.

--Hi, Larry. This is Amy.

--I didn't think I recognized the number. What's going on?

--Harry gave me your beeper number. Things are getting crazy here. Gerrit wants me to add some private security. The Sheriff Department is hit-and-miss. The locals are hopeless. He said you can do that.

--I certainly can. Do you have a security system?

--Ja. It was updated last year. We are keeping it on with the interior motion turned off.

--That's good. I'll need to come over to look so we can decide what level of security you need. I could be there around four. How do I find your place?

Amy gave him the directions.

At 4:00, wondering if Larry was lost, Amy looked out her front window, seeing him walk up to her front door with a dark-haired woman wearing jeans and a T-shirt. She was at least six feet tall with two hundred pounds spread evenly over her fit body, but she looked medium-sized next to Larry. Amy opened the door and let them in before they needed to knock.

--Hello, Amy. Do you remember my associate, Bonnie van Draght? She's a cousin of yours, I think. She's helping me with another case in Singapore, where she is undercover. She'll help me here, as well.

--Hi, Bonnie. I haven't seen you since we were kids. Where do we start, Larry?

--Tell me who you are worried about. Is there anyone else besides Theo?

--Another old friend has shown up. At least, he said he would be here next week. His name is Tony Triandos. All I'm sure of is that he is the grandson of a guy named Gus Martino, but I know he is involved in all the stuff that has happened. I don't know much, but he may want to ensure I don't become a witness. He's more dangerous than Theo. He called me unexpectedly, trying to be nice, but I assumed it was a threat.

--That's a reasonable assumption. Do you have any photos of either him or Theo?

--I could find something in one of my photo boxes.

--Okay, let's start there. You can look for the photos. We'll check the security system and then walk around inside and out.

After an hour, Amy and Gerrit, who had returned from grocery shopping, were waiting in the kitchen with several Polaroid snapshots when Larry and Bonnie arrived at the rear of the condominium. They had climbed up the fifty stairsteps from the beach and walked along the trail from the top of the dune to the complex. After stomping and brushing most of the sand off their shoes, they came in the patio door. Still breathing heavily, Larry looked closely at the pictures and handed them to Bonnie, who did not seem winded.

--These will work. The difficulty is that there are several points of access to your unit. To add some nighttime protection, we can narrow that down with several plug-in trip wire and spotlight setups on the side and beach. It'll be easy to bury the wires under the sand. The foot traffic is not heavy this time of year, but there is too much blowing vegetation to use motion detectors. We can also put in a plug-in motion light on your driveway. Your security system is top-notch, so the inside is well-protected. The big question is whether and how much staff to add. The lights and your security system give us a warning. Having an armed agent on-site twenty-four hours gives you actual protection.

--What do you think, Gerrit?

They waited for Gerrit to think it through. He asked Larry for a cost estimate. Larry calculated in his head and gave him a number.

--I think you need to do it, Amy. Hopefully, things will soon come to a head. We may only need it for a few weeks.

--When can you start?

--We can put in the warning spots tomorrow. Bonnie has already volunteered for the first shift this evening. I'll take the graveyard. Tomorrow, I'll work some others I've worked with into a schedule. They would all be ex-state police, like Bonnie. No amateurs. I see Theo in these pictures. He's the skinny one with the mean and hungry look, Bonnie. Is the good-looking younger guy Tony?

--That's right.

--Okay, I'll get copies to the Sheriff Department and the locals. Are we ready to go?

--Okay, let's do it.

--Great. It will relieve a lot of the fear that you are feeling. Right now, we have an appointment with another client. Bonnie will be back around seven for the first shift.

Gerrit looked more relieved than Amy.

--Thank you for your quick response. Bonnie, when you return, I can have a hefty salad bowl ready for supper. Veggies, quinoa, black beans, and miso.

Bonnie looked doubtful.

--Uh...I think I'll pick up something more substantial on the way back. I didn't have much for lunch.

Chapter 18—Pete, Third Friday, 1998

Wednesday and Thursday had been days of little progress on the DFG murders. It convinced Pete that he needed to let the state police and the FBI gradually take over the investigation into the various drug offenses. There were too many links outside the county and the state for his department to work with all the puzzle pieces. A Singapore County grand jury could not adequately gather the evidence necessary to indict all the participants. His focus and energy should be applied to the murders of Joe Berendts and Doug Mason. His responsibility was to name the suspects and supply the evidence for Sally Conners so she could indict and convict. He felt like he was treading water and needed to get moving again.

He spent most of Wednesday morning on routine management work, including making the changes to his budget that the committee had requested. Happy that he had been asked only to make minor tweaks, he penciled them in and passed them on to Priscilla to make the formal copy that would be sent back to the committee. He spent time with Brian going over staffing. They were two patrol officers short after their new hire. Anticipating normal attrition, transfers, and promotions, they decided it was time to plan a more robust recruitment program. Knowing that the state police were sponsoring a recruitment and new officer training seminar in early November, he asked Brian to sign up. Enough funds were allocated to training expenses in the current budget to pay for it.

His first call had been to Larry Vandevoss for the second consecutive day. After receiving the message that Pete had left at his son's house, Larry called back later in the morning.

--What can I do for you today, Sheriff? We brought you good news yesterday.

--I hope it's good news. Theo Bolinyk is still not found. Plus, Harv Nielson is still out of reach in Canada.

--Eventually, you'll get him. We're trying to find a way to get Harv to cross back into Michigan. We should have Amy call and tell him she has some money that Doug was supposed to pay him.

--I think that's a bad idea. It would just scare him even more. Harv's pill case belongs to Nederland County, as does Amy's marijuana farm investigation. Do you remember Alex Vega?

--Of course. What's he doing these days?

--He's helping the Colonel investigate organized crime throughout the state. He's interested in all this drug stuff in this county. I'm thinking I'll back off and concentrate on the murder cases.

--Murder cases plural?

--Yeah. George Bosch and Doug Mason. That's why I'm calling. There's a cleaning and maintenance crew that will be working on a boat at the Singapore Yacht Club that I'm interested in. I'm looking for someone to join them. Someone who knows what I might be looking for.

--I know one person who would be perfect.

Pete gave Larry the information for Betty Fields and an overview of what to look for. Larry said he would call back with confirmation. He also said he would devise a better enticement for Harv Nielson to come into Michigan, but he did not commit to backing off.

After an early lunch of microwaved leftovers of Flo's southwestern chili from the night before, he went to see Jimmy Dickerson again, timing his arrival toward the end of lunch at the center. Jimmy was still in the dining room, sipping coffee, waiting for staff to wheel him to his room for his daily nap.

--Hi, Pete. Have you come to bother me again? I told you all I know.

--I forgot something last time, Jimmy.

--What's that?

--Do you know Tony Triandos?

--Sure. He was Lydia's kid.

--What do you know about him?

--When he was younger, he hung around the back rooms, trying to pick up the working girls. He thought he was a real Romeo.

--What about later?

--He was the same, only scarier. The rumor was that he was an enforcer for the Boss.

--Who was the Boss?

--I never knew. Someone from Chicago.

--Did you know Lydia's father?

--Sure. He was around sometimes.

--Some people think he was the Boss.

--He was a serious guy. Everyone showed him respect. But I didn't think he was the big Boss.

--Do you think that Sam Morgan might know?

--Like I said last time. He knows a lot more than I do.

Pete thanked Jimmy and returned to the office to call Sam Morgan. His wife, Eva, said he was recovering from a medical procedure and couldn't see Pete until the next day.

Larry Vandevoss called again in the midafternoon. He had found an associate who would apply to Betty Fields at the yacht club to be part of the cleanup crew for Gus Martino's boat. The associate would apply on Thursday morning and join the team without delay. Pete knew it was a shot in the dark but worth taking. He told Larry to ask his man for anything he could find on Lydia's son, Tony Triandos, who might be coming to stay on the boat with her. Larry chuckled and said he would need to ask his lady, not his man. Pete said a woman would be even better. She would raise less suspicion and pay more attention to detail.

———————

Just after dawn on Thursday morning, Pete was already back at the DFG Club. The pumps were still running but working slowly, trying to suck water out of the remaining thick muck left over in the deepest part of the first pond. Thus far, nothing of interest has been uncovered. The pumps had been running since noon the day before. Tim Harvison's plan called for pumping as much water as possible into the largest pond on the other side of the club, which would allow most of it to be pumped back into the drained pond.

Later in the morning, the crew planned to return with a backhoe to dig into the rest of the muck after moving the hoses and pumps to the second pond. The backhoe with heavy tracks would move around the firmest edge of the mud while unloading one bucket at a time onto one of two shallow barges that could be pulled around the muddy pond. Each bucket would be carefully inspected for anything that resembled human bones. When one barge was full, water was added to allow a shore-based pump and flexible tubing system to send the sludge to a smaller third pond that the DFG decided to fill. Pete hoped that something would soon be found proving his theories about the murder cases to be correct.

When he returned to his office, Pete called Betty to tell her to be ready for a woman to come to apply instead of a man. Betty laughed and said that the woman was named Bonnie van Draght. Pete did not tell Betty that he was well-acquainted with Bonnie. He knew she would be more than competent because he had been her supervisor for several years when she joined the state police. Bonnie was already at the office, filling out the paperwork. He also asked Betty if she had seen a younger man hanging around the Dorothea. She had seen a young man, who seemed like more than an employee, show up several times with a crew that either brought the yacht in for the summer months or sailed it to Miami for the winter. She was not sure if he was family or not. She thought she remembered his name being Tony. Pete told her to also be on the lookout for him this week.

Next, he called Alex to update him on Theo. They commiserated over his ability to slip away. Alex told Pete he would update the state police looking for Theo. He also told

Pete to impound the rental car. He would send a crew to go over it in the next few days.

Later in the morning, he left to confront Sam Morgan. When he arrived, Eva asked if he would like to stay for lunch. She had plenty of homemade soup she was heating up for Sam. The aroma from the kitchen tempted Pete, but he knew he did not want to stay that long. She guided him to the den where Sam was watching a rerun of *Matlock*. He turned the high-volume sound down to normal. Pete still struggled to talk above the sound without yelling.

--I'm surprised you're watching a defense attorney, Sam. You were on the other side.

--It's the only thing that's on. It's okay. I like Andy Griffiths. Besides, I started as a defense attorney. My specialty was charging a lot to get rich drunks out of trouble.

--I only have one thing to ask you about.

--What's that? I told you I'm not giving you anything more.

--I've heard that Tony Triandos is coming back to town. What do you know about him?

Sam grabbed the remote and turned off the TV. He pointed to the chair next to him, allowing Pete to sit.

--How do you know that?

--Sources. His mother and grandfather are coming in, too.

--It's your fault for stirring all this up again. I'm going to need some protection.

--Why?

--What do you mean, 'Why?' He could kill me!

--You'll have to give me more than that. Why are you afraid of Tony? Do you know what I'll find tomorrow in the DFG pond? If you are in danger, you should change your story and tell me the truth so I can try to help you.

--My best chance is to keep my mouth shut.

--What if I bring you in for questioning?

--I have a lawyer who won't let that happen. If anything happens to me, it'll be on your conscience.

--I'll have a patrol car concentrate on your neighborhood, more to look for Tony than to protect you. That's all I can do unless you tell us everything you know. I'll let you know what we find in the pond. That might refresh your memory.

Pete picked up the remote, turned the TV back on, and left.

When he returned to the office after picking up an Italian sub at Subway, he found three faxes on his office machine. He sat down with his sandwich and studied them. The first was Jonnie Van Orden's military record.

He had not exaggerated his history in Vietnam. Jonathan Van Orden was awarded a Silver Star, a Bronze Star with Oakleaf Cluster, and, of course, a Purple Heart. He was treated and rehabilitated for over a year and then received a disability discharge due to severe leg injuries. The other details were routine: basic training at Fort Knox, advanced infantry at Fort Polk, marksman awards at both, and back to Fort Knox for a ten-week NCO course. He went to Vietnam and was already promoted to an E5 specialist pay grade. After his first two tours, he was indeed an E7 staff sergeant. There were no black marks and many more routine commendations.

Pete then pored over the medical examiner's report that had finally come in from Laura Denison in Lansing. He found the critical facts in the second half of the report. The rifle bullet had penetrated Doug Mason's skull from the front and had come partially out the rear. The shell was a Winchester .308. It was sent back to the investigation team for further analysis. The bullet was likely to have been lethal, but not at once. Doug may have been still barely alive when the shotgun blast hit him. The proximate cause of death was heavy bleeding from the shotgun blast, part of which severed his left carotid artery.

The report from John Newsome was also mostly routine and predictable. Two things stood out. First, partial palmprints were on the shotgun, and fingerprints were on the .308 bullet. They were not enough to find a match in a database, but if a suspect existed, the partials and the suspect's prints could be matched. Pete was hoping to focus on a suspect soon. If he did, the partials could become a definitive piece of evidence. John also told him that the location where the body was found was not the site of the shooting. The body had been moved. Pete had already thought that to be true. Nick Montez's bloody jacket found at Amy's farm now became significant. Pete suspected that the Mexican shooters whom Nick described were a fantasy. Pete would need to return to Amy's farm and look for something he had missed. John had also changed his mind. John was now recommending that the ponds be drained. Pete chuckled. He was way out in front of that recommendation. He hoped the next day would bring results.

Pete was about to leave the office, happy that there was a lull allowing him to check on his beavers on his mother's land before going to the high school to watch Star's volleyball game, when Mary Lu told him that Juanita Jones was on hold. He quickly picked up the call on his line.

--What's up, Ms. Jones?

--We have a Theo sighting, hopefully. I expect a considerable payback for Amy if this works out.

--If she helps us get Theo, we will give her credit. Tell me what you have.

--Call Amy. She'll give you the details.

After talking to Amy, Pete quickly organized a team of available deputies and police officers. With help from the Wakazoo PD, he filled four squad cars with two men in each. He had them wait in the county jail parking lot. Knowing that Benny Ramirez lived close to the office, Pete reached him at home, telling him to be ready for Pete to pick him up in his Bronco in fifteen minutes, dressed in plain clothes, preferably something for fishing. Pete instructed Brian to call Alex Vega and arrange state police backup. Brian would remain in the office, waiting for Pete to radio in with instructions for the patrol cars. After grabbing the photos of Theo from his desk, Pete raced home in his Bronco, put on some outdoor gear, picked up Benny, and arrived at the Singapore River Motel five minutes before the time Theo had given to Amy.

Not seeing anything close to the Camry rental described by Harry, Pete drove a mile past the motel before returning to the almost empty parking lot. After waiting ten minutes, he entered the door with a worn 'OFFICE' sign, leaving Benny in the car. He hit the desktop bell three times before hearing a voice.

--Hold on, I'm coming.

It took over a minute, but an old, thin man with a cane and two hearing aids finally arrived behind the counter. He talked slowly in a loud voice.

--How many rooms do you need?

Pete spoke just as loudly and slowly.

--None right now. I'm looking for a friend of mine. His name is Theo Bolinyk. Is he staying here?

--Not a name I know.

Pete pulled Theo's photo.

--This is what he looks like.

--Who's asking?

Pete pulled out his badge and ID.

--I thought it was you. I've seen you on TV.

--Do you know this person? He's missing.

--Sure. His name is Tom Bossly.

--When did you see him last?

--A couple of hours ago. He left in his car right away.

--Was it a blue Camry? Do you have the license number?

--It could've been a Camry. He was a regular. I didn't ask him for it.

--I need to look at the room.

--Do you have a search warrant?

--Don't need one. We're in hot pursuit.

--Too far for me to walk. I'll get the key.

Pete went to the room. He took one step inside after carefully unlocking the door. The space was empty and undisturbed. After searching the bathroom, he brought the key back to the office.

--What did you find, Sheriff?

--Nothing interesting.

--I'm not surprised. He always traveled light.

Pete arrived at the high school during a timeout in the second period of Star's volleyball match. He had left Benny at the motel just in case Theo returned to the motel before sending the four patrol cars in four different directions to look for the Camry. Finding it in a church parking lot on the south side of town took ten minutes. Theo had found a new ride after being spooked by something. Pete kept one team circulating Theo's photo in the neighborhood around the church to see if anyone had seen Theo being picked up by another vehicle before radioing Brian to have the Camry towed while also sending an update to the state police.

Flo seemed relieved and happy when he sat beside her in the bleachers.

--How are we doing?

--We won the first, 25-21. Now we're up 10-8 as you can see. It's been a tight match. As always, the Dordrecht girls average about six inches taller than us. Shirley has done a fantastic job with this team. They're all fighters.

--How about Star?

--Digging tough as usual. She's had some good sets, too.

--That's our girl! Am I stopping for takeout tonight?

--Unless you want to stop for groceries. I was planning to go tomorrow.

--Takeout it is. What would be good?

--We haven't had fish and chips from the diner lately. Star likes them.

--I had the burger there Monday. Fish and chips will work.

--Here we go. I hope we hold the lead.

Wakazoo maintained their advantage, taking the following two sets in close scores. The win put them in second place in the Division 2 Nederland-Singapore League. If they could hold that position over the last two weeks against weaker competition, they would have a bye into the district tournament for the first time. The family would have a small celebration, even though Pete's dragnet had come up empty.

———————

Early Friday morning, Pete was already at his desk trying to put the pieces of his two murder cases together. He received the telephone call he had hoped for from Tim Harvison, who was supervising the draining and dredging crew to ensure they followed regulations. They had found something. Tim told Pete that he should come right over and bring the medical staff because they found bones that looked human. Pete told him to back off and not disturb the site. He first called Alex Vega, who picked up.

--Hey, Alex, this is Pete McAdams.

--Hello, Pete, what can I do for you?

--As usual, I need some strings pulled.

--Okay.

--We've drained a pond at the DFG Club and have found some bones that could be human. How soon can I get a medical examiner?

--I might be able to get someone out early next week.

--That won't work. I need to get them out of the muck sooner than that.

--We have a contract doc with a Benton Harbor clinic. We use him for overflow. He's top-notch. I'll see how soon he can make it. He's usually anxious to make the extra money.

--Okay, try that. Let me know when he can come.

--By the way, something big has come up concerning Harv Nielsen.

--Tell me.

--He's turning himself in. Charley is supposed to pick him up at his uncle's house here in Middleburg late this morning. His uncle has him lawyered up.

--Is that Butch Bosch, George Bosch's son?

--Yes. Exactly.

--Thanks for the heads up. I'll get in touch with Charley later. Call the office to let me know when your guy can come. I'll be at the site. They'll get me on the radio.

When Pete arrived at the DFG, Tim was waiting. The crew was adding links to a weird-looking bridge with partially inflated pontoons resting on sludge instead of water. It almost surrounded the active area of the search. They carefully walked on the bridge closer to where the bones were poking out of the muck. Pete immediately felt that they were human. He could see what looked like a femur next to what seemed to be a hipbone. Although frustrated by the need to wait for the ME, the bridge gave him an idea. He hurried back to his unmarked car, radioed back to the office and waited for Brian to come on the line.

--Hey Brian, how many metal detectors do we have?

--Uh…One, I guess, maybe two.

--See if you can find some more. Bring them out here. Try to bring heavy-duty boots as well. You'll be walking in the muck of a drained pond. See if the detectors have extenders to expand their reach.

--Okay, Sheriff. I'm on it.

Pete asked for Mary Lu next so he could get his messages. Dr. William Saunders had already called. He and two techs would be at the DFG in ninety minutes. Jack Stevenson had also called. FBI profiles of Tony Triandos, Gus Martino, and Sal Broglio were faxed to the private fax machine in Pete's office. Pete told Mary Lu to make sure no one went into his office. The faxes were confidential. Now, Pete had competing priorities. He needed to stay put and watch what happened to the body, but he also was anxious to see the faxes. He changed his mind. He radioed back to Mary Lu and had her put the faxes in a sealed envelope for Brian to bring to him at the DFG.

Pete exited the car and wandered around the DFG, again picturing the ponds and their relationship to the two murders. He was expecting Buck Johnson to stop by the site again before noon. He and Buck were the only ones at the scene of both shootings before the bodies were picked up and the sites trampled on. He had asked Buck to return to the scene this morning so he could walk through it with him again to ensure he had not missed something. He needed a morale booster after losing Theo. Buck arrived at the DFG close to noon on Friday, just as a Lexus SUV pulled in behind him. Pete asked Buck to hang around while Pete went to greet the crew in the Lexus.

--Thanks for coming out on short notice. You must be Dr. Saunders. You'll find this situation to be very unusual.

--Please call me William, Sheriff. My two colleagues are Jerry Burrell and Stacy Kowalski, interns from the Lakeland Hospital in St. Joe They are working at my clinic this fall. This will be a great learning experience for all of us. You are lucky it's Friday. I don't have office hours. It's a catch-up day before our Saturday rush.

William was a Black man built like a bowling ball. Pete guessed about 5'9" by 290 pounds. Jerry and Stacy seemed like twins: a little taller than William, White and slim, with medium brown hair. Pete walked them down to the pond and introduced everyone to Tim Harvison. Tim pointed out the spot about thirty yards from the shore, where the backhoe had found the bones and stopped digging. The new arrivals all looked skeptically at the pontoon bridge. William sent the interns to the SUV for tools and heavy-duty plastic bags. When they returned, they carefully started to walk across the pontoons, following Tim and the driver. Pete expected William to wait at the shore, but he gamely followed the others, surprising Pete with his agility and balance despite his size.

When they all had gotten in position, the backhoe carefully lifted a small load of muck holding some of the bones so they could start the inspection. The interns had small head shovels, and William manned a heavy-duty grabber. They carefully picked out bones one at a time from the shovel before putting them in plastic bags. Pete could see that the process would take at least an hour. He was about to take Buck Johnson aside when he saw two of his patrol cars arrive.

Brian hopped out of one, walked over with the report from Jack Stevenson, and told Pete he had brought four metal detectors, including two new ones for the hardware store. Pete put the file under his arm and showed Brian the layout. He wanted Brian and his crew to use the detectors along the pond's shore. He saw that two of the deputies had brought hip boots. He told them to walk as far into the muddy pond as they safely could. The other two could work on both sides of the pontoon bridge. They would be looking for anything metal, especially a rifle and a handgun. The team quickly got to work, happy to be doing something different than their daily routine. Pete walked with Buck back to the tree where George Bosch and Doug Mason had been found.

--Buck, you saw both bodies before anyone else. Can you think back and remember anything that we haven't already talked about? I want to make sure that we aren't missing anything. You could walk around a little and see what memories might pop up.

--I walk around here all the time, Pete. I don't know what I could be forgetting. The most obvious difference is where the shooting specifically took place. I remember that George Bosch's body was moved from close to the pond to the tree where I found him. I have no idea about the exact location where this other guy was shot.

--We don't know, either. I have a hunch, but I can't prove it yet. Just let me know if you think of something.

--I will, Pete. I didn't mind coming out today. I am interested in what they may find in the pond. This is quite an operation you have going on.

--I hope it will prove to be worth the effort.

Pete watched the crew continue with their work. With no new findings imminent, he went to his car to read the reports in the folder. After he fought through the tedious details, he found them more enlightening than expected and wrote down a summary in his notebook:

> **Gus Martino is a significant player in Chicago organized crime, one step down from the top rung of the oligarchy. One of his areas of control is the gambling and drug trafficking operation along the southeastern shore of Lake Michigan, reaching north to Ludington. He could be the person called the Boss.

**Lorenzo Triandos, his son-in-law and Lydia's first husband, is one of his underlings who owned a restaurant and several bars in Chicago, each with a backroom gambling setup. He and Gus carved out a similar underground gambling club niche in Miami.

**Lydia's second husband, Jacob Epstein, was a mid-level player in several Miami gambling operations.

**Lydia was not known to be an active participant with her father or either of her husbands. Still, she would be targeted as a corroborating material witness if a case were built against the others.

**Tony Triandos is an up-and-comer who started as an enforcer for his grandfather, Gus Martino. He was once thought to be too much of a playboy to be a serious player, but that image was now considered a front. He was a dangerous person who was suspected in several eliminations of potential competitors and witnesses.

**Theo Bolinyk is an independent organizer of several drug supply networks. He had contacts in Chicago, Detroit, and Miami organized crime groups but was never an official member.

**Doug Mason was thought to be newly recruited by Theo Bolinyk.

Pete wasn't sure where it would all lead, but he felt it would all come together soon. As he thought through the possibilities, something troubling him about Buck Johnson came to mind. Buck had seen George Bosch's body being moved to its final location against the tree. Pete thought that was the case, but Sam Morgan and Jimmy Dickerson cut the investigation short. As far as he knew, Buck was not close to Sam and Jimmy. Still, he had been too afraid to tell Pete everything, which he could only have known if he had witnessed the shooting or its aftermath. He wanted to call Buck over immediately, but he thought twice. He didn't want to give Buck a chance to change his story until he had enough proof to lock it down.

As Pete collected his thoughts, he heard a yell from the pontoons. Standing on one of them, Brian had gotten a hit on his metal detector. Pete hustled to the shore. He saw that Brian was close enough to the backhoe that it could swing around and probe the muck where something metal sat beneath the surface. He hopped onto the pontoons to check the progress of the bone collection. William said they had recovered about eighty percent of the skeleton. The last few backhoe scoops had been empty. Some of the smaller bones might have been separated from the main skeleton. He wanted to try a few more before the backhoe could slide to the area near Brian.

Pete hopped off the pontoon bridge and waited for William and his crew to bring their cache of bones ashore.

--What did we find, William?

--From what I can tell on a superficial basis, we have a male body about 5'7" tall, according to the length of his femur. I noticed scattered damage on pieces of the ribcage that could be from a shotgun. I also found bullet damage on the femur I measured that could have been caused by a rifle or high-caliber pistol.

--Wow! That's great. When will you be able to verify it and find more details?

--I have office appointments tomorrow, but I can spend time with the body in the county lab on Sunday. It's a side job apart from my clinic. I should have something definitive for you on Monday morning.

--We need to keep it confidential, William. As few people as possible should know the details.

--That's the way I work. I'll fax reports only to you until you tell me otherwise.

--Thanks. What's your clinic like? I can tell that you know a lot about bones.

--I signed up for the Army after college to be trained as an orthopedic surgeon. I mainly worked with dead bodies in Vietnam. When I got back to the States, I had the shakes. Surgery was out of the question, but I stayed in the Army until I got my MD in family practice. My last hurrah in the army was picking up the bodies in the Iran hostage helicopter accident. Now, my family practice clinic is my life. It's primarily Medicaid and seniors on Medicare. Best thing I ever did. I still like doing medical examinations. The extra money helps, too. This one is interesting. It'll take all my experience to figure it out.

--It seems like we met before.

--We did. At the Free Press all-state announcements. Class A and Class B quarterbacks!

--Oh! You're Whizzer Saunders!

--And you were 'The Chief' back then and still are, I see. As you can tell from my size, I'm not Whizzer anymore. I had a deep hatred for that nickname all my life. I didn't get it because I was a whiz at anything. My granny gave it to me when I was two. You can imagine why.

--Uh…I think I get it. I hated 'The Chief' too. I like 'Sheriff' a lot better. How'd your college career go?

--I went to MSU. They flipped me to wide receiver. I was never first-string, but I got to play some when one of the starters got hurt. Keeping my scholarship was the most important thing.

--Same for me, except I was a linebacker. Here's my card, William. This is the one with my home number.

After Pete watched the crew pack the bones into the SUV, he turned back to watch Brian and the backhoe. Brian had borrowed William's grabber. On the third scoop, he grabbed what looked like a rifle or shotgun without a stock. He bagged it in one of William's bags and returned it to shore. When Pete saw it closely, he saw it was a badly rusted shotgun. He knew it had been in the water for twenty-six years.

By the time Pete had left Brian and his helpers to complete the cleanup at the DFG pond, it was almost two o'clock. He had already shut down the crew draining the second pond, which had been reduced to half its original size. He doubted anything else would be found, but he had Brian leave two of his men to continue with the crane and the metal detectors around the original mucky shore of both ponds. When he arrived at the Sheriff Department, he went to the breakroom to take a leftover container of Flo's chicken and rice casserole to his office to make phone calls. The first was to Alex Vega.

--How did it go this morning, Pete?

--We found an almost complete set of human bones. William Saunders from Benton Harbor came up to do the recovery. He'll send me a report on Monday.

--I suppose there is something else you need from me.

--There is. It could be helpful for both investigations.

--Okay. What is it?

--John Newsome sent me a report. He found partial prints on the shotgun next to Doug Mason and on the bullet stuck in his skull.

--That's not enough for an identification from the database.

--No, but if we have a suspect, it could be used for a one-to-one matchup. Has Harv been picked up yet?

--He has. Do you want us to match his prints, which we now have, against the partial on the rifle?

--Absolutely. I'd bet ten to one we'd get a match. The print on the bullet is sketchier, but I have a hunch.

--Which would be?

--We have Jonnie Van Orden's prints on his military record. He was a highly-rated sharpshooter, someone who could hit his target from a far enough distance away so that a high-powered round would lose some energy and not completely exit through the skull. He might have been with Nick Montez earlier than he's admitting. Like maybe when Nick was shot.

--It's a stretch, but worth a shot. Oops, that is a weird phrase to use in this situation.

--Very proper, I think.

--Okay, I'll send the prints to John; we'll see what happens.

Pete finished his casserole and quickly headed back out, telling Mary Lu that he would be right back. He had some more questions for Jimmy Dickerson. He was due for his time in the dayroom. The aide was wheeling him in when Pete arrived.

--Hi, Jimmy. It seems like we're best friends these days.

--What the hell do you want now, Pete? I've told you everything I know!

--Today, I'm just looking for information on Sal Broglio. You knew him.

--Yeah, I knew him, but not that well.

--First, I need a physical description. What did he look like?

--Dark skin and hair, a typical Italian, or more like a Sicilian. He was short. I was five-eleven back then. He was several inches shorter than me.

--What other characteristics did you notice as a professional sheriff?

--He had a bit of an accent. Something heavier than Chicago Italian. Like he was an immigrant, oh, and he was a gimp.

--A gimp?

--Yeah. He had a limp. And his left arm was useless. I remember him dealing cards with one hand. He would call them 'war wounds.' Then he would laugh and say he had never been in the Army. Rumor was that he got them protecting the Boss when they were younger.

--What do you think happened to him? It seems he disappeared.

--Who knows? He was a gangster. Another rumor had him going back to the old country. Just like Al Pacino in *The Godfather*.

--Thanks, you've been helpful today, Jimmy.

Pete went back to the office and found Brian.

--Hey, Brian. That shotgun we found is a Remington. Can we read its serial number without reducing its effectiveness as evidence?

--I've already checked. We'd have to take some of the crusty stuff off it.

--Don't do that. We need to get it to the lab in Lansing ASAP. Do we have anyone who could go today?

--Benny is here. His shift is over. He could get there before five. You know how much he loves overtime.

--Get him going. Make sure it's wrapped up and properly tagged. I'll call John Newsome to fill him in and let him know it's coming.

Pete picked up his messages for Mary Lu and went into his office. He called Sally Conners back first. He was surprised when she answered instead of her assistant.

--We need to find more for you to do. I don't have time to answer my phone calls directly.

--Lucy has something at her kid's school. Her backups have more important things to do. You know how it is.

--What do you have for me?

--Something surprising, I think. Juanita Jones called me. She said Amy Berendts is ready to tell us everything she knows.

--What does she want in return?

--No jail time. And added protection.

--I don't know what the state would say. The drug offenses are going to be theirs to work out. But we can't give away anything if she was involved in her boyfriend's death.

--That's what I told her. She has an appointment in Middleburg with Alex and his people on Monday. She wants to meet with us right after. She wants it to be a package deal.

--I wonder why Amy is ready to stop holding back.

--Juanita said that Amy now thinks being on our side is safer.

--We need to be at those meetings. Set up a time, and I'll work my schedule around it. While there, I'll try to get an interview with Harv Nielson. Have you heard that he turned himself in today?

--I did. That's good news. Okay, I'll set up a time and let you know. Now I'm anxious to hear about your morning. How did your big dig at the pond go?

--Incredible.

Pete gave Sally the details.

--Wow! My grand jury will be expanding its scope.

--Yup. Twenty-six years late.

Pete's next call was to Larry's beeper. While he waited for the return call, he spent an hour organizing and reorganizing the files on his desk that needed his attention. For the second time, Pete looked over the stack of messages that he had not returned. He realized what was bothering him. He needed to go back to Amy's farm one more time. It was two weeks later, but he knew that the inspection perimeter around the site of Nick Montez's bloody jacket needed to be expanded. He decided the files and his messages needing return calls could wait until Monday. Going to the farm would also give him a safe place to meet with Larry. He needed to keep Larry's undercover assignment between the two of them. When Larry called back, Pete asked him to meet at Amy's farm in about an hour.

On his way out of the office, he handed Mary Lu three of the most important calls and asked her to return them with Pete's apology. He told her he would stop at Amy's farm on the way home. They would hear from him on Monday. Mary Lu caught him in the parking lot before he got away.

--The guys at the DFG just radioed in. They have another find for you.

Pete raced back to the DFG. The deputies had found a corroded chain attached to about a similarly corroded one-hundred-pound boat anchor. He let it lay semi-submerged in the muck.

--Looks like we know how they kept the body down, Sheriff.

--Yes, we do. It also means they planned it.

--Shall we haul it out?

--No! Secure one end to the pontoons and let the site team check it out on Monday.

Pete continued to Amy's farm, arriving with enough time to begin his search. Starting by the bloody sand, still marked with yellow crime tape, he walked in a spiral pattern, looking for anything that may have been missed. The farmhouse was almost one hundred yards away. There was a pond about fifty yards in the opposite direction. There was heavy rain the day before the jacket was found and only a few light showers since so that any evidence on the ground had not been entirely lost. About one hundred feet from the center towards the pond, he walked around another ten-foot circle of crime scene tape with some random depressions in loose sand that may have been footprints. As he moved away from the center, small shrubs got in his way and slowed him down. He had gone almost seventy-five yards from the focal point when he saw Larry arrive at the house with a woman that Pete recognized as Bonnie van Draght. He stopped his ground search and walked over to the house.

--Thanks for coming out, Larry. Hi Bonnie, good to see you again. How did you get hooked up with this guy?

--We had a few years up in the same division in Saginaw. When he retired, he promised to make me rich in private security.

Larry grimaced and growled.

--So, you two know each other?

--Pete was my supervisor for several years when I got a posting in Jackson, closer to home.

--What do you have for us, Sheriff?

--I wanted to get a report on Bonnie's undercover work without prying eyes.

--I get it. She needed a view of the farm anyway. We've picked up another client related to the case, so we'll often be in your county. I hope you don't mind.

--Who's that?

--Amy Berendts. She feels she needs some extra protection. She doesn't think you have enough staff to do the job.

--She might be right. We have a whole county to protect. She made that job more challenging for us. What's your plan?

--I assume you and the city guys will continue with your drive-bys. We'll be inside, scanning the beach and doing some walkarounds. We should communicate our movements to your people and the locals.

--Absolutely. Just call them in to dispatch. I'll alert them. They'll pass it on to patrol. Now, about your assignment, Bonnie. Did I send you on a wild goose chase?

--Not entirely. I found some guns, but they weren't smoking.

--How many and what kind?

--Two thirty-eights, one in each bedroom, and a closet with two shotguns and a scoped rifle. As far I could tell, the rifle had been recently cleaned. The others had no evidence of recent use.

--That's more firepower than you'll find on most boats. Anything else?

--The bar was well-stocked. There was a food delivery today. They replenished the almost empty fridge. Someone must be coming in. One closet was half full of ladies' clothes, all designer labels, mostly size eight.

--There was also a captain's log. I didn't see anything unusual. I found photos on the walls and a box of more in the closet with the rifle. They looked like family and friends. I took snapshots of the ones that were out in the open. I took the box home last night and brought some to CopyMate to get copies. I picked them up this noon and returned the box to the cabinet. The film is being developed at the camera store in Singapore. They're doing a rush job for me. I'll get them tomorrow afternoon.

--Those would be helpful. Shall I have a patrol car pick them up?

--Sure. I'll give them a call. It might speed them up.

--Where are the copies from the box?

--In the car. Do you want them?

--Don't make me beg for it. Larry, when you get a schedule, please send us a copy so we know who's on duty.

--You got it. I was worried that you would resent private security getting involved. Bonnie has the evening shift today before I take the graveyard. I'll have a lineup for the next few days tomorrow.

--In this case, I think it's called for. I hope we'll wrap this up next week, so your services won't be needed long term.

--Do you think it could happen that quickly?

Pointing to his head, Pete replied with conviction.

--Things are coming together up here. Let me have those copies.

--Okay, Columbo.

As soon as Larry and Bonnie left, Pete resumed his spirals. On one side, he ran into a pond, which changed his route to half-circle loops. Large bushes and shrubs were impeding his progress as he moved away. He was thinking of giving up the hunt when, closer to the main house, with the brush on two sides and the pond across the way, he came to a large shed, which could have been used as a garage, with an overhang on one side. He decided to keep going until he reached the house. Going around the shed, something finally caught his eye: partial footprints in the sand and more on the dried, muddy concrete of the overhang. Round and straight markings were mixed in as if something had been dragged, picked up, and dragged again.

Pete went to his car to get his Polaroid camera, a roll of crime scene tape, stakes, and a tape measure. He took photos of the footprints and the other markings and then staked the scene tape around the shed. Finally, he measured back to the center of his search with his twenty-five-yard tape measure. It took five lengths of his tape plus another nine yards, 134 yards total.

He returned to his car, ready to quit for the day, when he saw a pickup driving in. It stopped on the narrow driveway and started to turn around when the driver noticed Pete's vehicle. Pete jumped in his car, turned on the dash flasher light, and called for backup as he followed the pickup down the driveway. Realizing he would not outrun what he now knew to be a police car, the driver stopped at the main road. Pete watched Nick Montez get out of the pickup. Pete's holstered weapon and soft armor vest were in the trunk, but he thought Nick would be unarmed. He stepped out of the car to meet him.

--What are you doing here, Nick? You're supposed to be staying with your cousin.

--They have three kids in a small double-wide. There's no room there. I figured I could crash here.

--I'm sorry, but you're violating your release conditions. You'll have to crash in my jail.

Nick shrugged with resignation as he heard another siren from an arriving patrol car. The deputies came over with handcuffs ready.

--Bring him in for not following his release conditions. He should go to a holding cell across the street for the weekend.

--Nick, I'll talk to you again soon. You should call your lawyer and tell him you want to cooperate fully. The truth is coming out about Doug's shooting. And yours, too. Don't get left holding the bag.

On his way home, Pete stopped at the office to switch to his Bronco, thinking that the next week would bring answers to his decades-old questions.

Chapter 19—Harry, Fourth Sunday, 1998

Harry woke up on Sunday morning at the River Haven B & B in Singapore with a vague feeling that he should attend a morning church service. He quickly dismissed the idea, telling himself that the Dutch subculture of his upbringing was seeping back into his mind. Since meeting with Amy on Wednesday, he had become more entangled with the various webs of Joe's life. Webs that he had avoided since moving away twenty-five years before Joe's death had woven him back in. At the same time, he had grown closer to Irma. Much closer.

On Wednesday evening, Harry returned to River Haven from the Snug Harbor diner on the river in downtown Singapore. It had become his go-to place for a quick meal. At first, he was content to sit and do nothing but watch the news and wait for the preseason televised game between the Nuggets and the Pistons to start. But halfway through the coffee he brewed for himself in the B & B kitchen, he began to feel alone. Having had enough of Larry and more than enough of Amy, he decided to act on a thought looming in his mind. Hank answered the phone when he called.

--Hi, Hank, this is Harry.

--Oh, hi, Harry. I suppose you want to talk to Irma.

--I could talk to you too, Hank. How are you?

--I'm the same. An old man like me doesn't change much. I'll get Irma for you.

Harry waited.

--Hi, Harry. What's up?

--I know you are off tomorrow. Do you have any plans?

--Big plans. Catch up on my laundry. Get my hair done. Go to the spa. Why do you ask?

--Well, I'm watching the news. They are saying that the colors up north are still at their peak. We could go for a drive. It's supposed to be a beautiful Indian Summer day.

--Where to?

--Does that mean you'll go? I'm not sure where.

--Ja, I think I would like to. I've always wanted to go to Leelanau. There's a lighthouse up there that I want to see.

--Where's that?

--At the top of the pinky on the map. Above Traverse City.

--I was at the thumb yesterday. The pinky would balance it out nicely. How far is it? Three hours?

--Closer to four, I think.

--That means we need to start early. Can you put up with me for that long?

--I'll force myself. I'll bring lunch. We can eat when we get there. Fruit and snacks, too.

--Great! That's why I asked you to go with me. I'll buy dinner on the way back.

--That closes the deal. Be here at eight. Bring a warm jacket.

--Yes, Ma'am. I brought one with me on this trip. We could also use some CDs for the drive. I have my rental. Do you have anything good?

--Hank has some Bill Gaither.

--Uh…What about Julie? She must have something listenable.

--I think she's into Destiny's Child and Usher. Not my cup of tea.

--I'm glad to hear that.

--I do have some boxes in Hank's basement. My ex had an excellent collection. I kept it, mostly out of spite.

--That sounds more like it.

———

Harry was five minutes late on Thursday morning. They loaded up the picnic basket, a cooler, a large camera bag, and the CD collection, which turned out to be the size of three large shoe boxes.

--I didn't have time to review them, so I took them all. They are cataloged. You'll be able to find what you like.

--That's a lot of music.

--He almost bankrupted us. He insisted on replacing his LPs and cassettes. He kept his LPs but didn't play them. He said they would be valuable someday.

———

The drive north was an advertisement for Michigan fall tourism. They took US-31 just past Manistee, where they turned onto M-22 to take the scenic route. They spent unplanned time finding the overlook at Sleeping Bear Dunes, where they stopped for the picnic lunch. The fall view gradually became more colorful as they drove north, reaching their peak at Sleeping Bear.

They had good FM reception for the first hour of the drive, so NPR's Morning Edition entertained them. When the news became repetitive, Irma opened one of the CD boxes, which were mostly pop favorites. They settled on the Beatles' *Revolver*, followed by Paul Simon. Irma read *The Poisonwood Bible* intermittently, but their conversations often interrupted her reading. She also had her Nikon SLR within easy reach. Harry had to turn around several times to return to the perfect photo opportunity. After Sleeping Bear, Irma found a small selection of jazz classics in another of the CD boxes, which pleased Harry. Brubeck, Miles Davis, and Stan Getz set the mood for the rest of the trip. The first half of the spectacular M-22 circle scenic detour took another hour, so it was almost two o'clock when they arrived at the Grand Traverse lighthouse on the peninsula's tip. While Irma took her photos, handling her Nikon like a pro, Harry enjoyed the postcard view of the lighthouse, the fall foliage, and the lake.

--This is worth the trip. Spectacular! Colorado doesn't have a lake like this. The color there is only groves of aspen gold scattered among the pines.

--This completes my lighthouse photo book. I saved the best for last. I've been to all the other lighthouses on this side of the lake.

--Let's find the facilities.

They walked around the grounds, taking in more color before visiting the lighthouse museum. It was time to begin their return trip to Dordrecht on the other side of the peninsula. Harry was surprised at how easy the trip seemed. Not only were their conversations comfortable, but the periods of silence seemed normal. They learned more about each other's families. They talked about their marriages and divorces, past careers, and hopes for the future.

--Do you see yourself as the head nurse at Covenant Rehab for the rest of your career?

--Absolutely not. I've been slowly working toward earning my DNP degree at New Leiden State. I can't hide with Hank forever. It's been a safe place after a traumatic marriage, but the danger is gone now. But I will need the money for housing and Jan's college. During our divorce settlement, my ex and I put cash into a 529 plan, which won't last for much more than two years. Of course, she wants to take pre-med at U of M, which means medical school later. I'll need to find a job that pays way more than I'm making.

--What's a DNP degree?

--Doctor of Nursing Practice. I won't be an MD like I hoped, but I'll at least be a doctor.

--Everyone will be begging to hire you. How long do you have left to qualify?

--Less than two years full-time, but three or four years, at the rate I'm going.

--I admire you for not settling for the status quo.

--What about you? Any more thoughts for the future?

--Not until yesterday. Rick Medendorp, an old high school friend, more of an acquaintance really, called me. He's now the COO of DeJong Systems. He's interested in starting a resale and recycling division. He wants to talk to me about running it.

--I thought you were glad to be done with all that.

--I thought I was, too, but I'm enjoying the ego boost. I would be interested in consulting. Something with a flexible schedule and limited hours on the job.

--Good luck with that. It sounds like something that could suck you in until you can't get out.

--That does concern me.

When they made a quick stop at the Eyaawing Cultural Center on the reservation of the Grand Travers band of Ottawa and Chippewa tribes, Harry realized that this was the reservation that Pete McAdams had mentioned that became the home of the last Odawa remnant that was forced out of Nederland County by the Dutch settlers. Like most West Michigan Dutch folk, Irma had never heard the story until Harry repeated what Pete told him about his mother's family. After finishing the short tour, they realized they would arrive in Traverse City at dinner time. Harry suggested that they find a decent restaurant.

--What's decent to you?

--Something a lot better than Denny's.

--A friend told me about a place called Amical.

--What's the menu like?

--I'm not sure. Expensive, she said.

--Perfect! Let's find it when we get into the city.

The restaurant was expensive, but Harry insisted it looked good to him. Since they were in a tourist town, there was no dress code. They saw others who had just come in from a hike. They started with a cocktail, followed by a lobster and filet combo for each, along with a shared bottle of wine. As they were finishing, Harry had a suggestion.

--It's at least a three-hour drive back to Dordrecht, we are both tired, and my alcohol level is approaching the legal limit.

Let's stay overnight and drive back in the morning. We could get two rooms, of course.

--We don't have pajamas.

--They have robes.

--We would need two rooms because two people who are just friends can share a car for twelve hours but not a hotel room.

--Touché. That 'friends' remark from last Sunday wasn't what I meant to say.

--Do you want to try again?

--First, I had to deal with an entangling relationship.

--And how is that relationship?

--Disentangled and in the relationship dumpster.

--And what else?

--You are enjoying this, aren't you? Watching me dig myself out of a hole that I dug for myself.

--Yes, I am. Please continue.

--Okay. You are way too gorgeous to be limited to a friendship. When I met you at the funeral, my heart rate spiked dangerously for a man my age.

--You covered that up very well.

--I didn't want to come on like just another guy on the make. I perceived you as someone not looking for a superficial relationship. I didn't want to spoil my chances by being too aggressive.

--What do you call buying me the two best dinners I've had in years and taking me on a day-long romantic drive?

--Being a friend first. Getting to know each other...was it romantic?

--It was.

--Am I forgiven?

--Hmm. Fifty percent.

--I'll take it. I still think we should get two rooms. Take it slow. Keep the pressure low.

--You're the tour guide.

--Let's get dessert to celebrate.

They split a tiramisu and left to go to the Park Place Hotel, once again following the recommendation of Irma's friend. When they got to the rooms, they turned toward each other. Harry asked.

--Is it okay for ex-friends to kiss goodnight?

--I think it's required behavior.

The kiss was tentative at first but became more passionate and lasted longer than most goodnight kisses. Irma found her speaking voice.

--Seventy-five percent.

--I'm going for a hundred.

They moved closer to one of the doors. Harry opened the door, and they kissed again in the entrance hallway with the door still open. Irma finally pulled away.

--I think we just wasted an expensive room.

--We can use both bathrooms in the morning. It'll help us get an early start.

———————

The drive back to Dordrecht on Friday morning had a different feeling.

--Why is there more room in the car today, Harry?

--I think that's because that bundling board is no longer between us. Please don't ask me where that image came from.

--I'm glad it's gone. This feels better.

--It's a good omen, though. This must be the right time and person for both of us. If it weren't, we'd be feeling worse today.

--It sounds like you've had experience.

--I'm just old. Fifty now, you know. You will feel the same when you're my age.

--I'm close enough now. Just being open to this is new to me. Coming off a damaging relationship while trying to raise Janice forced me into a sexual hibernation. Thank you for waking me up.

--Is that a Sleeping Bear/Sleeping Beauty reference?

--I think you could be my handsome prince.

--Why are we driving a new car? Where are those 1960s bench seats?

--Do you want to do the teenager thing? Park and make out now?

--My back and knees would not hold up. I need comfort at my advanced age.

--I am worried about one thing, though. If this is serious, what do I tell Jan? She already knows we had an overnighter, so I can't cover it up. I wouldn't want to call it a one-night stand.

--I would be miserable if it were a one-night stand or if it were covered up. Isn't she old enough to deserve the truth?

--Yes, she is. But she has been having issues that I haven't told you about.

--Boys?

--If only. It's more like girls. She thinks she might be gay.

--How are you handling that?

--We're scheduled to start counseling next week. She is in the 'I hope I'm not' stage. That may be because she's been bullied already. Boys have called her a dyke, partly because she is a good athlete but also because she isn't attracted to them. I feel it's real. The sooner we deal with it, the better.

--So, we have something else in common.

--Jennifer is gay?

--No. When we announced our divorce just before his senior year, David told us he was gay.

--Were you surprised?

--Yes. He didn't date a lot, but he had a group of friends that included girls. I guess I didn't know what the signs were. I felt guilty for not knowing him as well as I thought.

--What did you do?

--Tried to act as if it were normal. That wasn't easy at first for a man raised like I was. I think I'm doing better now. We are both getting more comfortable with each other. My divorce and his coming out made things difficult at first. He is still closer to Monica than to me.

--I hope I can handle it as well as you seem to have done.

--It's an ongoing process. What can I do to help?

--I've been thinking about that since we woke up. Can you come to supper tomorrow? It would be good for her to get to know you. I know she's free. I'm scheduled to work on Sunday.

--We could go out for pizza or something. Keep Hank out of it.

--No, I think Hank should be involved. Just make us an everyday thing. Get them used to the idea. No big deal. I hope I'm not being presumptuous or pressuring you.

--Speaking of pressure. We haven't talked about your feelings about church and religion.

--I'm working them out. I considered myself a lapsed Christian before I left my marriage. When I returned to Dordrecht, I thought I would get back into the church scene.

Hank certainly encouraged that. But it's not taken hold. I'm more of an agnostic than I realized. I find myself taking Sunday shifts whenever I can so I can avoid attending the services. I know what the reaction of the church people will be to Jan as well. That's why I want to move away from Hank soon. It's become limiting for both of us.

--Welcome to my world.

--So, what about tomorrow night?

--I'm up for it if it doesn't mean going to a church service on Sunday. We don't know where this fairy tale will end, but we need to follow the story.

Arriving back at River Haven at noon on Friday, Harry found a message from Allen Zuverink. He called him right back. Allen was with another client but picked up the phone to quickly ask Harry to stop by his office when he had time. Since he had time after he met with Rick Medendorp at DeJong, Harry said he could come by between three and four.

The meeting with Rick went quickly once they had exchanged memories from their high school days and updated each other on their current lives.

--Harry, I've had an idea in the back of my mind for a while. I think that DeJong should have its in-house component recycling division. If it broke even, we could keep our prospects from shopping around. We lost a few deals to clients who used firms like yours and moved away from us to our competitors. If we could take trade-ins ourselves, we could offer a turnkey service—in with the new and out with the old. So far, it's just an idea. When I brought it up, the executive committee was not excited about it, but when I heard that you had left your company and were hanging out in Dordrecht, I became interested again. Someone like you could set it up and manage it for us.

--It's a great idea. I've had similar thoughts. And I would be the most qualified person to do it. However, I am committed to not getting involved in a situation where I would once again be working and traveling too much. Consultant is the title that sounds good to me.

--What would that look like?

--I don't know, exactly. I would need to brainstorm it.

--I get that. I'm glad you seem willing to consider it. What would it take for you to outline a proposal without giving away your trade secrets, of course? Include what your level of involvement would be.

--I can do that, but to do it right would take some work and some access to your operations.

--How much time? I assume you would charge a fee upfront.

--How about if I answer those questions a week from today?

--That would work. I assume this will stay between you and me for now.

--Absolutely.

When Harry arrived at Allen's office shortly after three o'clock, he found Allen at his large desk with layers of folders spread out.

--I have found something curious, Harry.

--What do you mean by curious?

--I'm not sure what to make of it. Your dad received a thousand dollars each month from John Visser's companies for two decades. First from Visser Used Autos and then from Middleburg Visser Brothers Honda.

--That is strange. Do you know why?

--My dad dutifully recorded the payments as income. Copies of the checks were filed. At first, they were described on the checks and the entries as commissions but were always an even one thousand. Later, they were called consulting fees. Did your dad ever work for the Vissers?

--Not that I knew about.

--That's why it's curious, even suspect. Did he have any knowledge of the car business?

--Joe knew about many things, but I don't think selling cars was one of them. Especially Hondas. He was always big on buying Detroit iron, always GM. Do you think this was an under-the-table payoff?

--Something like that. I took one class in forensic accounting. Regular payments of even amounts outside of payroll or rent always bring attention from an auditor. Contracts for any regular service payments would be included in the file. There are no contracts included in any of Joe's files.

--I saw Visser at Joe's funeral, which brought back a memory of him being at my mom's funeral, too. I only know him because he was at some of my parents' pool parties. His daughters came, too. I had a crush on one of them.

--Me too, at Middleburg Christian. Unrequited, though.

--Of course. They were too cool for nerds like us.

--Still are. They're high society in Middleburg. What do you think we should do about this?

--It might be nothing, but I'll tell Sheriff McAdams. It seems like these different threads from Joe's life all wind up meaning something to the investigation. First, I'll check with my sister. She knows a lot about those days.

On Saturday morning, Harry was still sleeping at the River Haven Inn B & B when his room phone rang. He answered groggily.

--Hey, Watson. I need you. Aren't you awake? It's after eight.

--I am now. What do you need?

--I'm lifeguarding at Amy's. My replacement can't get here until the afternoon. I need you to cover for me while I round up some equipment.

--What do I need to do?

--Look for trouble and beep me.

--Okay, I guess. Let me get cleaned up before I go to the kitchen for breakfast. It's best here on the weekends. I'll be there as soon as I can.

After his shower, Harry was surprised to see the dining room full of customers and extra tables in the lounge. Rob had saved him a spot at one of them.

--Where did all these people come from?

--It's the weekend. Breakfast here is an event. Luke cooks instead of me. Some people stay with us just for Luke's breakfast. If we have room, locals are welcome. Here is a menu. Luke's wife, Lara, will bring coffee and take your order. Unless you know sign language, point to what you want. Unlike Luke, she doesn't wear hearing aids or speak. Luke's Eggs Benedict is a big hit. I like the hash. It's also fabulous and more filling.

--I'll need the hash. I'm unsure what kind of lunch I'll get at Amy's. Something vegan, I expect.

Harry introduced himself to others at the table: two women and three men. They turned out to be locals. Before his food was served, he had an invitation to a final week celebration at the yacht club the following Saturday night. As he was finishing his meal, Jeff Klaasen came over to his table with a short, stout man wearing a white chef's hat and smock with the 'Luke' embroidered on the pocket.

--Harry, do you remember Lucas Michmerhuizen from Christian grade school?

--I do remember! Hello Lucas, or I guess they call you Luke now.

Jeff signed to Luke. Luke's reply was mainly unintelligible. Harry thought he made out the words 'Flint' and 'name.' Jeff repeated that Lucas said he became Luke when he transferred to the Michigan School for the Deaf in Flint in eighth grade. Harry nodded his head up and down, trying to tell Lucas that he understood.

--Thank you for a great breakfast—the best I've had in a long time.

After Jeff signed, Lucas replied. Harry could understand the signed and spoken versions of 'thank you.' Jeff signed and spoke again.

--Harry is staying here for a while. You'll see him a lot.

--This time, when Lucas signed, Harry thought he got the gist. He replied with a thumbs up.

After they shook hands, Harry took a last sip of coffee before he rushed to meet Larry at Amy's.

When Harry arrived, he found Amy and Gerrit cleaning the kitchen after breakfast. Larry was on the back patio. He waved to Harry to come outside. He handed him binoculars and some photos.

--Take a good look at these, Watson. You know Theo, of course. The younger guy is Tony Triandos. They both have reason to keep Amy from being a grand jury witness, either in the state investigation that Alex Vega is running or the local grand jury that the sheriff and Sally Conners are setting up.

--Okay, who is Alex Vega?

--He was my boss at two different postings with the state. He's running a special team for the Colonel on organized crime. I talked to him earlier this morning. He's interested in Amy and her friends but considers them small potatoes. He thinks it could lead to bigger fish.

--Potatoes and fish. Are those professional terms?

--Don't act wise.

--Sorry. You sound like Raymond Chandler. Oh, and who is the Colonel?

--That is a professional term. It's the title of the head of the state police. That's enough questions. Shut up and listen. You will not only be looking for Theo and Tony. They could be sending someone else. Look for anyone who seems out of place, such as a service or delivery truck that stays too long or some guy down on the beach that seems wrong. Use binoculars to check the beach and along the top of the dune. Go to the front and look up and down the parking area. Check the entrance to the complex, too.

--What do I do if I see something?

--Beep me. If there is immediate danger, duplicate the call on this other beeper. It will alert the sheriff and the local police. And you can call your cousin. She needed some shuteye. She's in a hotel in town, five minutes away. All the numbers are near Amy's kitchen phone. Does that pocket phone of yours work out here?

--Nah, there's no reception. How long do you need me?

--If you can stay until five or six, Bonnie can get caught up on her rest. That'll allow me to take the graveyard shift tonight.

--I can stay until five. I have a date tonight.

--Who with this time?

--Irma Schroeder.

--You were with her yesterday. Is this serious?

--Maybe.

Shaking his head with a knowing smile, Larry left quickly, obviously on a mission. Harry went in to talk to Amy.

--Hello, Sis. Hello, Gerrit. You'll need to be nice to me today, Amy. I'm your protection.

--I'm in trouble now. Do they even trust you with a gun?

--No way. I'm just a lookout. Help is just a beep away. This should be the safest part of the day, though. The bad guys are still in bed.

--You might be right about that. We need to talk, anyway. My advisors want me to work out an agreement. They're afraid of your lawyer.

--They should be if his fees are any measure. I'd prefer not to give him the money if we agree to a fair deal.

--Let me think about it. I am meeting with the sheriff and the state guys on Monday. I will know more about where I stand after that.

417

--Okay. We'll put things on hold until then. In the meantime, I'll take my trusty binoculars and go on my appointed rounds.

Harry spent the next hour walking around the property. He felt a little conspicuous, wishing he had his dog, Evans, a light-colored golden retriever named after the mountain. It would give him some cover, allowing him to appear to be just a man walking his dog. Since Harry often traveled, he had to let Evans live with Monica. Harry was allowed to have him on some weekends when the dog was inconvenient for her.

He tried to act like a tourist as he took the dune trail to the stairs, practicing with the binoculars. He saw a few people on the beach and several sailboats out on the water enjoying the Indian Summer weekend that had started on Thursday for him on his trip with Irma. He was glad he was here today. The Sunday forecast was cold and rainy. Satisfied that he knew the terrain and nothing and no one seemed out of place, he returned inside and found Gerrit in the kitchen.

--Did you see anything out there?

--All quiet on the western front.

--That's good. Do you think we are overreacting?

--I'm not qualified to answer that. I've never been involved in anything like this.

--Me, neither. But Amy has told me things that make me think the danger is real.

--Like what?

Amy walked into the room, obviously having heard the first part of the conversation.

--Lots of stuff, Harry. We met with Juanita again yesterday at noon. We decided that I'm going to reveal everything I know on Monday. Theo has been involved in drugs and everything that comes with it, like surprising amounts of cash. I was part of it for a while. So was Dad. Theo was becoming more involved with Doug every day before he was killed. I've seen a lot. I know a lot that both investigations would like to hear about. Some of it would not be firsthand, but it could point them in the right direction.

--By the way, what do you know about Joe and his relationship with John Visser?

--I'm not telling you everything. But they were both mixed up in a lot of shit.

--Did you know he paid Joe a thousand a month for two decades?

--Ja.

--Why?

--To keep his mouth shut. It would be wise not to ask these questions of the wrong people.

The conversation ended as Harry saw Larry drive up in front of the garage. He went out to help unload boxes and bags of electrical and lighting components. They spent the next hours stringing lights around the three sides of Amy's condominium and hooking them up to power. Harry left while Larry continued to assemble a complicated switching system.

———————

Harry's Sunday morning reverie was interrupted by the ringing phone. It was Larry again.

--How did it go last night? Did you pop the question?

--Yes. I'm taking mom and daughter skiing after the first big snow in Boyne.

--I thought your knee was no good.

419

--It suddenly feels a little better since I have a new purpose in life. Plus, the Michigan hills are not the Rocky Mountains.

--How is ol' Hank taking this?

--He's looking at me with some suspicion now, like he's the father. He may pop the big question himself, for both of us. And answer it, too!

--What about church? Is she religious?

--Happily, she calls herself agnostic.

--Does her daughter approve?

--She warmed up once I brought up skiing. She's my best friend after I mentioned joining me and my kids in Vail during Christmas vacation. She's a good kid. She takes after her mother.

--Enough romance. I need you again today. Same plan.

--So, you can find time to see Lupe?

--I don't know where she is, but I think she went to Mexico to see her parents. She said she'll be back next weekend. In the meantime, I need some help finishing my warning system. I'll be there at noon after I stop at the sheriff's office and the police station. We can relieve Bonnie at the same time.

--I thought you had a team lined up.

--I do. But the other two guys can't start until tomorrow.

--That system seems complicated. Is that your idea?

--I've already applied for a patent.

Harry told Larry he would meet him at twelve. He went to his table in the lounge, which was starting to feel like home. This time, he had the Eggs Benedict with a side of pancakes while sitting with a couple from New Leiden. They were not as friendly as Saturday's group. After he finished breakfast, he checked out the mini library. He found a John le Carre novel that he had not read, *The Tailor of Panama*. He sat in a wing chair with a back garden view and started reading. Two hours later, he realized that it was time to meet Larry. Thinking ahead, he stopped at a family-run Mexican restaurant in a neighborhood just outside of downtown. Not knowing what lunch would be, he picked up four orders of mixed chicken and beef *grande* burritos. He knew Larry would be hungry.

Arriving before Larry, he found Amy in the cove off the living area set up as her home office.

--I'm here again. Ready to save the day.

--I hope it doesn't come to that. I would be in real trouble.

--I was hoping for a thank you. Where's Bonnie?

--Out on the dune, I think.

--I'll find her. She needs a break.

After Harry sent Bonnie back to her hotel, he made a circuit of the condo complex. When Larry arrived, they shared the burritos while he gave Harry an overview of the final steps in his security plan. Harry helped him place a tripwire assembly around the north and beach side of the condo. Larry then connected them to an electrical box that connected them to the lights on both sides and the motion detector lights in the front. Setting any one of them off would send up a small siren signal for each from each tripwire head, a louder siren where the systems connected, and the dozen security high-watt flood lamps on the three sides of the house. The lighting would only be active after dark. The work was complete by six o'clock as dusk was settling in. Larry told Harry to go in the house and tell Amy and Gerrit that 'holy hell' was about to break loose. When they looked out the window to watch Larry step on a wire, holy hell indeed sounded and flashed for the ten seconds it took Larry to run to his main assembly and cut the power. Amy and Gerrit were wide-eyed. Harry looked satisfied.

--We have an early warning system!

Larry puttered around the system, hiding wires and assemblies. He stopped often, seeming to stop and think, wanting to ensure he did not forget anything. When Bonnie arrived to relieve them around seven, Larry spent another half-hour showing her his handiwork. He also gave her the two beepers.

———————

Later that night, Harry and Larry sat in the Goose and Gander in Singapore, having a late dinner. Larry was getting ready to relieve Bonnie later in the evening for the overnight shift. As Harry sipped his coffee, Larry was halfway through a fudge brownie with chocolate swirl ice cream when his beeper went off. Harry watched Larry's face turn red and concerned as he checked the message.

--We need to go, Watson. We have trouble. Leave some money on the table.

Harry quickly tossed three twenties on the table and ran after Larry toward his Suburban.

--What's going on? Is something happening at Amy's?

--That message was from Bonnie. She used the emergency code.

Larry raced through town, showing skills he had developed as a state patrol officer. It took less than five minutes to get to the condominium complex entrance, where Larry swerved to a halt and jumped out, with Harry trying to keep up as he raced toward Amy's. Amy's complex had four buildings, each with four two-story townhouses. Hers was the last one to the north. They cut between two buildings rather than going to the front door. Larry slowed down, guided Harry into the dune grass, and stopped short of the tripwires. He moved slowly to the north, where they could see into the living area. They could see Amy, Gerrit, and Bonnie standing side by side. Bonnie had her hands in front of her in a 'don't shoot' stance. A man was facing them while waving a pistol around, surprisingly casual. Larry pulled his gun that Harry was unaware he was carrying. He whispered.

--It's fucking Triandos!

--I think you're right.

--Okay, Watson. Do you remember where we set up one of the tripwires toward the patio and to your right?

--Ja.

--Here's what you need to do. When you see me open that back door leading into the garage, you will count to ten, one count per second. Then you'll trip that wire, so the sirens and lights go on. Then you're going to bury yourself in that dune grass. Do you get that?

--Ja.

Harry looked through the window. The situation had stayed the same. They were talking, but Tony was still waving the gun. He watched Larry at the door. He remembered that Larry had the key to the front door. Hopefully, the back garage door was the same key. He waited for Larry to open the door before he started his count. When the count reached nine, he frog-walked, in as deep a crouch as he could manage, the six feet to the wire. He fell on it and grabbed it at the same time. Larry's entire light assembly flashed, and the sirens blared. Harry could not see as well in all the new light, but he could still see into the house.

He saw Tony startled and turned to the lights. Amy and Gerrit did the same. But Bonnie quickly jumped toward Tony as if she knew what would happen. She grabbed Tony's gun hand, which had also turned to the lights, with two hands, wrestling with him to control the gun. Harry heard at least two shots and the sound of broken glass. Meanwhile, Larry had burst through the kitchen garage door and raced fifteen feet to the living area. Rather than shoot, he held his pistol like a rock and, on the dead run, slammed its body into the side of Tony's head. Tony staggered as the gun dropped. Larry's blow, delivered on the run, had not connected with its full force. Tony recovered and saw the gun. He was the closest to it, but as he leaned down to grab it, Bonnie's boot caught him squarely on the jaw just before Larry leaped on his back. Larry's massive frame forced Tony into a face plant on the terrazzo tile surface.

Tony did not move, and neither did Larry, except to force Tony's arms behind his back. When she saw Larry in control, Bonnie jumped around the sofa and brought out a large black tool bag. In the time it took for Harry to get up and bang on the patio door for someone to unlock it, Tony's hands and feet were cuffed in plastic ties, and he was propped up in a corner, still unconscious. Amy and Gerrit turned toward the patio, still horrified, until they realized Harry was looking in. Gerrit's hands still trembled as he unlocked the door to let him in. As Harry walked over to Amy, she opened her arms to hug him, crying in relief.

The second beeper had sent a message to the sheriff's office and the police simultaneously. Hearing them starting to arrive, Bonnie went outside to greet them, letting them know the situation had been stabilized. Larry was on the phone with the sheriff's department, asking Pete McAdams to respond. Julie

Overweg, handling weekend dispatch, told him the Sheriff was already on his way.

Harry was the first to meet Sheriff McAdams on his arrival.

--What the hell happened, Harry?

Larry made his best tackle since he met you at the goal line. This time, Bonnie got to kick the field goal.

--Give me the details without the color commentary.

Harry described what happened from his view through the patio doors. Bonnie walked over and listened. When Harry took a breath, Pete turned to Bonnie.

--Does that sound right to you, Bonnie?

--Ja. That's the second half. Earlier, I was on the patio looking out at the beach with the binoculars. It was still dusk, and the weather was still calm. There were a few people still walking along the shore. A couple of fires were starting. When I looked south, Tony came behind me from around the garage. I heard the safety click before he said, 'Don't move.' Just like a movie. He walked me to the living area and then the kitchen, where Amy and Gerrit stood cleaning the dishes after we ate. He started ranting at Amy about Theo. That gave me a chance to press the emergency button on the two pagers I was carrying on my belt under my hoodie. He demanded to know where Theo was. Amy was frantic, trying to convince him she didn't know. She told him about Theo skipping the planned meeting last week and how she had no idea where he went. She calmed down a little and tried to be on his side. She said she would help him find Theo. She started flirting with him, even telling him she was more attracted to him than Gerrit. That bought some time. He even looked like he might buy it. But he still had the pistol aimed at Gerrit. Then he realized it was a ruse on Amy's part and turned the gun toward her. I tried to slip out of his view, but he stopped me. I don't know how long it took until the siren went off and the light flashed on. At the time, it seemed like an hour. Now, it seems like minutes.

Harry watched Pete walk over to the corner of the living area, where two local patrol officers stood over Tony, still propped up with his head hanging down. He checked the restraint and examined Tony's eyes. He was still knocked out. Pete gave out instructions.

--Get an ambulance out here. Keep these restraints on until you can cuff him to the gurney, both his hands and feet. We don't want him to come around and cause trouble. Have the ambulance go to Wakazoo Hospital. We have a secure bed there. One of our guys can ride along.

Pete then had a quick interview with Gerrit, who now seemed remarkably calm to Harry, while he backed up Bonnie's description of the confrontation. Finally, he walked over to Larry.

--This isn't the end of it, Larry.

--I know. It could be the beginning. I wonder if we should find Amy a more secure location for the next few days.

--She'll need to move anyway. We'll need to rope this place off for a few days until a state team can get here. A hotel would be safer. It's more public. They are less likely to try something. I'm thinking of those new bungalows at Riverview Lodge across the river. They're only accessible through a secure gate.

--Sounds expensive.

Harry added:

--Better safe than cheap, Larry. Plus, we won't have to add personnel. We can get two rooms and take turns.

--We? I thought you were just temporary help.

--I'm all in now. I bet they'll have openings on weekdays this time of year. We could get a deal.

--I'm glad to hear it. You are right. Let's talk her into it.

--Okay, guys. Let me know when you're there. Let's use the same warning system if you see any trouble.

Seeing that the Singapore police chief had finally arrived, Pete waved him over.

--Cory, this is Amy's private protection team: Harry Berendts, Larry Vandevoss, and Bonnie van Draght. They can update you on what happened here. I've talked to them and Amy and her friend, Gerrit.

--I know Amy and Gerrit.

--I need to ask you to take over here. My guys are all overworked right now.

--I'll take it from here, Pete.

--Thanks. We'll need the site secured until Monday when a crime scene team can do their thing. We'll need formal statements from participants here. Tomorrow is fine for that. The suspect is going to Wakazoo Hospital. Your team arrived immediately, so our warning system worked as well as possible. We'll continue it when Amy gets to a new location.

Harry watched Pete leave as Cory took over. He thought Cory seemed pleased to be included in the excitement, not to mention having the opportunity to pay special attention to Amy. Seeing everyone else still in shock, Harry went to the phone to call the Riverview Lodge. After using his bargaining skills with the night manager, he reserved two neighboring bungalows for the rest of the week.

Chapter 20—Pete, Fourth Monday, 1998

When he returned home on Sunday night after surveying the astonishing scene at Amy's condo, Pete realized that he had not obtained added information to help clarify his picture of the death of George Bosch. The drama of the arrest of Tony Triandos, following his intrusion into Amy's condominium, did not change the basic facts concerning either of his murder cases. Tony had gone to Amy's looking for Theo Bolinyk. He had used a gun to threaten her, thinking she would know where Theo was. But there was no new evidence about Tony's involvement with George Bosch or Doug Mason. The one helpful thing, however, was that he now had a reason to get a search warrant for the Dorothea. He took a chance at aggravating Sally Conners at home late Sunday night, trying to get a head start on what he expected to be a busy Monday.

--Hi, Sally. This will be quick. I just wanted to see if you could do some things for me first thing in the morning.

--Of course, Pete. I needed some more to do tomorrow.

--Think of how happy the entire sheriff's department will be with you. They don't like it when I'm in a bad mood. You have a chance to make me happy.

--Okay. Let me have it.

--We arrested Tony Triandos tonight on an attempted kidnapping charge. We placed him downtown in the only secure bed at the hospital because he was roughed up a bit by private security. I need a search warrant for his grandfather's boat that's docked at the yacht club.

--What do you hope to find?

--Evidence that would help us prove intent on the kidnapping charge.

--Okay, send me the paperwork. What else?

--Priscilla will get that to you in the morning. Another thing is that I have something that may make Nick Montez want to tell us what happened with Doug Mason. We have a partial print from Harv Nielson on the shotgun that might have been the kill shot. We also have a partial image of Jonnie Van Orden's fingerprints on the rifle bullet lodged in Doug's skull. I think that Nick would want to explain what happened. We could offer him a guarantee that we won't prosecute him for any drug offenses. I understand that we can't speak for the state investigation.

--I'll call his lawyer first thing tomorrow. His office is across the street. I'll see if he'll be available.

--Finally, that fingerprint of Van Orden means we need a search warrant for his farm. Can we get one for Nederland County?

--Probably, if a judge I know in New Haven will work with me. I'll give it a shot.

--We've got to stop using that phrase.

--Okay, okay. I get it. I'll let you know as soon as I get something.

Earlier on Sunday morning, Pete and the family had decided to take advantage of the last forecasted day of Indian Summer by taking the canoes out for a short paddle up the Singapore River in the opposite direction of their first trip. When they got to the Toussaint property, the kids claimed the birch bark while Pete and Flo each took a smaller fiberglass canoe. The river took them on a winding route through downtown Wakazoo to a state nature preserve on the west side of town. It was two hours of upstream paddling, but they were little more than two miles from their starting point as the crow flies. They stopped for lunch before returning downstream. They had taken Flo's Civic and Pete's Bronco so Pete could stay behind to check on the beavers. He had also called Buck Johnson to meet him at four o'clock. The creek still flowed smoothly around the beaver dam, so Pete had nothing to work on. He returned to his Bronco to wait for Buck, who arrived on time.

--Hi, Pete, how are your beavers doing?

--They're behaving today. Do you want to walk over there?

--Yeah, I'd like to see it.

As they walked, Pete changed the subject.

--You know, Buck, something you said on Friday is bothering me.

--What's that?

--You mentioned with certainty that George Bosch's body was moved.

--What about it?

--No one knew for sure that his body was moved. I suspected it was, but I didn't have enough proof without an

431

official crime scene inspection back in 1972. I know now that you saw much more than you told me. I want the whole story.

--I want to stay alive, Pete. No one knows I was there.

--That's why we're talking here instead of in my office. But when the grand jury gets started, you'll have to testify. Tell me the whole story now. Your identity will be protected. If you fight me on it, the subpoena will be public.

--Okay, I saw the body being moved.

--Did you see who did the shooting?

--Not the first one

--There was more than one?

--I heard the first shot. It took me a few minutes to carefully walk towards the sound. I thought it was just another trespassing hunter. I didn't want to catch a random shell.

--What happened then?

--There was a short, older guy and a younger, bigger guy doing the moving. I had seen the short guy a few times with George. I think his name was Sal. He was only using one arm. The younger guy did most of the work. They propped him against the tree and dropped the shotgun in his lap.

--Did you recognize the young guy?

--No.

Pete pulled a photo out of his jacket pocket.

--Is this him?

--Could be, I guess. That was twenty-five years ago.

--Things like that stick in your mind. What happened then?

--The young guy had another shotgun. He shot Sal, the little guy.

--We found him in the pond. How did he get there?

--They put him in the boat after they wrapped him in a chain with an anchor attached.

--They had the boat and the anchor?

--Yeah. The pond, we called it a lake back then, was a lot wider. We dredged it every year, so it was deeper, too. We stocked it with fish. Bluegills and sunfish for the kids to catch. We even put a raft out in the middle for them to dive and swim around. They got the rowboat and one of the anchors we used for the raft out of that shed on the other side of the pond from where George was.

--What happened next?

--I don't know. That's when I took off. Used the back exit. I thought they might spot me. I was scared shitless.

--What did they do with the boat?

--I came back the next day. Everything was cleaned up. The boat was back in the shed, and the padlock was back on it. There was only one anchor for the raft, though. I could see George still sitting on the other side of the pond. That's when I went to a phone at the closest farmhouse across the main road and called the sheriff's office. You were the one who showed up.

--You are saying 'they.' Were there other guys there?

Buck looked stunned. He remained silent.

--C'mon, Buck. You've told me this much. Let me have it all.

--There was a guy in the boat.

--Who was he?

--It might have been Sam Morgan. He was too far away to recognize for sure.

--Someone not only knew about the shed and the boat, but also had a key.

--One guy stayed back by the shed. It was too far away for me to recognize.

433

--You know John Visser. Was it him?

--I didn't know him that well back then. He was tall and skinny like John.

--Okay, Buck. I need to think this through. Don't tell anyone we talked about this.

--Don't worry. I'm already sorry I've told you. I'll be looking over my shoulder from now on.

When Pete returned home, Flo had a Reuben sandwich supper waiting for him. She and the kids had eaten theirs earlier. They all watched the end of the Lions game while he gobbled his down. The kids went to their rooms to study and take turns calling their friends while Flo returned to grading papers. Pete went to his office to gather his thoughts, trying to fit Buck's news into the mental picture he had painted. He was thinking of going to bed early when his police radio squawked. An emergency call for a patrol car to back up Singapore police at a condominium complex in Singapore. Pete knew it would be Amy's. He grabbed his jacket and ran out to his Bronco. He did the twenty-minute drive in fifteen minutes, which gave him time to consider everything he had learned the day before.

When Pete arrived at his office on Saturday in the darkness of a fall day at six in the morning, he already had a message from Jack Stevenson telling him to call back as soon as he received the message. Pete dialed the direct number.

--Hi, Pete. Thanks for calling.

--How'd you know it was me?

--I put you in our system. Our tech staff will load a national database in the next few months.

--Is that even legal? What about privacy laws?

--Everyone signed their rights away to the phone companies when they got their first phone line.

--Unbelievable! What do you have for me that is important enough for an executive like you to work on Saturday?

--We are all here for the culmination of an investigation in Jersey. Watch the national news tonight and tomorrow. But I have something for you that you won't like.

--I haven't had breakfast yet, but tell me anyway.

--Our Midwest division picked up your guy Theo Bolinyk as a material witness. He's concealed and protected for now.

--How long does 'for now' mean?

--Depends on what they have on him and what he can give them. Potentially months or even years.

--That does suck. Will they even let me talk to him?

--Not right now. But they might come and talk with you. They might be willing to exchange information.

Pete had not planned to work on the weekend, but he needed to spend some quiet time with Bonnie van Dracht's copies and the photos from her camera. He spent Saturday morning organizing them on the empty table in what passed for a conference room for the sheriff's department. He locked the door from the inside so no one would accidentally see the compromised material evidence. It had to be his eyes only. He heard a knock on the door as he tried to glean information from the photos. Julie Overweg, the weekend operator, had a call from John Newsome for him. Pete was amazed at the apparent power Alex Vega wielded. It would usually take more than a week to get results from Lansing. After remembering to lock the conference room door from the outside, he went to his office and answered.

--Hey, Pete, this is John Newsome.

--Hey, John, what do you have for me?

--Well, you didn't hit a home run, but you got a couple of first downs and threw an interception.

--That's a fantastic mixed metaphor. What does it mean?

--Just making sure you're awake. The partial prints are first downs. It's not good enough to get a conviction but enough to investigate further.

--Specifically?

--There are partial matches to the prints you sent us. Van Orden to the .308 bullet and Nielson to the shotgun print.

--That's the best I hoped for. It'll keep me on track in the Doug Mason case. What was the interception?

--We got the serial number off the old shotgun. We called Remington to check the original purchase. They have records reaching way back.

--So, who bought it?

--It was you! Or, back then, in '68, Jimmy Dickerson was the Singapore County Sheriff. He bought twelve shotguns. This was one of them.

--That's a real curveball to return to your original metaphor.

--I should have thought of that one. Anyway, I wanted to let you know. You'll get the paperwork faxed over later today.

--Thanks for the update and the speed. It was a three-point shot.

As soon as Pete put the receiver down, Julie knocked again. Harry Berendts was on the phone.

--Hi, Harry. I'm sorry I couldn't get back to you yesterday. I had lots of stuff going on.

--Like what? Anything I should know?

--Not yet. What can I help you with?

--I hope I'm helping you. I have some information that may be meaningful for the George Bosch suicide or murder if that's what you're calling it now.

--It is murder, as of yesterday.

--Okay, murder it is. My friend, Allen Zuverink, is helping me fight with my sister over Joe's estate. His father was Joe's accountant before Amy fired him about four years ago. Allen has all of Joe's records until that time.

--I want those.

--I told Allen that you would say that. He won't fight a court order or a grand jury subpoena. I'm telling you one thing that stood out. For over twenty years, starting shortly after the Bosch murder, Joe received one-thousand-dollar monthly checks from Visser Used Autos and later from Visser Honda. There is no backup for them in the files. They were listed as consulting fees.

--That may mean something. I have been talking to John Visser. Now, I need to speak to him again. Do you have Allen's business information? I'll work on getting a warrant. The grand jury is still a few weeks away. Does Amy know anything about the payments?

--She must know about them. She managed his affairs for the last four years. I'm going to see her later today. I'll bring it up. And I'll get Allen to fax his information to you.

--Thanks. Keep me informed. Larry told me that he is building a protection team for her. Are you part of it?

--Hell, no. Not officially, anyway. I'm filling in during the day until he finds someone qualified. My only experience was as a clerk in the National Guard. A typewriter was my only weapon. I even tried hunting again last week. I missed a literal sitting duck. I'm just helping where and when I can. I'm on my way over there now.

--Be careful. This could get serious.

--I'm aware of that.

Pete hung up from Harry and immediately dialed Alex Vega, hoping he was also putting in extra time. Pete got the answering machine. He left a message asking Alex to get a subpoena in Nederland County for Joe Berendts' financial records from Allen Zuverink based on his conversation with Harry Berendts. Pete also wanted to enlist at least two state police officers to help him execute a possible search warrant for Jonnie Van Orden's farm as early as possible on Monday after his scheduled interviews with Amy Berendts and Harv Nielson. He told Alex to expect a fax on Monday with the necessary legal information and approval for the warrant.

Pete went back to the conference room to focus on the pictures again. He recognized several of the subjects. Most of them seemed to be taken on the Dorothea. Joe Berendts was in more than a dozen with Lydia. One showed both of them with a young man who looked enough like Lydia that Pete assumed he was Tony Triandos. The same man was in another photo with Lydia and an older man, probably Gus Martino. There were several snapshots of Amy with either Joe, Theo, or all three–one with just Amy and Tony. There was one which was more recent that pictured Amy and Doug. The most surprising photo was of Joe and Lydia with several people in the background, two of whom Pete recognized: John Visser and Sam Morgan.

These photos were a questionably obtained cache he could not use to interrogate anyone or get a warrant to search the yacht. To make them useful, he would need a separate, legitimate reason to obtain a search warrant, allowing him to use the cache as evidence. He placed the photos in a large, expandable file folder and brought it outside to his Bronco. For now, only he and Bonnie van Draght would see them.

———————————

Just before ten on Monday morning, Pete was getting back into his routine after the excitement at Amy's condo on Sunday night. He was again looking over the photos from the Dorothea. Having a few minutes before a meeting with Nick Montez and his lawyer, he wanted to see if he had missed anything on Saturday morning when he had spent hours reviewing the photos and other aspects of his potential murder cases. After interviewing Nick, he would need to rush to Middleburg for the interview with Harv Nielson, followed by another with Amy Berendts and her lawyers. Not finding anything new, Pete slipped the photos back into the folder and called in Brian Chatfield.

--Brian, I've got two things for you. I appreciate your extra work while I try to make sense of these shootings.

--Whatever I can do.

--First, we need to review our weapon inventory history. You may need some help from Priscilla on this. Jimmy Dickerson bought twelve Remington shotguns in the 1960s. Here are the serial numbers. I need to know where they are now. One of them was the one you found in the pond.

--That shouldn't be difficult. We update that inventory every year.

--I'm betting that it has been missing for a few decades. Maybe others are missing too.

--I'll check that out.

--Next, get a team ready to execute a search warrant for a yacht at the yacht club this afternoon. It's named Dorothea. John Baker is familiar with it. Put him on the team. The warrant should be approved later this morning.

--Sounds like fun. What are we looking for?

--Officially, evidence related to the kidnapping charge against Tony Triandos. We could also stumble on evidence of involvement, including intent and motive, in the shootings of Doug Mason and George Bosch. The yacht belongs to a guy named Gus Martino. Gus's daughter, Lydia, is staying there. Tony is her son.

--Okay. I've got something new for you, too. Doug Mason's pickup was towed in from Saginaw last night. The state crime scene team went over it this morning. The bed had been washed, but they found traces of blood. They don't know whose it is yet.

--They'll be a match for Doug. It will help prove he was moved to the DFG.

--Probably. They've already found more traces on the ground at Amy Berendts' farm. It looked like someone had tried to cover them up.

--So, if they are a match for Doug, we'll know his body was moved to the DFG.

--Yup.

Pete rushed to Sally Conners' office after finally receiving her call that Nick Montez and his lawyer, James Velez, had arrived and were waiting in her conference room. Once again, Velez did not wait for Pete or Sally to open the conversation.

--I must object, once again, concerning your harassment of Mr. Montez.

--This is not harassment, Counselor; I saw Nick violating his release conditions.

--He was still in the county, just looking for a quiet place to sleep.

--That may be, but the essential reason for this interview is that Nick has not told us the truth. We need to know who shot him in the shoulder. We now have evidence that Doug Mason was moved from Amy's farm to the DFG, where we found Nick's bloody jacket. That means he is a prime suspect in Doug Mason's murder. It's time for Nick to tell us the truth.

--We'll need five minutes to confer.

Pete and Sally left the room. Pete told her about Doug's pickup and the other early evidence that Amy's farm was the crime scene. Sally decided to try to move up the grand jury date. James Velez opened the door and waved them back into the conference room.

--My client will admit he was at the scene. He did not have a gun or shoot Doug Mason. What is your offer for cooperation? He will use his Fifth Amendment rights and refuse to answer questions or testify without something meaningful.

Sally held up a hand to Pete and spoke directly to Velez.

--Nick could be the first person to tell the complete truth. If he waits, the others may try to implicate him. He is already an accessory to a pending murder charge. If he pleads guilty and cooperates, we will ask the judge to show leniency in the sentencing.

--We need something better than that.

This time, Pete answered first.

--That's not the best advice to give your client. But I'm on my way to Middleburg to interview other suspects. Nick may find himself offering us too little too late.

———————

After the meeting with Nick, Pete stopped by Amy's farm to check on the results of the crime scene investigation. He found John Ditmer, who was once again supervising. None of the evidence they found contradicted Pete's concept of what had transpired. He asked if they had checked the edges of the closest pond for a pistol. Ditmer frowned and said they had not brought the right equipment. After telling him it would not be necessary, Pete thanked John for his quick response and headed for Middleburg for the meeting with Amy Berendts and her attorneys. He stopped for a Big Mac as he entered the town and wolfed it down before walking into the Nederland County branch office. The receptionist said they were expecting him and buzzed the conference room. Pete could hear Alex tell her they would be ready for Pete in about ten minutes. It was fifteen minutes before Pete was ushered in. He was surprised to see Reggie Robinson sitting beside Amy and Juanita.

--Hello, Reggie. Good to see you again.

--Good to see you, Pete. Are you attending the Red Men Lettermen's Banquet at homecoming next week?

--Are they still calling it Red Men? I thought they changed the name to accompany our new official mascot, the Pikes.

--They haven't changed the name of the banquet yet. The alums will vote again this year. Now that they are letting the women in, I'm sure both names will get changed this time.

--That's good. I've always felt I was the only one who belonged.

442

Alex cleared his throat.

--Let's reminisce later, gentlemen. I have places to be. Pete, we have been here for two hours. We can send you a transcript. I know you have questions about your cases concerning the deaths of George Bosch and Doug Mason. We'll let you take the lead at this point.

Juanita interrupted.

--Alex, we would prefer that this part of the interview be confidential between Sheriff McAdams and us so that anything said will not affect the proposed agreements we have discussed. We would prefer that your group not be involved.

--Is that okay, Pete?

--Sure, leave the recorder with a new tape.

When the Nederland County group, a uniformed state police captain, and Alex left, Pete started the cassette recorder and the interview by reviewing the opening formalities before proceeding with his questions.

--I am glad to see you here, Amy. That was a traumatic experience last night. Are you sure you're up for this?

--It has not been easy, but I want to be finished with it. Gerrit and I woke up early today to meditate. It helps.

--That's good. Do you have questions for me before we start?

--Why are you here, Sheriff?

--We have information about both the murders that Alex mentioned. Please tell us what you know about them.

--I thought they were both suicides.

--I've never thought that. Now, new evidence proves that they were not suicides.

--But I'm still not involved in either one. I have nothing for you.

--Your father was a material witness in the George Bosch murder. Your ex-husband is still wanted for questioning. You gave us a meeting location with Theo on Thursday. He was gone when we arrived. Did you warn him?

--Why would I do that if I told you where he was?

--They call it playing both sides against the middle. Do you know where he is now?

--No.

--Why were you going to meet him?

--He said I owed him money. I was going to give him part of it. Then I got scared that he would want all of it.

--Why did you owe him money? Was he extorting you?

Juanita answered before Amy had a chance to reply.

--This line of questioning is approaching the line we set at the beginning. Let's move on to something else.

--Do you know the location of any of his assets?

Amy hesitated and looked at Juanita and Reggie. This time, Reggie answered.

--You will have to be more specific, Pete. What kind of assets? Otherwise, move on as Ms. Jones suggested.

--Okay. One more thing about Theo Bolinyk. He had a business arrangement with Doug Mason. Did he have a reason to kill him?

--Nothing that I know about. Doug and Theo made their arrangement behind my back. I was not involved in their schemes.

--Nick Montez, Harv Nielson, and Jonnie Van Orden are persons of interest in the death of Doug Mason. You have had a business arrangement with all three of them. We have evidence that places them at the scene of Doug's shooting. What can you tell us about that murder scene?

Reggie again answered.

--Be more specific in your questioning.

--Sorry. Did you know that the four of them planned to meet?

--No.

--Do you know about any conflicts between them?

--Only Nick. When he was arrested at my store, he mentioned that Doug owed him a lot of money. I haven't seen Harv or Jonnie in over a month.

--Back to George Bosch. Theo and your father had breakfast with him the morning he was shot. Did either one tell you anything that would aid our investigation?

--No, nothing that they said. But I could tell they were upset and nervous about it. Now that you are so sure that it was murder, I have a better understanding of why.

--What would that understanding be?

--I think they feared they would be next in the line of fire. If they knew anything, they would not talk about it.

Pete opened the notebook in front of him before taking a deep breath.

--I am sorry to bring up last night again. How well do you know Tony Triandos, your attacker?

--Not well. I met him a few times in Miami when I visited my dad. He was dating Tony's mother.

--That would be Lydia Epstein, who has a yacht at the Singapore Yacht Club.

--Yes.

--I understand she arrived there this weekend. Coincidence?

--I have no idea.

Pete turned a page of his notebook and then closed it.

--Do you know why John Visser was paying Joe a thousand dollars a month for decades?

--Not specifically. I know they were involved in some illegal stuff when they were younger

Reggie held up his hand again.

--That's approaching the line again, Pete.

Pete hesitated for a short but uncomfortable moment.

--I still think you know more than you're telling, Amy. I could not describe you as a cooperating witness if anyone asks, like the prosecutors in the parallel organized crime case. Please think about that. Let me know if any sudden memories come back to you.

Pete left the office and headed to the restroom. He wanted the meeting to end on a serious note without the usual pleasantries that could give Amy and her lawyers the wrong signal. Reggie was on his way in when he came out of the restroom. They exchanged only a nod.

As Pete waited outside the conference room for his following interview, a man he recognized came out and sat a few chairs away.

--Butch Bosch! It's been a long time. Remember me? Pete McAdams.

--Hello, Pete. It has been a long time. I take it you're here to interrogate Harv.

--I am. I didn't realize until a few days ago that he's your nephew. Or that George Bosch was your dad. I was a rookie deputy when I found his body at the DFG, so I've been involved in these cases for a long time.

--Do you think there is a link between Harv and my dad?

--Some of the same names come up.

--I never accepted that my dad killed himself.

--Neither did I. Now we know he didn't.

--Really! Why haven't I heard?

--We just found more evidence on Friday. We won't publicize it until the investigation is complete. But you deserve to know.

--Thanks for that. What's going to happen to Harv? I'm trying to get him in a treatment program instead of prison.

--He could work out a deal if he cooperates with the task force. It's a little more challenging to get a deal for my case. He was at the scene of Doug Mason's shooting with your dad's shotgun, the second of a pair. Someone tried to make it a copycat of how we found your dad. That was a setup, too.

--It sounds like you're making headway on my dad's case.

Once again, the receptionist told Pete they were ready for him in the conference room.

--Good to see you, Butch. I'll go as easy as I can while questioning Harv.

When he entered the conference room, Pete was introduced to both Harv Nielson and his lawyer, Terry Dykema, who Pete recognized as another Dordrecht High alumni and Butch's teammate. Alex asked Pete to start the questioning.

--I'll cut to the chase, Harv. There was a rifle at the scene of Doug Mason's shooting on which were found partial fingerprints that match yours. That rifle is precisely like your grandfather's with a sequential serial number. We know he owned a matching pair. How did it come into your possession?

Harv looked at Dykema, who nodded his okay to answer.

--My mom took it when my grandpa died. She thought my stepdad would want it. When they divorced, he left it behind for me. I used it when he took me hunting a couple of times.

--We have evidence that Nick Montez, Jonnie Van Orden, and you were at Amy Berendts' farm, where you confronted Doug Mason. What was the argument about?

--He owed us money. A lot.

--How much?

--Thousands. Each.

--Did you threaten Doug with the rifle?

--No. It was still in my truck.

--Did Doug threaten you with his pistol?

--Kind of. When we walked over to him, he pulled it out as soon as we got close. He was afraid he couldn't handle both of us.

--All three of you?

--No. Jonnie stayed with his truck. It would have been hard for him to get there with his walker. He stayed back near the driveway.

--How close to Doug were you?

--I don't know. About the length of this room.

--Is that when Doug threatened you?

--Not right away. He waved the gun around while we argued about the money.

--What happened then?

--Nick took a couple of steps toward him. Doug pointed and shot at him.

--And then what happened?

--I heard a shot from behind us. Doug just dropped to the ground, like one of those people balloons that loses its air.

--Whose idea was it to move the body?

--I was freaked out. I said it reminded me of my grandpa. Jonnie said it gave him an idea. We could move the body to the DFG and make it look like a suicide or an execution. We wouldn't be suspects. We wouldn't be linked to the DFG.

--How did you move him?

--Nick said there was a wheelbarrow in the shed. While Jonnie helped Nick with his shoulder, I loaded Doug into the wheelbarrow and put him into the back of his pickup.

--What were you thinking while you did that?

--Jonnie had gone through a change. He was barking out orders. He said we were pussies. That this was nothing compared to 'Nam. I just did what he said. I followed orders like we were in the Army or something.

--How did you know where to put him?

--One time when we visited, when I was about twelve, my uncle Butch took me fishing with my cousin. He showed us the spot where my grandpa died. I remembered it.

--Who put Doug by the tree?

--Me and the wheelbarrow.

--Who shot him in the face?

--I didn't want to, but Jonnie kept yelling at me. It reminded me of some Vietnam movies I've seen. He told me to go to the pond and wash the shotgun with my shirt to get my fingerprints off.

--Where's the wheelbarrow?

--In the barn back at the farm. We washed that in the pond, too.

--You drove Doug's pickup when you left Amy's farm?

--Yeah. Jonnie told me to run it through a carwash twice. I did it three times. Except for the washes and gas, I didn't stop until I got to Saginaw.

--Where's your pickup?

--In a barn at Jonnie's.

Pete looked around the table while he gathered his thoughts.

--I think I have what I need for now. Harv's rendition rings true. I wasn't ready for the wheelbarrow. We'll need to keep him in custody until we can issue an arrest warrant for disturbing a crime scene. I'll let the prosecutors decide which county's cases take precedence.

When Pete's interview with Harv Nielson had concluded, he found a phone and called Sally Conners in her Wakazoo office. She gave him the good news that she had obtained the approval for both search warrants. He quickly found Charley Vredevelde talking in his office with Alex Vega.

--Sally Conners has just obtained a search warrant for Jonnie Van Orden's farm. I need help exercising it ASAP.

Charley seemed doubtful.

--What are we looking for? Who authorized it?

--Sally used a district judge in New Haven to make sure there would not be any jurisdictional issues. We are looking for his rifle. His fingerprints were on a bullet lodged in Doug Mason's skull.

--Why didn't we know about that?

--We held some things back on a need-to-know basis.

Alex looked at Charley.

--You better find a couple of deputies and go with him, Charley. This could affect our case as well. One of our patrol teams will follow.

Thirty minutes later, Pete and Charley pulled into Jonnie's long driveway in Charley's official town car cruiser. Two sheriff patrol SUVs followed them, along with a state police cruiser. Pete was the first out of the cars and was on the way to the front door when Jonnie opened it and came out onto the porch with his walker.

--Did you need to bring a whole squad, Sheriff? What can I help you with?

--It's just procedure, Jonnie. We have a warrant for your arrest. For now, the charge is disturbing a crime scene. We have another warrant to search for rifles and ammunition in your possession. We also need to take Harv's pickup and have it towed in.

--I get it. I didn't expect Nick and Harv to hold out for long.

--Where should we look first?

--You don't need to tear everything apart. There are two rifles and ammunition in that first shed over there. The pickup is in the barn next to it.

Pete pointed Charley and the officers to the shed and barn.

--You've already been read your rights. We know you have an attorney. We need to take you in.

--I'll say one thing and then shut up. Doug had his pistol aimed at Nick and Harv. You know he got a shot off and hit Nick. He would have shot Harv next and then come after me. I had to take him out. It was self-defense.

--That was a hell of a shot.

--Not really. Routine, when I was in 'Nam. It has triggered some old PTSD symptoms, though. I've been sleeping even worse than usual.

451

--As I said, the current charge is disturbing a crime scene. Was it you or Harv who masterminded the copycat of George Bosch?

--No comment.

--That charge could change if we find that you, Nick, and Harv were the aggressors and Doug was the victim. The county prosecutor will evaluate that. I'll try to get her to act quickly. We can list this as being a voluntary arrest on your part. I can come inside with you so you can grab what you need. If you have prescriptions, the officers will take them along for you. Make sure the labels are legit and current. I'll even let you make a call to your lawyer. I have an ADA van coming, so you can use a wheelchair or your walker. We also have an ADA cell waiting for you.

--Thanks for that. I will take my chair. I'm tired.

The rifles and ammunition were bagged and marked. The van arrived with a state police escort. Pete rode in the van to escort Jonnie back to Wakazoo for his booking. Charley and two deputies stayed at the farm to search for other evidence.

When Pete had Jonnie safely booked after they arrived in Wakazoo, he went directly to the yacht club. He found Brian, John Baker, and the rest of the crew already midway through the search process at the Dorothea. Pete saw that the weapons Bonnie had described were bagged and tagged, along with a desktop CPU and several file boxes filled with folders of documents. Closet doors and cabinet drawers were left open. Pete casually walked past the drawer with the photographs Bonnie had copied for him before continuing to the other levels on the yacht. He found Lydia Epstein a level above the

452

main deck, sitting beside the helm in an oversized captain's chair.

--You know you're going to get sued for this, Sheriff. My lawyer is on his way.

--Hello, ma'am. Sorry for the intrusion. Your lawyer is welcome. He can sit quietly next to you. I'm Sheriff Pete McAdams. You must be Lydia Epstein.

--I didn't know I was on your radar.

--You're not. But your boyfriend, Joe Berendts, was on it for a long time.

--Really? What for?

--A material witness to the murders of George Bosch and Sal Broglio. I'm sorry for your loss. Were you and Joe still close?

--I lost Joe a few years ago. His daughter wouldn't let me see him after his stroke.

--That sounds like something Amy would do.

--What do you mean by murder? George killed himself. Sal just disappeared.

--New evidence says otherwise. You haven't asked me about your son.

--What about him?

--He's being transferred to Lansing's high-security intensive care bed.

--What the fuck! Did you shoot him?

--You haven't heard? We arrested him last night for attempted kidnapping. He was trying to get Amy Berendts to give up Theo Bolinyk's location. I assume Theo was on his hit list. Two of my former state police colleagues had to disarm him forcibly. He has severe concussion syndrome, and there might be permanent brain damage.

--Jesus Christ. I didn't even know Tony was in town. He was supposed to come next week. You didn't take our car, did you? I need to get to Lansing.

--We have an order to impound it. Who do you know that could take you? Amy might be willing.

--Fuck you! I thought you arrested her.

--She's starting to cooperate. They could loosen her bail restrictions.

Brian called from the lower deck up to Pete.

--Someone is here to see the man in charge, Sheriff.

Pete descended the stairs and found a man dressed in a custom-tailored suit.

--Sheriff, I'm Leonard Caputo, attorney for the owners of this boat. I must insist that this search be stopped. I will have a court order shortly.

--By owners, I assume you mean the LLC, GM Enterprises. Would you name its principal partners for me?

--It sounds like you already know.

--How much more time, Captain?

--We're about done, Sheriff. We are waiting for the tow truck so we can impound the car.

--There you go, Counselor. We'll be out of your way shortly, but the boat will still be off-limits for at least another day. A team of state experts is coming tomorrow. Captain Chatfield will have an inventory for you to sign. Since you seem so concerned about her, your client, Mrs. Epstein, is upstairs by the helm. She needs a ride to Lansing to check on her son and a place to stay tonight. I think Mr. Martino would appreciate it if you helped her out.

Pete watched Lenny go up to the helm to see Lydia.

--Arrogant SOB acts like he doesn't recognize me. He was Joe Berendts' lawyer back in the day. I'm taking off, Brian; thanks for handling this. Since we're here, why don't we pack up those photos on the shelf and in the box in the office closet where the gun case is? There could be something we could use.

--Will do.

Brian caught Pete's eye and followed him off the yacht to the dock.

--Priscilla was able to find the old inventory records. You were right. The last time the shotgun from the pond was listed on an inventory was 1970.

———

Pete went back to the office just as the daytime staff was leaving. Priscilla handed him fax copies of a report that William had sent to the coroner. He skimmed through it to find the conclusions. The body was estimated to have been in the pond between twenty and thirty years, based on the disintegration of the skeleton. There was damage to the hip and shoulder bone consistent with bullet wounds. Some surgical work had been done in both areas. If a missing person's medical records could be found, they could be used to check for a match.

Pete found Priscilla still working at her desk. He asked her to send the report to Jack Stevenson at Quantico, with instructions to check for any medical information he had for Sal Broglio. He returned to his desk, remembering he had promised to be home for dinner, which was planned to be takeout tacos from Avilas, the family-owned Mexican restaurant on M-22. It previously had been a well-known local diner that had finally run out of generations to keep it going. Pete had been assigned to do the pickup. He called Flo, who he knew would just be arriving home from picking up Star at volleyball practice, to tell her he would be home at seven sharp.

After a busy week of missing each other, Pete appreciated the sense of family togetherness. They were still talking until almost 8:30. Pete went to his office to make notes while Flo graded more papers. Star and Mike claimed to have homework. It was a little before10:00 on Monday night when Pete finally came out of his home office, only to find Flo asleep on the couch. He gently woke her up.

--Hey, let's both go to bed.

--Did you have something in mind?

--Now that you mention it, I do.

--If you carry me, it's a deal. I don't want to spoil my dream.

--What were you dreaming?

--I can show you.

Pete carried her to the bedroom.

Chapter 21—Pete, Fourth Tuesday, 1998

S hortly after midnight on Monday, Flo was fast asleep; but Pete was still restless. As he went to the refrigerator to look for a snack, he heard a squawk from the police radio in his office. He could not make out the words until he went through his office door and heard 'Shots fired!' repeated. He grabbed the mic for the radio and asked for another repeat. A call describing gunfire had come from a citizen on Forest Drive. Pete's immediate thought was Sam Morgan, who lived on Honeysuckle Lane, just two houses from Forest Street. He hopped into a pair of jeans and ran to the front closet, frustrated with the time it took to put in the serial number to unlock the gun case. He finally belted his holster with its Colt .45 caliber pistol and ran to his Bronco while simultaneously trying to get his arms into his official sheriff's leather jacket. He turned on the police band radio in his Bronco and raced toward Sam's neighborhood. He heard the chatter, the sound of some gunshots, and 'Officer down!'

He swerved with squealing tires onto Honeysuckle only to slam on the brakes, stopping just before hitting a city patrol car turned sideways to block the narrow street. He saw an officer on the ground. Fifty feet in front of him, he saw the partial back of a man ducking behind an SUV with a long gun in his hands. He was slotted between the car and an open door protecting his back. The angle prevented Pete from recognizing either the man or the type of his rifle. Beyond the SUV was a sheriff patrol car blocking Honeysuckle in the opposite direction. He knew that only one deputy patrol officer would be behind it. He watched the shooter rise above the SUV and fire several shots at the sheriff's patrol car. Getting an unobstructed view of the profile and magazine, he realized the rifle was an AR15-style assault weapon. The man had glanced back in Pete's direction but seemed to ignore him. Pete realized that he thought the old Bronco belonged to a civilian who would not be much of a threat.

Pete crouched low as he jumped from the Bronco to check on the officer. He was on his side, breathing heavily. Pete recognized him but only knew his last name.

--Where are you hit, Moreno?

Officer Moreno could only manage a whisper.

--It's my hip. I can't move.

--Stay down. Dispatch is sending an ambulance.

--I was stupid. I didn't take cover. I didn't know he had a big gun. He was coming to finish me off when your guy pulled up on the other side.

--That's okay. We're going to get him.

Pete crept toward the patrol car, his pistol in his hands. He was able to peek with only half his head exposed. He watched the shooter rise again to look toward the Sheriff's patrol car. But he did not raise his rifle and ducked back down before Pete could get into position to shoot. Pete knew there would be a shotgun in the patrol car's trunk, but there was no way he could get to it. His .45 would have to do the job. But the deputy on the other side had managed to get to his shotgun. Suddenly,

Pete saw him stand up and get off two blasts. They wreaked havoc with the windows on the SUV but caused no severe damage to the shooter, who raised his rifle to counterattack. Pete leaped up, putting his elbows on the patrol car's hood to steady himself. He got off three rounds and watched the man fall.

He quickly came around the patrol car and approached the SUV as fast as he could while keeping his crouched stance, with both hands holding his pistol in the ready position. He saw his deputy, who he now realized was Benny Ramirez, doing the same from the other direction, purposely widening his approach to keep Pete out of his potential line of fire. When Pete reached the SUV, he put down his pistol, realizing the fight was over. At least one of his shots was a direct hit between the skull and the nape of his neck. Pete did not recognize the shooter. He felt his pulse with no result. Benny came around the side, pointing his shotgun down, as well.

--Wow! Nice shot, Sheriff.

They heard ambulances. Gradually, neighbors were turning on lights. Pete told Benny to help Officer Moreno and direct one of the arriving ambulances to Sam Morgan's driveway. Apprehensively, Pete walked toward Sam's front door. He rang the bell and tried to open the door. There was no answer. He walked around the garage to the back door. It was standing open. He slowly walked in, announcing himself as Sheriff McAdams. Still no answer. He went through the rear family area to the kitchen, the dining room, the front living area, and Sam's office. Still no answer. He climbed slowly up the stairs. He noticed one door open to a bedroom where he saw Sam on the floor. There was a .38 pistol close to one of Sam's hands. Pete observed heavy bleeding from one side of his torso and blood on his scalp. Sam was lucky that the shooter had not brought in his semiautomatic rifle. It would have caused a lot more damage. Pete was feeling a pulse for the second time in minutes. This time, he got a response. He ran back down the stairs to meet the ambulance crew. He told them to rush up a gurney.

Pete followed them back up the stairs. When he watched the crew work Sam onto the gurney, he noticed a series of what he thought were bullet holes in the wall next to the door and in the hallway wall across from it. He also saw a closet door in the bedroom slowly opening. Eva Morgan peeked out. As the door opened further, Pete saw another .38 pistol in her hand, pointed at the ground. He carefully took it out of her hand as she sat on the bed, looking down at the floor where Sam had been lying.

--I shot the fucker. I think I hit him.

--It looked like you did. Sam is still alive. This crew will take him to the emergency room.

--We heard him sneak in the back door. He came in shooting. He had a silencer. He jumped back in the hallway when we shot back. He just stayed there. I don't know how badly he was hurt. But we didn't dare go out. Sam made me hide in the closet. Finally, he jumped back in. That's the shot that hit Sam. I thought he was dead. I opened the closet door and kept shooting. He went back out in the hallway. I went back into the closet. He finally left when he heard the sirens. By that time, I was too scared to do anything. I was petrified.

Eva's eyes became dark and focused as she looked up to face Pete.

--Did you kill him?

--I did.

--Thank you. I'm glad it's you in charge instead of that asshole, Jimmy.

--Is there a place you can go, Eva? I can't let you stay here alone. Do you have family close?

--Just my daughter in Plainway.

--I'll have an ambulance bring you to the hospital for observation. Could your daughter come to get you tomorrow? Can I call her for you?

--Her number is on the wall by the kitchen phone. She just moved. I can never remember the new one.

Pete went to the kitchen and called Julie. He asked for one more ambulance, non-emergency, for Eva. He also asked her to call Brian to find two other deputies to come with him to secure the shootout scene for the investigators. He called home. Flo picked up in a sleepy voice. He gave her a partial description of his night. He wanted her to know that he was okay but that he would not be able to get back home for several hours. His call to Eva and Sam's daughter was more difficult. He told her what happened as calmly as possible. After being shocked into silence for a few seconds, she said she would be at the hospital within an hour.

He went back upstairs and knocked on the bedroom door that was now closed.

--Are you in there, Eva?

--Just a minute, Pete. I'm getting dressed.

Pete waited for her, marveling at her resilience. When she came out, he led her down the stairs and passed her on to the third EMS crew that had just arrived. Turning back to the street scene, he saw that Benny had been joined by another patrol car that came from Singapore. Pete walked over to Benny.

--At this point, we better let the other guys manage the scene, Benny. We're participants.

--Okay, Sheriff. I was getting them started.

--Brian will be here in a few minutes with a crew. We'll need to give him our weapons. You handled yourself well tonight.

--It reminded me of Desert Storm. I was in some firefights there, too.

--You were a Marine?

--Semper Fi.

--I've been looking at photos of many people involved in this mess. I don't recognize this guy. We'll let Brian check for ID when he gets here.

Pete and Benny watched the other deputies put up the crime scene tape while they waited for Brian. Some neighbors had come out to the street to watch with them. Others had turned off their lights and gone back to bed. When Brian arrived, Pete and Benny gave him their guns, which he quickly bagged and put in his trunk. Pete pulled him aside to give him a quick replay of the gun battle. Brian made some notes before going to Benny for his perspective. He returned to Pete to get his statement on what happened inside the house. After Pete outlined that scene, he gave more details.

--Since I fired my weapon, you must take the lead. The shooter used a pistol in the house. It may be in the SUV or on his person. You'll find two more .38s upstairs in the bedroom that belong to Eva and Sam. When I arrived, I touched Eva's when I had to take it out of her hand.

--How are they?

--Sam has severe wounds. Irma is fine physically, but I also sent her to the hospital for observation.

--I'll talk to her in the morning when I go there to check on Sam.

--What I want you to do now is to check this guy and the car for ID. We need that because we can't be sure he was acting alone.

Brian went over to the shooter on the ground. One by one, he searched the man's pockets as carefully as possible. They all were empty. He went to the car. The driver's door was still open. He and Pete saw the silenced pistol on the seat and an 8 x 11 sheet of paper.

--That'll be the pistol he used inside. Can you grab that paper? Bring it out in the light so we can read it.

Brian grabbed a corner with his gloved hand. He brought it to the spotlight on one of the patrol cars that lit the scene. It was a black-and-white photo of Sam Morgan on half the page. Sam's address was handwritten on the bottom. Pete saw some small print at the top. He asked Brian to turn it toward him and bring it closer. He took a pad and pen from his pocket to write the printed fax information along the top: time, date, and the 'to' and 'from' fax numbers.

--Okay, Brian. The scene is yours. I have my Polaroid in the Bronco. Take a snapshot of what's left of this guy's face for me when you can get a good angle. I'll borrow a patrol car so Benny can take me to the office to make calls. I'll pick up my official vehicle and bring back some coffee.

When Pete arrived at the office, Julie had a coffee thermos ready and was working on a second. He left messages for Alex Vega and John Newsome, asking for a crime scene crew as soon as possible, stressing the seriousness of the situation and the necessity to clean up a residential neighborhood. He found the number for William Saunders and redialed the after-hours emergency number recorded by the message. He was able to leave his name and number with a live operator. He took a few deep breaths as he took out his notepad. Trying to gather his thoughts, he stared at the phone numbers. William called back before anything crystallized.

--Thanks for calling, William. I have another body for you. This one is still warm.

--I was having a bad dream anyway. Let me have the condensed version of the rest of the story.

Pete gave him the details, asking if William wanted the body taken to the morgue.

--No, I always want it where it lies if possible. I'll grab a few more hours of sleep and can be there around seven. Daylight is better.

Pete gave William the directions and told him to ask for Captain Brian Chatfield. When he hung up, he looked in the bottom cabinet of his bookshelf for the county phone book. The area code list was in the front. The fax had been sent to a number in Miami at 8:55 AM, less than twenty-four hours ago, on Monday morning. He already knew it was sent from the area code for western Michigan. He thought he recognized the following three numbers as well. Looking through his Rolodex, he confirmed that it was sent from a Middleburg number. A feeling of clarity came over him. He felt the DFG murders were finally going to be resolved. He asked Julie to cancel the hearse until William arrived in the morning, picked up two thermoses of coffee, and returned to the shooting scene.

Pete was back in the sheriff's department by nine on Tuesday morning after watching his staff process the scene and getting three hours of sleep. Now, he walked over to the coroner's office to check on the progress of William's examination of the still-unnamed shooter. He found William as he was washing up.

--Anything interesting, William?

--Nothing we didn't already know. It was a clean kill, as we used to say in 'Nam. Someone shot a .45 bullet in the back of his neck. Another .38 bullet lodged in his clavicle after penetrating his pecs and ribs from the front. He didn't suffer.

--That's too bad. The .38 round came first, so he did suffer some. It slowed him down. It came from his target's wife in the house. When my deputy drew the shooter's fire, I could take my time and take him out. Did you find anything to help us determine who he is and who might have sent him?

--Fingerprints, of course, if he's in the system.

--I would be surprised if he's not. In addition to the usual channels, we should send the prints to Alex Vega at the Middleburg state police branch. He's running an organized crime task force. And then to Jack Stevenson at Quantico. He is doing the same nationally. They'll speed up the process. My office manager, Priscilla Morrison, has their information.

--Will do.

--Thanks for coming out. You're a lifesaver.

--I couldn't save this guy. No thanks needed. You'll get my bill. I've got three kids ready for college in the next few years, so I know where the money will go.

Pete returned to his office to find Lenny Caputo waiting for him, dressed in another hand-tailored suit.

--What can I do for you this morning, Counselor? You're up and about early.

--I'm getting a court order to lift your blockade on the Dorothea. Mrs. Epstein had to stay in a hotel last night. Her father is due today. You are depriving them of the use of their property.

--It's a crime scene.

--You've already done your search and found nothing.

--We suspect Tony Triandos stayed there to plan the attack on Amy Berendts.

--Number one, Tony has not stayed on the boat for over a year. Number two, I am filing assault charges for him against his attackers, who brutally beat him.

--Tell you what I can do for you. I don't have enough people to guard the boat, so your clients can move back later today after a team from Lansing checks it out. But the Coast Guard also has a hold on it, so it stays in the harbor.

--Under whose authority?

--A national organized crime task force with a federal court order. I assume they have a legitimate reason.

--It can't stay in the water in the winter.

--That gives them at least a month to impound it. I have one more thing to discuss with you. I need to talk to Mrs. Epstein and Mr. Martino. When can we all meet? On the boat would work for me.

--Mr. Martino is arriving this afternoon.

--I can be available after 4:00. Will that work?

--Let's get it over with. They have nothing to hide.

Pete checked in with Mary Lu. She had nothing new for him except a callback request from Sally Conners. He found the duty roster to check the available patrolmen for the day. Brian had several helping him control the crime scene until John Ditmer arrived from Lansing with his team, which was being diverted to Honeysuckle Lane before processing Amy's condo and the Dorothea. Brian had already called in backup help to fill the daily patrols, including Benny Ramirez, who was already back in and ready for duty. When he got to his office, he first called the hospital to check on Officer Moreno. Pete was relieved that he was in stable condition and that the damage to his hip could be repaired. He also found that Sam Morgan was still critical and in the ICU. They expected to transfer him to Kalamazoo. His next call was to Sally Conners.

--Hello, Pete. You had an eventful day and night yesterday.

--Too eventful. We need to figure out where we are on all this.

--Okay. One at a time. There will be an inquiry into the shooting last night. I sent Donovan over to the site. You did the right thing in handing that over to Brian. Nice shot, by the way. Did you hear that Sam is still critical?

--Yes. What about Tony Triandos?

--I like that he is in Lansing. I don't know if our hospital or jail would be a safe place for him. While you were out yesterday, I got the local police report regarding the shooting at Amy's condo. I called Harry Berendts and Larry Vandevoss. They came in for an interview along with Gerrit Gerritson. Amy was in Middleburg. She's coming in this morning. Their descriptions have been consistent. Harry had a clear view of the finale. I've added attempted murder to the charges. His gun was fired. That will keep him in custody. I've talked to the state PA about taking over the case. We're getting overloaded here. John Ditmer's team will look at that crime scene after they finish at Sam's place. The locals have it taped off.

--Thank you for all that. That's a load off of all of us. The feds will also want to get in on the Triandos case. The important thing is to keep him in custody. What about the Doug Mason shooting? The three amigos are claiming self-defense.

--After which they moved the body.

--And posed it. Do you think you could make a murder charge of some level stick?

--It would not be easy. We'll go with disturbing-the-scene for now. I talked to Alex Vega already this morning. He wants them for his organized crime task force on drug charges. Mostly so they can get their testimony. It's best to let them run with it first.

--That leaves us with the George Bosch case and the coverup. I'm sure Sam Morgan's shooting was part of it. The body we found in the pond is probably Sal Broglio. The feds are trying to find his medical records so we can match them up to William Saunders' examination results. I'm finally getting somewhere.

--Enough for a grand jury?

--Not yet. I have more trees to shake. Amy Berendts, for one. She knows more than she's telling. Theo Bolinyk, if I could get him out of witness protection. And two more that only I know about.

--Who are they?

--I'm not divulging that until I've pinned it down. I don't want to get your hopes up. Or put you at risk.

--I'll accept that for now. Don't get yourself too far out on a limb with no backup.

When Pete ended the call with Sally, Mary Lu knocked on the door. Jack Stevenson had called and wanted a quick call back. Pete dialed right away.

--Thanks for the quick callback, Pete. I have something for you, and I need something from you.

--Let me have it.

--Our Chicago office has Sal Broglio's medical records for you. They've had them filed since he disappeared in '72. They're being faxed over to you as we speak. We also found something you want to know about the Honda dealership in Middleburg.

--Which is?

--Gus Martino owns almost half of it.

--Thanks, I can use that. What can I do for you?

--We are ready to arrest Gus Martino. We think he might be headed your way.

--That should be easy. I have an appointment to meet him and his lawyer on his yacht at four o'clock. We had a search warrant for his boat for information on Tony Triandos. A state team is going in today. What's the charge?

--Justice has enough for a general RICO charge in Miami. We'll organize a posse to go with you to your appointment. Hold all the information obtained from the search warrant for me.

--I want Gus for first-degree murder conspiracy.

--Can you make it stick?

--Not yet.

--I guess you'll need to take a back seat.

--Story of my life lately. It does make my job easier. I'll return to issuing traffic tickets and arresting kids drinking on the beach. It'll be a lot safer, too.

--Don't forget political corruption. That'll get you reelected.

--That worked the first time. Where should I rendezvous with your posse? The parking lot at our jail would work. It's a fifteen-minute drive to the yacht club. Can they get here by 3:30?

--Count on it. I'll fax some documents for you to pass on to them, including the arrest warrant and a new federal search warrant.

--I'll take care of it.

When Pete finished with Jack, Mary Lu knocked on his door again.

--Amy Berendts called raising heck. She wants to get back into her condominium. Here's the number. She's at the Riverview Lodge.

Pete sighed and dialed.

--Hello, Amy. This is Sh...

--When the fuck can I get back in my home? This place is expensive!

--I am working on it. Things went crazy last night. If you haven't heard, a hired gun tried to kill Sam Morgan last night. He's in critical condition. The crime scene crew from Lansing was diverted to that scene. They will get to your place this afternoon.

--Shit! Is he coming for me next?

--No, we got him. He won't be doing any more shooting. We think he was a substitute for Tony since he was no longer available.

--No thanks to you. I had to hire Larry.

--Hey, I trained Bonnie back in the day. Give me some credit. Amazingly, your brother and second cousin helped save you.

--Get me out of this hotel. It is expensive! Even worse, Lydia showed up in the dining room last night. She's staying here too.

--You can blame that on me. We have her yacht taped off, too. You showed up in a photo album we found. I didn't know you were friends. Lydia took lots of pictures. You also looked more than friendly with Tony.

--That was all about my dad and Theo. I was tagging along.

--But it means you know much more than you tell me. It's time for you to cooperate with us completely.

--That's bullshit. My lawyers are close to a deal with Alex Vega and the state crime force. Talking with you will screw it up.

--That deal won't cover a murder charge.

--I had nothing to do with Doug's shooting. You found that out yesterday. It wasn't even murder.

--I'm still working on George Bosch. You know something.

--I keep telling you I don't know anything about that.

--I'll let that go for now. You'll want to know that the feds have expressed interest in what we found on the boat. They'll be talking to you.

--Fuck! Will this ever be over?

--The sooner you tell all, the quicker it will disappear. Stay by the phone. We'll call you when you can get back into your home.

--Maybe I'll see you. I'm going to the PA's office to give my statement.

--I'll be out. I have people I need to talk to.

On Tuesday noon, Pete stopped to pick up a Subway Italian on his way to Middleburg to meet with John Visser again. He had called to tell Visser he had a few more questions. When he arrived, he again used the public entrance to the showroom. Seeing Pete's wearing his sheriff's jacket, the greeting sales associate waved to him as he walked in.

--You're back! Are you ready to buy a car, Sheriff?

Pete smiled and pointed up the stairs. When he reached the top, the receptionist quickly escorted him to Visser's office. Pete guessed that Visser did not want anyone to notice a sheriff hanging around his office.

--Good afternoon, Sheriff. I can't imagine what else I can help you with.

--We have some loose ends. Quite a few loose ends.

--Like what?

--Let's start with a piece of information I came across. Your Honda dealership is forty percent co-owned by a holding company called GM Enterprises.

--Why would that mean anything?

--The GM is Gus Martino. You told me you have nothing to do with him.

--It's a simple business deal. I'll be buying him out next year. It's also confidential information. How did you get it?

--It's a public record. We know where to look. We found it in Florida. There will be a grand jury empaneled as early as next week. Your business records will be subpoenaed.

--Good luck with that.

--We also have several recent photos showing you with Martino and other questionable folks in the last few years, including Theo Bolinyk. You didn't tell me the truth when you said you were no longer involved with these folks.

--How could you get photos like that? That's invading my privacy!

--Lydia Epstein likes to take pictures at the parties she throws on Martino's yacht.

--That doesn't prove anything.

--That's true, not by itself. Would you like to hear what's been happening to some of those guys?

--Why not? Go ahead and tell me.

--Tony Triandos is being transferred to a secure hospital ward the state police have in Lansing. He has severe concussion symptoms. He had a collision with a couple of ex-state police officers. He's being held on attempted murder and kidnapping charges.

--Who cares? I have nothing to do with him.

--Next, the legal rumor mill has Theo Bolinyk in witness protection with the feds. Who knows where? How much does he know about your activities?

--Nothing.

--Amy Berendts knows a lot about Theo. And her father, Joe Berendts. She spent yesterday morning with a state task force. I bet your name came up.

--You don't know that.

--How about Sam Morgan? He was just moved to intensive care in Kalamazoo. Two bullet wounds. He'll soon be talking. It's time to get ahead of the momentum and tell us what you know.

--You must think I'm crazy. None of these people will dare to talk. Even if they did, they would have nothing to say about me. We all know what happens to people who do talk. Do you know what Tony Triandos told me once?

--I can imagine.

--I asked him if he planned to kill me. He said no. He would kill my grandkids and make me live with it. That's why I still deal with those people. But now, I only do legal things. They like it that way. They want to be legitimate.

--Good luck to them, although they know how to run restaurants. One more thing. We shot the guy who shot Sam. Unfortunately, he died before he could talk. Here's a snapshot. His name was Chester McPherson. The FBI knows him to be a contract killer. Did you know him?

--Heck, no.

Pete stood up and leaned across Visser's large desk.

--Strange, here's a copy of the note he had on his passenger seat. As you can see, it's a photo of Sam Morgan with his address. Check out the fax number scrolled across the top.

John Visser's face turned from pink to white.

--This was a quick deal. You needed a substitute because Tony Triandos was put out of commission on Sunday night. Mistakes were made.

Visser hesitated before answering.

--This is the last time we talk without my lawyer. Get out of my office and my showroom.

--One more thing. I have uncovered a witness who saw what happened at the pond. Someone who looked like you was at the DFG boat shed when George Bosch was killed. You were there with Sam Morgan and Tony Triandos. You made a mistake when you let us drain the pond. We found the missing raft anchor. You were the guy with a key to the shed, where they got the chain and anchor to sink Sal Broglio after Tony shot him. That was after Sal shot George.

Visser's face was now bright red.

--I'm on my way out. Be on the lookout for the grand jury subpoena.

Pete walked out of the office and down the steps to the showroom. The salesperson slowed him down.

--Have you seen the new CRX? You'd look good in it.

Out of curiosity, Pete walked over to look at the sticker and sat in the driver's seat.

--My wife would like this. I'll let you know. I'll have to ask the county for a raise.

Just as he reached the exit door, a shot rang out. Pete's first reaction was to duck behind an Accord and reach for his weapon, but he came up empty. It was still impounded from the shooting the previous night. He caught his breath and realized the shot had come from the upstairs offices. He raced back up the stairs while pushing aside two other salespeople, staring up the stairs in shock. Several office staffers appeared from their cubicles to the left of the reception desk. Reaching Visser's office, he gently pulled the stunned receptionist away from the closed door. He turned the handle and gave the door a push before quickly standing to the side. When nothing happened, he pushed the door completely open and peered in.

John Visser was twisted and slumped over the left arm of his executive desk chair. Once again, Pete looked at a face partially destroyed by a gun blast. He saw a pistol on the floor as he walked around the desk. Without expecting to find one, he reached for Visser's left wrist to feel a pulse. There was none. He saw an almost blank Visser Honda ecru letterhead paper on the desk. In a neat, legible longhand, Visser had written:

> *I have hope for redemption, that my faith will make me free.*
> *This is for my grandchildren. May they live in peace.*

--Pete walked quickly out of the office and closed the door.

--Would someone please call 911 and ask for the local police and the local sheriff to send officers? Tell them there has been a shooting and a death.

Picking up a side chair from the reception area, Pete returned to John Visser's closed office door to sit down and wait.

Pete arrived back in Wakazoo five minutes late for his rendezvous with the FBI team. There had been a considerable commotion at the Honda dealership. John Visser was an important man. The Middleburg police chief had shown up in person. Charley Vredevelde had arrived simultaneously, letting everyone know that the Nederland County Sheriff, Ronald Dillingham, was coming from New Haven. Pete made his statements to the chief and the sheriff. When pressed, he showed them the copy of the sheet of paper found in the shooter's vehicle in front of Sam Morgan's home. He also told them about Visser's comment about Tony Triandos threatening his grandchildren. He knew that would be reason enough for his suicide.

It was after 3:00 before he was able to leave for Wakazoo. When he arrived, he was surprised that Jack Stephenson was part of the FBI team waiting for him in the jail parking lot.

--This must be a huge deal, Jack. How did you get here this fast?

--I rushed to the airport to catch a flight to Chicago. I got there just in time to meet up with these guys. This is James Wainright, the agent in charge. How do we get to the yacht club?

--Hop in with me, Jack. I'll lead you all to it.

Pete stopped in the yacht club parking lot in front of a caravan of five black SUVs. They stopped at the office to see Betty Fields. Two agents went in with Pete to serve the office search warrant for records about the Dorothea, Augustus Martino, or GME LLC. He led the rest of the team to the Dorothea at the end of the dock. At that point, he stayed behind and let Wainright take the lead. He watched them confront Lenny Caputo, Lydia, and an older man, all of whom had been waiting on the dock to gain access to the Dorothea. The man, who he assumed was Gus Martino, growled out in a loud voice.

--What the fuck is this? I thought we were just meeting with that goddamned redskin sheriff.

Wainright read Gus his rights and presented Caputo with the search warrant. Two agents cuffed Martino, who was now silent, and escorted him past Pete back to the FBI vehicles. The rest were already fanning out on the yacht. Pete shook Jack's hand.

--I think this will do it for me. Are you heading back?

--Yeah. I have a flight out of Chicago tonight. Martino will go directly to Miami. Let's try to get together in the UP around the holidays.

--Let's make that work. I'm heading to the office. I have a lot to clean up.

———————

Pete was tired and thought his day was almost done, but he found Eva Morgan and a forty-ish man waiting for him. The man was carrying what looked like three shoe boxes.

--How is Sam doing, Eva?

--They say he's fifty-fifty. Let's go to your office. We have something for you.

--Pete led them in.

--What do you have there?

--Sheriff, I'm Sam's son, Gerald. I came in from Detroit today. My dad was able to talk a little. He told us about these boxes stored in a floor safe in our garage. Decades ago, just after Nixon's tapes were revealed, he told me he wanted something like that for his office to protect himself from people who might be out to get him. I couldn't do anything as fancy as the White House, but I hooked up a cassette recorder and a speakerphone so he could record conversations. These are the ones he kept.

Eva leaned in with her finger on top of the boxes.

--He said there's some dangerous shit in there, Sheriff. He wants you to use it to protect me and to keep him out of jail.

Pete stared at the boxes, apprehensive about what he might find.

--Thank you, I think. We need to lock these up. A team will need to listen to them, catalog them, and transcribe them.

478

Then, we can see what can be used as evidence. If he pulls through, I can't guarantee it will keep him out of jail, but they could help. He's being investigated for conspiracy to murder.

--Can you use them to get the Boss? That's what he wanted.

--The FBI got the Boss an hour ago. His name is Augustus Martino. Hopefully, this is another lock on his jail cell or even a nail in his coffin if all the murder charges hold up. Have a seat for a few minutes. We need to get a signed receipt for you.

Pete called Priscilla to bring over a voluntary physical evidence form so she could record the material Eva and Gerald brought in. He used his office Polaroid camera to photograph the boxes and their contents. When the preliminary documentation was completed, he had a warning for Eva and Gerald.

--Only we four, plus Sam, know these tapes exist. The prosecuting attorney, Sally Conners, will be brought into the loop. For our safety, and especially yours, do not tell anyone else. Even if he is in prison, Gus Martino will still have contacts who will do his bidding.

By the time he ushered them out of the office and the rest of the office staff had left, he and Priscilla locked the properly labeled boxes in a chest in the evidence room. Pete took a big breath before heading to the exit door.

--I'll see you tomorrow, Priscilla. I'm more than done for the day. I'm hoping things will soon return to normal.

Chapter 22–Harry, Spring, 1999

Early Thursday morning, Harry drove his new BMW 328 into Amy's condominium complex with its trunk and back seat packed with suitcases and boxes. This was Amy's day to report to the Wakazoo Courthouse for the start of her eighteen-month sentence negotiated with the trial court and Alex Vega's organized crime task force. She had pled guilty to cultivating more than twenty marijuana plants on her farm. The penalty could have been seven years and a $500,000 fine. Her guilty plea and cooperation in other investigations had earned her a reduced sentence and a $50,000 fine.

It had been Harry's idea for him to rent her condominium during her incarceration. He had been staying at the River Haven B & B between trips back to Colorado, including Christmas and spring vacation ski weeks with David, Jennifer, Irma, and Janice. Harry's life had become increasingly centered in Michigan, but he was still not settled enough to make any permanent plans. Since the B & B was about to get prohibitively more expensive as peak season approached, renting Amy's home was a viable solution. He gradually brought half of his Colorado clothes on his flights from

Denver. The BMW was a luxury he allowed himself so he could leave his five-year-old Acura in Colorado.

Harry entered the front door to find Gerrit carrying two suitcases to the garage.

--Can I help, Gerrit? How soon are you leaving?

--I have everything packed and ready. I'll hit the road as soon as Amy is incarcerated this afternoon.

--You're driving?

--I am. I'll be there for six weeks. I'll need a vehicle. I'll fly back to Harbor Springs in May for the summer. I have another van there that I can use. I plan to spend winters in New Mexico in the future.

--I thought you were going to be in Colorado.

--Technically. The ashram is just over the border north of Taos. I think of it as still being in New Mexico.

--Because it sounds more exotic?

--That could have something to do with it.

--Is Amy ready? We're due at the title company for the closing in half an hour.

--I am. Let's check on her. She may need help moving her last things to the loft bedroom.

Since he did not think he would need it, Harry had agreed to let Amy use the third bedroom above the garage as storage while she was away. He also agreed to keep her Lexus convertible in the garage. He could tell that it gave her comfort to have part of her life waiting for her when she came back. He was more reluctant when she tried to enlist his help in keeping Mode du Jour open for what could be two peak seasons before she returned. He held off until Jeff Klaasen joined the team. Jeff knew that one of his employees, Benson Blok, who had worked at Marshall Fields in Chicago, wanted to return to women's fashion. The store could be operational along with Judy Marsden and one more hire. Harry and Jeff would share the management duties and any profits.

--Are you ready, Sis? We need to get going.

--I'm not in a hurry to give away my farm and go immediately to prison afterward.

--I'm sure you're not. But you'll need to get used to not having choices.

--F you, Harry. I think you're enjoying this.

--I'm not. Really. I am trying to make it easier for you. You should be realistic. Getting through this will take all your mental energy. Feeling persecuted and resentful will be counterproductive, right, Gerrit?

--Yes, but I think Amy is already aware of the conditions of her life's next phase. She also has the mental strength and the tools to deal with it. She tends to get back to reality after blowing off some steam. I think she has been making good decisions. She will be able to resume her life afterward.

Amy had already calmed down.

--Sorry, Harry. Knowing you are taking care of the store is a load off my mind. It's not like I can do anything else when I return. I'll be a convicted felon. It still feels like a hanging, but let's go. Gerrit is ready to be transactional.

They were ushered into a small conference room at the title company when they arrived. Pete McAdams introduced them to John Aishike, representing the Grand Traverse Band of Ottawa and Chippewa Indians, who were technically Gerrit's Farm purchasers. Per the land contract, Amy was nullifying her option to buy in return for twenty-five percent of the purchase price, which would net her thirty-eight thousand dollars, twelve thousand more than the capital payments she had made. She needed the money to pay her fine. Gerrit would use his portion as a nest egg to start his New Awakening ashram in Colorado. After completing the process without difficulty, Amy looked at Pete with resignation.

--I suppose you'll be there this afternoon, ensuring I am properly incarcerated.

--No, I don't need to be there. I didn't work out your deal. I may even have been more lenient. You let yourself get caught up in events you could not control and with people with bad intentions. The PA's office and the jail staff will handle everything. They don't need me.

Harry changed the subject to allow the title company representative to start the process. After it all proceeded smoothly to completion, Harry again kept the mood upbeat.

--Congratulations are in order, John. This is a start on your band's southern reservation.

--It won't be a reservation. We plan to call it the Odawa Winter Hunting Grounds Preserve. We have our eyes on other sites that will create a meaningful chunk of land along the river.

--How about the DFG property?

--We met with their committee last night and agreed on a potential deal. All we need now is for the DFG board and our elders to give it the final okay. We also need the Sheriff here to make a deal for his family's plots. That will complete the rectangle.

--You know that I'm not the hold-up, John. It's up to my mother and two of her cousins. They are okay with the idea but have doubts about how the band has handled projects in the past. They don't want to line the pockets of a few governing elders who have been in charge too long.

--I know more about that than anyone. Some of us younger members are organized now. We've made some changes for the better, but change takes time.

--You don't have to tell me. I'm dealing with the same stuff in my county.

--This will be an educational project for our young people. We already have beavers returning. We'll let the ponds go natural and stock them with original fish species. We'll do our part to help the state clean up the Singapore River. We'll plant heirloom corn and recharge wild rice growth. We are anxious to get underway.

Noticing Amy fidgeting, Harry once again changed the subject.

--This is interesting, but I have just enough time to let Amy have her last meal as a free person.

As they were leaving, Pete pulled Harry aside.

--Thanks to you, Larry's plan has worked. The sting is supposed to happen tonight. Are you coming along?

--No way. I would rather not be known as a plant. They won't assume I was involved if I'm not there when you arrest them.

--True. We'll let you know what happens.

The first week of January, Larry had come to Harry asking for a favor.

--I need you again, Watson.

--What for this time?

--I need someone to pose as the owner of a nice twenty-foot cabin cruiser.

--That's sounds easy. What's the catch?

--I'm on the cusp of wrapping up my case at the boat docks and yacht clubs along the coast.

--Fill me in. You've been very secretive about it.

--Okay, here's the deal. Last summer, the insurance company I've been working for began to experience a sudden rise in theft up and down both sides of the Lake Michigan coast. Mostly, newer boats and supersized outboard motors were being taken. They suspected an inside job. I got a good recommendation from a former boss at the state police, so they hired me. That was the job I told you about in the fall.

--I started examining the claims, looking for patterns. Bonnie went undercover as a clerical in the claim office. The first thing I did was to visit the security departments of their two competitors in maritime insurance. They were experiencing a similar increase in theft claims. Bonnie found one inconsistency that turned out to be true for all three insurance companies. A few major companies in maritime finance financed the stolen boats.

--On a hunch, I checked on the credit history of the owners of the stolen boats. Surprise! All the owners were behind in their payments. The thefts were a good deal for everyone except my clients. After the owners receive the insurance settlements, the finance company gets their money or more, and the owners get out from under an unpayable debt. The thieves set up an easy score, arranging easy access to a boat after planning the time and place with the owners. They even give the owners a cut. That's where you come in.

--Doing what?

--Almost nothing. We'll get you a fake identity and a boat at the yacht club, insured by one of our companies. When the season resumes, you can even take Irma for a joyride. A credit file showing your alter ego with overdue payments will be created. You sit back and wait for the thieves to call. You'll listen to their pitch and wait a week before you agree so you don't seem too anxious. Then, you set up a time and place. Me and the law will be waiting for them.

--I don't quite get it. Which insurance company has an inside person who gives the names of the targets? Or does each company have a person?

--See, you're a natural at this. The answer is none of them. But Bonnie discovered that the finance companies work with the same collection company. That's where the inside person is. We think it may be one of the partners. Stealing a boat is easier and more lucrative than receiving a percentage for the tedious collection work, especially if the boat owner is in on the deal.

Larry's plan was ready to play out its last act three months later. The delay was caused by the time it took to set up the title, insurance, and financial details and by ice on the big lake. The wait was also a good thing for the investigation. It gave Larry and Bonnie time to narrow their focus to a group of suspects. The sting would close the deal for Sally Conners and a grand jury. It would also mean big bonuses for Larry and Bonnie.

The previous Monday, Harry had played his part as Howard Baanveldt perfectly when he received a call from a woman named Heidi. She claimed to find boats for a buyer who would buy them from owners behind their payments. At first, Harry told her he wasn't interested, but when she persisted, he agreed to meet with her the following day at the Singapore Yacht Club, where the boat that Larry had set up for him was docked.

Heidi was an attractive brunette with a very professional appearance and businesslike manner. Harry was glad he had taken the boat for a trial run when she asked to take it for a ride to assure her buyer that it was in good condition.

During thirty minutes of cruising the river, Heidi had become more friendly and personal, a step away from blatant flirting. Harry was happy to play along.

--Howard, I like your boat. We could take it for a longer ride sometime.

--I don't know how long I can keep it.

--How far are you behind? I don't get the exact information.

--It'll be six months, next week. Exactly how long it's been since my divorce was final. I should have insisted that she take the boat. I planned to live in it. She got the house, but I had to rent an off-season room when I got claustrophobic after a week of living on the boat.

--We better act fast before the repo man shows up. If we can make a deal, you will save your credit rating.

--Will your buyer give me what I need? It's close to being underwater. Figuratively, of course.

--It's a nice boat. You're a nice guy. I'll try to get you as much as I can.

--What happens now?

--I'll call you tomorrow.

Harry got the call shortly after noon on Wednesday.

--Howard, I have a deal that could work out for you. Can you meet me at the G & G around five?

--I look forward to it.

This time, Heidi was dressed, less businesslike than the first time, in a red shift dress that showed off her figure, including more than a bit of cleavage and thigh. She ordered a martini while Harry had his usual Old Fashioned. She had a contagious smile and a way of looking Harry in the eye, almost making him wish they were not conning each other.

--Howard, I have some unwelcome news, but I have another possibility.

--Let me have it.

--My buyer is going to pass on this one. He doesn't think the market is good right now for your size boat. But I know someone who could solve your problem.

--Who would that be, and how could he help?

--Is your insurance up to date?

--It is now. I have a payment next month that I will need to skip.

--Great! Here is how it works. You give me a set of keys. On an agreed night, you leave the boat uncovered, gassed up, and ready to go. It will disappear. You will make the theft report and your insurance claim the following day.

--I don't want to do anything illegal.

--Howard, it's a way out for you. My person will even give you a couple of grand for your trouble.

--Now you're making me nervous.

--But I saw a twinkle in your eye. This would fix your debt problem with no risk.

--Let me think about it.

Heidi had lost her smile and was no longer flirting.

--My guy doesn't allow that. It'll happen on Thursday night. That's tomorrow. If you don't help, he may take it anyway and set you up for it.

--He can do that?

--Yes, he can, Howard.

Harry looked dejected and let his eyes look down.

--Well, I need the two thousand. I'm even behind on my rent at the B & B.

--Good choice. Remember, it will be tomorrow evening, before dark. With the keys available, it will look like a typical boat ride. Leave them with the life preservers under in the deck compartment.

--When do I get my share?

--I have five hundred for you now. That makes you part of the deal. We won't meet again. They'll find a way to get you the rest after the insurance company pays off your loan. There may even be a few leftover dollars to sweeten your deal.

Harry took a deep breath. Heidi passed him an envelope.

--What do they do with the boat?

--Don't ask or think about it. Everything will be fine, Howard. Just make sure you leave the keys. You don't want to make these people upset with you. You'll feel better when you make that insurance claim, and your loan is paid off. I'm disappointed that we can't meet again. We could've had some fun together.

Harry watched her leave while he paid the bill before returning to his room at River Haven. He followed his orders from Larry and Pete and ran a stop sign while driving fifteen mph over the limit. He was relieved to hear the siren and see the flashing lights behind him. After both vehicles pulled to the side of the road, the officer waited at least five minutes, appearing to check the registration before he came to Harry's car window.

When Deputy B. Ramirez casually asked why he was in such a hurry, Harry told him he had a package for Sheriff McAdams. Benny returned to his patrol car and looked as if he were filling out a ticket form, which he took to Harry's car. It was a cash receipt. He watched Harry write in the amount and slipped the envelope into his shirt. If Harry were being followed, it would look like a routine traffic stop.

After the conferral with Pete at the Thursday morning meeting, Harry caught up with Amy and Gerrit as they walked across the street to the Wakazoo Grill for lunch. He was up for the hamburger plate and knew that there were several salads on the menu that Amy and Gerrit might find tolerable. Amy seemed doubtful.

--This is my last meal before being locked up in Ypsilanti. I was hoping for something better, Harry.

--We would need to be somewhere other than Wakazoo. The atmosphere here is better than the grocery store deli.

--No doubt. Do you think they'll have vegan options at the women's facility, Gerrit? They tell me I will be in one of the least restrictive pods.

--They might surprise you. But you'll need to change your perspective about food. You will need to eat what's in front of you. Ingesting sufficient calories will be the goal. You can cleanse when you get back to the real world.

--Enough about food. I've heard they have a music program. It might keep me sane.

--Don't forget to keep up your meditation and yoga. You could improve your mental health during your time inside.

--I will remember that. Do you have any questions about the store or my accounts, Harry?

--No, I get most of it. As far as the store is concerned, we have the staff we will need. Judy and Benson are capable in the front end. Jeff's backroom person will be able to also cover your store for receiving and stocking. Shirley's daughter, Laurie, is working with her now. She'll be spending more time in the store handling your office duties. I'll sign the checks and act like a boss.

--Do you feel okay about it?

--I'm good with most of it. I'm a little unsure about your other interests, most of which now coincide with mine. I hope I won't regret our fifty-fifty deal.

--You got the best of it. I had to give in on a lot of stuff. I won't be around to fight about it. At least we won't be paying lawyers.

--I have Allen, and you have Bill. It's their job to figure it out so we come out even. Remember, the final signoff has not happened yet. If neither of us is happy, we can go back to fighting.

Gerrit held up his hands.

--Don't let that happen. You both will have enough money to live how you want. Don't let pettiness get in the way.

--You're right. But, Harry, promise me you'll ensure Lydia keeps paying her rent.

--Unless you see her in Ypsilanti with you. She's not entirely in the clear, you know.

--You have no idea how much I'd love to see that.

Their lunch arrived. Harry's burger was not as good as he remembered. He ate slowly while Amy and Gerrit were picking at their Garden-Fresh Salad and Garden-Fresh Fruit Dessert. Amy was unusually quiet. Harry had no idea what to talk about. Gerrit filled the void with a detailed description of his ashram plans, hoping to give Amy something comforting to expect. Part of her plan for her after-prison life was to spend much of her off-season time in the ashram.

The walk to the jail was short. They had only a few minutes together inside before she was separated from Harry and Gerrit. Harry saw the tears in her eyes as Gerrit spent a long moment hugging her and whispering close to her ear. They watched her bravely walk into a restricted area with her intake officer.

———————

As Harry drove back to Amy's condo, which he was still not thinking of as his home, he remembered a meeting with Larry at Allen Zuverink's office in early January. When he arrived, he found Larry already sitting in the conference room with several file folders in front of him. Four file boxes were on one end of the oval table. Allen walked in just as Harry was sitting down across from Larry. Allen pulled out the chair across from the file boxes.

--Welcome, gentlemen. As my eighth-grade math teacher used to say, it's time to turn our brains on. This may get complicated.

Larry closed the file folder he was perusing. Harry appeared worried.

--That's what I'm concerned about. I don't know if I can afford the on-the-clock time.

--That's one thing you don't have to worry about. We've found enough assets in Amy's accounts to make the search worthwhile. I suspect there is even more, but it would take legal action and detective work to find it.

Larry's eyes widened.

--That's why I'm here. Right, Harry?

--I guess, but you're not cheap either. Let's not get too deep in the weeds, Allen. Let us have the summary.

--Okay. There are four bundles to review. Let's take them one at a time.

--The first holds Joe's more apparent assets, for which Bill Snyder included backup documents. They add up to more than we thought. They are still tied up in probate for a few more months.

--We've also found documentation of the cash that Amy had improperly siphoned away from Joe before he died. If they want to avoid legal battles, we have some leverage to reclaim your share. Her power of attorney agreement included fiduciary responsibility. She did not have carte blanche authority to use his money for personal gain.

--Third, there are hints found that other accounts exist. There are transfers from several shared accounts in a Miami bank: one for Joe, another for Amy, and a shared account. There is also a shared account with Amy and Theo Bolinyk. This might have been a slip-up on Theo's part. The account numbers are included. I think your power of attorney could allow you to at least access the records.

--Finally, in another slip-up, there is a record of a safety deposit box in South Bend. We may need Larry to help uncover that.

Harry's attention focused on the last folder.

--Last fall, Amy wanted me to go to South Bend to pick up some money for her and Theo. I told her I wouldn't get involved with Theo's business. I knew it could be illegal. What do you think would be our next step, Larry?

--I wouldn't say I like the smell of any of this. You're right. If Theo's involved, it's dirty money. Let's get your high-priced lawyer and the probate court involved. They can do it legally if Joe's name is on it. We could try to use Harry's power of attorney on the other accounts, but it's limited.

--These are your copies, Harry. I would give them to Gerald Brooks and follow his advice.

--Okay. I have an appointment with him next week. I'll include these files. Larry, I'll let you know if we can use your help.

When he arrived back at River Haven, Harry pulled out the files and paged through them, struggling to concentrate. Putting them aside, he called the Brooks law office to alert them to the latest information. He agreed to bring them to the office the following day to give Gerald time to review them before their scheduled meeting a week later.

At that meeting. Gerald surprised Harry by suggesting that Rose's trust was not rock solid. If Amy were to contest it, she could win. Even if she failed, it would be tied up in court for a long time, delaying the entire probate resolution. Gerald recommended that Harry pursue a settlement to package the whole estate into one bundle. A fifty-fifty result would be satisfactory. It could work in Harry's favor. After reviewing the rest of Allen's work on the possible Joe and Amy links to the Miami accounts, he suggested that Harry share them with the law enforcement agencies still involved in the ongoing organized crime investigation. Knowing that the inquiry involved Theo and Amy, Harry thought it would be best if Amy turned them over, thinking she would get cooperation credit that could reduce her sentence. Gerald called Reggie Robinson to gauge his interest. The call was sent to Juanita Jones, who agreed to meet Harry later the same day.

Needing to remain in New Leiden for several hours, Harry went to a movie to kill time. He found the noon matinee he sought at a new Cinemark theater complex twenty minutes away. He and David had seen all the Star Wars movies together, but now they were separated. David had already seen *Star Wars: The Phantom Menace* without him, so Harry wanted to catch up. He arrived at Juanita's office with renewed energy at four o'clock.

After quickly reviewing Harry's files, Juanita was on board with Harry's idea. She needed to get Amy's agreement, but she formed a plan for Harry, Gerald, and her to meet with FBI investigators, the Michigan Organized Crime Task Force, and Pete McAdams. Harry was relieved. It could help Amy, and he would avoid being implicated in covering up criminally tainted accounts.

It took Juanita's persuasion, but Amy realized she had no choice but to cooperate despite fearing retaliation from Theo. They met with Pete, Alex Vega, and FBI Agent-in-Charge James Wainright. After the meeting, the FBI took charge of the case. It took almost two months to unveil the accounts and open the South Bend safety deposit box. They found nearly two million dollars in cash deposits, stocks, and bonds. Harry had no idea how much of it was legally obtained and belonged to Joe or Amy, which could mean some would belong to him. He hoped it would be enough to pay Gerald's bill.

When Harry drove up to 'his' condo after leaving the courthouse and stopping at River Haven for the last of his belongings, Larry was waiting for him, helping Gerrit put the final boxes into his Jeep. After they said their goodbyes as Gerrit drove off, they walked inside.

--Gerrit said that Amy's incarceration went smoothly.

--It was sad. But she is in a collected frame of mind, as much as could be expected, anyway.

--I can only imagine what it would be like. I hope she can keep that frame of mind during the rest of her time. But let's get back to you. I like your new wheels. You're stepping up in the world. It would be best if you didn't drive it to Denver. Your ex may want an adjustment to your settlement.

--That's a done deal. I told her she wouldn't need to contribute any added money to the kid's college expenses. She was happy with that. We all even skied together in Vail. She and Matt liked Irma and Janice.

--Imagine that! Three happy blended families.

--I hope it stays that way. Are you going to the party at the yacht club tonight? I told Pete I wanted to stay out of the spotlight.

--We'll all be watching from a distance. If it goes according to plan, there won't be any arrests. The state police and the feds want to stand back and let them get away. They are more interested in who is receiving it at the next level. We have cameras covering the boat and a tracking device attached to it. They'll follow it as far up the line as possible before arresting anybody.

--Do they know where Heidi is, if that is her real name?

--I'll tell Irma about your interest in her.

--I don't want her to send her friends to deal with me.

--She was headed south on the interstate. That's all they'll say.

After Larry left, Harry prepared two cups in Amy's French coffee press. Wanting to relax, he found a stack of newspapers, including the morning edition of the New Leiden Daily Record, to which Amy subscribed, mainly to keep up with the fashion ads. The Sunday edition of the Chicago Tribune was also on the desk, appearing untouched. But he chose to read the current week's edition of the Wakazoo Gazette when he saw Pete McAdams' photo on the front page. As he was reading the article, Amy's ringing phone startled him. Wondering if it was for Amy or if someone had tracked him down, he reluctantly picked up. It was Pete McAdams.

--Hi, Harry. I have some news I should share with you.

--I am reading about you in the Gazette. Nice photo!

--Thanks, I was hoping to make a good impression.

--How did you find me?

--I'm the Sheriff. It's what I do.

--Oh, ja, I forgot. Is something happening with our sting? I'm hoping Heidi forgets about me.

--Not yet. This is a different issue you should know about.

--What could that be?

--Theo Bolinyk is on the move again. He left the witness protection program without notification. He has a lot of law enforcement and others looking for him. Because of your involvement with us, I thought you should know.

--What does that mean for me, Pete?

--For one thing, be on the lookout for Theo, in person or by phone. He could try to meet up with Amy or get to her house for some reason. He may not be aware that she has started to serve her time.

--What do I do if I see him?

--Avoid him and call me. I'll send in the cavalry.

--Really? I thought you were on the other side.

--Ha! Good joke. Don't forget the Scottish part of my heritage. The feds will be covering the Miami and South Bend banks.

--Okay, thanks. Congratulations, by the way. I see you've made some progress on cleaning up the Board of Supervisors. That should seal up your reelection next year.

--Maybe not. It's making me an enemy of some influential people. The two we've arrested are low-hanging fruit. We have a lot more work to do. You'll hear next week that Cory Epperson will be resigning along with Grover Lukasen, my lead detective, making my life easier. I've spent the last three years keeping them away from important cases.

--What did they do?

--As the investigation proceeded, we discovered Grover never got an anonymous phone call about Amy's farm. He knew about it for months. He got pissed because Doug wasn't paying him enough to look the other way. He only wanted to pressure him to pay up. He was shocked when it became a big deal, eventually exposing himself. We also found that Cory had been on Theo Bolinyk's payroll for years. His last favor was switching our rental cars for him.

--Another success for you! If Theo shows up here, you'll be my first call.

Harry returned to pour his coffee before sitting in Amy's vintage ChairWorks lounge chair and ottoman to peruse the newspaper.

———————

Saturday morning, Harry went back to River Haven for his weekly breakfast appointment with Larry. Larry only had to experience one of Luke's weekend breakfasts to insist on signing up for every Saturday morning. Since Larry was their best customer, Rob and Luke had allowed him to reserve a spot when only guests were accommodated as peak season approached. Larry was already seated when Harry arrived, giving his order to a young server. Harry had not seen her before.

--Harry, this is Luke's daughter, Miriam. She has joined the team here. I already ordered breakfast for you.

--Welcome, Miriam. I take it you have completed your classes at Western?

--Almost. I'm taking my final two classes this quarter. I can walk in June.

--Congratulations! I know Luke and Lara are enormously proud of you. What are your plans for your future?

--We were talking about that. I am planning to open a restaurant with my parents here in Singapore.

--They told me that they were looking for a location. That's a big step.

--True, but not that big. I have six years of experience as a server and bartender to accompany my business degree. Mom and Dad have a generation of working in the kitchen. A nice, small spot on the riverwalk with outdoor seating is available. We plan to work our butts off in the peak season and have

500

reduced hours in the winter. Dad can still work for the schools. Plus, I can translate when needed.

What about capital? Have you saved up enough?

--We have some saved. We also have a couple of investors. We could use another one. Mr. Vandevoss said that you might be interested.

--Oh, he did?

--When could we show you our business plan? We have great menu ideas.

--Ah, it would have to be next week. I can't promise anything. A lot of my funds are still tied up in probate.

--How about Monday at 3:00? We could meet at the site.

--At least you know how to close. I'll see you then.

Harry turned to scowl at Larry as she went back to the kitchen.

--Thanks a lot. I didn't realize that you are now my financial advisor.

--I'm just trying to get you involved in the community so Watson will be there when I need him.

--I see we have three place settings. Do we have a guest?

--Lupe and I have tickets to the Blackhawks playoff game tonight. We'll be taking off from here.

--Great! I need to see her. She owes me some rent.

At that moment, Lupe came to the table from behind Harry.

--I heard that, Harry. You should pay me. I'm built-in security for you. Besides, you could live there yourself. I could be your guest.

--Larry would disapprove. Plus, security is not a concern in Dordrecht, and I've given you a great deal. I also promised myself that I would never live in Dordrecht again.

--If I had known you would be here, I would have brought the check to you. It's in the mail.

--If not, I now know an effective collection agency.

--Ooh. I'm scared. Larry told me all about Heidi.

Their four breakfast orders arrived. Larry, as usual, had ordered both the omelet and the pancakes. The conversation started again after they had taken a few bites.

--Let's change the subject. What's the latest on your brother, Lupe?

--He's finally reached an agreement with that task force. His lawyer has been very forceful in his defense. Nick must continue to testify at upcoming cases, but he'll avoid prison time if he continues to play his part.

--Good for him. He was just a pawn for Doug Mason. What about Harv?

--Not good so far. The rehab center is playing the victim big time. They're pressuring the prosecution not to settle. His uncle Butch told me the other day that it would go to trial.

--He has a good lawyer. He could get by with a light sentence. Speaking of the three amigos, Larry, what do you hear from Jonnie?

--He's in the clear. Sally Conners finally took Doug's shooting to the grand jury last week. They didn't bill it. Self-defense. Anything else they had on him was past the statute of limitations.

--That's another good thing. With Theo on the loose again, Amy is the only one serving significant time.

--Theo is on the loose?

--Ja, Pete called me on Thursday to be on the lookout for him.

--That's unbelievable. That guy is like a ghost. Also, don't forget Gus Martino. He hasn't gone to trial yet. He could get off.

--Pete McAdams hopes he does. He would love to bring him back from Miami to be tried here for conspiracy in the George Bosch murder. Of course, since Sam Morgan died in January, the other suspects are all dead, except Tony Triandos. He was at that scene as well as ours. Have you heard anything about him, Larry?

--Ja, he's still in rehab and unfit for trial. They claim his brain isn't working right.

--Thanks to you and Bonnie.

--It could be a big fake by Tony. Are you done there, Lupe? We need to get going.

--Yes, *Jefe*. How can you eat twice as much as I do in half the time?

--It's a talent. See you next week, Harry. Think about being a restaurant owner.

--I might be interested. Let me know if you see Theo the Ghost. Harry went to the kitchen to check in with Luke and Lara about a personal matter.

He returned to the condominium to reluctantly return a phone call from Lydia, who had left a Saturday callback time on Amy's machine on Friday. She answered on the second ring.

--Thanks for calling, Harry.

--You must have one of those ID things. I need to get one on this line to screen out calls meant for Amy.

--I see she has you doing her bidding. She was always good at that.

--I'm just trying to help. What's up?

--I'm just letting you know that I'm moving out. I'll be gone by Monday morning. Papa has leased a big house on the bay and needs my help.

--Won't he be in jail soon?

--No time soon. This mess will be going on for a long while. Because of his age and health concerns, he was granted bail with conditions restricting him to his residence so he found something comfortable. I'm also trying to get them to move Tony here so I can take care of him.

--Meanwhile, you are breaking your lease. It has eight more months to go, I think.

--You are welcome to sue me. Good luck. My movement is restricted, too. I'm regarded as a critical witness and even suspected of being a co-conspirator. I'm becoming an expert at pleading the fifth.

--Amy will be happy to hear about your travails. I won't sue. It'll be easy to find someone to lease it. I don't need the hassle. I'll need something in writing, though. You can send it to our agency where you pay the rent. I'll release you from the lease to make it legal. Speaking of Tony, how is he? I've heard he is making the most of his injuries.

--Not well, thanks to you. That's why I'm trying to get him moved down here. Three different states want to get their hands on him. He should be with us.

--You'll get no sympathy from me. He tried to kidnap my sister, and you think his problems are my fault? I just tripped the wire.

--Fuck you!

--Goodbye to you, too!

———————

After a long walk on the beach, Harry spent the rest of the morning cleaning the condominium for a special occasion. After lunch, he took a quick afternoon shopping trip to New Leiden. At five, he returned to the condo with a bottle of champagne and two bottles of Napa County merlot. Both were among the most expensive selections at the wine store recommended by Luke. He also had a small box. He was just in time to meet the delivery van from the floral shop to receive two large bouquets, one for the dining buffet and the other to be placed on the top of the fifty-inch rear projection TV that Doug had left behind. Harry hoped it would make the sitting area a little more romantic. Having never planned an occasion like this before, he was unsure of his ability to pull it off. He went to shower and put on his best suit, skipping the tie. Luke, Lara, and Miriam arrived at 5:45 with the catered dinner Harry had arranged with Luke. Luke had promised a server would stay. That turned out to be Miriam.

Irma arrived at 6:00 wearing what appeared to Harry to be a new dress. He had told her he was planning a special dinner event at the yacht club while 'Howard Baanveldt' was still a member. Harry ushered her into the living room just as Miriam came in with the champagne and a caviar tray. She expertly popped the cork.

--What's going on, Harry?

--Let's have a seat and celebrate. There's been a change in plans. I didn't want to hang out with the yacht club crowd. We will be dining at home tonight.

--I got all dressed up to dine in?

--It'll be worth it. You go with the flowers, champagne, and caviar, not to mention my best suit, except you are the most beautiful.

--Okay, you're forgiven. This is very romantic. Thank you. I am starving, so let me start on the caviar before I guzzle the champagne.

--I'll pour while you spread.

Harry handed her a flute.

--We need to toast.

--To?

--To you and me and our future.

Irma sipped and leaned over for a quick kiss before she started in on the caviar.

--What is the future, Harry?

--That would be the critical next step. If it goes well, the whole evening will be a success.

--And the next step is?

Harry reached over to an end table drawer to pull out a box. This is for you. It's not a present because it comes with strings.

Irma slowly inspected the box.

--I don't see any strings, Harry.

--I'm the strings. The contents and I are a package. I'm in love with you. I know that is not going to change. I want us to be married.

Irma opened the box to find a diamond and sapphire ring. Her eyes teared up. She was speechless.

--Don't say no! At least say you'll think about it.

--What are you thinking, Harry? I would never say no. I'm in a state of shock. I feel the same as you.

--Oh my God. I wasn't sure.

Irma slipped the ring on her finger.

--It fits.

--You can exchange it!

--Are you kidding? It's perfect! You know, it was good that you arranged this little party to go with it. The flowers, the champagne, and the caviar put you over the top.

--I'm happy about that. Hey, we need a real kiss and another toast.

After the kiss and toast, Irma returned to her car to grab her Nikon. Miriam was drafted to photograph the replay. Irma took many more photos, including the table setting and the entrée. Miriam took a few more of the lucky couple. When the lobster meal was finished, Irma was ready to get serious.

--What about the details, Harry?

--I don't care. I would be delighted to be engaged for the rest of our lives.

--I don't mean a wedding. We've both been through that before. We can go to the courthouse. I mean the big questions. Where do we live, and what about Janice? What about your new job at DeJong?

--One thing at a time. I decided yesterday to pass on the consultant position at DeJong. I realized that I did not want to be in marketing again, even part time. I was only good at it when I would imitate my dad and use his 'Joe' personality. My true self was more inward like my mother. I am more comfortable with myself now. I have a store to run for Amy, a restaurant start-up to help with, and Larry wants me to be his business manager.

--That's all happening in Singapore.

--It is. I can live anywhere with you but would prefer not to live in Dordrecht. And I have an idea that could make Singapore the solution.

--You are always one step ahead, aren't you?

--A half a step this time. I sat next to Flo McAdams at the softball game yesterday. She asked about the Dordrecht High freshman playing second base that I had come to watch.

--How did she do?

--Fine. Dordrecht won four-two. Jan scratched out a single and handled a couple of ground balls cleanly. She almost turned a double play. I told Flo that she was also an excellent student and that you were exploring options for next year.

--I am?

--Well, we are now. She bragged about the new Wakazoo High School building that will be ready next year. The sophomore class will be over two hundred. The business park has also attracted a lot of companies, which raised the school tax base. She's excited about a new AP program that Western cis helping set up. Plus, she's the basketball coach. She's recruiting.

--You have a house in Dordrecht, too. Jan could stay where she is. However, I must admit that living in Dordrecht can feel like a time warp, a completely different dimension.

--So, we have those two options. Long term, Colorado could be the third choice. Janice would go for that. Problem solved. We need to choose one. Let's send Miriam on her way and celebrate some more. It would be best if you weren't driving after the champagne and wine.

--I wasn't thinking of going anywhere.

--Excellent. Waking up for a spring morning walk on the beach may convince you that this should be the place.

--You are beyond romantic. I'm going to enjoy this and save decisions for another day.

ABOUT THE AUTHOR

The setting for *Dordrecht Dimension* was inspired by the West Michigan area where Jim Otte was raised. After a fifty-year odyssey managing designed-oriented furniture stores in Michigan, Colorado, Texas, and Arizona, Jim and his wife, Nancy, a retired Deaf Education teacher, live in Portland, Oregon.